Antoinette de Mirecourt

Universitas Press
Montreal

www.universitaspress.com

Canadian Classics Series Editor: Cristina Artenie

Hardcover first published in November 2024

ROSANNA LEPROHON

Antoinette de Mirecourt;

or,

Secret Marrying and Secret Sorrowing.

A Canadian Tale.

Universitas Press
Montreal

CONTENTS

Introduction

Sylvia Hunt

Rosanna Leprohon was one of the first successful nineteenth-century Canadian authors. However, despite a prodigious literary output and positive contemporary reviews, few today have heard of her. On one hand, she is described as "a Canadian phenomenon—genuinely bilingual and bicultural ... presenting the story [of the British conquest] from a French-Canadian point of view . . . moving effectively between the traditions and languages of the two founding cultures" (McMullen 14). On the other hand, J.C. Stockdale states that "though her novels have little appeal now, they retain some of their charm if taken for what they were: amusement for women readers of early Canada" (np). This dismissive view of Leprohon's novels, in particular the three that deal with pre- and post-conquest Quebec, negates their political and cultural importance in the presentation of Canadian history from a French perspective.

Of Irish descent, Rosanna Eleanor Mullins (1829-1879) was born in Montreal to Francis Mullins, a successful ship chandler,[1] and his wife Rosanna Connelly. After graduating at the age of seventeen from the Convent of the Congregation of Notre Dame[2] where she received a solid education in history, language, literature and religion, Leprohon published her first poems in the

---

[1] The *Montreal Herald* of 28 November 1837 includes an advertisement for the sale of a "neatly finished clinkered built PLEASURE BOAT" by "Mr. Francis Mullins, Steam Boat Wharf, Montreal." The Montreal City Directory for the year 1844 includes only one Francis Mullins and he is listed as a grocer and ship chandler living at 67 Commissioners Street (144).

[2] The Congregation of Notre Dame in Ville Marie (now Montreal) was founded in 1658 as a religious order dedicated to the education of the colony's girls and young women.

Literary Garland, a popular Canadian literary periodical.[3] After this successful foray into writing for publication, she regularly submitted poetry, short stories and, later, serialized novels to the *Garland* until it ceased production in 1851. That same year she married Jean-Baptiste-Lucien Leprohon (1822-1900), a medical doctor; the couple moved to Saint-Charles-sur-Richelieu where they lived until 1855 when they permanently returned to Montreal. For the first eight years of her marriage, Leprohon ceased writing, probably due to the demands of her young and growing family.[4] After their return to Montreal, however, Leprohon resumed her literary production. She died 20 September 1879 and is buried in Côte-des-Neiges Cemetery in Montreal. Outside of these details, there is little meat to hang on this bare-bones outline of a literary life. Because her letters were burned after her death, there is nothing else except her published works and parish documents that give insight into her life. The author whom Susanna Moodie described as "the pride and ornament of a great and rising country" (quoted in McMullen 21) is now virtually unknown.

Leprohon began her literary career writing stories set in England. Influenced by authors like Frances Burney and Jane Austen, her plots generally revolve around young women entering society, encountering social humiliation and, eventually, finding happiness in marriage. However, in 1859, she published in serial format *The Manor House of de Villerai: A Tale of Canada Under the French Dominion.* Following in the footsteps of authors like Sir Walter Scott (1771-1832) and James Fenimore Cooper (1789-1851), this historical novel presents the conquest of Canada from the perspective of the French and their political concerns in the aftermath of the Seven Years' War. This was followed by *Antoinette de Mirecourt; or Secret Marrying and Secret Sorrowing* (1864) which focuses on cultural relations after the conquest, and *Armand Durand; or A Promise Fulfilled* (1868) which deals with Lower Canada

[3] Published by John Lovell and John Gibson, the journal, subtitled "A Repository of Tales, Sketches, Poetry, Music, Engravings," ran from 1838 to 1851. Its specific aim was to be a "vehicle of Canadian literary expression," the masthead stating its purpose as "A fragrant wreath composed of native flowers/ Plucked in the wilds of Nature's rude domain." Leprohon's first poem was "The Young Novice" which appeared in Vol. 4, No. 11 (Nov 1846) edition (page 524). Her poetry appeared regularly and, in 1849, her first prose piece "Alice Sydenham's First Ball" appeared in issue 1 of that year (1-14).

[4] Leprohon had thirteen children.

in the early nineteenth century. These three novels were written in English and then translated into French[5] and were immensely popular with both English and French readers.

Leprohon lived in what might be termed a culturally liminal space. Coming from an Irish-Anglo background and marrying into a prominent French-Canadian family,[6] she had a unique perspective on French-Canadian life. This access to the two cultural worlds of Lower Canada acted as a form of literary bridge between these two solitudes.[7] Her novels which feature French-Canadian characters show a great respect and understanding of their culture and history, presenting the need for cultural survival in the face of British domination. As McMullen states, "in Canada there have been few writers who moved this effectively between the traditions and languages of the two founding cultures" (14). She is thus able to sympathetically and realistically portray French-Canadian characters for an English-speaking audience.

---

[5] The translation of the novel was done by Leprohon's nephew Edouard de Bellefeuille, a young law student. In 1859, he presented and published his thesis *Sur les mariages clandestins* [On Clandestine Marriages]. In it he states that "mais malgré cela la mariage continue toujours d'être d'abord un contrat naturel et un Sacrement; et c'est pour cela que, quand on parle du mariage, on ne parle pas d'un contrat ordinaire, comme le contrat de vente, le contrat d'éxchange, de louage, etc" (5) [but in spite of this, marriage still continues to be first of all a natural contract and a sacrament; and that is why, when we speak of marriage, we do not speak of an ordinary contract, such as the contract of sale, the contract of exchange, of hire, etc]. In this novel, the marriage is the latter form of contract, one which binds Antoinette to silence and secrecy. Like the cities of Montreal and Quebec during the Seven Years' War, she is under siege and brutalized by her husband. She is a territory to be acquired and controlled, wanted only for her financial potential.

[6] Her husband, Lucien Leprohon is just as interesting a figure as his wife. As a medical practitioner, he began *La Lancette Canadienne* (1847), a French-language medical journal and the first medical journal in Canada, in the hopes of connecting the French medical community. In 1855, after returning to Montreal, he worked with the military as a physician, before returning to private practice. In 1870, he helped found the Women's Hospital of Montreal. Active in local politics, he was particularly interested in sanitation. In 1871 he became professor of hygiene at Bishop's College in Lennoxville. He was vice-president of the College of Physicians and Surgeons of the Province of Quebec.

[7] This term was coined to describe the divided society of Canada; it was popularized by Hugh MacLennan in his novel *Two Solitudes* (1945).

Historical Context: Conquest and Confederation

The historical contexts of both the novel's setting and its composition are necessary in order for readers to fully understand Leprohon's intentions.

The setting

The novel is set at the end of the Seven Years' War (1756-1763). This was a global conflict between Great Britain, Prussia, and Hanover on one side and France, Austria, Sweden, and Russia on the other. Since only the colonies of England and France are of concern for this novel, we will concentrate on the North-American theatre of war.

Great Britain's expansion beyond its original thirteen colonies in North America was impeded by France's occupation of all territory along the Mississippi river basin. Of particular contention was the fertile land in the Ohio River valley which was under French control. In order to protect this asset, France began constructing forts along the Ohio River, and manning them with militia units. This militarization worried British settlers and negotiations between the two European nations proved futile. In May 1754, British colonial militia, led by a young Lieutenant George Washington, attacked Fort Duquesne (present day Pittsburgh, Pennsylvania), marking the beginning of what was termed by the English as the French and Indian Wars, the North-American front of the Seven Years' War.[8] Because the British colonists outnumbered the French (2 million versus 70,000), alliances with Indigenous peoples were essential.[9] In 1756, Britain declared war on France and the European theatre of conflict opened.

Initially, British troops concentrated on protecting their own territories in North America. However, with the end of the Ohio conflict in 1758 which resulted in a British victory, they turned their attention to the French territories to their north, specifically the cities of Quebec and Montreal. In 1759, Quebec was captured, followed by the capitulation of Montreal in 1760.

[8] In Quebec, the conflict is known as La Guerre de la Conquête.

[9] The French allied themselves with the Wendat (Huron) people while the English allies were the Haudenosaunee (Iroquois) nation.

Although the war in Europe continued for another three years, the conflict in North America was over. In February 1763, the Treaty of Paris was signed and, in that treaty, France ceded its North-American territories to Great Britain. The treaty guaranteed the roughly 70,000 French-Canadians generous terms including freedom of worship, their French civil law, and freedom from deportation.

The novel's writing

The novel was written during the Confederation process of the mid-nineteenth century. In 1841, after the violent rebellions of Upper and Lower Canada,[10] the two provinces were united under the Act of Union into one unit: the Province of Canada. To the dismay of French-Canadians, the original joint government was replaced with one government with equal representation. Unfortunately for French Canada, this meant that they would be underrepresented in government.

In 1858, George-Étienne Cartier (co-prime minister of Canada) and John A. Macdonald argued that it would be best to split the two Canadas into provinces, joining each one to a federal union along with New Brunswick, Nova Scotia, Prince Edward Island, and Newfoundland. The reasons were practical: running the country would be more efficiently done if the federal government looked after national decisions while the provinces administered to local issues. Additionally, confederation would strengthen the economy. There were also fears of American military reprisals after England supported the southern states in the American Civil war (1861-1865). For these reason, as well as the need for a transcontinental railway to connect the provinces, confederation was seen as a necessity.

Despite the obvious need for a union, not everyone was supportive of the proposal. In Quebec, Jean-Baptiste-Eric Dorion (1826-1866) began the newspaper *L'Avenir* as a public forum for

---

[10] The rebellion in Lower Canada was far more violent than in Upper Canada. Louis-Joseph Papineau and his Patriotes demanded responsible government, control over government spending, and limiting the control of the Roman Catholic Church. French-Canadian farmers suffered through an economic depression in the 1830s. Protests led to armed conflict between the French and English, resulting in the burning of French-Canadian homes and businesses. For more historical depth on these uprising, see Allen Greer's *The Patriots and the People: The Rebellion of 1837 in Rural Lower Canada* (1993).

opposition to the plan. He and others believed that "conflicts will always be resolved in favour of the general government and to the detriment of the often legitimate claims of the provinces" ("Confederation's Opponents"). The Roman Catholic church supported the confederation proposal, arguing that confederation and the division of the country into specific provinces would give French-Canadians their identity and a provincial capital. For the rest of the population, under the old union Quebec had forty percent of the population but shared equally in governance which gave them a cultural security. The new legislative changes meant that Quebec, which now had only thirty percent of the population over the four provinces, would have less representation and less security at the federal level. As a result, forty percent of Quebec's eligible population voted no to confederation; the sixty percent who voted yes did so because it was seen as "la moins mauvaise des choses dans un monde fort mauvais" [the least bad thing in a world of bad things].

Manners, morals, and politics

On its surface, *Antoinette de Mirecourt* is a novel of manners in the style of Frances Burney's *Evelina* (1778) or Jane Austen's *Pride and Prejudice* (1813): a young, beautiful heroine, naïve to the ways of the world, must navigate the marriage market with little guidance. Morals, manners, and behavioral conventions are of primary concern and direct readers' reactions to the various characters as to whether they meet those expectations or not. In general, these novels deal with the private sphere—the home is central to the feminine action; men leave or withdraw into masculine spaces where women are not allowed by convention.[11] *Antoinette de Mirecourt* follows these well-established conventions. Much like *Pride and Prejudice*, where a unit of militia is stationed in the village of Meryton during the Napoleonic Wars, British troops established a garrison in Montreal that was maintained for almost a century after 1763. Like the officers in Austen's novel, these men, now with

[11] If the novels of Jane Austen are used as examples of the novel of manners, *Pride and Prejudice* only presents the action from the female characters' points of view. Readers never enter Mr. Bennet's library because it is closed to his wife and daughters; we do not follow Mr. Collins or Mr. Darcy into their spaces of work or study. In addition, Austen's novel *Northanger Abbey* (1816) includes a chapter 5, just like this novel, which interrupts the plot by presenting, in Austen's case, a vindication of the novel genre.

little to do, disrupt normal life. It is the bicultural content and the after-effects of conquest that complicate the simple marriage plot. In this novel, marriage is not a domestic ideal, but instead used as a metaphor for conquest and confederation. Quebec is symbolically represented by Antoinette. Of marriageable age, she must find the most suitable spouse, just like the *habitant* in the editorial cartoon below.

LE MOMENT PSYCHOLOGIQUE
LE CANADA: Me voilà homme maintenant et il me faut un habit neuf. Lequel vais-je choisir. Celui de l'impérialisme est trop large et pas assez long; celui de l'annexion est trop long et pas assez large. Je crois qu'une bonne tuque et un capot d'étoffe, sont encore ce qui m'irait le mieux.

The Psychological Moment. **Canada**: I am a man now, and I need a new suit. Let's see what I will choose. Imperialism is too large and not long enough; annexation is too long and not large enough. I think the good tuque and a cloth hood are still what suits me best.

The British garrisons in Montreal and Quebec meant that there was a strong military presence in the territory. Once hostilities were resolved, the inevitable interaction between the French and English helped to ease former antipathies. These interactions also created some serious issues romantically. Young soldiers, away from home and dealing with homesickness and boredom, naturally turned to the local French-Canadian ladies for companionship. Parties, concerts, and sleigh-rides were the perfect locations for the blossoming of young love. The young ladies who partook in these occasions were colloquially known as muffins[12] and the fear of muffinage (marriage to one of the local ladies) was real. According to a report by Field-Marshall Viscount Garnet Wolseley, "several impressionable young captains and subalterns had to be sent home hurriedly to save them from imprudent marriages" (115-116). Thus, the secret marriage in the novel is not implausible in this atmosphere of social co-mingling. As a mother of young daughters, Leprohon was probably well aware of these dangers.

Major Audley Sternfield is a young, attractive marital possibility. A dashing officer, he is described as having a "tall and splendidly-proportioned figure... [and] faultless beauty"—a veritable "Apollo." The reader quickly learns that there is mendacity behind that handsome exterior. He pressures Antoinette into a secret marriage, an arrangement she cannot acknowledge until it has been paternally approved and sacramentally confirmed. After gaining his prize, Sternfield transforms into a "cruel and heartless tyrant." Just like the former French colony, Antoinette was besieged, conquered and reduced to submission by her "new master." His name, Sternfield, implies an uncompromising field of conflict. Allegorically, this type of merger is not based on equality, respect, or honesty. Instead, it is a complete surrender to overbearing authority.

Antoinette's second option is her childhood friend Louis Beauchesne. Handsome, French, Roman Catholic as opposed to the "aliens . . . to the [French] race, creed, and tongue," Louis is, on the surface, a perfect match. However, Antoinette feels she cannot marry him because she views him purely as a brother. This quasi-incestuous union would be paternally sanctioned, but would be without the love Antoinette desires in a marriage. By the end of the novel, Louis must flee the country and return to France after dueling with Sternfield. Allegorically, Louis represents the old regime of France, Louis and Antoinette being the names of the monarchs at the time of the French Revolution. Unlike the political cartoon which represents independence as the best suit, Leprohon implies that to remain politically and culturally isolated in the new nation of Canada is not viable.

[12] The term comes from a bastardization of *ma femme*.

Finally, Colonel Cecil Evelyn proves to be the only suitable match. Initially presented as handsome but moody and dauntingly gruff with a reputation as a misogynist, he quickly comes to respect Antoinette after witnessing her calm demeanor during a life-threatening crisis. This respect evolves into love; combined with a common moral base (he is Roman Catholic), he becomes the ideal partner for Antoinette. He "fearlessly brave[s] the world's judgement" about her secret, scandalous past and marries her despite public opinion.[13] If we continue the political allegory, Evelyn is the perfect new suit for the new nation of Canada: deferential, honourable, and equitable. Domestic felicity is assured in such a union. The masculine world of war and politics is domesticated and feminized with Evelyn's submission to the French Antoinette.

In 1769, Frances Brooke (1724-1789) published *The History of Emily Montague*. Set in Quebec just after the English conquest of the city, the novel also uses the marriage plot as a backdrop for serious political discussion about how best to govern the French-Canadian population. Instead of conciliation or placation of the French, the novel recommends that religion, language and culture need to be Anglicized and anglicanized. The romantic plot eliminates intermingling of the cultures; the main male character, Colonel Edward Rivers, initially considers marriage to a wealthy French-Canadian widow Mme Des Roches. However, despite her wealth, intellect, and beauty, Rivers leaves her in the Canadian wilderness, opting instead to marry the very British Emily Montague. In the end, all the English characters return to England and domestic tranquility. Leprohon's novel is almost a rebuttal to Brooke's work; instead of the negative portrayal of the French *habitants*, they are presented as hardworking and helpful. The English soldiers are stripped of their heroic appearance and presented as largely tyrannical or ridiculous. Instead of retaining cultural purity and returning to England as the best landscape for domestic felicity, the ending of Leprohon's novel presents Canada and the intermingling of the cultures as not only possible but desirable. In feminist and post-colonial studies, Leprohon is a largely forgotten novelist. However, her three historical novels dealing with French Canada before and after the conquest are important contributions to the discourse on nationhood and identity.

[13] In many ways, Evelyn is like Austen's Mr. Darcy—proud to the point of rudeness, he is eventually the cause of good for the Bennet family, rescuing Lydia from ruining scandal.

Works Cited.

Literary Garland. https://www.canadiana.ca/view/oocihm.8_06178

McIntosh, Andrew. "Confederations Opponents". *The Canadian Encyclopedia*.

McMullen, Lorraine and Elizabeth Waterson. "Rosanna Mullins Leprohon: At Home in Many Worlds". Silences Sextet: Six Nineteenth-Century Canadian Women Novelists. Montreal: McGill-Queen's University Press, 1992: 14-51.

Montreal Herald. Tuesday, November 26, 1837. https://numerique.banq.qc.ca/patrimoine/details/52327/3130490

Montreal Directory (1842-1843). http://more.stevemorse.org/montreal_en.html

Stockdale, J.C. "Mullins, Rosanna Eleanora (Leprohon)". *Dictionary of Canadian Biography*. University of Toronto, 1972.

Wolseley, Garnet. *The Story of a Soldier's Life*. New York: Kraus Reprint Co., vol 2. 1971.

CHRONOLOGY

1829 – Rosanna Mullins is born on 12 January in Montreal.

1839 – Begins studies at the Convent of the Congregation of Notre Dame

1846 – Publishes her first poem ("The Young Novice") in *The Literary Garland.*

1847 – Serializes her first novel, *The Stepmother* in *The Literary Garland* (February-June).

1848 – Serializes her second novel, *Ida Beresford; or, The Child of Fashion* in *The Literary Garland* (January-September).

1849 – Meets the Leprohon family.
Publishes her first short story, "Alice Sydenham's First Ball," in *The Literary Garland* (January).
Serializes her third novel, *Florence Firz-Hardinge; or, Wit and Wisdom*, in *The Literary Garland* (February-December).

1850 – Serializes her fourth novel, *Eva Huntingdon*, in *The Literary Garland* (January-December).

1851 – Serializes her fifth novel, *Clarence Fitz-Clarence; Passages from the Life of an Egoist*, in *The Literary Garland* (January-May).
Marries Dr. Jean-Lukin [known as Lucien] Leprohon (1822-1900), a French-Canadian physician practising in Saint-Charles-sur-Richelieu.
The Literary Garland closes in December.

1852 – Her first son (Lucien) is born and dies.

1853 – Her first daughter (Gabrielle) is born.

1855 – The Leprohons settle in Rosanna's native Montreal.
Her second son (Rodolphe) is born.

1856 – Her third son (Claude) is born.

1857 – Her second daughter (Geraldine) is born.

1859 – She resumes publishing with the novella "Eveleen O'Donnell," which appears in *The Pilot* in Boston (January-February).
The Manor House of Villerai (her sixth novel) is serialized in *The Family Herald* (November 1859-February 1860).
She begins publishing poems in *The Journal of Education.*
Her fourth son (Édouard) is born.

1860 – *Le Manoir de Villerai* (the French translation of her sixth novel) is her first novel to be published as a book.
She translates Edouard Sempé's cantata for the Prince of Wales's visit to Montreal.

1862 – Her fifth son (Joseph Arthur Lukin) is born but dies in infancy.
An entry on "Mrs. Leprohon" appears in Henry J. Morgan's *Sketches of Celebrated Canadians.*

1863 – Her third daughter (Gertrude Ida) is born.

1864 – *Antoinette de Mirecourt* (her seventh novel) is published by John Lovell of Montreal..
Edward Hartley Dewart's anthology *Selections from Canadian Poets* includes five poems by Rosanna Leprohon.

1865 – *Antoinette de Mirecourt* appears in French translation.
Her fourth daughter (Marie Antoinette Selby) is born but dies in infancy.

1866 – Poems by Leprohon are selected in the anthology *The Harp of Canaan.*

1867 – Her fifth daughter (Eleanore Florina) is born but dies in infancy.

1868 – Serializes her seventh novel, *Armand Durand; or, A Promise Fulfilled*, in *The Daily News* (also published as a book by Lovell the same year).
Her sixth daughter (Marie Florence) is born.

1869 – Serializes *Ada Dunmore; or, A Memorable Christmas Eve* (her eighth novel) in *The Canadian Illustrated News* (December 1869-February 1870). The French translation appears in book form.

1870 – Publishes "My Visit to Fairview Villa" in *The Canadian Illustrated News* (May).
Her sixth son (Jean de Niverville) is born.

1872 – Serializes *The Dead Witness; or, Lillian's Peril* (her ninth novel) in *The Hearthstone* (August-October).
Publishes the short story "Clive Weston's Wedding Anniversary" in *The Canadian Monthly and National Review* (July-August).
Her seventh daughter (Maude) is born but dies in infancy.

1874 – Publishes "Who Stole the Diamonds?" in *The Canadian Illustrated News* (January).

1877 – Publishes "A School-Girl Friendship" in *The Canadian Illustrated News* (August-September).

1879 – Rosanna Leprohon dies of heart failure on 20 September in Montreal.

1881 – *The Poetical Works of Mrs. Leprohon* (probably edited by John Reade) is published posthumously.

Note on the text

This edition is based on the original version, *Antoinette De Mirecourt; or, Secret Marrying and Secret Sorrowing. A Canadian Tale*. By Mrs. Leprohon (Montreal: John Lovell, 1864).

Spelling that seems unusual or wrong today but that was in fact accepted at the time when the novel was written (e.g., "enthral," "woful," "wofully," "secresy," as well as alternative participles like "sprang" for "sprung") has been preserved. Similarly, we have preserved the wavering spelling of some words (both "gray" and "grey," "enquire" as well as "inquire").

Typographical errors ("requsite" for "requisite" or "exqusite" for "exquisite," quite common in the nineteenth century) have been tacitly corrected. Missing diacritics in the numerous French phrases have been tacitly incorporated.

A list of sources for the footnotes can be found at the end of this volume.

In an Appendix we have included Rosanna Leprohon's last known literary production: the short story "A School-Girl Friendship," which was first published in *The Canadian Illustrated News* (Vol. 16, 8-11, 25 August-17 September 1877, 118, 134, 158, 174).

The reader will find striking similarities and interesting differences between that story and *Antoinette de Mirecourt.* Typographical errors have been corrected or are explained in the story's footnotes.

Antoinette de Mirecourt;
or,
Secret Marrying and Secret Sorrowing.
A Canadian Tale.

ROSANNA LEPROHON

PREFACE

The simple Tale unfolded in the following pages, was not originally intended to be issued with any prefatory remarks. Advised, however, that it is usual to do so, the author, having no wish to deviate from the established custom, will merely say:

Although the literary treasures of "the old world" are ever open to us, and our American neighbors should continue to inundate the country with reading-matter, intended to meet all wants and suit all tastes and sympathies, at prices which enable every one to partake of this never-failing and ever-varying feast; yet Canadians should not be discouraged from endeavoring to form and foster a literature of their own.

More than one successful effort towards the attainment of this object has been made within the last few years, and more than one valuable work, Canadian in origin, subject, and sympathies, has been produced and published among us. To every true Canadian this simple fact must afford no little gratification, and any fresh contribution will not prove unwelcome. Therefore, remembering that the smallest stone employed always helps a little in the construction of even the loftiest building, the author, not altogether without some hope of a favorable reception, ventures on introducing to the public this work; satisfied that if ANTOINETTE DE MIRECOURT possesses no other merit, it will, at least, be found to have that of being essentially Canadian.

Chapter I.

The feeble sun of November, that most unpleasant month in our Canadian year, was streaming down on the narrow streets and irregular buildings of Montreal, such as it existed in the year 176—,[1] some short time after the royal standard of England had replaced the fleur-de-lys of France.[2]

Reflecting back the red sunlight in the countless small panes of its narrow casements, stood a large and substantial-looking stone house, situated towards the east extremity of Notre Dame street, then the aristocratic quarter of the city.[3] Without going through the ceremony of raising the ponderous knocker, we will pass through the hall-door, with its arched fan-light overhead,[4] and, entering the mansion, take a short survey of its interior and inmates. Despite the lowness of the ceilings, so justly incompatible with our modern ideas of elegance, or even

[1] Though the year remains unspecified, there are several clues in the novel that suggest the story begins in 1763, during the military occupation of Montreal, at a time when the Seven Years' War was not yet over.

[2] Montreal was surrendered to the British on 8 September 1760. The official transfer of sovereignty was recognized in the Treaty of Paris of 1763.

[3] Notre-Dame Street, which runs parallel to the Saint Lawrence River, is one of the oldest streets in Montreal. In the 1760s, its "east extremity" would have reached today's Bonsecours Market.

[4] The fanlight window (usually called a transom window in the US) is a semicircular window (often glazed) placed above the entrance door of a house and divided by narrow bars into several sections, which gives it the appearance of an open fan.

comfort,[5]—despite the rough wood-carving and tarnished gilding encircling the doors and windows, and the quaint, useless wooden architraves running round the walls of the different apartments,[6] there is a stamp of unmistakable wealth and refinement pervading the abode.

Glimpses of fine old paintings, costly inlaid cabinets,[7] antique vases, and other objects of art, revealed through the half-open doors, confirm this impression, even before we are told that the mansion is inhabited by Monsieur D'Aulnay, one of the most distinguished among the few families of the old French *noblesse*,[8] who continued to dwell in any of the principal cities after their country had passed under a foreign rule.[9]

The master of the house, a plain-featured but gentlemanly-looking man, was seated, at the moment in which we introduce him to the reader, in his large and well-lighted library. The three sides of this, his favorite apartment, were covered, from ceiling to floor, with compactly-filled shelves, whilst a few well-executed busts or good portraits of literary men were the only ornaments of any sort which

[5] A late-Victorian architect (and Leprohon's contemporary) explained that "Modern taste, trained in modern Gothic notions, loves height" and that a "cause of the great height of our modern houses is our liking for high ceilings" (Stevenson II, 145).

[6] In classical architecture, architraves were beams placed on top of columns, but in modern times they have become a kind of moulding above doors and windows. They are described here as "useless" since they continue "round the walls."

[7] Richly inlaid furniture (with arabesques of tortoiseshell, brass and pewter) was mostly the invention of the Frenchman André-Charles Boulle (1642-1732). Cabinets made by him or his apprentices were very popular in the houses of 18th-century French aristocracy.

[8] French for "nobility" or "aristocracy."

[9] About 30% to 40% of the French nobility (some three hundred families) left Quebec after 1754 (when the French and Indian War started). See Gadoury 156-159 and Larin 101-102. Such figures are complicated by the fact that some of the people who left during or immediately after the war came back, and that many Acadian refugees came to Quebec around the same time.

the room contained. The serviceable, dark bindings of the volumes, innocent of gilding or gaudy lettering, betrayed they were valued by their owner more for their contents than their appearance; and in his earnest, unostentatious love of literature, might have been found the key to the tranquil placidity of character which distinguished him under circumstances which would have often severely tried the patience of less philosophic men. When hosts of his personal friends and relatives urged him, after the capitulation of Montreal, to do as they were doing, and return to *la vieille France*,[10] or at least seek the solitude of his wealthy seigneurie in the country,[11] and bury himself there for the remainder of his days, he looked round his library, sighed, and shook his head. In vain some fiery spirits indignantly asked him how he could brook the arrogance of the proud conquerors who had landed on their shores? how he could endure to meet, wherever eye or footstep turned, the scarlet uniforms of the epauletted heroes who now governed his native land in King George's name.[12] To their indignant remonstrances he sadly but calmly rejoined he should not see much of them, for he intended establishing himself henceforth permanently in his beloved library, and going abroad as little as possible. When farther pressed on the subject, he referred his friendly persecutors to Madame D'Aulnay; and as it was well known that that fair lady had on several occasions expressed her fixed determination to never bury herself during life in the country, though she

[10] French for "old France." The original contains a misspelling, as it reads "vielle."

[11] Also spelled "seigniory" in English. The seigneurial system in New France involved a special kind of land tenure in which landlords (the "seigneurs") were allotted large holdings, out of which they rented out long lots along bodies of water (also known as "ribbon farms") to peasant farmers.

[12] Allusion to British soldiers, also known as "redcoats" because of the color of their uniforms, and to the first British governors of Canada, who were all generals who had taken part in the conquest. George III was king from 1760 to 1820.

had no objections to their burying her there after death, he was generally, at this stage of the argument, left in peace.

As we have said, Mr. D'Aulnay was seated in his library, absorbed in the perusal of some abstruse and learned work, no political regrets or projects disturbing for the moment his intellectual enjoyment, when the door of the apartment opened, and an elegant looking woman, on the shady side of Balzac's admired feminine age of thirty,[13] and dressed with the most exquisite taste and care, entered.

"Mr. D'Aulnay," she exclaimed, laying a dainty, heavily-ringed hand on his shoulder.

"Well, what is it, Lucille?" and he half closed his book with a regretful though not impatient look.

"I have come to tell you that Antoinette has just arrived."

"Antoinette," he absently repeated.

"Yes, you moon-struck man," and the little hand inflicted a playful tap on his cheek. "My cousin Antoinette, whom I have been vainly begging of that cross uncle of mine, for the last six months; and who has been at last granted a chance of seeing a little of life under my auspices."

"Do you mean that rosy, good-humored little girl I saw two summers ago, in the country, at Mr. De Mirecourt's?"

"The same, but instead of a little girl, she is now a young lady, and a wealthy heiress besides. Uncle De Mirecourt has consented to her passing the winter with me, and I am determined that she shall see a little society during that time."

"Ah! I understand too well what that means," groaned Mr. D'Aulnay. "So our present domestic rules are to be subverted, the house completely upset, and the whole place overrun with idle young fops, or unknown men with swords clashing against their heels, as you have been studiously hinting to me for some time past. Alas! I thought

[13] In *A Woman of Thirty* (*La Femme de Trente Ans*), first published in instalments between 1830 and 1832, Honoré de Balzac (1799-1850) praises the woman of thirty for being sophisticated and mercurial.

when the Chevalier de Lévis and his gallant epaulettes left the country,[14] there was to be an end to all this military fervor or fever; and I must to my shame acknowledge, that if anything could have tended to console me during that darkest episode of the history of my country, it was the supposition I have just mentioned."

"What would you, *cher ami*?"[15] plaintively questioned Mrs. D'Aulnay. "Have we not mourned in sackcloth and ashes, as it were,[16] for many a long and dreary month since; but people must live, and to live they must see society. I really would as soon assume the garb of a female Carmelite, and see you don a Trappist's cowl and robe at once,[17] as live any longer in the cloister-like seclusion in which we have been vegetating for an interminable time past."

"Nonsense, Lucille! As to the Trappist's cowl and robe, I think they would be more suitable to my age and tastes, and certainly far more comfortable, than the silk stockings and ball-room costume which your new projects will compel me so often to assume. But to discuss the matter seriously, surely you who used to talk so pathetically over the woes of Canada with the brave French soldiers who have left our shores—who used to enthral your listeners by your eloquent and patriotic denunciations of our enemies and

[14] The Chevalier de Lévis (François Gaston de Lévis, 1719-1787) took command of the French forces after the Marquis de Montcalm died in the Battle of the Plains of Abraham (1759) and unsuccessfully tried to retake Quebec. He left the country in 1761 and lived his remaining years in France. The city of Lévis, on the south shore of the Saint Lawrence River opposite Quebec City, bears his name.

[15] French for "dear friend."

[16] Sackcloth and ashes are mentioned several times in the Bible as an outward sign of mourning or repentance.

[17] Neither the Carmelites nor the Trappists had any monasteries in Canada at the time. However, they were both famous monastic orders. The Carmelites were founded as a male order during the Crusades, but the name was later associated more often with nuns, whose order was founded in the 15th century. The cowl is a long, hooded garment worn by monks.

oppressors, and were compared by Col. De Bourlamaque[18] to one of the heroines of the *Fronde*,[19]—surely you are not going to entertain and feast those same oppressors now?"

"My dear, dear D'Aulnay, I again repeat, what alternative have I? I cannot invite clerks or apprentices to my house, and our own people are nearly all dispersed in one direction or another. Those English officers may be tyrants, ruthless oppressors, what you will; but they are men of education and refinement; and—conclusive argument—they are my only resource."

"Pray, tell me, then, when this reign of anarchy is to be inaugurated?" questioned Mr. D'Aulnay, silenced though not convinced.

"Oh, on that point, my dear André, I am certain of meeting with your approbation. The good old Canadian *fête* of *la Sainte Catherine*, a day which our ancestors from time immemorial have joyously observed,[20] will be the evening I will choose for again opening our doors to something like life and gaiety."

"And I fear closing them against peace and comfort; but, do you know any of the men who are destined henceforth to fill our *salons*[21] and to eat our suppers?"

---

[18] Misspelled in the original as "Bourlamarque," here and elsewhere. François-Charles de Bourlamaque (1716-1764) was a French military commander of Italian origin. After the defeat of New France, he became governor of Guadeloupe.

[19] The Fronde was not one, but two revolts against the crown in mid-17th-century France. Many aristocratic women took part in the revolt (see Vergnes, for example, for an account of their participation).

[20] The feast of St Catherine (25 November) was first attested in the 13th century in France, where it is traditionally seen as a celebration of girls. In Quebec, the feast was mostly an occasion for spinsters (young women older than 25) to find a suitable husband. Madame D'Aulnay uses the term "Canadian" in the sense of French Canadian, which was the accepted meaning in the 18th century.

[21] The salon is the great ballroom in French palatial dwellings and, by extension, the largest room in any big house. In the 18th century especially, the term also referred to the people who usually gathered in such a room.

"Yes; Major Sternfield called here yesterday with that young Foucher, who, in times past, would scarcely have obtained admittance into my house; but, alas! society is so reduced in point of numbers, we cannot afford to be too exclusive now."

"Was that long-legged flamingo I caught a glimpse of in the hall, Major Sternfield?" questioned Mr. D'Aulnay.

"Long-legged flamingo!" reiterated the lady, petulantly, "what an extraordinary choice of unsuitable epithets. Major Sternfield is certainly one of the handsomest and most elegant men I have ever met; and, what is more to the point, he is a perfect gentleman in manner and address. He expressed, in the most deferential terms, the earnest, anxious desire of himself, and many of his brother officers, to obtain entrance into our Canadian *salons*—"

"Yes, to pick up any heiresses among us, and after turning the heads of all the rest of the girls, jilt them," grumbled Mr. D'Aulnay.

"Ah, you are mistaken," rejoined his wife with animation. "Myself and country-women will take good care that in all cases they shall be the sufferers, not ourselves. Antoinette and I shall break dozens of their callous hearts, and thus avenge our country's wrongs."

"Heaven preserve me from a woman's logic!" muttered the sorely-tried husband, hurriedly re-opening his book, and settling himself back in his chair. "There, there, invite them all, from General to Ensign, if you will, but leave me in peace."

Chapter II.

Elated by her success, Mdme. D'Aulnay traversed, with a light step, the long, narrow corridor, leading from the library, and turned off at the right into a pretty, airy bed-room, furnished with every possible attention to comfort. The apartment, however, at the moment in question, was in considerable confusion. Shawls and scarfs lay scattered on the chairs; whilst a half-opened trunk, with innumerable band-boxes,[22] lay heaped upon the floor.

Standing before the tall *Psyche*,[23] adding a last smoothing touch to her rich waves of hair, stood a young girl, with a slight, exquisitely-formed figure, and very lovely, expressive face.

"Dressed already, my charming cousin!" smilingly exclaimed Madame D'Aulnay. "You have done much with very little;" and she glanced significantly, if not contemptuously, at the dark gray dress, as simple in its fashion as it was in material, which the young girl wore. "But, come, let me look at you well. I had only a glimpse of you, just now;" and, suiting the action to the word, she drew her guest towards the window, first pushing entirely back the heavy damask curtains that hung before it.

"Why, Antoinette, child, do you know that you have grown positively beautiful? Such a complexion—"

[22] A band-box was used to store ribbons and, later, hats.

[23] Psyche was a Greek goddess of the soul, better known however as Cupid's beloved in Apuleius's version of her story.

"Mercy, mercy, Lucille!" laughed the object of this eulogium, deprecatingly raising her pretty little hands before her face; "just what Madame Gérard prophesied before I left home."

"And, pray, what did that tiresome, punctilious, scrupulous old governess prophesy? Come, tell me;" and, placing her young companion in a cushioned *fauteuil*,[24] she drew another towards her, and sank into its soft depths.

"Well, first of all, she did all in her power, talked more in one week than I have heard her do in months, to induce papa to prevent my coming. She spoke of my youth and utter inexperience—the dangers and snares that might beset my steps, and then, dear Lucille, she spoke of you."

"And what did she say of me?"

"Nothing very terrible. Simply that you were graceful, accomplished, and fascinating ('tis your turn to hide your blushes now), but that you were eminently unfit for the responsible office of mentor to a girl of seventeen. Whilst you were imaginative, thoughtless and impulsive, I was giddy, childish and romantic; so she argued that nothing good could come of committing me six long months to your guidance."

"And what said Uncle De Mirecourt to all this?"

"Not much at first, but I am tempted to think poor Madame Gérard said too much. You know papa always says he possesses a good share of the firmness—to use a mild term—constituting from time immemorial one of our family attributes; and when Mrs. Gérard became so urgent and earnest, he began to say just as decidedly that, as I was seventeen, it was time I should see something of society; or, at least of town life,—that Madame D'Aulnay was his niece, and an amiable, kind-hearted woman,—with many other flattering speeches, of which I will spare you the recital. Still, the day was beginning to go against us, for he thinks a great deal of Mrs. Gérard's judgment; and he

[24] French for "armchair."

concluded by remarking that I might postpone my town visit to another winter,—when I, overwhelmed by this sudden disappointment of all my hopes and prospects, burst into tears. That decided the matter. Papa declared he had already half engaged his word to me, and that unless I chose myself to free him from his promise, he must keep it. Then Mrs. Gérard turned to me, and for two days her kindly-meant entreaties, and gentle counsels, made me the most miserable little girl in the world. Indeed, I had finally made up my mind to yield to her wishes, when your last urgent, kind letter arrived. After its perusal, I embraced her tenderly,—for she has been, from my early childhood, a true and loving friend,—and implored her to forgive me this once for disobeying her. She said—but, no matter, here I am!"

"And most welcome you are, you dear little creature! I declare, I would have had neither heart nor courage to enter on this season's campaign, without some such auxiliary as yourself. You are a wealthy heiress, high-born and handsome, and you will meet here the very *élite* of those elegant English strangers."

"English!" repeated Antoinette, with a slight start. "Oh, Lucille, papa hates the very name."

"What of that, child! If we do not have them, who are we to have? Our darling French officers have left us for ever,[25] together with the flower of our young *noblesse*. Any that remain of the latter are dispersed throughout the country parishes, burrowing in dismal seigniories or lonely old family mansions,[26] and would prove at best but uncertain and occasional visitors. Surely, then, I am not to fill the drawing-rooms that have been crowded, night after night, with men like De Bourlamaque and his chivalric

[25] French regulars troops left after the British conquest of New France.

[26] Parishes were understood as small administrative units; seigniories (the English version of a word that first appeared in its French version; see note 11) usually included a manorial house.

companions, with such creatures as the occupants of the inferior government or other offices, which our English masters have judged too paltry to be worth destituting. But, tell me, area the two Léonard girls coming to town soon?"

"Yes; I receiving a few lines yesterday from Louise, mentioning they were both coming to spend a couple of months in Montreal with their aunt."

"*Tant mieux!*[27] They are handsome, elegant-looking girls, and will be quite an addition to our circle. But, I must warn you in time that you must have a charming evening dress ready for next Thursday, the purchase and making of which, by the way, I must superintend myself. I intend that we shall celebrate *la Sainte Catherine* with all possible splendor. In the meantime, if you should feel lonesome, or find yourself at a loss for amusement, you have only to look from the window at any hour in the afternoon, and you can see the fine imposing figures of our intended guests, lounging up and down our rough pavements."

"Do you know any of them yet, Lucille?"

"I have made the acquaintance of only one; but if he is anything like a fair specimen of the rest, I assure you we shall waste no more sighs on any of De Lévis' gallant followers. Major Sternfield,—that is the name of my new military acquaintance,—and (*par parenthèse*)[28] he has placed the whole regiment at my disposal, guaranteeing that they shall make themselves equally useful and agreeable;— Major Sternfield, then, is superbly handsome, polished and courteous in manner, in short a most accomplished man of the world.[29] He got young Foucher to introduce him here; and though I received him somewhat coldly at first, my reserve soon yielded to the deferential homage of his

[27] French for "all for the better."

[28] French for "as a side note."

[29] The 18th-century gentleman was also expected to be a "man of the world," even though the two notions sometimes clashed. This was famously expressed in Lord Chesterfield's *Letters to His Son on the Art of Becoming a Man of the World and a Gentleman* (1774).

address, and the delicate flattery of his manner. By way of climax to his many perfections, the dear creature speaks French charmingly. He told me he had spent two years in Paris. In taking leave, he asked permission to return soon with a couple of brother officers, who specially desired an introduction."

"And what says cousin D'Aulnay to all this?"

"Why, like a true philosopher, and a good, sensible husband as he is, he grumbles, but—submits. And 'tis better for us both he does so, for though scarcely a shadow of real sympathy exists between us (he is matter-of-fact, practical, and intensely literary, whilst I am romantic, enthusiastic in temperament, and cannot endure the sight of a book, unless it be a novel, or volume of sentimental poetry), we are still, in spite of such startling dissimilarity of tastes and character, happy, and mutually attracted to each other."

"Were you very much in love, then, with cousin D'Aulnay, when you married him?" questioned Antoinette, hesitatingly, for she felt she was treading on what had hitherto been almost forbidden ground to her young imagination.

"Oh dear, no! My parents, though kind and indulgent in other respects, showed me no consideration in this. They simply told me Mr. D'Aulnay was the husband they had chosen for me, and that I was to be married to him in five weeks. I cried for the first week almost without intermission. Then, mamma having promised me I should select my own *trousseau*,[30] and that it should be as rich and costly as I could desire, a different turn was given to my feelings, and I became so very busy with milliners and shopping, that I had not time for another thought of regret, till my wedding day arrived. Well, I was happy in my lot, for Mr. D'Aulnay has ever been both indulgent and generous; but,

[30] Also known as the "trousseau de mariage," it consisted of a woman's lingerie, as well as bedding and all sorts of house linens that were part of a bride's dowry.

my darling child, the experiment was fearfully hazardous,—one which might have resulted in life-long misery to both parties. Remember, Antoinette," continued the speaker, with a pretty air of sentiment, "that the only sure basis for a happy marriage, is mutual love, and community of soul and feeling."

Apparently, mutual esteem, moral worth, and prudence in point of suitable choice, counted for nothing with Madame D'Aulnay.

Well might the trustworthy governess have raised her voice against entrusting to such a mentor, Antoinette De Mirecourt, with her childish inexperience, rich, poetic imagination, and warm, impulsive heart.

Chapter III.

Having introduced our heroine to the reader, we will devote a few pages to her parentage and precedents.

Twenty years previous to the opening of our tale, on a golden October day, general rejoicing and gaiety reigned throughout the *seigneurie* and Manor-House of Valmont, in which Antoinette first saw the light, and which had belonged to her family from the early date at which the fief had been conceded to the gallant Rodolphe De Mirecourt. This *beau gentilhomme*,[31] who had landed in Canada possessing little else than a keen bright sword and a pair of shining spurs, soon found himself installed, in return for some services rendered the French crown, lord and owner of the rich and fertile demesne[32] of Valmont, which had descended since in direct line to its present owner, Arthur De Mirecourt. Arrived at the age of manhood, the latter yielded to a natural desire to see that gay sunny land of France, that polished brilliant Paris of which he had heard such marvels recounted. But though the splendor of the latter at first dazzled, and its countless attractions fascinated him, the young man soon began to weary of its glittering dissipation, and to long for the simple pleasures, the quiet life of his own land. Despite then the entreaties, the

[31] French for "handsome gentleman."

[32] A demesne was the land managed directly by a lord of the manor (not including the land rented to tenants); see also note 11.

indignant representations of his gay young Parisian friends; despite the reproachful glances of the dark eyed graceful dames who used to shed such pitying glances on him when allusion was made to the land of "snow and savages,"—he returned to his native country, fonder and more devoted to it than when he had left its shores. His sojourn in the brilliant French capital, had in no degree changed the simple healthful tastes of his boyhood, and never had he entered into the varied amusements of a Parisian *fête* with more buoyancy of spirit, and freshness of enjoyment than he did into the simple rejoicings succeeding his return to his own quiet home in Valmont.

Warm and loving hearts were waiting there to welcome him back,—the widowed mother, who had found so powerful a solace in his thoughtful affection, for the loss of the husband and children who lay sleeping beneath the seigneurial pew from which Sunday or holiday so rarely found her absent; friendly neighbors and censitaires[33] too, not omitting the orphaned Corinne Delorme, a young girl distantly related to Mrs. De Mirecourt, whom the latter had brought up with a mother's care, and whom he had always looked on as a dear sister.

This same Corinne, though possessing a graceful figure and regular small features, had never obtained the title of a beauty,—a circumstance which may have arisen in part from her total want of that gaiety and animation in which Canadian girls are so rarely deficient, or from a certain look of languor and pallor, the result of a very delicate fragile constitution.

A more exacting woman than Mrs. De Mirecourt might have occasionally taxed her young *protégée* with ingratitude, so undemonstrative, so quiet was she in word and manner; but then it must be remembered that the young girl never forgot those silent unobtrusive attentions, that respectful

[33] The "censitaires" were the lord's tenants (who paid him the "cens," i.e., the seigneurial dues).

deference which daughter owes to parent. Never perhaps had Corinne's constitutional coldness showed itself more plainly, or in a more annoying form to her benefactress, than on the occasion of Arthur De Mirecourt's return to his native land. Whilst household, friends and neighbors, were planning festivities and rejoicings to duly honor the expected arrival, she alone displayed a provoking calmness amounting to indifference; and on the morning of his return, when he turned towards her, after tenderly folding his mother in his arms, and drew her towards him in a brother's frank friendly embrace, she evinced no more emotion or joy than if they had only parted the day previous. Happening to touch upon the circumstance, in one of the pleasant confidential conversations which his mother declared amply repaid her for the loneliness she had experienced during his absence, Madame De Mirecourt found a dozen excuses for the delinquent. Poor Corinne was so sickly—subject to such frequent headaches—such great depression of spirits,—which benevolent pleas meanwhile did not prevent the young man from setting down the object of them as a cold unamiable egotist.

It might have been expected that Mrs. De Mirecourt, having but recently recovered her son as it were, would have been in no hurry to share the large place she held in his heart with any rival, and yet such was really the case. No sooner was he fairly installed at home than a restless desire to see him settled in life,—married, took possession of her. Acting on this maternal wish, a hint was given here and there to lady friends, and Arthur was soon besieged by invitations in every quarter, certain of meeting, wherever he went, fair young faces which would have looked to singular advantage in the low dark rooms of the old Manor-House. Arrived at the age of twenty-eight, rejoicing in a heart and fancy entirely free, young De Mirecourt by no means sought to keep aloof from these social meetings; and before long, he began to acknowledge secretly to himself, that he returned in some slight degree, the evident partiality that a certain graceful young heiress, possessed of radiant health and spirits, bestowed upon him. Matters not advancing however with that rapidity which Mrs. De Mirecourt desired, that wily lady determined on inviting the young girls she had privately selected as a future daughter-in-law, together with a few other young people, on a fortnight's visit. The visit was now drawing to a close, and nothing tangible had come of it. Arthur had indeed talked, danced and laughed a great deal with Mademoiselle De Niverville, who, in reality, was as good as she was charming, but that was all. No honeyed word, no tender love-vow had fallen from his lips; and she was now about returning home, and both parties were as free as if they had never met. Still the young man sincerely admired her, indeed he could scarcely do otherwise; and more than once, as the sweet gaiety, the winning kindness of her disposition, showed itself in such striking contrast to the apathetic indifference of Corinne, who seemed to grow colder and more reserved every day, he could not help wishing for his mother's sake, whose life-long companion the young girl, if she continued to be single, was destined to be, that she more nearly resembled the fair young heiress of De Niverville.

Meanwhile, Mrs. De Mirecourt, anxious and uneasy about the success of her matrimonial plans, bethought herself of seeking the co-operation of Corinne, and asking her to urge the dilatory Arthur to come to an understanding with Miss De Niverville before she left Valmont. Mrs. De Mirecourt would willingly have done this herself; but the two or three attempts she had made in that direction had been so firmly though laughingly parried by her son, that she deemed it unavailing. Corinne accepted, though perhaps somewhat reluctantly, the delicate mission confided to her, and sought one morning the breakfast room, in which Arthur, always an early riser, was reading alone. Very patiently he heard her, for her manner possessed more sisterly kindness than it usually betrayed; and she earnestly enlarged on Louise's merits and many good qualities—the hopes and expectations which she and her friends had probably founded on the attentions he had lately paid her, and on the happiness he would confer on his devoted mother by fulfilling the wish nearest her heart.

The quiet yet persuasive eloquence with which Corinne spoke, surprised whilst it half convinced her auditor. He made no answer, however, beyond smilingly replying that he had ample time yet, that the party were all going out sleighing that very afternoon; and as he intended driving the fair Miss De Niverville himself, he had a splendid opportunity for satisfying public expectation generally. Seeing that Corinne still looked very earnest, he took her hand, and added more gravely:

"Laughing or jesting will not prevent me, my kind little sister, from seriously reflecting, and perhaps acting on your recent kindly-intended counsels. The drive this afternoon will certainly afford a most favorable chance, if I can only make up my mind to avail myself of it. Of course you will join us?"

"I fear I cannot. I have a letter to write, and it is better for me to get rid of the task during the day, so that I may be free to join you all in the drawing-room on this, the last night that our guests will be with us. For this morning I have more work laid out than I can possibly accomplish."

What charming weather it was for a drive! How smooth were the dazzling white roads, how glorious the sunshine! Even Madame De Mirecourt had been induced to join the party, and buried under bear-skin robes, in her own comfortable roomy *carriole*,[34] looked as cheerful as the light-hearted Louise herself.

---

[34] In French Canada, the "carriole" (in the original it appears in the Anglicized version of "cariole") is a horse-drawn sleigh, though its original meaning is that of a light carriage.

Corinne, true to her previous determination, remained behind; and as she stood at the window waving them a friendly farewell, looking so pretty with that quiet smile on her delicate colorless features, and the sun-light gilding her rich silky hair, De Mirecourt again thought what a pity it was that so little feeling or warmth of character lurked beneath that fair exterior. But these thoughts were soon forgotten in the excitement of starting, and in the pleasurable duty of attending to his fair companion, and gathering the sleigh robes carefully around her. But, behold, after they had driven a short distance, the pretty Louise took it into her graceful head to imagine that she felt cold, and commenced bemoaning the want of a certain dark grey shawl, whose thick warm texture was a certain protection against the coldest of wintry blasts. Of course, a gallant cavalier like De Mirecourt instantly proposed returning to the house for it, and the sleigh was soon drawn up again at the starting point.

"I will hold the reins, Mr. De Mirecourt, whilst you run in for it. I left it in the little sitting-room. Pray do not be angry with me for being so forgetful and troublesome?"

The young man replied to the charming speaker with a dangerously tender smile, and then entered the house. Lightly and rapidly he ran up the staircase, into the apartment indicated. There, on the end of the sofa, he perceived the object of which he had come in quest; but as he hastily caught it up, the sound of a low though passionate sob fell on his ear. Surprised and startled, he glanced around. The sound again repeated, came from an inner chamber opening off the sitting room, and which a couple of book-cases had invested with the dignified title of library.

Who could it be? What did it mean? Suddenly, through the half open door, his eye fell on a mirror suspended opposite him, on the wall of the library; and clearly reflected in that mirror, was the figure of Corinne Delorme seated on a low stool, apparently in the utter abandonment of grief, her face bowed over some object which she held tightly clasped in her slender fingers, and on which she was showering impassioned kisses. That object was his miniature, a gift which he had brought his mother from France.[35]

All was madc clear to him now. The coolness, the indifference, was all feigned—an icy veil assumed to hide the devoted love that had grown with the young girl's growth, and become an engrossing sentiment of her life, a sentiment, however, which maiden pride and modesty had taught her so effectually to conceal. Yes, loving him as she did, she had found courage enough to plead the cause of another—to dismiss him with smiles when she supposed him on the point of offering the prize of his love to a rival.

Very quietly, very softly, De Mirecourt retreated, and when he rejoined Miss De Niverville, his face was much paler and graver than was its wont. During the drive, notwithstanding his utmost efforts, he was unusually preoccupied, and had to bear, in consequence, a considerable amount of raillery from his fair companion; but whatever course the conversation took, no profession or vow of love escaped his lips. Arrived at home, he soon made his escape from the lively group that gathered around the large double stove,[36] and it was not till a couple of hours after that he rejoined them.

The first person he met on entering the drawing room was Corinne; and with a quiet smile on her pale still face, she "hoped he had enjoyed his drive."

"Tolerably; but shall I tell you, sister mine, whether I followed out your counsels or not?"

---

[35] Portrait miniature was very popular in the 18th century and it continued to be more and more popular well into the 19th century, until the invention of photography.

[36] Double stoves included an outer case and a furnace (or inner stove). The fuel was burned in the inner stove while the outer case heated the air around it and thus heated up a large room or a series of adjoining rooms.

Brave young heart! Not the quivering of a feature, not the twitching of an eyelash, betrayed the terrible anguish that reigned within!

Softly, distinctly, the answer came:

"Yes; tell me that you have fulfilled the wishes of the best of mothers—of all your friends."

He looked earnestly, searchingly, in her face.

"Will *you* congratulate me, Corinne, if I have done so, and if my suit has prospered?"

A crimson flush, fading as rapidly as it rose, overspread her face, and turning away, she rejoined in a quiet, almost cold tone:

"Why should I not? Your choice is one against which no objection could possibly be raised."

Without openly avoiding him, Corinne contrived that, during the course of the evening, she and De Mirecourt should not find themselves again in proximity. He could read aright now, however, that apparent indifference and egotism which he had till lately so greatly misjudged and so strongly condemned.

The following day, Louise De Niverville left Valmont, and her tardy suitor had not spoken. With De Mirecourt's delicate sense of honor, his chivalrous generosity of character, it seemed to him that he was no longer free, that he belonged of right to her who had lavished on him unsought the hidden wealth of her secret love. After a week's quiet reflection, during which he found his fancy for Miss De Niverville had taken no root whatever in his heart,—a week during which Corinne had endeavored unceasingly to avoid him, struggling all the while as only a woman can struggle against that affection which was daily gaining in intensity and depth,—he sought her side one snowy winter evening, as she stood at the sitting room window, silently watching the white flakes falling outside, and, without many vows or protestations, asked her to be his wife.

She turned fearfully pale, and after a moment's silence whispered, "was she, a poor dependant, the bride his mother would choose, his friends approve of?"

"That is not what I ask you, dear Corinne. I do not marry to please either friends or mother; and besides, the latter loves me too well to find fault with choice of mine. Tell me, simply, do you love me well enough to become my wife?"

Slowly, hesitatingly, as if the secret, so long and so jealously kept, could scarcely be yielded up, came the little monosyllable—yes; and a few weeks later, they were married, quietly and without pomp, in the little village church,—Mrs. De Mirecourt, the first disagreeable sensation of the surprise over, easily sacrificing her own private wishes to those of her idolized son.

Once married, the indifference and coldness of Corinne's character vanished like snow before April sunshine, and never was wife more loving and more devoted. De Mirecourt never told her that he had surprised her secret, never told her that she owed as much to pity as to love; and soon his generosity met its reward, for an affection as ardent as that which his young wife had so long secretly cherished for him, sprang up in his heart towards herself. Alas! that union, blessed and trusting as theirs, was doomed to be so soon severed! Two years of domestic happiness, unclouded by look or word of estrangement, during which period Antoinette was born, was accorded them, and then the young wife, always delicate and fragile, began to droop.

No affection, no care could save her; and before many months had elapsed, she was taken from De Mirecourt's loving arms, and laid in her last earthly home. Ere the first anniversary of her death had arrived, Madame De Mirecourt had joined her, leaving the Manor-House as gloomy and silent as a tomb. The appointed time of mourning over, friends began to hint to the young widower that his home required a mistress, that he was too young to devote himself to a life-long sorrow.

Mr. De Mirecourt, however, remained deaf to all such friendly suggestions; and after procuring in the person of the estimable Madame Gérard, a suitable governess for his infant daughter, he subsided into the quiet country life he had led ever since.

Fortunate beyond measure was the little Antoinette in having found so kind and prudent a guide to replace the mother she had so early lost; and notwithstanding the excessive indulgence of her father, and the impulsive thoughtlessness of her own disposition, she had grown up an amiable and winning, though not wholly faultless character.

Chapter IV.

It was St. Catherine's Eve, that day always marked in French Canadian homes, whether in the *habitant*'s[37] cottage or the *seigneur*'s mansion, by innocent mirth and festivity, and which answers so nearly to our Hallow-E'en.[38]

On the night in question, Madame D'Aulnay's abode was blazing with waxen tapers[39] and resounding to the strains of lively cotillion and contre-danse;[40] whilst her handsome rooms, filled with glittering uniforms, and gauzy, perfumed dresses, presented a brilliant and enlivening scene.

Leaning gracefully beside the mantle-piece of the grate, the bright reflection of whose clear fire cast a most becoming glow on her really fine features, stood the elegant hostess herself, engaged in conversation with a tall, fine-

[37] A "habitant" (literally, "inhabitant") was a term applied to French-Canadian peasants.

[38] Allusion to the custom of preparing "St Catherine's taffy" ("tire de la Ste-Catherine") on 25 November. According to legend, the custom was initiated by Marguerite Bourgeoys, one of the founders of the city of Montreal, in order to attract young (indigenous) children to her school.

[39] Tapers were slender candles, usually too thin to stand upright and therefore kept in holders. In the 18th century, tapers made of wax were a symbol of gentility, since most people used tallow candles.

[40] Usually spelled "contredanse." It had dancers move in pairs arranged in files or in squares. The dance probably originated in France, from where it was imported in England and became a "country dance," and was then brought back to France in the 17th century by English dance masters.

looking man, whose clear bright color and dark blue eye betrayed his Anglo-Saxon descent. The lady had brought the whole artillery of her charms to bear on her companion, speaking glances, bewitching smiles, and sweetly modulated tones; but though he was courteous and attentive, she felt she had made little or no impression; and to the courted and fascinating Madame D'Aulnay this was indeed a mortifying novelty.

Meantime, whilst she was thus vainly lavishing her powers of attraction on her unimpressionable guest, her cousin, Miss De Mirecourt, was succeeding much better with her partner of the hour. The latter was Major Sternfield, "the irresistible," as he had already been styled by some of the fairer portion of the company; and certainly as far as outward qualifications went, he almost seemed to deserve the exaggerated title. A tall and splendidly-proportioned figure—eyes, hair and features of faultless beauty, joined to rare powers of conversation, and a voice whose tones he could modulate to the richest music, were rare gifts to be all united in one happy mortal. So thought many an envious man and admiring woman; and so thought Audley Sternfield himself.

A fitting partner for this Apollo was the bright-eyed, graceful Antoinette De Mirecourt, whose rare personal charms were doubly enhanced by the witching *naïveté*,[41] and shy vivacity of manner which many found more fascinating than even her beauty itself. Major Sternfield was bending over her, apparently heedless of every thing but herself, and certainly leaving her no cause to complain of the devotion of *her* partner; when, skilfully enough for such a novice, changing the tone of the conversation from the shade of sentiment to which Sternfield, even in that early stage of their intercourse sought to bring it, she exclaimed:

"Pray tell me the names of some of your brother officers? They are all strangers to me."

[41] Misspelled in the original as "naivété."

"Willingly," he smilingly rejoined, "and their characters too. It will be but a proper preliminary step to their introduction to yourself; for they have all vowed, with but one exception, that they will not leave this evening till they have obtained, or attempted to obtain, an introduction to you.

"To begin then. That dark, quiet-looking man on your right is Captain Assheton, a very amiable and very harmless sort of person. The good-humored, ruddy personage beside him is Doctor Manby, surgeon of ours, who would amputate a limb as smilingly and cheerfully as he would light a cigar. That very pretty, very exquisitely-dressed young gentleman, dancing opposite us, is the Hon. Percy Delaval; but, as I have promised to introduce him to yourself, provided you will permit it, when this dance is over, and he will probably claim your hand for the next, you will have an immediate opportunity of knowing and judging for yourself.

"But who is that stately-looking, gentleman talking with Mrs. D'Aulnay?" and Antoinette glanced towards the mantle-piece where the hostess still stood, conversing with her impassible companion. "That is Colonel Evelyn:" and as Sternfield pronounced the name, an expression of mingled dislike and impatience flashed across his face. It was instantly repressed however; and in a lower tone he rejoined:

"In the first place, he is the *one* exception I hinted at just now, who did not pledge himself to become acquainted with you this evening, if possible. Is not that enough; or, do you still wish to know more of him?"

"Decidedly. He interests me now more than ever."

"A true woman's perverse answer," inwardly thought Sternfield: but with a low bow, he replied:

"Well, your wishes must be obeyed. In a few words then, confidential of course, I will tell you what Colonel Evelyn is. He is one who believes neither in God, nor man, nor yet in woman."

"You almost frighten me! Is he an infidel?"

"Not perhaps in open theory, but in practice he certainly is. Born and brought up a Catholic, he has never, in the memory of the oldest member of the regiment, entered church or chapel. Cold and distant in manner, he is on terms of friendly intimacy with no man; but worst and greatest crime of all," and here the chivalrous speaker deprecatingly smiled, "he is a professed, incorrigible woman-hater. Some disappointment in a love affair, early in life, the particulars of which none of us have ever heard, has embittered his character to such a degree that he openly declares his contemptuous hatred for all of Eve's daughters, vowing they are all equally false and deceitful. Pray, forgive me, Miss De Mirecourt, for uttering such shocking sentiments in your presence, even whilst condemning them heart and soul; but you commanded me to speak, and I had no alternative but to obey. But here comes Mr. Delaval to solicit an introduction."

The usual formula was gone through, Antoinette's hand asked by the new-comer for the ensuing dance, and then Sternfield turned away, first whispering in the young girl's ear:

"I yield my place with such regret, that I shall soon venture on claiming it again."

If Major Sternfield had chosen his successor with the intention that he should act as a foil to himself, he could not have succeeded better in his choice.

The Honorable Percy Delaval was a golden-haired, pink-cheeked, delicate-featured youth of twenty-one summers. Lately come into a considerable fortune—belonging to an old and wealthy family in England, and possessing, as before hinted, considerable personal attractions, Lieutenant Delaval was as thoroughly infatuated with himself as ever lover was with mistress. To his natural gifts he had added some acquired ones, such as a lisping, drawling form of speech, a lounging mode of standing or reclining (he rarely sat, in the proper acceptation of the term), and a peculiar mode of languidly half closing his large blue eyes, or occasionally calling up into them an abstracted vacancy of gaze and expression,—all of which numerous and varied attractions, rendered him, at least in his own estimation, more irresistible than the handsome Sternfield himself. Such was the young gentleman, who, after a protracted silence, during which his eyes had listlessly wandered round the room, apparently unconscious of the existence of his partner, at length turned towards her, and half patronizingly, half languidly, enquired "if she were fond of dancing?"

"That depends entirely on the species of partner I chance to have," replied Antoinette, with as much truth as spirit.

The infatuated Percy, however, saw only in this plain speech, an implied compliment to himself; and after another five minutes' imposing silence and abstraction, he resumed—"They say it is intolerably cold here in the winter!"

To this proposition there was no reply beyond a slight inclination of his companion's head.

"What do the men wear to protect themselves from the Siberian rigor of the climate?"

"Bear skin coats," was the laconic reply.

"And the women—haw—I beg pardon, the ladies—the fair sex, I should have said?"

"Blankets and moccasins," rejoined Antoinette, slightly tossing her pretty little head, for she felt her patience rapidly giving way. The Honorable Percy stared.

Was it really the case; or could this "obscure little colonial girl," as he inwardly characterized her, be quizzing him?[42]

Oh, the latter supposition was improbable—totally out of the question. It must be that in some of the country parts,

[42] "Quiz" is used here in the old sense of "mock, poke fun, pull someone's leg."

the women still wore the singular costume just mentioned, a reminiscence probably of the peculiar customs of their Indian predecessors.[43]

Returning to the charge, he resumed with more impertinent *nonchalance* of tone and manner than before:

"They say that for eight months the ground is covered to the depth of four feet with snow and ice, and everything freezes. How do the unfortunate inhabitants contrive to support nature during that time?"

Antoinette's first feeling of irritation was fast giving place to one of amusement, and she smilingly rejoined:

"Oh, if provisions are very scarce, they eat each other."

Heaven and earth! It was then possible, nay, actually true. She *was* quizzing him! His very breathing seemed suspended by the discovery, and for a considerable time, indignant amazement kept him silent. But, he must condignly punish, annihilate his audacious partner; and calling up as contemptuous a sneer as his pretty, effeminate features would permit him to assume, he rejoined:

"Well yes, Canada is as yet so utterly out of the pale of civilization, that I am not surprised at your tolerating any custom, however barbarous."

"True," serenely replied Antoinette; "we can tolerate everything here but fops and fools."

This last sally was too much for Lieutenant Delaval, and he had not recovered from the effects of the shock it had given him, when Major Sternfield hurried up to again claim Miss De Mirecourt's hand for another dance.

Antoinette carelessly placed her arm within that of the new-comer, and turned away, totally unconscious that Colonel Evelyn, who had been examining some prints at a table behind them, having succeeded in making his escape from his hostess, was an amused auditor of the whole of the preceding singular dialogue.

[43] Here, the author inserted the following footnote: "The reader will please remember that this was nearly a century ago, when such a thing was possible, though not probable."

"Well, what think you, Miss De Mirecourt, of the Honorable Mr. Delaval?" smilingly enquired her present partner. "If you remember, we decided that you should form your judgment of him unbiassed by any previous opinion of mine."

"I request of you, Major Sternfield," was the petulant reply, "to introduce me in future to no more foolish boys. They make tiresome partners."

Sternfield's eyes sparkled with suppressed mirth; and that evening the mess room rang with jokes and laughter which made the Honorable Percy Delaval's ears tingle with mingled wrath and desire of revenge.

Chapter V.

And now will our readers forgive us if at the risk of being thought tedious, or, of repeating facts with which they may be as well acquainted as ourselves, we cast a cursory glance over that period of Canadian history which embraces the first few years that followed the capitulation of Montreal to the combined forces of Murray, Amherst, and Haviland[44]—a period on which neither victors nor vanquished can dwell with much pleasure.

Despite the terms of the capitulation, which had expressly guaranteed to Canadians the same rights as those accorded to British subjects, the former, who had confidently counted on the peaceful protection of a legal government, were doomed instead to see their tribunals abolished, their judges ignored, and their entire social system overthrown, to make way for that most insupportable of all tyrannies, martial law.[45]

[44] In the Montreal campaign of July-September 1760, the British attacked from three different directions, with troops commanded by James Murray (who advanced from Quebec City), Jeffery Amherst (coming from Lake Ontario), and William Haviland (moving north from Fort Crown Point, on the border of New York and Vermont). Jeffery Amherst (1717-1797) was commander-in-chief of the British forces in North America from 1758 to 1763. He and Murray became the first two governors of the British Province of Quebec. Back in his native Kent, Amherst commissioned a mansion called Montreal Park.

[45] The British military regime in New France lasted from 1760 until the Treaty of Paris of 1763.

It is true that the new government may have thought these severe measures necessary, for it is well known that the Canadians, for three long years after King George's standard floated above their heads, still persisted in believing and hoping that France had not abandoned them, and that she would yet make a final and succcssful cffort to regain the province when the cessation of hostilities should have been proclaimed. This last hope, however, like many others that the colonists had fixed on the mother country, was doomed to disappointment; and by the treaty of 1763 the destinies of Canada were irrevocably united to those of Great Britain. This circumstance determined a second and more extensive emigration of the better classes of the towns and cities to France, in which country they were received with marks of special favor, and honorable places found for many of them in the government offices, in the navy and the army.

Never perhaps was government more isolated from a people than was the new administration. The Canadians, as ignorant of the language of their conquerors as these latter were of their own cherished Gallic tongue, indignantly turned from the spurred and armed judges appointed to preside among them, and referred the arrangement of their differences to their parish clergy or some of their local notables.

The installation of the English troops in Canada had been followed by the arrival of a host of strangers, among whom unfortunately were many needy adventurers, who sought to build themselves positions on the ruined fortunes of the vanquished people. Of these, General Murray, a stern but strictly honorable man, who had replaced Lord Amherst as Governor General, remarks: "When it had been decided to reconstitute civil government here, we were obliged to choose magistrates and select jury-men out of a community composed of some four or five hundred merchants, mechanics,[46] and farmers, unsuitable and contemptible on account of their ignorance. It is not to be expected that such persons can resist the intoxication of power thus unexpectedly placed in their hands, or refrain from showing how skilful they are (in their peculiar way) in exercising it. They hate the Canadian *noblesse* on account of their birth and their other titles to public respect; and they detest other colonists, because the latter have contrived to elude the illegal oppression to which it was intended to subject them."[47]

The chief-justice Gregory, drawn from the depths of a prison to preside on the bench, was entirely ignorant not only of the French language but also of the simplest elements of civil law;[48] while the attorney-general was not much better qualified for the high charge he held.[49] The power of nominating to the situations of provincial secretary, of council recorder, of registrar, was given to favorites, who rented them to the highest bidder.

---

[46] In the obsolete sense of "laborer, manual worker."

[47] Leprohon took this quote from the second volume of a translation by Andrew Bell of François-Xavier Garneau's *Histoire du Canada* (published by Lovell in 1860, with a second edition in 1862). Garneau abridged a much longer letter by Murray, which had been quoted at length in John MacGregor's 1832 *British America,* and in which the governor speaks of the original British colonists as "traders, mechanics, and publicans" and as "contemptible settlers and traders. . . . It would be very unreasonable to suppose that such men would not be intoxicated with the unexpected power put into their hands; and that they would not be eager to show how amply they possessed. . . . The Canadian noblesse were hated, because their birth and behaviour entitled them to respect; and the peasants were abhorred, because they were saved from the oppression they were threatened with" (II, 382, 386-387).

[48] William Gregory, Chief Justice of the Province of Quebec from 1764 to 1766. Leprohon follows here Garneau's *Histoire* again (Garneau mentions Gregory's former imprisonment). However, he was an established lawyer in London and (like so many at the time) had simply been detained in a debtors' prison.

[49] George Suckling, Attorney General of the Province of Quebec from 1764 to 1766.

It is true the governor was soon compelled to suspend the chief-justice, and to send him back to England; but this, and one or two other conciliatory measures failed to counteract the painful impression which had been made on the minds of the conquered people, that such a thing as justice no longer existed for them. The dismemberment of their territory was a point that grieved them almost as much as the abolition of their laws. The islands of Anticosti and Magdalen, as well as the greater part of Labrador, were annexed to the government of Newfoundland;[50] the islands of St. John and Cape Breton were joined to Nova Scotia;[51] the lands lying around the great lakes, to the neighboring colonies;[52] and finally New Brunswick was detached, and endowed with a separate government and the name it bears to-day.[53]

Royal instructions were received to compel the clergy and the people to take an oath of fidelity under penalty of being obliged to leave the country, as also to deny the ecclesiastical jurisdiction of Rome, which every Catholic is bound in conscience to acknowledge and submit to.[54]

[50] The sparsely populated Anticosti Island, Magdalen Islands (Îles de la Madeleine) and the coast of Labrador were annexed to Newfoundland in 1763 but they were returned to the Province of Quebec in 1774. Labrador was re-annexed to Newfoundland in 1809. The border between Quebec and Labrador is still in dispute today.

[51] Cape Breton is still an important part of Nova Scotia, while St. John (Île Saint Jean) split off in 1769 and was renamed Prince Edward Island in 1798.

[52] The French forts and settlements in the area around the Great Lakes (known in French as "les pays d'en haut") are now in Ontario, Michigan, Illinois, Indiana, Wisconsin, Ohio, and Minnesota.

[53] New Brunswick was split off from Nova Scotia after the deportation of the French-speaking Acadians and became a new province in 1784.

[54] Between 1763 and 1774, the same Test Acts that had been in place in England since the Restoration were imposed in the Province of Quebec, effectively banning from public office any individual who did not swear allegiance to the king and did not abjure the Catholic faith.

They were also summoned to yield up all their weapons and defensive arms, or swear that they had none concealed. These latter orders, which were equally severe and unjust, the government hesitated about enforcing. A spirit of restless dissatisfaction, of open murmuring and complaints began to take possession of the people, hitherto so submissive to their new rulers. These latter felt it was necessary to relax the severity of their measures; and when at a later period, the American colonies broke out into the revolt which ended in the establishment of their independence, Great Britain, either through policy or justice, finally accorded to Canadians the peaceful enjoyment of their institutions and their laws.[55]

[55] Through the Quebec Act of 1774, free practice of Catholicism was guaranteed and the use of the French civil law was restored.

Chapter VI.

Madame d'Aulnay and her young cousin were now fairly launched into that life of fashionable gaiety in which they were so well fitted to shine, and an *entrée* to madame's pleasant salons was sought as a singular favor and advantage. Of course the lady's new military acquaintances were assiduous in their visits. Among the latter, Colonel Evelyn occasionally came, but father intimacy made no change in his grave, quiet demeanor, nor did it soften, in any degree, his remarkable reserve. He never danced, and scarcely ever addressed a word to Antoinette or any of her pretty young rivals. Though refined and courteous in manner, he never paid a compliment—never uttered any of those commonplace gallantries which pass current in society as successfully as remarks on the weather. Surely Major Sternfield was right; and this man, so reserved, so inaccessible, had little faith or trust in woman.

Ample amends however did Audley Sternfield make for his Colonel's indifference, and few days passed without his presenting himself, under one pretext or another, in Mrs. D'Aulnay's drawing room. A project deferentially proposed by himself, and acceded to by both ladies after some pressing on his part, farther increased their intimacy. This was his becoming their preceptor in the English tongue. With the latter language Mrs. D'Aulnay was but slightly acquainted; but Antoinette, however deficient in point of pronunciation, possessed a very accurate knowledge of its grammatical construction, thanks to the lessons of her governess, who, though experiencing, like most foreigners, great difficulty in pronunciation, read and wrote it with perfect accuracy.

What dangerous means of attraction were thus furnished Major Sternfield in his new capacity. To sit daily for hours with his fair pupils at the same table, reading aloud some impassioned poem,—some graceful tale of fiction, whilst they listened in silent enjoyment to the rich intonations of a remarkably musical voice; or watched the expressive play of his regular, faultless features. Then when he arrived at some passage of peculiar beauty or fervent sentiment, how eloquent the rapid glance he would steal towards Antoinette—how ardent, how devoted the expression of his dark speaking eyes.

Was it to be wondered at that the young and inexperienced girl, thus exposed to such powerful and novel temptations, learned lessons in another lore than that of languages; and that after those long and pleasant hours of instruction, she often sat wrapped in silent reverie, with flushed cheek and downcast gaze that plainly told something more interesting than English verbs and pronouns occupied her thoughts.

It was the first really good sleighing of the season, for the few slight falls of snow that had hitherto heralded winter's approach, descending on the muddy roads and side-walks, had lost at once their whiteness and purity, and becoming incorporated with the liquid mud, formed that detestable combination with which we Canadians are so familiar in the spring and fall, and which we recognize by the name of "slush." A hard frost, however, succeeded by a sufficiently abundant fall of snow, had filled with rejoicing all the amateurs of sleighing; whilst a clear blue sky overhead, and brilliant sunshine, flooding the earth with light if not warmth, left nothing to be desired.

Before Mrs. D'Aulnay's door was a tiny, exquisitely-finished sleigh, whilst a pair of glossy black ponies of the pure Canadian breed,[56] stood tossing their gayly-tasseled heads, and ringing out musical peals from the host of little silver bells adorning their harness. 'Tis unnecessary to say that this fairy-like equipage was waiting for Mrs. D'Aulnay and her cousin, who were both in the former's dressing-room, adding the finishing touches to their elegant and becoming winter toilettes. On a chair, lay a pair of lady's riding-gauntlets, which the fair lady of the mansion took up, exclaiming:

"You may safely trust yourself to my driving, Antoinette, for I am a practised hand. My ponies too, though pretty, spirited-looking creatures, are very gentle, and admirably broken in."

From this speech it will be seen that Mrs. D'Aulnay, amongst her other accomplishments, possessed that of driving two in hand;[57] and though few ladies of the time either sought or admired this gift, Madame D'Aulnay was a leader of fashion, and did as she pleased.

"Do you know, *petite cousine*,"[58] she remarked, glancing complacently in the mirror, "those dark furs of ours are very becoming! They harmonize well with even my sallow complexion, whilst they become your glowing carmine cheeks divinely. But what have we here, Jeanne?" and she turned towards a middle-aged woman who entered with a couple of letters in her hand.

"For Mademoiselle Antoinette, madame"; and the new-comer placed the epistles in the young girl's eagerly out-stretched hand.

Jeanne was a somewhat privileged person in the household, for she had lived with Mrs. D'Aulnay in the

[56] The Canadian horse is descended from a few individuals sent by King Louis XIV from France at the end of the 17th century. In recent decades it has been considered close to extinction. Many Canadian horses were exported to the United States and were killed there in the Civil War as cavalry horses in the Union Army (see Hendricks 101).

[57] This refers to the ability of driving a pair of horses (two horses harnessed abreast, i.e., side by side).

[58] French for "little cousin."

capacity of lady's-maid before the latter's marriage, and had followed her to her new home, probably never to separate from her; for she was fondly attached to her mistress, and frequently favored her with proofs of her devotion in the shape of remonstrances and reproachful counsels, which the petted and capricious Madame D'Aulnay would have borne from no one else.

Antoinette hastily opened her letters, both of which were very long and closely written; and as Mrs. D'Aulnay's glance fell on the well-filled pages, she somewhat impatiently exclaimed, "Surely, dear child, you do not intend waiting to read those folios through now! There, there, put them away: they will keep till our return."

"Not so, dear Lucille. They are from papa, and poor Mrs. Gérard, both of whom have been but very little in my thoughts for the last couple of weeks; so, by way of penance, I intend remaining at home, and reading the letters over till I have them by heart."

"What nonsense!" exclaimed her hostess. "Do you really mean to lose this beautiful afternoon, and the first good sleighing of the season? Surely you will not be so absurd!"

"It must be, dear friend, for this once; so forgive me."

"Ah!" rejoined Mrs. D'Aulnay, half pettishly, half playfully, "I see you possess a considerable share of the family firmness, or, to give it its true name, obstinacy; but I must make up my mind to exhibit myself in Notre Dame street alone this afternoon. Well, adieu!" and with a light step she descended the stairs.

Chapter VII.

Antoinette, after Mrs. D'Aulnay's departure, hastily divested herself of her out-door clothing, and then entered on the perusal of her letters. The first, which was from her father, was kind and affectionate; spoke of the void her absence made in the household; told her to enjoy herself to her heart's utmost desire; and ended by warning her to watch well over her affections, and bestow them on none of the gay strangers who might visit at her cousin's house, for assuredly he would never under any circumstances countenance any of them as her suitors. A burning blush suffused the girl's cheek as she read this last sentence; and she hastily laid down her father's letter, and took up the other, as if to banish the peculiar thoughts thus suddenly evoked. But the second epistle was still more unfortunate in the reflections it gave rise to; and as Antoinette read on, the glow on her cheek deepened to a feverish crimson, and the large bright tears gathered in her eyes, and ell one by one on the paper.

No harsh reproaches, no severe denunciations, had found place in Mrs. Gérard's letter; but with gentle firmness she spoke of duties to be fulfilled, of errors to be avoided, and then implored her pupil to question her own heart narrowly, and find in what and how far she had been unfaithful since she had entered on the gay life she was now leading. For the first time since her arrival beneath Mrs. D'Aulnay's roof, Antoinette entered on that trying task of self-examination; and at its close, she stood before the tribunal of her own heart, self-condemned.

Was she really the same innocent, guileless little country girl, whose thoughts and pleasures a few weeks previous had been as simple as those of a child?—she, whose long conversations with Mrs. D'Aulnay ever turned on dress, fashion, or silly sentiment; who lived in a round of glittering gaiety, that gave no time for serious reflection or self-examination? What amusements had replaced her former quiet country walks and useful course of reading—her religious and charitable duties? Aye! blush on, Antoinette! for the answer is one both condemning and humiliating;—the perusal of silly novels and exaggerated love-poems; the conversation of frivolous men of the world, whose whispered flatteries and lover-like protestations had become so familiar to her ear that they had almost ceased to make her blush; and idle day-dreams, planning equally idle pleasures for the future.

Whilst the remorse evoked by these thoughts was busy at her heart, Jeanne entered to say that Major Sternfield wished to see her.

"Impossible!" sharply replied Antoinette, for the fascinating Audley had much to answer for in her present severe self-retrospect.

"But, Mademoiselle," expostulated Jeanne, endeavoring to explain that the gentleman, certain of admittance, had unceremoniously followed her into the hall, and now stood outside the threshold of the adjoining apartment, which was one of the drawing-rooms, awaiting her appearance.

"I tell you, 'tis impossible, Jeanne," was the quick impatient reply: "I have a headache, and can see no one."

The clear ringing tones of the speaker certainly indicated nothing like severe suffering, and considerably disconcerted, the visitor retraced his steps. At the hall-door he paused, and, suddenly turning to the dark-eyed *soubrette*[59] who stepped forward to open it for him, expressed his earnest hope that "Mademoiselle De Mirecourt was not very ill."

"Well, no sir," hesitatingly replied Justine, touched alike by the dark appealing eyes and perfectly spoken French of the handsome interrogator. "Mademoiselle received some letters from home a short time since; and they may have contained some unpleasant news, for, on passing the half-open door, I could see that she was crying." The gallant Sternfield bowed his thanks, and passed into the street.

"Letters from home and crying over them!" he murmured to himself. "I must find out from Madame D'Aulnay, to-morrow, what it all means. My little country beauty is too great a prize to be let carelessly slip through my fingers."

A half-hour afterwards, Mrs. D'Aulnay in the highest spirits returned home. Not finding Antoinette in the dressing-room, where she had left her, she hurried up to the latter's apartment, meeting Jeanne on the way, who informed her that Major Sternfield had called during her absence and had been refused admittance.

"Why, what new phase of my little cousin's mood is this?" she inwardly asked herself. "I suppose she has received a long epistolary lecture from home, which has given her over a prey to vexation or remorse."

Antoinette was lying on a couch, on which she had purposely thrown herself, intending to feign headache, and thus escape the remarks and suppositions of her hostess. The latter, however, without appearing to notice the swollen eyelids of her young companion, expressed her regret at her indisposition, and then entered on an animated description of her afternoon's drive. "It had proved delightful; she had met everybody worth meeting, and had organized with

[59] The soubrette is a stock character in comedy and opera (that of a mischievous or flirtatious maidservant), but the term was also used in French literature as a synonym for a housemaid.

Madame Favancourt, a driving-party to Lachine[60] for the following day. Major Sternfield, whom she had met on the way, was to see to the whole affair; and, in short, they would have a most delightful excursion. But now," she continued, in a still livelier strain, "I have come to the cream of the story. Whom should I meet in the Place D'Armes,[61] in a splendid sleigh, driving a pair of superb English bays, but our misanthropic Colonel! The temptation of adding such a faultless turn-out to our expedition to-morrow was irresistible, and, raising my whip, I beckoned him towards me. The bays champed and curvetted[62] as if they hated the sight of a pretty woman as much as their master does; but reining them in with an iron hand, he courteously listened to my invitation, evidently seeking all the time for some plausible excuse for refusal. Thinking frankness best with such an extraordinary character, I laughingly declared that our resources in the way of handsome equipages and horses were somewhat limited. He eagerly commenced assuring me that his were entirely at my disposal, not only to-morrow, but whenever I should require them. Seeing, however, what the gentleman was at, I quietly interrupted him, by exclaiming,

"Not without the owner, Colonel Evelyn: both or none!"

"You never saw a man so much put out. He bit his lip; reined in the bays till he almost made them stand perpendicularly on their hind legs; and at length, seeing that I awaited determinedly his answer, he rejoined in a hurried constrained tone that he would do himself the pleasure of joining us on the morrow. He is a perfect barbarian;—but I will leave you now, awhile, for quiet will do you poor head

[60] Now a Montreal borough, Lachine (on the southwestern portion of the island of Montreal) was then a small village.

[61] Place d'Armes is a famous square in Old Montreal (see also note 110).

[62] To curvet means to leap about or frolic.

good," and, lightly pressing her lips to the fair young cheek pillowed on the couch, she left the room.

Antoinette wearily sighed as the door closed upon her, and murmured: "Oh, if I wish to be again what I was, I must return home! The temptations of this gay house, the society of my kind-hearted but pleasure-loving cousin, are too much for my weak heart and feeble resolves."

Chapter VIII.

A gay cavalcade of prancing horses and richly-decorated sleighs were drawn up the following day, about noon, in front of Madame D'Aulnay's mansion. Conspicuous among these was the magnificent equipage of Colonel Evelyn; but the owner himself was standing near it with a moody, constrained expression, that plainly betokened he was there against his will. Most of the party were already in their respective places, laughing and chatting in the highest spirits; when the door of Mrs. D'Aulnay's residence opened, and that fair lady issued forth, dispensing sunny smiles and friendly bows on all sides. In her wake came Antoinette; but the usually sparkling gaiety of the latter was strangely clouded, yet many thought this new and pensive shade of her beauty became her even better than the olden one.

As the elder lady stepped on the pavement, Colonel Evelyn approached her, and, in a tone which he vainly endeavored to render *empressé*,[63] requested her "to honor his sleigh by occupying it."

She smilingly bowed assent, and then turned aside to answer some polite enquiries from some cavalier near. Suddenly Major Sternfield sought her side, and begged her to give him a seat with herself as he had something very particular to say to her. The truth was, he was most impatient to know why Antoinette had refused seeing him the previous day; as well as to learn, if possible, the cause of the tearful grief of which Justine had spoken. Mrs.

[63] French for "seemingly eager to help, keen to appear zealous."

D'Aulnay good-naturedly answered in the affirmative, not very sorry at the same time to inflict a passing slight on the ungallant Colonel, who seemed to think it so severe a hardship to share the occupancy of his sleigh with her charming self. Having previously, however, intended that Antoinette and Major Sternfield should drive together, whilst she should head the cavalcade with Colonel Evelyn, she now felt momentarily embarrassed how to arrange matters. After a moment's thought, she tripped up to the Colonel, and smilingly told him "that as Major Sternfield had thrown himself on her charity, she had no resource but to take him in her own little equipage. Here, however, is my substitute," she archly continued, drawing suddenly forward the embarrassed and astonished Antoinette, who had been looking around her for the last few minutes with a listless pre-occupied expression, which seldom rested on that sweet face.

Completely taken by surprise, and at the same time indignant beyond measure at being thus arbitrarily forced on the society of so unwilling a companion, Antoinette drew back, vehemently declaring "that she would not consent to such an arrangement,—that the horses looked too restive!"

With an almost imperceptible curl of his lip, Colonel Evelyn hastened to assure her "that the steeds, though spirited, were thoroughly broken in," whilst Mrs. D'Aulnay impetuously whispered in her ear,

"Do you want openly to insult the man? Get in at once."

Antoinette unwillingly complied; and as Colonel Evelyn arranged the rich robes carefully around her, he contemptuously thought within himself, "What a well-got-up[64] piece of acting! Young as they may be,—guileless as they may look,—they are all alike!"

Whilst backing his horses to let Madame D'Aulnay and Major Sternfield (who, by the way, on seeing the last arrangement, heartily regretted his precipitancy) take

[64] Well fashioned, smartly dressed (sometimes used to describe people, but most frequently the appearance of a book).

precedence, the lady insisted on Evelyn's keeping the lead, declaring his magnificent bays were just the thing for opening the procession.

Proudly, gaily, the party swept on, making the air musical with the sweet ringing of bells, and, after proceeding down the length of Notre Dame street, passed through Recollet's gate,[65] which gave them egress outside the wall encircling the city, and they soon found themselves[66] in the open country, on the road to Lachine.

Colonel Evelyn's moodiness and Antoinette's vexation yielded after a time to the charms of the brilliant blue sky and sunshine,—the beautiful appearance of the wide-spread fields covered with their glittering snowy mantle, and sparkling as if some enchanter had strewn them with diamond-dust. There was something, too, peculiarly exhilarating in the rapid pace of the steeds, and in the keen bracing air itself, that insensibly communicated its influence to both parties; but still, strangely enough, both remained silent. The scene was entirely new to Evelyn, and talking commonplace platitudes would have marred his enjoyment; whilst Antoinette, on her part, was determined to show him, that, though forced in a measure on his society, she had no intention of profiting by the circumstance in any manner.

At length they neared the Lachine Rapids,[67] the roar of whose restless waters had been for some time previous

[65] The Recollet Gate ("La Porte des Récollets") was one of the eight gates of the Ramparts of Montreal, which were torn down in 1804-1817 (see also note 66).

[66] Here, Leprohon inserted the following footnote: "This wall, which was originally built to protect the inhabitants of the town from the hostile attacks of the Iroquois tribe, was fifteen feet high, with battlements. After a time, it was suffered to fall into decay; and it was ultimately removed by an Act of the Provincial legislature, to make way for some judicious and necessary improvements."

[67] Rapids on the Saint Lawrence River, between the Island of Montreal and the south shore. They are actually close to the borough of Lasalle, not to the borough of Lachine.

sounding in their ears; and as the broad wreaths of foam, the snow-covered rocks with the black waters boiling and chafing up between them, or eddying round in countless different currents and whirlpools, burst upon their view, an involuntary exclamation of admiration escaped Colonel Evelyn's lips. The scene was indeed grand, sublime in the extreme; and the lonely wooded shores of Caughnawaga opposite,[68] the tiny islets with a solitary pine-tree or two growing from their rocky bosoms, and standing where they had stood for ages, calm, unmoved by the wild tempest of waters so fiercely raging around them, gave fresh food to the thoughts, whilst they added increased grandeur to the scene.

In the eager admiration of the moment, the Colonel unconsciously relaxed his grasp on the reins, when a shot, suddenly discharged from the gun of some country sportsman near, startled the spirited steeds, that instantly set off at a most fearful pace. The peril was imminent, for the road led close along the bank of the rapids, rising in some places several feet above the chafing waters. Still, the hand which held the reins was one of iron, and its form and vigorous grasp was a considerable check on the headlong career of the terrified animals.[69] After the first moment of alarm, Evelyn turned towards his companion to deprecate by some encouraging word, the piercing shrieks, the fainting fit, or other tokens of feminine alarm, which would greatly have heightened the dangers of their position; but Antoinette sat perfectly upright and quiet, her

[68] Today Kahnawake, a First Nations (Mohawk) reserve on the south shore of the Saint Lawrence River. It was originally founded as a Mohawk "seigniory" managed by the Jesuits. In 1762, as Jesuits were banished from North America, Thomas Gage, the military governor of Montreal, reorganized it as an Indian Reserve.

[69] The word "career" had been used as a figurative term for the course of someone's professional life since the end of the 18th century, but the old meaning of "speed" (especially in reference to the gallop of a racehorse) was still more common.

lips slightly compressed, and in nor way betraying her secret terror, save in the marble-like pallor of her face.

Noting the anxious glance Evelyn had just turned on her, she quietly exclaimed, "Do not mind me: attend to the horses." "What a brave little girl!" he inwardly thought; and assured of her perfect self-possession, he devoted every straining nerve and sinew to recovering his control over the runaways. Clear eye and strong hand were alike requisite, for they were now approaching a spot where the bank became steeper and the road narrower. An overturned cart, rising up black and unsightly by the wayside, added a fresh impetus to the terror of the already half-maddened animals. With a desperate plunge they sprang forward, and the wild effort caused the reins, already stretched for a considerable time past to the utmost tension, to snap asunder. In that moment of deadly peril there was no time for etiquette or ceremony, and, quick as thought, Evelyn snatched up the light form of his companion, and murmuring "Forgive me," threw her out on the snow-covered ground. He instantly leaped out after, narrowly escaping entangling his feet in the robes, and stumbling forward with considerable violence. His first though was of Antoinette, who had risen to her feet, and was now leaning in silence against the trunk of a tree, her lips rivalling her cheeks in their death-like pallor.

"Are you much hurt?" he hurriedly enquired.

"Oh, no, no," was the piteous toned reply; "but the horses, the poor horses!"

Colonel Evelyn looked eagerly around. Aye, where were they? Down at the foot of the steep bank, maimed and bleeding, and still desperately struggling amid the rocks and shallow water, into which they had rolled. Evelyn dearly prized his beautiful English bays, perhaps over-valued them as much as he under-valued women; but it is only rendering him justice to state, that in that moment every thought of regret for their fate was absorbed in secret gratulation that the helpless girl committed for the hour to his charge, was safe.

"Take my arm, Miss De Mirecourt," he gently exclaimed, "and we will seek for assistance at yonder little cottage."

Antoinette complied, and their knock for admittance was followed by an invitation to come in. On entering, they found themselves in a bare, scantily-furnished room; the walls and hearth of which, however, were spotless, the small narrow panes glittering like diamonds, and the whole place shining with that exquisite cleanliness and order with which the Canadian *habitants* soften, if they do not conceal, their poverty, wherever it exists. Peacefully smoking beside the huge double-stove sat the master of the household, whilst half-a-dozen round-eyed, swarthy-cheeked children, of all ages from one to seven, played and tumbled like so many dolphins upon the floor. On seeing his unexpected visitor, the man instantly rose, and, without betraying half the astonishment he secretly felt, removed the blue *tuque* from his head,[70] and politely answered in the affirmative to Antoinette's request for assistance. Looking suddenly, however, towards the group on the floor, he explained, in a somewhat hesitating tone, that his wife had gone from home on business, and made him promise that he would not leave the children in her absence, lest they should burn themselves. The absent wife's fears were fully justified by the state of the stove, which was nearly red hot; but Antoinette with a smile wreathing her still white lips, assured him she should take every possible care of the little ones during his absence. Smiling his thanks, the man left the cottage, accompanied by Colonel Evelyn; and Antoinette found herself alone with her young companions. Her first act was to bend her knee in heartfelt gratitude to Providence for her late escape, and then she turned her attention to consoling the youngling of the flock, who set up a lamentable outcry a moment after its father's departure. The task was not difficult, for childhood's tears are easily dried; and a few moments after, he was installed on her lap, timidly fingering

[70] Tuque is a French Canadian term for a knit cap.

the golden trinkets suspended from her neck, the heat of the room having forced her to lay aside her furs and mantle; whilst the other children grouped around her, listened eagerly to a wonderous tale of a stupendous giant and a lovely fairy, feasting their eyes meanwhile on the beautiful face and elegant dress of the speaker, whom they inwardly set down as belonging to the very class of fairies she was telling them about.

Chapter IX.

Some time after, Colonel Evelyn entered the cottage alone, and, as his clouded gaze fell on the group before him, he involuntarily smiled. The little one on Antoinette's lap nestled closely to her breast on seeing the tall stranger enter, and clung there as naturally as if his little curly pate had always been accustomed to lie next a silken boddice, and press jewelled ornaments. Very lovely Antoinette appeared at the moment; and the gently play of her features, as she kindly looked from one little auditor to another, invested her with a charm which her beauty had never, perhaps, possessed in saloon or ball-room.

On seeing Evelyn, she eagerly inquired about the horses.

"Our host is attending to them," he carelessly replied, "and will join us in a few moments. But tell me, are you really none the worse in any manner for our adventure? Do you not feel any pain or ache?"

"No—yes—there is something like a dull pain here," and baring her rounded beautifully-shaped arm to the elbow, she disclosed a large discolored bruise upon its soft surface. Colonel Evelyn's countenance betrayed considerable emotion as he looked down on that frail arm, so indicative of almost childish helplessness, and remembered the undaunted courage the brave young owner had exhibited throughout the whole of that trying ordeal.

"Yes," he said, "I must indeed beg your forgiveness for my rough handling; for you must have received that bruise when I threw you from the sleigh. It would have been as easy for me to have sprang out with you in my arms, but I dreaded that in doing so, my feet should become entangled in the shawls and skins filling the sleigh, and thus entail our mutual destruction. Can I do anything for you now? Let me bath it in cold water."

"Oh, no: 'tis a mere trifle, which Jeanne will attend to when I get home," she smilingly rejoined, but coloring as she hastily drew down her sleeve.

A momentary pause ensued, and then Colonel Evelyn, who had been earnestly regarding her, exclaimed—

"Do you know that you have behaved throughout like a perfect heroine? Not a start, not even a single exclamation of fear; and yet I am certain, from the expression of your countenance, that you were greatly alarmed."

Antoinette hesitated a moment, and then an irrepressible smile broke into countless dimples around her pretty mouth as she shyly rejoined:

"They say one great fear almost neutralizes another; and terrified as I was by the mad career of our steeds, I was almost equally afraid of yourself."

"How, of me?" he wonderingly exclaimed.

"Yes. In the first place I was in your sleigh merely on sufferance: I had been, as it were, forced on you, undesired and unsolicited, and consequently felt doubly bound to behave well. No, do not interrupt me," she playfully said, as Evelyn essayed a few dissenting words, remembering at the same time with something like remorse, the harsh judgment he had inwardly passed on her previous to their setting out. "Then, secondly,"—but here the speaker paused in some slight embarrassment.

"And what, secondly?" questioned her companion, considerably amused.

"Well, I had been told that you were an inveterate woman-hater, and consequently presumed that you would show but little indulgence to a woman's fears or fancies."

A look of mental pain instantly chased the smile from Evelyn's face, and almost involuntarily he rejoined: "The unenviable character you give me, has been won and borne my many, merely because they have practiced a prudence taught them by past experience."

The words were uttered in a low, constrained tone, and the speaker immediately walked to the little window as if to terminate the subject.

Suddenly, two loud reports of a gun, fired in quick succession, startled Antoinette, whose nervous system, notwithstanding her apparent-calmness, had been considerably shaken by the late adventure, and an exclamation of terror escaped her lips. Evelyn winced as the shots rang through the air; but instantly recovering himself, he turned to his companion, kindly exclaiming:

"Do not be alarmed: 'tis our host, who is performing an act of mercy, and putting my poor maimed horses out of their pain."

"What! both killed!" and the girl involuntarily clasped her hands.

"Yes, I examined them well, and seeing that prolonged life would only be prolonged agony to them, I sent our kind assistant to borrow a gun at some neighboring cottage, and left to him the painful task of releasing them. I was too cowardly to wait myself for the accomplishment of the sacrifice.

After a moment's pause, Antoinette exclaimed in a low agitated voice:

"I need not say how deeply sorry I am, Colonel Evelyn, for you, as well as for the indirect share I may have had in this unfortunate event; nor how grieved I am that thought or remembrance of myself should be connected in your memory with the most unpleasant circumstance that will probably mark your sojourn in Canada."

"Do not say that, Miss De Mirecourt," he hurriedly replied. "Rather felicitate me on the fortunate chance which ordained that you should have been my companion, instead of Madame D'Aulnay, or some other timid woman whose weak fears would have infallibly destroyed two lives more precious than that of a couple of carriage-horses. But one woman out of many could have displayed the self-command you did to-day, and which tended more to our mutual preservation than any skill or horsemanship of mine. But here comes our humble friend with the wreck of our late equipage."

Antoinette approached the window and saw their host, aided by a couple of men whom he had called to his assistance, bringing forward a handsomely carved dash-board, and the rich tiger-skin robes. These latter, being thoroughly saturated by their late immersion, were instantly spread to dry on the low stone wall surrounding the garden of the cottage. Through their united efforts they then succeeded in dragging up the body of the sleigh from the foot of the bank, and placing it beside the rest of the *débris*.[71] Whilst the men were standing round the latter, and passing some sage remarks upon the accident, the loud tinkling of numerous sleigh-bells became audible, and the driving-party soon came dashing up. Suddenly, Major Sternfield, who was driving Madame D'Aulnay, caught sight of the broken sleigh lying by the road-side, and recognizing the rich sleigh-robes, he reined up his horse with a precipitate violence which elicited a loud scream from his companion, and sprang to the ground. Hurriedly beckoning the men, he addressed some rapid enquiries to them, the answers to which seemed in some degree to reassure both himself and Mrs. D'Aulnay, who at the first hint of the accident seemed dreadfully alarmed. Sternfield helped her to alight, and they entered the cottage, soon followed by the remainder of the party, who were all equally curious and excited.

---

[71] Leprohon spells the word the French way and places it in italics, though it had entered the English language a long time before and was often spelled without the sharp accent.

Expressions of sympathy with Miss De Mirecourt's late fright and congratulations on her escape, were of course the order of the day; but most of the gentlemen were equally sincere in their condolences with Colonel Evelyn on the loss of his fine bays, to which professions of regret the latter listened with more impatience than gratitude. A consultation regarding the return of the actors in the late adventure was then held, and it was decided that Mrs. D'Aulnay's servant should yield his place behind to Major Sternfield, who should in turn give up his seat beside Mrs. D'Aulnay to Antoinette. Colonel Evelyn, instinctively avoiding any of the sleighs containing members of the fairer portion of humanity, found part of a seat in a narrow cutter[72] already nearly filled by the portly Dr. Manby and a brother officer, but he contrived to cling on to it till they reached Lachine.

Here the party halted for rest and refreshment at the inn of the place, which was a very indifferent one; but through Sternfield's foresight, a large hamper containing choice wines and other refreshments had been placed in one of the sleighs, and was heartily welcomed when produced.

The early sunset of December was illuminating the front of Mrs. D'Aulnay's mansion when the party stopped before it. Friendly farewells were smilingly interchanged, and then the members of the party sought their respective homes. Colonel Evelyn kindly shook hands with Antoinette, earnestly reiterating his hope that the morrow would find her completely recovered from the effects of her late alarm; but Major Sternfield, less easily satisfied, implored Mrs. D'Aulnay to grant him permission to enter with them, or at least return that evening. This the lady smilingly but positively negatived, declaring that Miss De Mirecourt's pale cheek plainly betrayed she wanted immediate and complete repose.

[72] An open, lightweight sleigh.

That evening, Mrs. D'Aulnay passed with Antoinette in the latter's apartment, and, after some questioning and cross-questioning regarding the day's mis-adventure, she enquired if there would be any indiscretion in asking to see the letters her cousin had lately received from home. Somewhat reluctantly the latter put them in her hand, but the elder lady caressingly exclaimed as she wound her arm round the young girl's neck, "You must have no secrets from me, my little Antoinette! You have neither mother nor sister to confide in; choose me then as your friend and counsellor."

Mr. De Mirecourt's letter she read slowly over, and then refolded without further comment; but after a rapid glance at the contents of Mrs. Gérard's epistle, she crushed it up in her hand, and, opening the stove door, threw it in.

The act had taken Antoinette so completely by surprise that the paper was in ashes before she had fully comprehended the companion's intention; but recovering from her indignant amazement, she exclaimed, whilst her cheek flushed crimson:

"Why did you do that, Madame D'Aulnay?"

"Simply because I will not have my darling little cousin made miserable by dwelling over and pondering on the prosy letters of any narrow-minded, strait-laced old woman. Why, that absurd epistle caused you a head-ache and crying-fit yesterday; and, think you, I will run the risk of a repetition of the same thing to-day, especially whilst you are in such a nervous, exhausted state?"

"You did very wrong, Lucille," replied the girl, reproachfully; "but I will say no more on the subject, as I doubt not you intended well."

"Many thanks, little one, for your prompt forgiveness; and in return for it, I will impart to you a secret which I have just discovered. Why do you not ask what it is? Well, I will reveal it without any pressing. It is the pleasant fact that you have made a complete conquest of the handsomest and most fascinating man in the circle of our acquaintance. Audley Sternfield is deeply in love with you."

A rosy flush instantly overspread Antoinette's face, whilst Mrs. D'Aulnay archly added:

"And to follow up my discoveries, I do not think he loves in vain."

Eagerly the young girl strove to refute the charge, but her blushes and confusion increased, till at length she desisted and listened in silence to her companion's raillery. When the latter finally paused, she gravely resumed—

"Lucille, I am sincere in saying I do not think I love him. I admire him very much, prefer his society to that of most other men"—

"Why, you delightfully innocent little creature, what is all this but love? I did not feel the half of it for Mr. D'Aulnay, when I married him. Seriously, you are very fortunate, and will be an object of envy to all the young girls of our acquaintance. Independent of his matchless personal gifts and accomplishments, he belongs to an excellent family, and, despite his comparative youth, his military rank is high. Why, before you are six years married to him, you will probably be a Colonel's wife."

"Married to him, Lucille! how can you talk so thoughtlessly?—Have you not just read my father's letter?"

"What if it, child? Who ever heard of fathers in real or fictitious life,—on the stage or off it,—doing what they ought to do, or acting in a kind and reasonable manner? They are always either striving to force their daughters into marriages which would ensure their misery, or seeking to prevent them contracting those which would procure their happiness. A girl must have spirit, and allow no authority to come between herself and the man she loves, especially if he be a passable match in a worldly point of view."

The practical suggestion contained in the latter part of Mrs. D'Aulnay's speech seemed somewhat inconsistent with the previous romantic tenor of her eloquence; but Antoinette, without noticing the discrepancy, quickly rejoined:

"You should not speak thus, Lucille. I do not know what some fathers may be, but I know that mine has always been kind and indulgent,—has always acted in a manner calculated to ensure my deepest love and respect."

"All very well, child, whilst you have submitted, as heretofore, to his will in everything; but wait till you venture to oppose or differ from him on any material point. Believe me, dearest, I know more of life than you can possibly do; and you will yet acknowledge the correctness of my opinion."

Alas, what a dangerous guide and companion had fallen to Antoinette's lot! How little chance had her simple childish reasoning against the refined sophistries of this accomplished woman of the world!

Chapter X.

The following morning Colonel Evelyn called to enquire how Miss De Mirecourt was, but he did not ask to see her, merely leaving his card.

"Well, that is more than I would have expected from such a semi-barbarian, especially after the loss of his splendid horses," was Mrs. D'Aulnay's qualified encomium.

In the afternoon the ladies went down to the drawing-room, and soon after Major Sternfield entered. There was an indescribable gentleness in his manner, which made Antoinette imagine she had never yet seen him appear to such advantage; and she began to think Mrs. D'Aulnay must be right, and that she really did love him. Contrary to her usual wont, the hostess left the room on some trifling pretext, after a half-hour's conversation, and Antoinette, with a feeling of unusual nervousness, caused probably by a recollection of the secret her cousin had imparted to her the day previous, found herself alone with Audley Sternfield.

The latter was not one to lose an opportunity he had eagerly sought and desired, and, after alluding in eloquent words, rendered still more persuasive by the musical tones in which they were uttered, to the agitation and alarm her late accident had caused him, he poured forth protestations of love and devotion into the ear of his blushing listener. 'Tis not to be wondered at that such terms of impassioned devotion, whispered for the first time to a young romantic girl, should be fraught with dangerous power; and when we remember that the speaker was one endowed with the rarest personal gifts, we will cease to wonder if Antoinette sat confused and silent, feeling that she did, she must reciprocate in some measure the ardent love lavished on herself. Still the answer, the little monosyllabic "yes" that Sternfield so earnestly implored, came not; and feeling that moments to him of golden worth were rapidly passing, he suddenly knelt beside her, and taking her hand in his, renewed his petition with more impassioned fervor than before.

At that moment the sound of a door closing at the end of the passage fell on Antoinette's ear, and she hurriedly exclaimed "Rise, for heaven's sake, Major Sternfield; rise! I hear some one coming."

"What of that, Antoinette? Here will I remain till I receive some hope—some word of encouragement—till you whisper me, yes."

"Yes, then yes," was the girl's quick, almost indistinct reply. "Rise at once."

"Thanks, my own," murmured he, raising the hand he still held, to his lips, and rapidly passing on one of the slight fingers a splendid opal ring, the seal of their mutual betrothal.

Here Mrs. D'Aulnay entered, and a slight but well-pleased smile flitted across her face as her glance passed from Sternfield's handsome features, glowing with happy triumph, to the embarrassed, averted countenance of her cousin. The gentleman did not greatly prolong his stay, for his quick tact told him that his absence just then would prove a great relief to his shy betrothed; but as he took leave of Mrs. D'Aulnay, where she stood a little apart, looking from a window, he whispered:

"How can I ever thank you sufficiently, my true and generous friend! My suit has been favorably received."

A kindly smile was his answer, and then, as the door closed upon him, Mrs. D'Aulnay approached and threw herself on a sofa beside her companion. The latter however seemed in no mood for conversation; and unwilling to compel her confidence, the lady touched lightly on indifferent topics, passing, apparently without design, a warn eulogium on Sternfield, which almost set at rest sundry uneasy doubts and reflections which even then were agitating Antoinette's mind. That night, however, when the young girl, according to her wont, bade an affectionate good night to her hostess, the latter took her hand, and, glancing significantly at the brilliant ring that sparkled there, imprinted a kiss on her fair young cheek, whispering at the same time words of earnest joyful gratulation, to which Antoinette replied only by blushes and a slight pressure from her tiny fingers.

A day or two after, Jeanne entered the drawing-room to announce a visitor for Mademoiselle Antoinette, and her smiling, satisfied look presented a marked contrast to the grim disapproval with which she ever heralded the approach of any of King George's gallant officers, for whom she entertained, individually and collectively, a profound antipathy.

"Who is it, Jeanne?"

"A young gentleman, Mademoiselle. One much nicer than any we have seen about here for some time past."

Mrs. D'Aulnay quietly smiled at this unceremonious speech, but uttered no remark, whilst the privileged Jeanne continued, "I am sure Mademoiselle will be pleased to see Mr. Beauchesne."

"Louis Beauchesne!" quickly repeated the lady of the house. "Oh, he brings you letters or special messages from home, Antoinette, so I will go to the library for a little while, as I wish to speak to Mr. D'Aulnay, but I will return soon. Jeanne, show this favored young gentleman up at once."

Shortly after, a young man of five-and-twenty with a clear ringing voice and open handsome countenance, entered the apartment, and accosted Antoinette with a degree of familiarity which betokened that great intimacy, if not friendship, existed between the two parties. The first few moments of friendly questioning over, it suddenly struck the young girl that there was an unusual degree of constraint about her companion's manner; and she was on the point of frankly asking the cause, when the latter drew a letter from his breast-pocket and handed it to her, exclaiming, in a somewhat embarrassed voice, "From you father, Antoinette"; after which brief piece of information, he rose and walked towards a window.

Antoinette's quick glance rapidly scanned the contents of the epistle; and astonishment, perplexity, and annoyance successively passed over her countenance as she read on.

At length she sharply exclaimed, "Are you acquainted with the contents of this letter, Louis?"

"I might hazard a guess at its purport," Beauchesne hesitatingly rejoined, "though your father did not show it to me."

"No prevarication," was the quick reply. "You know as well as myself, that my father informs me here in the most sudden and unexpected manner, that he has chosen you as my future husband, and that I am to receive you as such."

Beauchesne's dark cheek slightly flushed, but he made no reply, whilst his companion petulantly resumed; "Why do you not speak? Surely you agree with me that the whole thing is most absurd and unreasonable?"

"Pardon me, Antoinette," and the young man's tone plainly betrayed both mortification and wounded feeling. "Pardon me, but I really see nothing so very ridiculous in the proposition. Moving in the same circle—belonging to the same race and creed—intimate together from earliest childhood—"

"Yes, there it is," she hastily interrupted. "The friendly familiarity in which we have grown up together, has taught us to love each other dearly, but only as brother and sister."

"Again, pardon me," and this time an almost imperceptible smile curved the corners of his handsome mouth. "On that point, at least, I am fully competent to judge, and can assure you that my love is something more than brotherly in its fervor and warmth."

"How provoking you are, Louis! you speak in that strain merely to annoy me."

"Antoinette, be petulant—unkind if you will, but do not be unjust," he replied, approaching close to her chair, and fixing his earnest gaze upon her face. "I *do* love you, and my affection is not the less sincere that it is unaccompanied by any of those frenzied outbursts of passion which all lovers in romances and melodramas are bound to indulge in."

Poor Louis! At that moment the perverse Antoinette was mentally contrasting, and greatly to his disadvantage, this really rational, truthful declaration of affection with the late impassioned words and looks of Audley Sternfield. Perhaps something of what was passing in her mind, betrayed itself in her countenance, for Beauchesne continued with a slight touch of bitterness:

"But, I forget, you may perhaps have been listening of late to the love-vows of those who are proficients in the art in which I am only a novice. What chance of success has my simple, unstudied speech against the polished eloquence of those gallant gentlemen of the sword, who have perhaps made love in a dozen different climes to as many different women? You forget, Antoinette, I labor under the singular disadvantage of your being the first idol of my heart has worshipped—your ear the first into which I would pour promises or vows of love."

The truth of some of the allusions contained in Louis's last speech, dyed the young girl's cheek with tell-tale blushes, and she was too much confused to venture on a reply. Beauchesne partly read the truth in her embarrassment; and he quickly resumed, in tones in which regret had replaced the bitterness which had marked his previous words:

"Surely it is not really so, Antoinette? Surely you have not given so quickly to a stranger the love you refuse to the tried friend of childhood?"

"It matters not how that may be, Louis dear," she replied, deeply touched by the appealing gentleness of his last words; "but do not be angry with me if I frankly and truly declare I never can return your love."

"So be it," he calmly rejoined, but his lip slightly quivered as he spoke. "'Tis better we should understand each other at once. May the one you have chosen prove one half as true and faithful as I would have done."

A pause followed, which was broken by Antoinette exclaiming in a troubled voice, "I fear papa will be very angry with me. Did he seem exceedingly anxious for our marriage?"

"So anxious that he never even counted on the possibility of my failure."

"I suppose, then, that whenever he learns the real state of things, he will hasten here in great anger, and terrify me to death"; and her eyes filled with tears at the prospect her fancy had thus conjured up.

The kind-hearted Beauchesne, touched, notwithstanding his late grievous disappointment, by the childish fears of his companion, encouragingly replied, that he felt assured Mr. De Mirecourt was too just and indulgent to blame his daughter for refusing her hand where she could not give her heart.

"Ah! I do not know that. Papa is kind, but he does not like opposition of any sort. Louis dear, if you would only be generous enough to help me!" and she looked up eagerly in his face.

"How?" he briefly questioned.

"When you return, tell papa, what of course you ought and do secretly feel, that as my affections are not yours, you will no longer seek my hand."

"Most assuredly, Antoinette De Mirecourt," he rejoined, irritation and amusement struggling for the mastery in his breast, "I will do no such thing: be thankful that I do not tell him I am willing to wait for you, even seven years long, as Jacob waited for his bride."

"Well, then, tell me Louis, that you forgive me for what has just passed between us. Promise me that we shall remain as fast friends as we have hitherto been!"

There was no resisting that entreating look, that pleading, coaxing tone; and the young man frankly grasping her hand, rejoined, "I promise willingly. Yes, as we cannot be lovers, we shall at least remain friends. But I must leave you now: I have imperative business to attend to."

"You must not go without seeing Madame D'Aulnay. She would be quite angry with you."

"Frankly, I would rather forego that pleasure to-day. Lucille is no great favorite of mine."

"Nonsense! she expects you to remain here, and will be vexed with me if I allow you to leave without her seeing you. Wait but one moment: I will bring her immediately," and Antoinette hastened from the room.

During her absence, another visitor, Major Sternfield, was shown into the drawing-room. On his entrance, young Beauchesne, with his usual frank courtesy, bowed, preparatory to exchanging some commonplace remarks with the new-comer; but the latter, falling back on the sublime dandyism which he had the tact to keep in abeyance when in the society of Mrs. D'Aulnay and her cousin, or of his own intimate friends, inquiringly stared at this unknown candidate for the honor of his acquaintance; and then sinking back in the deep easy-chair which Antoinette had just vacated, and on the arm of which her perfumed handkerchief still lay, industriously commenced dusting his well-fitting boot with his tiny, agate-headed cane.

Beauchesne, humorously determined to show the Exclusive[73] that supercilious impertinence was not the

[73] A popular term in the first half of the nineteenth century for socialites.

special prerogative of any class or profession, lounged across the room to the mantle-mirror, and commenced pulling up his collar and running his hand through his thick raven curls with a self-concentrated solicitude, an utter forgetfulness of time and place, which successfully rivalled in impertinence even Sternfield's super-refined dandyism. On the entrance of the ladies, Louis, exercising the prerogative of intimate acquaintance, turned languidly towards them, listlessly hoping they were well, and then sank on a couch with a wearied *nonchalance* which was a tolerably faithful reproduction of the manner in which Major Sternfield had just performed the same action.

The latter seeing at once that this daring *provincial* was actually turning him into ridicule, darted a covert flashing glance upon him, and Mrs. D'Aulnay, comprehending the position of affairs, quickly exclaimed:

"Oh! come here, Louis, I want to ask you a question about Uncle De Mirecourt."

She retreated into the hall as if to ask or impart something of a confidential nature, and when the somewhat unwilling Louis had joined her, she caught his arm and playfully shaking him, enquired in a whisper: "What sort of an impression did he intend giving her guest of Canadian politeness."

"As good as that which he has given me of foreign breeding," was the cool reply. "But tell me, Lucille, in heaven's name, is yonder handsome coxcomb the chosen lover of Antoinette?"

"He is certainly a great admirer of hers, and I believe a somewhat favored one," was the hesitating reply; "but, Louis, you must not talk of, or treat Major Sternfield so contemptuously: he is a man of rare gifts, and—"

"There, there, Lucille, that will do," and he strove impatiently to shake off the little hand that still rested on his arm. "God help her, poor child! she will learn soon that what she takes for pure gold is but dross. No, I cannot stay to-day. Do not urge me further. Say farewell to Antoinette for me. *Au revoir*"; and breaking from the hand that still sought to detain him, he hurriedly left the house.

Mrs. D'Aulnay mused a moment, and then murmuring, "Certainly a disappointed suitor!" slowly turned back into the drawing-room, thinking what a terrible sacrifice it would be to give Antoinette to such a lover.

Chapter XI.

Major Sternfield, whose equanimity had been considerably ruffled by his meeting with Louis Beauchesne, did not stay long; and after he had taken his departure, the letter which Louis had brought was again read, and its contents discussed by both ladies. The somewhat arbitrary though kindly tone of the epistle was triumphantly pointed out by Mrs. D'Aulnay as an irresistible proof of the truth of her theory respecting the unreasonable tyranny of fathers, where their daughters' affections were concerned; and her conjectures with regard to the extremities of Mr. De Mirecourt would proceed to in order to enforce his wishes, put Antoinette into a state of feverish restlessness which effectually banished sleep from her pillow that night. A severe headache, which confined her the ensuing morning to her room, was the consequence; so that when Sternfield called with some book or trifling message for her, he found no one but Mrs. D'Aulnay in the drawing-room. His visit, however, proved anything but wearisome; for his companion took advantage of their *tête-à-tête* to frankly communicate to him the contents of the letter of which Louis had been the bearer; informing him, at the same time, of Mr. De Mirecourt's intense prejudices against foreigners, and of his formally declared determination to never allow his daughter to marry one. Sternfield's stay was unusually protracted; and towards its close, had any curious eye glanced into the drawing-room, it would have seen him in the act of holding Mrs. D'Aulnay's hand, whilst voice and eyes were alike eloquent in preferring some request. For a long time the lady hesitated and wavered; but at length, touched by his entreaties, she bowed her head in token of assent.

"Thanks, thanks, my true and generous friend!" he vehemently exclaimed. "You have saved Antoinette and myself."

"I do not feel so sure of that. I can do but little for you. Everything depends on your influence with my fair cousin herself; but you can call again this afternoon, and I will give you an opportunity of pressing your suit."

Mrs. D'Aulnay kept her word; and when Major Sternfield repeated his visit at a later period of the day, some inevitable writing obliged her to leave the room shortly after his entrance, whilst, singularly enough, though several acquaintances called, none found their way into the drawing-room. After a time Sternfield took his departure, whilst Antoinette, with a flushed cheek and contracted brow, escaped to her own room. Thither she was soon followed by Mrs. D'Aulnay, who found her pacing the apartment with quick, nervous steps, and heightened color.

"What is the matter, Antoinette? Are you still ill?" she enquired in a kind tone.

"Ill, and unhappy," was the hurried, agitated reply. "Shall I, or shall I not, confide in you?" and the speaker looked earnestly, wistfully into her cousin's countenance, which wore a look of innocent unconsciousness.

Oh! could Antoinette's better angel have spoken then, how he would have urged her to turn from that dangerous mentor, and place her confidence in those who would have proved more worthy of the trust. But it was the soft musical tones of Mrs. D'Aulnay that made themselves heard, as she gently insinuated her affection for Antoinette, and her earnest desire to promote the latter's happiness in all things. Little by little she at length drew from the young girl a confession, that Sternfield, who seemed by some wonderful instinct (so poor Antoinette in her simplicity said) to have divined the contents of the letter which Louis had brought, had been using every possible entreaty and argument to induce her to a secret marriage.

"And what answer did you give him, dear?"

"Of course, I peremptorily refused," was the petulant reply. "Why, you are almost as bad as Sternfield himself, Lucille, to ask me such a question."

"Well, child, abuse me if you will, but I really do not condemn his proposal as strongly as you seem to do. Once wedded, your father would have no alternative but that of forgiving and receiving you again into favor; whilst now, he may forbid your union with Sternfield, under threats so severe, that you dare not disobey him."

"Well, if he does so, I must submit," rejoined Antoinette, moodily. "I cannot, I dare not, deceive him to such an extent."

"What, submit! Yield up the man you love for a father's whim,—sacrifice the happiness of your whole life to a mere prejudice!"

"Filial duty and affection are neither whims nor prejudices," retorted Antoinette indignantly. "Papa has always been kind and indulgent, and to deceive him so terribly would be indeed but a poor return for all his affection."

"Perhaps you are right, child," was the quiet reply; "and I begin to think it would be as well on the whole to obey him on every point. Louis will make a good, humdrum sort of husband; and even if your connubial happiness occasionally prove somewhat monotonous—even if you regret at times the never-to-be-recalled past—your filial duty and your own conscience will prove your reward."

"Lucille, you are very provoking to-day! Rejecting a secret marriage with Major Sternfield is one thing, and wedding Louis Beauchesne is another."

"Oh! you will find them synonymous, cousin mine. Uncle De Mirecourt is not a man to be trifled with, and your refusal to wed the suitor he may choose for you will prove as unavailing as would the struggles of a linnet against the strong grasp that seek to place it in a cage. But you look flushed and feverish, dear child. Seek your pillow, and take counsel from it."

Alas! Antoinette did so, instead of seeking direction from that unfailing source of light which would have guided her footsteps so unerringly amid the snares into which they had wandered. Still, for two days she scrupulously avoided any mention of Sternfield's name, evading, with equal care, all further discussion regarding him with Mrs. D'Aulnay; and the latter began to think the handsome Englishman's chance was a hopeless one, when help came to his cause from a quarter, the very last from which it might have been expected. This was in the shape of a very severe, very imperious letter from Mr. De Mirecourt to his daughter, mentioning that he had just heard from a lady who had recently left Montreal, of the notorious flirtation she was carrying on with some English officer, and that he was coming to town in a week to put an end to the affair by hurrying on her marriage with the husband he had chosen for her.

This letter, most certainly ill-judged and arbitrary, corroborating so fully all Mrs. D'Aulnay's late predictions, had a most pernicious effect on Antoinette's already wavering mind, and she had recourse again to her cousin for advice and encouragement. 'Tis needless to say in what shape the latter administered it; and she now openly and constantly spoke of an immediate and secret marriage as the only alternative left.

Chapter XII.

Additional cause of mental trouble and anxiety presented itself in the absence of Major Sternfield, who, since Antoinette's indignant rejection of his proposal, had not returned to the house.

Whether this was the result of disappointment and wounded feeling, or that of simple calculation on his part, it is impossible to say. If the latter, he certainly proved himself a clever tactician, for his absence served his cause far more effectually than his presence could have done. Left almost entirely to herself—for she felt too unhappy to see any of the general run of "callers" who daily presented themselves in her cousin's *salons*—half distracted by fears of her father's forcing on her marriage with Louis, or visiting on her the full weight of his anger if she resisted, she missed with an acuteness, a feverish anxiety, she would have heretofore deemed impossible, the honeyed words, the tender protestations, which of late Audley Sternfield had so constantly breathed into her ear.

Mrs. D'Aulnay, who, partly out of kindly feeling to Antoinette, as well as to Sternfield, whose mutual happiness she thought could be alone secured by marriage—partly out of a silly sentimentalism, seeking excitement of some sort of other—was determined to bring about their union, if possible; so far from doing anything in her power to alleviate Antoinette's very apparent wretchedness, strove rather to increase it. Now, affecting to look on the latter's marriage with a suitor she did not love, as inevitable, and pitying her in consequence; then, gently blaming her timidity, her obstinacy in refusing to wed the one she did. These exhortations she always concluded by repeating that once her young cousin was united to Sternfield, they would have no difficulty in obtaining her father's forgiveness, though the latter would inevitably keep his word of wedding her to Louis if no obstacle, beyond his daughter's unwillingness, presented itself. Another time she would wonder, and comment on Sternfield's protracted absence—hint, that discouraged by Antoinette's coldness and contemptuous rejection of his suit, he had abandoned it, or perhaps turned his attentions to some other quarter where they would be more flatteringly received; and then she would leave Antoinette to reflections which dyed her brow with humiliating blushes, and made her heart ache as if had never ached before. It was at the end of such a conversation, that Mrs. D'Aulnay rose to dress for a drive, in which Antoinette had petulantly declined joining her, saying,—

"Well, it is probably better for all parties that Sternfield has ceased his visits here, for what could they avail but to render you both more wretched. In two days at farthest, your father will arrive; and before another month, you will be Louis's very obedient, very loving wife."

"Never!" she vehemently exclaimed. "I shall live and die single first."

But as reflection brought up before her the inflexible determination of her father's will when once fully bent on any point, the passionate flush on her cheek faded, and she wearily leaned her head on the small table near her, faint and sick at heart. From her father, her thoughts turned to the recreant Audley, who had wearied so soon of a lover's supplicating attitude, and the quickened beating of her heart as his image mentally rose before her, even though irritation mingled with the warmer feelings she entertained for him, whispered more energetically than aught else could have done, "that now, at least, she ought not to become the bride of Louis." The opening of the hall-door, announcing the probable advent of some visitor, but increased the morbid irritation of her feelings; and as the door of the apartment in which she was sitting unclosed, she impatiently exclaimed, without raising her head from the arm on which it was bowed:

"Not at home, Jeanne, not at home to any one."

"Still less of all others to me, Antoinette," whispered a deep musical voice beside her; and her quickly raised, startled glance, encountered the dark eyes of Audley Sternfield, fixed in pleading, deprecating entreaty upon her.

"Forgive me, my beloved, this once, for thrusting Jeanne aside, and forcing myself on your presence unannounced, but I have just learned that Mr. De Mirecourt arrives to-morrow, and I have that to say to you which must be said. Tell me, first, though, that you forgive me"; and he caught Antoinette's hand, which she passively suffered him to retain, averting from him, however, her pale and troubled countenance. "I have come, mine own, to implore your forgiveness for the annoyance I caused you in our last interview—to atone for my madness and folly."

"You have taken time to do so," returned his companion, her delicate lip nervously quivering.

Oh! unwary, inexperienced Antoinette, how much was unconsciously implied, acknowledged in that childish reproach! Major Sternfield's triumphant glance told he took in its full import; but in tones of softest humility, he continued, as he seated himself beside her:

"You ordered me from your presence, my own Antoinette, and I dared not seek you again till your anger, which my presumption had perhaps justly evoked, was somewhat appeased."

But why follow that wily man of the world through his course of passionate entreaty, deprecation, and well-feigned despair? What change against him had the yielding, child-like Antoinette, unsustained as she then was by the religious principles, to whose holy suggestions she willfully closed her heart? As might be foreseen, the tempter triumphed; and on his again repeating, for the twentieth time, his proposal of an immediate marriage, she at length bowed her pale cheek on his shoulder, and burst into a passionate flood of tears.

"This evening, my beloved," he whispered, as he pressed her cold, still half-reluctant hand to his lips, again and again.

Antoinette's tears flowed still faster, but she spoke not. Her silence, however, was answer enough for her lover, and he continued: "kind Mrs. D'Aulnay will befriend us as she has ever heretofore done; and here, in her drawing-room, Doctor Ormsby, the chaplain of our regiment, will unite us by those sacred bonds which will give me the blessed right to call you all my own."

"Dr. Ormsby," repeated Antoinette, with a bewildered look, which told the peculiar circumstances of a secret marriage now fully dawned for the first time upon her. Yes, it must indeed be so. No Catholic priest would or dared marry her thus privately and secretly. Her father, too, was daily expected—no farther time allowed for hesitation, for delay. Wofully as the young girl had retrograded from the standard of truth, and pure, strict uprightness, which had been hers when she first arrived beneath Mrs. D'Aulnay's roof,—negligent as she had latterly grown in prayer, and in the fulfilment of all her religious duties, enough remained of olden feelings and principles, to make her shrink from the idea of a clandestine marriage, unhallowed by a father's blessing, and that religious benediction, which she had been taught from childhood to regard as so solemn and necessary a part of the marriage service. Sternfield saw her increased trouble, and divined at once the cause. Eloquently he spoke of Doctor Ormsby's worth and goodness, and gently insinuated how little mattered slight differences of ceremonies.

"Ah! yes," interrupted his companion, with a slight shudder, "to you it is but a ceremony,—to me it is, or ought to be, a sacrament."

"But, my beloved, our nuptials shall be blessed and solemnized again, if you wish it, by a clergyman of your own faith, whenever your father shall have been informed of our marriage,—nay, before then—to-morrow, if you will. Antoinette, my own Antoinette, what is there that love like mine would hesitate to grant you?"

Silenced, though not convinced, she made no reply, for passion at that moment spoke louder in her heart than principle; and now every obstacle vanquished, every objection overcome, Sternfield poured forth his ardent expressions of love and gratitude, unmindful, almost careless in the proud height of his triumph, that tears were still flowing down her pale cheek, and that the little hand he held so closely was as cold as one of her own Canadian icicles. This singular lover's interview was brought to an end by Mrs. D'Aulnay's entrance, some short time after; and a glance at Sternfield's happy, triumphant countenance, so forcibly contrasted by the pale, agitated face of his companion, enabled her to form at once an accurate guess at the real state of matters. Antoinette rose on her cousin's entrance, and left the room, but not before Sternfield had imprinted a kiss on her hand, whispering in an audible tone:

"This evening, my Antoinette, at seven."

"Well, Major Sternfield, I see you have diligently improved your time. So day and hour are settled!" exclaimed Mrs. D'Aulnay, fixing a penetrating glance on her military friend. Perhaps the exultant triumph that beamed on his handsome face, slightly jarred with her sentimental ideas of what a lover's reverential devotion should be, infusing probably, at the same time, some uneasy fears into her mind, regrading the absolute certainty of Antoinette's future wedded happiness,—a thing of which, till the present moment, she had never entertained even the shadow of a doubt. The quick-sighted Sternfield detected at once the could on Mrs. D'Aulnay's countenance, slight as it was, and, probably divining the cause, instantly advanced towards her, exclaiming,

"My dear, kind Madame D'Aulnay, you, who have listened so indulgently, so patiently to all my doubts, hopes, and fears, will not wonder that I am nearly intoxicated with joy, when I tell you that Antoinette has consented to become mine by the holiest of all ties, this very evening. Oh, best and dearest friend, I could kneel to you, if you permit it, to pour forth my thanks—my unbounded gratitude."

The handsome speaker seemed very much in earnest, and the lady, completely appeased, smiled kindly upon him, as she rejoined:

"Enough, Major Sternfield: I believe in your sincerity. And now, if this solemn affair is really to come off this evening, I must send you away, for I have a great deal to do."

The young man kissed the fair hand held out to him; an act of gallantry which the speaker, who was equally proud of her pretty tapering fingers, and splendid rings, seldom objected to, and hurried away. Mrs. D'Aulnay did not at once seek Antoinette, for the one glance she had obtained of her tearful, pale face, on entering the drawing-room, told it would scarcely prove a propitious time for consultation or discussion, yet. Instead, she proceeded to her own chamber, and rang for Jeanne, with whom she was closeted a half-hour, giving her some household directions. Then she sought Mr. D'Aulnay, and chatted another half-hour with him, incidentally mentioning that she and Antoinette expected a couple of gentlemen friends in the evening, a precaution which she knew would infallibly keep her husband in his library. The early winter evening was rapidly closing in; and giving a passing glance at the drawing-rooms, to assure herself that lights and fires were brightly burning, she sought her young cousin's room.

The latter was standing near the bed-room window, her forehead pressed against the panes as if she were watching the snow-storm wildly raging without, the falling flakes of which, caught up by the fierce wind, were whirled against the casement, or blown about in blinding masses, obscuring for the moment everything in earth and sky.

"Good heavens, child!" exclaimed Mrs. D'Aulnay, almost angrily, "what are you dreaming about? Five o'clock, and priest and bridegroom expected in a couple of hours!"

Her annoyance was excusable, for Antoinette still wore the soft dark stuff she had put on in the early part of the day, and no ribbons, flowers, or lighter garments lying about, betokened any intention of assuming a more suitable costume. But as the young girl slowly turned her pallid, tear-stained face, towards the new-comer, the heart of the latter smote her, and she felt she must console and encourage, instead of finding fault.

"Come here, Antoinette, darling, to the fire," she kindly exclaimed: "you will take cold near the window. It is time to think, too, about what you will wear this evening, for you must look your very best."

The bride-elect made no reply, but the expression of wretchedness on that usually bright and sparkling countenance, told how indifferent all minor details were to her then. A violent struggle, fierce as that of the storm she was watching, had been passing in her breast during the previous hour; and better thoughts, and good inspirations had been combatting powerfully for the mastery. The strife was not yet over; for as Mrs. D'Aulnay, alarmed at her pallor and silence, drew her towards her, repeating her questions, she whispered,

"Lucille, I cannot, I dare not venture on this terrible step! 'Twould be a union unblessed by God or man."

Mrs. D'Aulnay sank into a chair, in speechless amazement and indignation. Antoinette De Mirecourt's destiny was trembling then in the balance. One word of good advice, one encouraging look, would have given her strength to have drawn back from the precipice on which she was standing; but, alas! that strengthening word or look came not, and instead, her companion burst forth:

"Are you mad, utterly mad, Antoinette? Your consent, your promise given—your lover, with the clergyman, whose assistance he has asked, on their way here—"

"But my father; oh, Lucille, my father!" gasped forth the girl, her cheek turning to still deathlier whiteness.

"Don't speak to me about your father!" retorted Mrs. D'Aulnay, now fairly roused to anger. "The harm, if harm there is, is entirely his doing. What right has he to dispose of you to Louis Beauchesne, as if you were a farm or field he wished to get rid of? Decide, now and for ever, between the husband he has selected for you, and the one your heart has chosen. Aye! choose between Louis Beauchesne and Audley Sternfield. But I am wasting words, my poor little cousin," she added in a softened tone: "your final choice is already made, though that wayward heart shrinks from acknowledging it. I see I must be your tire-woman[74] for the occasion; and 'tis as well, for I am determined Audley shall feel proud of you."

[74] A lady's maid (especially one that helps her lady get dressed) or a female dresser in a theatre ("tire" is an old variant of "attire").

Chapter XIII.

Turning to Antoinette's ward-robe, she hastily selected a rose-colored silk dress, and, bringing it forward, exclaimed:

"You are too pale for white this evening; besides, as we are comparatively alone, it might excite the remarks of the servants. This soft, war color will give something of that glow to your complexion in which it is so sadly deficient to-night."

Under Mrs. D'Aulnay's skillful fingers, the process of dressing was a speedy one; but if hours had been lavished on the task, the result could scarcely have been more successful. Major Sternfield had indeed a lovely bride.

"Come to the drawing-room, now, you little nervous creature," the elder lady smilingly exclaimed. "You must be seated there quietly for a half hour at least, before they come in, for I can hear the beating of your heart as plainly, almost, as the ticking of yonder pendulum."

Once in the drawing-room, Mrs. D'Aulnay took good care to leave her companion little time for serious reflections; for she passed from one subject to another, with a vivacity and rapidity of utterance, which almost overpowered Antoinette's already overtasked brain. Once, however, perhaps from weariness, she suddenly paused, and a long silence ensued. Antoinette's eyes were fixed on the floor, and, by the light of the lamp on the table near her, in whose full radiance she sat, Mrs. D'Aulnay earnestly scrutinized her features. There was something in their peculiar set expression which sent an uneasy fear through that lady's heart as to the wisdom of the step on which she was strongly encouraging, if not almost forcing the young girl committed to her charge, and suddenly, impulsively she exclaimed:

"Tell me, Antoinette, darling, do you not truly, deeply love Audley Sternfield?"

For the first time that day, something like a smile flitted over the girl's face, as she replied: "Why, you have told me yourself a hundred times that I did, after questioning and cross-questioning me more strictly than any lawyer could have done."

"Yes, but does not your own heart tell you that you do?" was the rapid, almost agitated inquiry.

For a moment Antoinette was silent; and then, as memory called up before her the fascinating handsome Sternfield, with all his boundless devotion to herself, a shy smile played round her lips, and she murmured, "yes."

"Thank you, sweet cousin, for the avowal!" replied Mrs. D'Aulnay, throwing her arms around her; and feeling almost as delighted with the acknowledgment, in her new-born anxiety, as Sternfield himself could have done. "Thank you a hundred times; and now I will ring for Jeanne to bring you a glass of wine. You look bent on being nervous and provoking, by and bye."

It was Jeanne who answered the summons, and when her mistress exclaimed, "Let tea be given in the drawing-room: I expect a couple of friends," she rejoined, "Oh, madame, nobody that could help it would venture out to-night: 'tis most fearful weather!'

Her mistress quietly smiled in reply, inwardly thinking how terrible would be the storm which could prevent *one* of their expected guests from coming. As the door closed upon Jeanne, a furious blast struck the casement, and caused Antoinette to give a nervous start.

"'Tis all for the best, dearest," was her companion's smiling remark. "We need be under no apprehensions of unwelcome intruders dropping in. Ah! there are our friends," she added as voices and footsteps sounded in the hall, and sundry stampings betokened the new-comers were endeavoring to divest themselves of the snowy covering with which the storm had favored them. In another moment Major Sternfield and his companion Dr. Ormsby were in the drawing-room, and the ceremony of introduction was gone through. The clergyman, a young, intellectual-looking man with dark earnest eyes, replied briefly, almost coldly, to Mrs. D'Aulnay's flattering welcome, and, as soon as they were seated, stole an earnest scrutinizing glance towards Antoinette, beside whose chair Sternfield was already bending. Neither the pink hue of her dress, the heated atmosphere of the drawing-room, nor yet the presence of her lover, had brought color to her cheek, or animation to her eye; and the minister's earnest gaze grew yet more serious and his expression more thoughtful, as he watched her. Rapidly, imploringly Sternfield whispered in the girl's ear; and at length, when Mrs. D'Aulnay, whose patience was almost exhausted by the want of gallantry of her clerical guest, exclaimed, "Antoinette dear, we must not trespass on Dr. Ormsby's valuable time," she briefly, almost irritably replied, "I am ready."

Mrs. D'Aulnay turned quickly to the door, which she noiselessly fastened, and then moved to the table near which the remainder of the party were now standing. For a moment Dr. Ormsby's calm, earnest glance rested on Antoinette, and he then gently said:

"You are very young, Miss De Mirecourt, and 'tis a life-long engagement on which you are about to enter. Have you weighed well its duties and its purport?"

"It seems to me that your question, Dr. Ormsby, is a very singular and unnecessary one," interrupted Sternfield, with a dark frown.

"I am but doing my duty, Sir," was the grave, stern reply; "or rather, I fear I am about to overstep it, in keeping the promise I have given you. However, as I am here, if Miss De Mirecourt is still determined to wed you thus privately and hurriedly, 'tis not for me to raise opposition now."

Antoinette again repeated in an almost inaudible voice, "I am ready." In a few moments, those solemn words, "They whom God hath joined let no man put asunder," rang in their ears, and Antoinette De Mirecourt and Audley Sternfield were man and wife. After a few brief words of felicitation, Dr. Ormsby rose to take leave. In vain Mrs. D'Aulnay begged him to remain to partake of some refreshment—in vain the handsome bridegroom, who had now completely recovered his equanimity, repeated her entreaties: he was resolute. As he shook hands with Antoinette, she laid her little hand on his arm, and whispered in a tone inaudible to her companions:

"Promise me that you will keep my secret."

"That promise," he kindly rejoined, "I have already tacitly given Major Sternfield, and to you I now repeat it. Need I say it shall be sacredly kept?'

"Thank you, and bear witness, Doctor Ormsby," she rejoined in a louder though more agitated tone, "that I tell Major Sternfield in your presence, that till the marriage shall have been publicly acknowledged to the world, and celebrated again by a Roman Catholic priest, he and I shall be but friends to each other."

Dr. Ormsby gravely, kindly bowed his head, and then left the room; and as the yawning domestic showed out the tall stranger, he carelessly wondered at his early departure, little dreaming what a powerful, life-long influence his stay, short as it had been, had exercised over the future destinies of two of the occupants of the drawing-room. Meanwhile the parties in question were standing quietly around the table as if nothing unusual had happened; and Mrs. D'Aulnay and Major Sternfield were exchanging some commonplace remarks about Dr. Ormsby's gentlemanly manners and appearance; but the lady stole many a secret, uneasy glance towards the silent bride, the pallor of whose cheek had given place to a feverish vivid scarlet, such as the keenest wintry air, or the most violent exercise, had never perhaps yet called to it.

When the door closed upon the clergyman, Antoinette abruptly withdrew from Sternfield the hand he had immediately caught in his, and poured herself out a large glass of water, which she swallowed in a single draught; but the little fingers trembled so violently in raising it to her lips, that part of its contents were spilled on her bridal dress.

Mrs. D'Aulnay, naturally thinking that the lovers might wish to exchange a word alone, had, at first, quietly turned to leave the room; but a quick glance from the bride, half imploring, half authoritative, had warned her to stay. Unwilling to increase the agitation she read so plainly depicted in the latter's face, she addressed some commonplace observation to Sternfield, and then walked to the window; whilst Audley, probably actuated by a similar dread, repressed the ardent words that rose to his lips and continued to address her in the subdued strain of gentle affection which he justly divined would alone prove welcome at the moment to his trembling bride.

"What a fearful night!" exclaimed Mrs. D'Aulnay as she drew together the crimson curtains shading the window near which she was standing. 'Tis snowing, storming, and drifting in a manner that will effectually block up the roads for days to come. Your father, Antoinette, cannot possibly arrive to-morrow."

"A welcome respite!" was the secret thought of all parties, but a thought to which no one gave expression; and then Major Sternfield took occasion to enquire, with much seeming interest, how many miles it was to Valmont. Shortly after, Mrs. D'Aulnay rang for tea, which was quickly served up, and all three continued to affect a composure and calm which none really felt. Another hour passed over, all circumstances considered very heavily; and then the hostess warned Sternfield by a glance towards the time-piece, that it was time for him to leave.

After a friendly clasp of the latter's hand and a few whispered words of gratitude, he turned to his shrinking, girlish bride, and, folding her in his arms, murmured, "My wife, my own!" For a moment that bright young head rested on his shoulder, and then with a convulsive sob, or rather gasp, she faltered:

"Audley, Audley, never give me cause to repent the irrevocable step I have taken to-night!" Another embrace was his only reply; and he left the apartment with a light step and a proud triumph in his face which was certainly not reflected from the countenances of his companions.

"Come to rest, Antoinette, darling!" exclaimed Mrs. D'Aulnay, when they were alone. "I will go with you to your room, and wait to see you in bed."

The girl passively obeyed; and when her gay evening-dress was laid aside, and her rich heavy braids of hair gathered up beneath the little snowy cap which made her fair young face look doubly youthful, she knelt before her prie-Dieu,[75] but only to rise from it a moment afterwards, vehemently exclaiming, "Oh! Lucille, I cannot, I dare not pray to-night!"

"And, why not, you dear, fanciful little creature?" It seems to me prayer is doubly incumbent on you now that you have a handsome, devoted husband to pray for. But do not mind it to-night: I see you are really ill and your hand is burning. Lie down at once."

Antoinette passively submitted, but the step brought no repose to mind or body; and for several hours her cousin sat at her bed-side, listening anxiously to the moaning and incoherent ravings which immediately ensued whenever

[75] A prayer desk (sometimes very elaborate; sometimes only a very narrow kneeling bench, but with room above for elbows or a book). Its name is French (literally, "pray God").

sleep overpowered her, or soothing the nervous fancies or terrors which marked her waking moments. At length, about an hour after midnight, she sank into a deep, dreamless slumber; and Mrs. D'Aulnay retired to her own couch, more anxious and troubled than she would acknowledge even to herself.

Chapter XIV.

The following morning, the young girl awoke with an intense, overpowering head-ache which kept her prisoner in her room the whole of the forenoon, much to the annoyance and disappointment of Sternfield, who called at an early hour; and who, when refused admittance by Jeanne, turned from the door with a lowering frown which excited that worthy woman's wrath to a high degree.

"One would think he was the master of the house," she resentfully muttered, as she closed the door upon him. "Why, he looked as if he was about to push me aside and force himself in as he did the other day when he wanted to see *Mademoiselle*."

She failed not on the first subsequent opportunity to communicate her ideas on the subject to her mistress, whose smooth brow contracted as she listened to the tale, in a manner which proved more satisfactory to Jeanne than it would have done to Major Sternfield had he witnessed it. Antoinette came down to dinner; and just as the ladies had sought the drawing-room, and Mr. D'Aulnay his library, the tinkle od sleigh-bells stopping before the door announced an arrival.

"My father," murmured Antoinette, turning pale as marble.

"Yes, it is indeed he," rejoined her companion, taking a hasty *reconnaissance*[76] through the window. "Who would

[76] The act of reconnoitering (misspelled in the original as "réconnaissance").

have expected him with such roads? And now, dear child, no tremors—no nervousness. If, by ill-fortune, your father happen to be in an unpropitious humor, do not run the risk of confessing your marriage now: precipitancy might spoil all."

Ere long, Mr. De Mirecourt—a carefully-dressed, stately-looking gentleman of the old French school—entered; and his daughter, dreading to meet his penetrating glance, instantly threw herself into his arms. He embraced her affectionately, and then gently raising her face, he looked earnestly into it, exclaiming, after a moment:

"'Tis as I feared, little one! This gay, fashionable life does not agree with a simple country girl like yourself. Why, you look three years older than you did when you left home; and though your cheeks are rosy enough, these burning little hands tell that your roses are more those of fever than of health."

"Antoinette did not rest well last night, dear uncle," said Mrs. D'Aulnay, who was standing beside the new-comer, her hand resting caressingly on his shoulder. "She is unusually nervous."

"There it is, my fair niece," was the smiling reply. "The usual fine lady's cant. Why, my little Antoinette, who used to give me breakfast every morning in the country at seven, and help to eat it too, with excellent appetite, scarcely knew then what the term nervous meant."

"But, *cher oncle*,[77] Antoinette was scarcely more than a little girl a few months ago. She is a young lady now."

"A fine lady, you mean, Lucille. But it is not that alone: I find an indefinable change in her that I cannot describe. Perhaps it is that she is more graceful, more elegant in her style of dress; in short, more like my charming nice, Madame D'Aulnay," he good-humoredly added. "However, let my little girl's external appearance pass, 'tis well enough; but I cannot say I am well satisfied with her on other points.

[77] French for "dear uncle."

Aye, you may well blush!" he added, as Antoinette's face became painfully crimson. "I have two serious accusations to bring against you. But to begin with the first: What is the reason you reject Louis Beauchesne, the husband I have chosen for you—to whom I promised you?"

"Because, dear papa, I do not love him sufficiently well to marry him."

"Ah, Lucille, Lucille, this is your work," exclaimed Mr. De Mirecourt, reproachfully shaking his head at his niece. "Just what Mrs. Gérard foretold, when we discussed the propriety of accepting your invitation for Antoinette."

"But, dear uncle, I know you are too just, too kind, to force my cousin into a marriage with a man she does not love."

"She loves Louis quite as well as you did Mr. D'Aulnay when you wedded him; and who will presume to say that you are not a very happy couple? But *trêve*[78] to this nonsense! I have made up my mind; and though I give her her own way about pocket-money, household matters, and other minor details, on this point I must have mine. She has known Louis long, always treated him with affectionate kindness, and is as well acquainted as I am with his irreproachable character. He is an excellent *parti*[79] too in a worldly point of view, and I do not intend sacrificing so many combined advantages, in compliance with a girl's sentimental whim. So prepare to return home with me to-morrow, my daughter; or if I leave you another week here, it will be only to give you the chance of at once selecting your *trousseau*,[80]—for, before this day month, Louis Beauchesne will be my son-in-law."

"But, dear dear papa," pleaded Antoinette, with tearful eyes, throwing her arms about Mr. De Mirecourt's neck

[78] French for "truce" or "break."

[79] French for "match."

[80] See note 30. However, the "trousseau" was usually prepared long before marriage. Families often began putting it together as soon as a girl was born, rather than buying it in the weeks before wedding.

as she spoke, "forgive me if I say I cannot marry Louis. I will do anything else you wish me to do—return with you to the country to-morrow, live as quietly as a hermit there"—

"Pshaw! enough of this folly!" interrupted Mr. De Mirecourt, unwinding, though not unkindly, the little arms encircling him. "I have overlooked your singular, I might say rather undutiful letter of last week, informing me that you could not, would not, listen to my wishes; but, Antoinette dear, you must not try my patience too far!"

A pause ensued, and then the young girl unclosed her lips twice as if to speak, but her resolution failed her, and she directed a pleading look towards Mrs. D'Aulnay, mutely asking her to enter on the dreaded explanation.

"Well, it is all settled then?" cheerfully enquired Mr. De Mirecourt, misinterpreting the momentary silence into a token of consent.

"Ah! I fear not, my dearest uncle," and Mrs. D'Aulnay's hand was again laid caressingly on his shoulder. "There may be an invincible obstacle to this union—one which, perhaps, cannot be overcome!"

Mrs. D'Aulnay had scarcely calculated on the effect her words would produce, or she might have hesitated before uttering them. Dashing off her hand, Mr. De Mirecourt sprang to his feet, and, looking angrily from one to the other, sternly repeated,

"Invincible obstacle! What do you, what can you mean, Lucille? But, pshaw!" he continued, less violently, "'Tis only your romantic, exaggerated style of speech; unless, indeed,"—and here his gaze grew darker than before,—"that Antoinette has become entangled in a ridiculous love-affair with some of the gay military gallants who are probably allowed to over-run the house. I have heard a whisper of the flirtations and nonsense going on here of late."

"Uncle, dear uncle!" gently remonstrated Mrs. D'Aulnay.

The simple appeal, uttered in the softest tones, somewhat calmed Mr. De Mirecourt, but he continued, still firmly enough, "'Tis of no use, Lucille. Soft words and pleading looks will not prevent me saying what I have to say; and again, I repeat, I hope that my daughter has not forgotten herself so far as to enter into any secret love-engagement with those who are aliens alike to our race, creed, and tongue."

"But if she should have done so, dearest uncle—if she should have met with some noble, good man, who, apart from the objection of his being a foreigner, should have proved himself worthy in all other things of inspiring affection—"

"Then, Madame D'Aulnay," he interrupted, striking the table so violently that the vases and other ornaments on it shook again, "the first thing she has to do is to forget him; for never, never will she obtain either my consent or my blessing."

"Now is the moment," inwardly groaned Antoinette; "now, we should undeceive him—tell him it is beyond earthly power to prevent the union he so utterly condemns." So thought Mrs. D'Aulnay too; but Mr. De Mirecourt had wrought himself up to a degree of anger most unusual with him, and they tremblingly recoiled from the thought of exasperating him farther.

"Listen to me, daughter Antoinette, and you, my too officious niece, bear witness," he resumed, after a short pause, which had been merely a lull in the tempest. "I must be plain, explicit, with you both. I forbid you, child, to have any intercourse, beyond that of distant courtesy, with the men I have mentioned; and if you have entangled yourself in any disgraceful flirtation or attachment, break it off at once, under penalty of being disowned and disinherited."

"Oh! my father!" faltered Antoinette, clasping her trembling hands, "For God's sake, retract those cruel words: they are too terrible!"

A vague fear stole over Mr. De Mirecourt's heart at this passionate appeal; but as is frequently the case, it only increased his irritation, and seizing his daughter's arm, he violently repeated, "I shall not retract them, disobedient, wilful girl!"

At that moment the drawing-room door opened, and Louis Beauchesne entered. A look of mingled dismay and indignation flashed across his face as his glance took in the scene before him; but Mr. De Mirecourt, still under the influence of his late fierce excitement, exclaimed,

"I have just been telling this wilful girl that this day month,[81] willing or unwilling, she shall become your wife."

"Oh, Mr. De Mirecourt," he replied, with a look of mingled bitterness and pain. "I seek not an unwilling bride—one forced to the altar against the wishes of her own heart. But are you not exacting too speedy a submission from Antoinette? Scarcely a fortnight has elapsed since you first mentioned your wishes to her, and you must accord her a little time to make up her mind. Why, she will require a month to recover from the effects of to-day's scolding"; and he glanced compassionately towards Antoinette, who was leaning against a chair, her cheek pale as marble, and every feature quivering with agitation.

Mr. De Mirecourt's heart smote him. During the seventeen years that his daughter had passed under the protecting shadow of his parental love, he had never addressed as many unking and harsh words to her as he had done within the last ten minutes; and unacquainted with the secret fears and anxieties torturing her heart, he attributed her overwhelming emotion entirely to his own severity.

"Sit down Antoinette," continued Louis, reading, at once, the relenting expression stealing over her father's face. "Sit down, and I know Mr. De Mirecourt will promise to grant six months instead of one, to prepare your mind and your *trousseau*."

[81] An obsolete phrase meaning "one month from today."

"You are a philosophical wooer, Louis," exclaimed Mr. De Mirecourt, sarcastically; "more so than I would have been at your age; and seem to be in no hurry to seal your happiness."

"Because I seek Antoinette's happiness before my own," he rejoined, whilst the old bitter expression clouded his countenance for a moment. "But speak, Mr. De Mirecourt, is it not settled that you will give her six months longer for reflection; at the end of which time let us hope that your wishes and mine may be fulfilled."

Poor Louis! he knew well the futility of that hope; but in his generous abnegation, he only thought of procuring a respite for the pale trembling girl before him.

"Be it as you wish then," returned Mr. De Mirecourt, with an attempt at carelessness. "Since the expectant bridegroom is satisfied, so also should I be. But, Antoinette, remember that of what I have just told you concerning foreign lovers or suitors, I retract nothing. What I have said, I have said; and if you disobey me, neither blessing nor inheritance will ever be yours. And now enough on this chapter. Where is Mr. D'Aulnay?"

"I will seek him, dear uncle," rejoined Mrs. D'Aulnay, hastily rising, for her quick ear had caught the sound of the hall-door opening. On leaving the room, instead of proceeding to the library where her husband was, she rapidly descended the stairs in time to arrest Sternfield, who was divesting himself of his outer coat, preparatory to seeking the society of the ladies, Jeanne having received no orders to exclude him.

Mrs. D'Aulnay drew him hurriedly into a small ante-room off the hall, and in a few rapid words recounted the stormy interview which had just passed up stairs. The major's flushed cheek and contracted brow betokened the intense annoyance the recital caused him; and had his companion been as quick-eyed as she generally was, she would have perceived that at her mention of Mr. De Mirecourt's threat of disinheriting his daughter, the listener's cheek gained a deeper glow, his eyes an angrier light. "Can you tell me," he irritably enquired, "how long this tyrannical old man is going to stay, for see my wife I must and shall."

"Hush, hush, do not speak so loud. I think he will leave to-morrow morning; and till he has taken his departure, you must remain exiled from her presence. Do not get impatient; for, believe me, our penance meanwhile will be severer than yours."

Dismissing Sternfield with a friendly pressure of the hand, she turned now to the library where she found, as she had expected, her husband; and immediately entered on a narrative of the late scene in the drawing-room, condemning Mr. De Mirecourt's harshness in no measured terms, and concluding by imploring Mr. D'Aulnay to use all his influence in inducing this *père sauvage*[82] to leave poor Antoinette a little longer with them. "Believe me, dear André," the lady pathetically added, "she will be scolded and worried into her grave, if she goes back with her still irritated father. Request, then, the prolongation of her visit as a personal favor; and if you are sufficiently persevering, uncle De Mirecourt will scarcely refuse you."

"Well, I will do as you ask me, Lucille, for I am really fond of the little girl; but still I cannot help thinking she would be better at home, than flirting and fluttering about with the military cavaliers that you and she both so strongly affect."

[82] French for "wild father" ("wild" in the sense of unsophisticated, uncivilized).

Chapter XV.

The meeting between Mr. D'Aulnay and his guest was cordial in the extreme, for they had been fast friends from early boyhood, and, though dissimilar in many points of character, resembled each other in being both honorable, kind-hearted men. On Mr. De Mirecourt's mentioning that he was about to bring his daughter back to the country, his host, with a warmth and earnestness for which the guest was unprepared, insisted that Antoinette's visit should not be shortened in so sudden and unreasonable a manner.

"It must be, my dear D'Aulnay. Your house here is too gay for an inexperienced country-girl, such as she is; and I cannot trust her any longer among the fascinating English gallants whom report says find their way so frequently into Madame's *salons*."

"But surely where I trust my wife, you may safely trust your daughter?"

"Scarcely, André. My fair niece has a store of experience and worldly knowledge which my little girl has not had time yet to acquire."

"Well, even so, you will not refuse to leave her with us a couple of weeks longer?"

Mrs. D'Aulnay here joined her entreaties to those of her husband; and after considerable pressing, Mr. De Mirecourt consented, though with considerable reluctance, that Antoinette should remain another fortnight in town, at the end of which time she was to return without fail to Valmont. The evening passed pleasantly enough to most of the little party; for Mrs. D'Aulnay and the good-natured Louis, whom the hostess had almost tearfully pressed to remain, exerted themselves to amuse the others. Antoinette alone was silent and sad; but the scene of the morning, fortunately, accounted sufficiently for her unusual depression. No allusion to that event was made by any one, except once, when she herself whispered to young Beauchesne: "My dear, kind Louis, how can I ever thank you sufficiently for your generous interference this morning!"

"Aye! Antoinette, you *may* thank me, for the effort cause me a sharp, bitter pang. I am not quite the cold philosophical wooer your father thinks me. But no more of this now: it would only agitate you. Enough to say, that if I cannot be your lover, I will still continue to be your friend."

His companion's beautiful eyes, so dangerously eloquent in their gratitude, drove poor Louis from her side, but only to see him soon return again; and as Mr. De Mirecourt's watchful glance followed their long-whispered conferences together, his smiles became more genial, his laughs more frequent and prolonged. In the course of the evening he consulted his host on the project so dear to his heart, informing him at the same time of Antoinette's opposition to his wishes.

"Well, my opinion," replied Mr. D'Aulnay, as he directed, by a slight movement of his head, his companion's attention to the two young people who were standing at a distant window conversing in a low tone—"my opinion is, that you have only to let them alone, and they will soon be more anxious even than yourself to fulfill your wishes. I know very little of womanly character or peculiarities, but I have read the works of those who have most deeply studied the question, and they all unite in asserting it to be a most difficult thing to force a young girl to love a suitor against her own will. They indeed go farther, and say that to warn her against, or forbid her loving any particular individual, is the most effectual way of ensuring her attaching herself to him."

Mr. De Mirecourt smiled at this doctrine, and thought it might possible be somewhat exaggerated; but still he had sufficient respect for Mr. D'Aulnay's opinions, to accept his counsel of leaving his daughter unmolested for some time to come, on the subject of her marriage, convinced that such would be the most effectual means of bringing it about. He would have felt more anxious respecting the truth of his theory had he chanced to overhear the conversation going on at the distant window, in which Louis, in reply to his companion's whispered avowal that she loved Major Sternfield, resigned then and for ever, all hope of her hand; promising, at the same time, with the innate generosity which formed so striking a feature in his character, to always do whatever he could to aid and befriend her. Mr. De Mirecourt left early the following day, despite the condition of the roads; and Antoinette, anxious to escape from her own harassing thoughts, seated herself at her tapestry-frame, where her white fingers were soon moving with as much rapidity as if no graver care engrossed her mind than the formation of the miniature lilies and roses she was tracing on the canvass. Bending over her frame, her thoughts as busy as her fingers, she heard not the servant's announcement of a visitor, and it was only when enfolded in Sternfield's arms that she was aware of his presence.

Startled, surprised, she abruptly withdrew herself from his close clasp, and then, with crimsoned cheek, she asked, "Why did you do that, Audley?"

"Why did I embrace my bride," he repeated with a forced laugh. "A singular question that, Antoinette!"

"Listen to me," she gently though firmly rejoined, and this time there was no tremor in her voice, no nervousness in her manner. "I again repeat what I have once before told you, that till our marriage shall have been acknowledged in the eyes of the world, I shall be nothing nearer to you than I was as Antoinette De Mirecourt."

"You are unkind, unjust to treat me thus!" he vehemently rejoined.

"Not so, Major Sternfield," exclaimed Mrs. D'Aulnay, advancing towards them. "Antoinette is right; and should I find that till the time she mentions has arrived, you should in any way annoy or grieve her, rest assured that much as I esteem you, much as I have done and would do for you, I should be obliged to deny myself the pleasure of seeing you beneath my roof. Remember, Antoinette is under my protection, and I must shield her from unnecessary annoyance."

"Good heavens!" impetuously interrupted Sternfield, "is it thus you threaten, speak to me about my own wife! It passes human patience! it passes belief! Nay, I must, I *shall* speak," he continued more violently than before, shaking off at the same time the hand which Mrs. D'Aulnay, partly in warning, partly in deprecation, had laid on his shoulder. "Think you that after a clergyman has declared us one—after I have solemnly placed on her finger the wedding-ring that now glitters there, I am not to be allowed to speak to her—to even kiss the hem of her garments without permission?"

Antoinette, terrified by this hot outburst of passion, stood motionless with changing cheek and beating heart, but Mrs. D'Aulnay, wholly undismayed, quietly replied: "Be calm, Major Sternfield, and do not compel me already to regret the share I have had in bringing about your union. Yes, it must be as you say; and till your marriage is openly proclaimed, I will run no risks of having my cousin's spotless name made a bye-word by servants and scandal-mongers through too attentive civilities on your part. Rather than that such a thing should happen, I would close my doors at once upon you."

"By heaven! you will drive me out of my senses!" he fiercely retorted. "I will not, I shall not submit to such intolerable tyranny. Antoinette, were the solemn vows you uttered before God the other evening, a mere farce, an empty mockery?"

"Oh! no, no, Audley," and the soft pleading look, the low earnest tones of the girl somewhat calmed even his fierce wrath. "Surely, I have already given you a great, a mighty proof of my love; but understand, till the conditions mentioned by me and subscribed to by yourself at the time of our marriage shall have been published, I will not look on the latter as completed—as ratified."

"And when is this ratification to take place?" he questioned, though somewhat less violently than before.

"Whenever you wish. Perhaps we had better write a full confession to my father at once," but a slight shudder ran through her frame as she spoke.

"Beware of precipitation!" exclaimed Mrs. D'Aulnay. "After yesterday's terrible scene, reflect carefully before venturing on such a step. He might cast you off—disinherit you at once. Even Major Sternfield, excited as he is at the present moment, will join me in condemning so hasty a proceeding. The way must be prepared first; your father soothed and humored till he is in a mood to receive such a communication more favorably. Am I not right, Audley?" Sternfield, who had no wish that his bride should be portionless, felt the full justice of her remarks, and moodily replied in the affirmative.

"Well, since such is the case, let us all make up our minds to be tolerant with one another. You, Audley, will promise to look on Antoinette merely as your betrothed, till a public repetition of the marriage-service in her own church shall have made her entirely and wholly yours."

Sternfield made ne reply, but walked to a window, near which he stood for some moments in sullen thought. This constant harping on the incompleteness of their marriage made him both anxious and uneasy, and, after serious reflection, he returned to the spot where his pale young bride still stood, and exclaimed: "'Tis a hard and trying ordeal, Antoinette, to which you and Mrs. D'Aulnay wish to subject me; and you would yourselves despise me, if my heart had not at first rebelled against it. If you wish it so, however, I must endeavor to submit. In return, you must both solemnly promise, nay, swear that you will not reveal our secret union, till I shall deem the time advisable."

Mrs. D'Aulnay, giddy and thoughtless, at once rejoined, "Certainly: I see nothing wrong in that. I promise you, Audley, in the most solemn, the most binding manner that it shall be as you say. But excuse me one moment: there is Jeanne at the door, waiting to consult me on some household topic."

"Now, Antoinette, it is your turn," said Major Sternfield, as his hostess left the room. "I consent to waive, for the present, a husband's authority and privileges; to look on you, treat you—hard task!—as a stranger, instead of my own dear wife, as you really are. In return, you will bind yourself never to breathe the secret of this marriage to any one, nor to allow Mrs. D'Aulnay to reveal it, till I give you leave."

"Oh, Audley!" was the imploring rejoinder, "why must we surround ourselves with more secresy—more mystery? Alas! have we not enough already around us?"

"It must be so, dearest, for your sake as well as mine. But this mystery, as you call it, will not last long, for my impatience to openly make you, call you mine, will brook no long delay. Promise, then!"

"I do, most solemnly," she earnestly repeated.

"By this sign, which I know you hold so sacred," he added, raising to her lips a small gold cross which she always wore suspended from her neck.

She kissed it, and repeated again, "I promise," adding afterwards, with a shudder, "My vow is indeed a binding one, that cross was my mother's dying gift."

"And I know you will keep it sacredly; but sit down, Antoinette, darling, and we will talk quietly, kindly together, just as if we were but simple acquaintances; as if our destinies were not united beyond the power of aught on earth to ever part them."

When Mrs. D'Aulnay returned, she was enchanted to find Antoinette quietly seated at her frame, looking like her olden self; whilst Sternfield, on a low ottoman beside her, was reading aloud from some volume of love-verses, such passages as he deemed most suitable to the circumstances. This was something like the realization of her romantic dreams for her young cousin—something like the *piquant*[83] mystery she delighted in; and resting her hand lightly on the young man's rich dark curls, she said with a half sigh, half smile, "What would some wives not give to have their husbands make love to them thus!"

Audley Sternfield glanced towards his young bride, and though the long lashes veiled the downcast eyes, the sweet smile that stole over her lips, the soft crimson that suddenly flooded even her ivory neck, told that she, too, inwardly thought with Mrs. D'Aulnay, it was indeed very pleasant.

[83] French for "stimulating" (the 1864 text had "piquante," i.e., the feminine form of the adjective, which is corrected here).

Chapter XVI.

The stated fortnight, with its hours of pain and pleasure, passed rapidly over; but alas! poor Antoinette found that for her at least pain predominated. Apart from harassing doubts regarding the possibility of her father's proving implacable; apart from the remorse she experienced for the manner in which that kind, good father had been deceived and disobeyed, there was much in her lover's conduct to grieve and wound her. Ever passing from one extreme to another, he was either all tenderness and passion, or else a prey to the most gloomy irritability; and whilst under the influence of the latter mood, he would reproach her with her coldness and cruelty, in terms which made the girl's eyes overflow, and her heart throb with mingled grief and indignation. Her approaching departure for the country was a continual source of recrimination and upbraiding; but despite all his remonstrances, her resolution remained unchanged. She knew, if Major Sternfield did not, that her father was not a man to be trifled with.

The last day of her stay in town had arrived, and Mrs. D'Aulnay had invited a number of guests, intending that Antoinette's closing evening should be as pleasant as possible. All was gaiety and glitter—promising a time of complete enjoyment; but one young heart was destined to learn, during the course of those mirthful hours, a new and keen suffering from which it had as yet been exempt.

Antoinette had of course danced the first dance with her lover, and as they promenaded slowly round the room, he abruptly exclaimed:

"Were you speaking seriously yesterday evening, when you told me that you could not possibly say how long you would remain in Valmont?"

The reply was so low toned that he guessed, rather than heard its purport; and he rejoined irritably: "I tell you that so prolonged, perhaps uncertain an absence is more than I can patiently bear. However possible for you, it would be impossible for me; so I shall soon run over to see you."

"And what would papa say to that?" she questioned, in alarm.

"He would know nothing of it. I could go under a feigned name, and stop at some village-inn near, or at some farmer's house. You would have nothing to do then but to take your walks or drives in the right direction."

"Audley, Audley, I dare not—I cannot do that. The sharp eyes, the busy tongues, of village-gossips would soon make our meetings known, not only to papa, but to all the world."

"So you refuse me even this paltry concession! Beware, Antoinette: you are trying me too far!"

"What can I do?" she urged, turning an appealing, tearful glance upon him.

"What can you do!" he retorted, untouched by that pleading look. "Prove by your actions that you are a woman, not a silly child; prove that you really feel, in some slight degree, the love you so solemnly vowed me a fortnight since. Surely, I do not ask much. Permission to meet, to see you for a short hour; and yet even that you heartlessly refuse me. If you continue thus insensible to pity, to common justice, I shall soon insist on your showing me both."

"These reproaches are intolerable!" gasped his companion, turning deadly pale. "Audley, I will confess all to my father at once, and throw myself on his mercy. Better his open though terrible anger, than this unceasing secret wretchedness."

"No, you will not confess to Mr. De Mirecourt yet. Remember your solemn promise. When the favorable time comes, and not till then, shall I release you from that vow."

"Oh, Major Sternfield, in what a net-work of deceit and mystery you have bound me!" she rejoined with involuntary bitterness.

"Perhaps you are already beginning to weary of your bonds," was the cold reply. "Well, I acknowledge I am a tiresome lover, too devoted, too fond; I must endeavor to amend, however."

Silence followed this remark, and soon after he led her to a seat, leaving her without further comment. In another moment, she saw him by the side of a graceful, dark-eyed brunette, whispering in her ear with the devotion he usually vouchsafed herself. An uneasy feeling smote her, but she resolutely combatted it, and accepted the hand of the first partner who presented himself. The dance over, her gaze involuntarily wandered in the direction of her lover. He stood just where she had last seen him, bending over his beautiful companion, toying with the flower she had given him from her *bouquet*, and adding, by his whispered flatteries, additional brilliancy to the bright flush that glowed on her cheek. Ah, now indeed, a keen, sharp pang shot through Antoinette's heart; but too proud, too maidenly to show it, she went calmly through the penance of another dance with a wearisome partner, who almost bewildered her already aching brain by his overwhelming flood of weak, small talk. It came, however, to an end, and then the slow measured strains of the minuet, so different to the rapid polka, waltz, and galop of our days, struck up, and Sternfield and his companion pressed forward to join it. Still Antoinette bore all bravely. Another partner came up, and, though she declined dancing under a plea of fatigue, he retained his post beside her. Nothing daunted by her discouraging silence, he stood his ground, determined to have her hand for at least once during the evening; and when the music of the contra dance, which succeeded the minuet,[84] commenced playing, she unwillingly stood up with him. By some unpleasant freak of fate, the place that fell to her lot was very near the couch on which Sternfield and his partner were now resting; and during the course of that interminable dance, she had to stand an apparently unconcerned spectator of that mutually engrossed couple, who seemed at the moment so entirely wrapped up in each other. Notwithstanding her close proximity, never once did Sternfield's glance wander towards herself; and as she silently watched them—how could she help it! she ever and anon asked her aching heart, "Is that man really my husband? Must I see all this, bear all this, and not even dare to complain—this too, the last evening that we shall be together for perhaps many weeks! Bring me to the other room, it is too warm here," she abruptly said, when her partner, noticing her excessive pallor, asked her at the close of the dance if she were ill.

With a sentiment of relief, she entered a small sitting-room, specially appropriated to Mrs. D'Aulnay's use, which at the moment chanced to be vacant; and, longing for a moment's solitude to school her looks and voice to the calmness they ought to wear, she eagerly assented to her partner's proposal that he should procure her some refreshment. He was scarcely gone, when the clanking of approaching spurs told that an intruder was at hand. It proved to be Colonel Evelyn, who had accepted (an unusual circumstance for him) Mrs. D'Aulnay's invitation for that evening; and who now, without perceiving Antoinette, threw himself on the sofa with a wearied *ennuyé*

[84] The minuet consists of four straight, ceremonious steps. The contra dance (see note 40) uses livelier music.

look.[85] His glance, however, in carelessly wandering round the room, suddenly fell upon her, when he started up, exclaiming,

"What, you here, Miss De Mirecourt, and all alone?"

"Oh, I have only just entered. Mr. Chandos has gone in quest of coffee and cake."

Colonel Evelyn at once detected that her carelessness of manner was assumed, and, as he looked at her more narrowly, there was something in the pallor of her cheek, the constrained look of her beautiful but unusually pale lips, that brought vividly back to memory the eventful drive they had once taken together, and the feeling akin to interest which she had awoke in his breast at the time. Instead of quietly escaping from the room, as was his wont when by any chance he found himself *tête-à-tête* with a pretty woman, he drew nearer, and, whilst uttering some of the commonplaces of conversation, which he generally avoided, secretly wondered at the shadow which had fallen on that young face, at the involuntary look of pain it wore.

"You have wearied soon of dancing, to-night," he said, after a short pause.

"Yes, I must keep my strength for to-morrow's journey. I will start for Valmont immediately after breakfast."

"Ah, you are leaving us then. What will your friends and admirers do in your absence?"

"Forget me," she apathetically rejoined.

The listener inwardly thought that where she had once inspired love, she was not one to be easily forgotten, but he merely said, "As you will doubtless forget them."

Ah! would she? There was *one* that now she never could, never must forget; and yet how he had grieved, how he had trampled on her feelings, though the course of that painful evening!

[85] "Ennuyé(e)" was borrowed from French as a counterpart of "ennui" in the 1750s and was often understood as a synonym for "bored," though the word is quite versatile in French.

She made no reply to her companion's chance remark; but the tide of vivid crimson that rushed to her cheek, the look of intense mental pain that suddenly contracted her features, told how deeply it had moved her. Interested, touched by the evidence of suffering thus involuntarily betrayed, Colonel Evelyn gently changed the subject; inwardly thinking what a pity it was that a few more months' experience of fashionable life would teach that guileless young nature to dissemble completely the emotions it now so clearly revealed.

Had Antoinette been in her usual state of health and spirits, smiles irradiating her beautiful face, Evelyn would soon, if not almost immediately, have left her side; but he had known deep and bitter anguish himself, and moody, misanthropic as he appeared at times, coldly, impatiently as he turned away from human mirth and friendship, suffering or sorrow always touched his heart.

At this juncture Mr. Chandos returned with a well-loaded salver, and, as he pressed some of its contents upon Antoinette, expressed a hope "that she would soon be able to accompany him to the ball-room."

"If Miss De Mirecourt would rather remain here a little longer to rest herself, I will be happy to wait upon her," exclaimed Colonel Evelyn.

Mr. Chandos engaged for the next dance to a sprightly young lady, who was probably already impatiently awaiting him, mentioned his engagement, and joyfully withdrew. Antoinette, after making a pretence of tasting some fruit, rose with a vague, unhappy feeling that she ought not now to sit thus alone with Colonel Evelyn, or indeed with any other.

"What, anxious to go already, Miss De Mirecourt? Pray take my arm, and we will walk through the rooms till you are sufficiently rested to return to the partners who are probably growing impatient at your absence."

The forced smile with which poor Antoinette endeavored to meet this remark was more painful to see than even her late expression of misery; and Evelyn, remembering her calm, unflinching look in an hour of mortal peril, sorrowfully thought that bravely as she might meet physical danger, she was one apparently whom mental suffering would soon prostrate. Walking slowly through the rooms, he exerted himself in a manner most unusual with him, to interest and amuse her, and he partly succeeded.

Colonel Evelyn possessed a rare and powerful intellect, and, though his conversation was wanting in the graceful strain of compliment, the witty and constantly recurring epigram, which imparted such brilliancy to that of Sternfield, to a refined and cultivated mind, it was infinitely more interesting. Antoinette quietly listened, unconscious that in the short, simple observations she occasionally made, her companion found a freshness, a transparent candor which charmed him far more than the wittiest repartees could have done.

In passing through one of the apartments, dimly lighted by rose-colored lamps, and abounding in niches and angles which seemed to make it a very temple of flirtation, they saw Major Sternfield seated on a *causeuse*[86] beside a pretty, child-like creature of sixteen, whose blushing, embarrassed face, and downcast eyes betrayed she was totally unused to the new strain of adulatory conversation in which he was initiating her.

As they passed on, Evelyn's lips curled, and he abruptly asked,

"Do you admire Major Sternfield?"

"How little he imagines," inwardly thought poor Antoinette, "that Major Sternfield is now the sole arbiter of my destiny—my future life"; but the Colonel, without perceiving her sudden embarrassment, or, careless of

[86] A sofa for two people, a love seat (from a French word meaning either "one who chats" or "a place to chat").

hearing her reply, rapidly went on,—"Of course you do, and so also do three-thirds of the ladies present to-night. He is handsome as an Apollo, dresses, dances, and flirts irreproachably;—surely, that is enough. Still I think I would rather labor under the imputation of being a woman-hater, as you once told me I was regarded, than a woman or rather lady killer. One is not more heartless than the other. But now, I must yield you up, for I see a claimant for your hand approaching, and I will say farewell, for I intend soon leaving this gay scene."

"Good bye! You have been very kind to me to-night," she simply said, tendering her hand.

He clasped it in a friendly pressure, and whispered, "Your last words encourage me to venture on offering you a counsel which otherwise you might have regarded as impertinent; a counsel at least disinterested, for it comes from one who has ceased to seek or care for ladies' smiles and approbation. It is this: Remain in that happy country home, in which you have grown up candid and truthful; remain with the tried, wise friends of your girlhood. You will meet none such in the gay, heartless life on which you have lately entered."

"Too late!" inwardly sighed Antoinette, but she merely replied by a sad slight shake of the head; and Colonel Evelyn turned away, acknowledging to himself that such a thing as truth or worth in woman might still possibly exist.

Antoinette, on her part, accepted without word or comment the partner who had just presented himself, and doubly wearisome did his platitudes appear after the engrossingly interesting conversation of her previous companion. Soon her thoughts wandered back to Audley Sternfield, to his studied, cruel neglect of herself, his open devotion to others; and the olden pained look came back on her face, stronger than ever. At the end of the dance, supper was announced. That over, came a cotillion, some singing; and, finally, when the greater part of the guests were taking leave, Major Sternfield sought her side.

"How have you enjoyed yourself?" he asked; "I left you to do so, untrammelled by my wearisome attentions."

"You have made me very unhappy, to-night," she rejoined, with a quivering lip.

Sternfield read as clearly as Colonel Evelyn had done, the traces of mental anguish on that pale face, and his heart somewhat smote him.

"Forgive me, Antoinette," he tenderly whispered; "but what is the slight annoyance my conduct may have caused you to-night, compared to the suffering your coldness continually inflicts on myself?"

"I act as I do from principle, Audley; but you have grieved, tortured me to-night, either through retaliation, or through an idle wish to see how much you could make me suffer—how much I could bear."

"Not so, my little wife; but I thought the harsh lesson might render you more merciful to me than you have hitherto been. You will not surely now refuse me permission to visit Valmont?"

"Visit Valmont if you will, Audley, but come openly, without disguise; and even at the risk of incurring papa's anger and reproaches, I will receive you with friendly welcome: but to meet you in inns or lonely walks, I will not, I cannot consent."

"So be it. I shall speedily commit myself, according to your wishes, to the mercies of your father's hospitality. Meanwhile, how shall I pass the time of your absence?"

"Oh, you have many resources," she bitterly replied: "witness to-night."

"What, jealous, Antoinette!" and an almost imperceptible smile flitted over his face.

"I do not know that I have felt so; but I know that I have been very wretched during the course of the last few hours; and have asked myself more than once in alarm, can the love you profess for me be really sincere—can it even really exist whilst you treat me thus? Oh, imagine Audley, with what agony—what anguish such a doubt must have filled my heart, now, that we are irrevocably united together!"

"Yes—; fortunate indeed that it is so!" he rejoined, his eyes flashing with a moody triumph.

His companion shuddered. "Fortunate, you should say, Audley, as long as confidence and affection reign between us."

"I make no exception—fortunate in any and every case. Even with distrust, coldness, irritation, clouding our mutual relationship, 'twill always be a welcome thought to know that you are entirely, irrevocably mine!"

The words were merely one of those exaggerations of passion which sound pleasantly enough, in general cases, in the ear of a young bride of a fortnight; but they blanched the cheek of Sternfield's girlish wife, and filled her heart with nameless dread.

"What, am I not right?" he continued, almost fiercely, noticing her sudden pallor.

"For mercy's sake, Audley, do not speak so wildly! God forbid that either distrust or anger should ever arise between us now! I will be true, faithful, and devoted to you,—ah, do you, on your part, be kind and forbearing with me. Sport not with my feelings, as you have so mercilessly done to-night—"

"Even as you are constantly doing with mine," he whispered. "But, here comes our hostess. Pray, dearest, try and look more cheerful; or I shall have to undergo a private court-martial at her hands."

"What are you two conspiring about in this desolate corner?" Mrs. D'Aulnay smilingly asked. "Why, Antoinette, you look wretchedly ill! You will surely be unfit for your journey to-morrow."

"There, Major Sternfield, say good night at once, for I am certain it is you who have worried all Antoinette's roses away with your melancholy fretting and grumbling. Say good night and good-bye!" and she good-naturedly turned from the lovers, still interposing her stately person between them and the half-open door of the adjoining room in which some of the guests still lingered.

"Farewell, my own Antoinette," whispered Sternfield, as he tenderly pressed the young girl to his heart. "Forgive and forget the pain I have so cruelly inflicted on you to-night."

Forgive and forget, aye, the request was easily spoken, but was it as easily granted? Antoinette's sleepless, tear-stained pillow could have answered that.

Chapter XVII.

Another day saw our young heroine installed in her own home, surrounded by her father's affectionate cares, the gentle ministerings of her devoted governess, and the friendly attentions of Louis Beauchesne, who was of course a privileged visitor of the Manor-House. Still, despite the triple wall of affection thus surrounding her—despite her return to the regular hours and calm healthful pursuits of country life, she retained the fragile delicate look she had acquired during the last few weeks of her residence in Montreal. Mr. De Mirecourt felt little anxiety on the subject, persuaded as he was that a fortnight's rest would make her as strong as ever; but Mrs. Gérard was far from being as sanguine, or as easily satisfied.

What pained and alarmed her far more than the pallor of Antoinette's cheek or the slowness of her step, were the frequent fits of melancholy abstraction in which she so often indulged; as well as her indifference, if not aversion to the charitable as well as intellectual pursuits which had formed the chief pleasures of her guileless life before her recent visit to Mrs. D'Aulnay. Gently, patiently, lovingly, as a mother would have done, did she endeavor to win the confidence of her beloved pupil; but the latter shrank with terror from every overture: and Mrs. Gérard, finding the invariable result of any such effort was to drive Antoinette to the seclusion of her room for half the day, abandoned the attempt, contenting herself with daily pouring forth prayer to Heaven in private, for the support and direction of that heavily-burdened young heart, sparing, at the same time, no effort to cheer and distract her sadness.

A source of unceasing regret and annoyance to Mrs. Gérard, was the constant correspondence kept up between her charge and Mrs. D'Aulnay. This annoyance was well-founded; for the reception or writing of a letter generally left the young girl a prey to a fit of absorbing melancholy, or to a severe headache. How much would her anxiety have been increased, had she but known that half of the letters thus received from, or sent under cover to Mrs. D'Aulnay, formed part of a correspondence with Major Sternfield.

A gentle, half-playful request on her part to be permitted to see some of the epistles in question had met with a cold reply from Antoinette, accompanied by an assertion that she had promised Mrs. D'Aulnay to show her letters to no person. Really alarmed, Mrs. Gérard applied to Mr. De Mirecourt; but the latter, grown doubly indulgent towards his daughter since her return, impatiently rejoined that Antoinette must not be worried or vexed about trifles. She was too old to be obliged to submit to inspection a harmless correspondence with her cousin, as if she were still a school-girl.

So had it always been with Mr. De Mirecourt, whenever the governess had appealed to him; and if his child had hitherto proved a gentle and submissive pupil, it was owing entirely to her own natural sweetness of disposition, not to parental constraint. It was well for the young girl's jealously-guarded secret, that her father's time and thoughts at the present period were entirely taken up by other matters, or he could not have failed noticing the great and unaccountable change which had come over her.

We have already remarked that the greater part of the French Canadians, instead of having recourse in their difficulties to judges who understood neither their laws nor their language, were accustomed to refer them to the arbitration of the *curé*,[87] or to that of some leading person in the parish. In Valmont, Mr. De Mirecourt was universally beloved and respected; and he found himself constituted judge and umpire in all the differences which happened to arise amongst his co-parishioners. No appeal was ever sought from his decision, for all felt that he acted with the strictest justice and impartiality.

"A letter for you, little one," he smilingly said, entering one morning the cheerful though old-fashioned sitting-room in which the ladies of the household were passing the hours of the forenoon. "As heavy a despatch as the provincial secretary ever receives."[88]

No answering smile brightened his daughter's face as she took the epistle and slipped it into the folds of her dress, with a slight word of thanks. Mr. De Mirecourt, who had an unusual number of cases *en délibéré* that morning,[89] soon took his departure, and a moment after Antoinette rose also.

"Why not read your letter here, my child?" questioned Mrs. Gérard. "I promise to neither speak to nor look at you during its perusal."

The young girl murmured some apologetic, half-unintelligible reply, and left the room. Ah, those letters of hers were not letters to be read under the eye of any one whose scrutiny she feared. They brought crimson flushes to her cheek, tears to her eyes, too often for that. They

---

[87] The parish priest in a French Roman-Catholic church. Not to be confused with the English term "curate," which usually refers to the assistant of a parish priest.

[88] The provincial secretary was a senior member of the executive council of colonial British North America. He was responsible for communications between the provincial government and the Colonial Office in London and acted as the province's registrar-general, keeping track of civil records of the population as well as all kinds of business licenses and land registration.

[89] In the French judicial system, during a judgment "en délibéré" only judges are meeting to deliberate. Neither party (lawyers included) may attend this procedure.

sent too many shades of pain and pleasure (alas that the pain should have so constantly predominated) flitting over her expressive face to permit her to let any eye study her features whilst she read them.

Alone in her room, she turned the key in the door and opened the envelope which contained, as she had previously divined, two letters, one from Major Sternfield, the other from her cousin. We will give the latter—a pretty accurate illustration of the mind and character of the writer—in full.

"My darling Antoinette, for Heaven's sake, make every effort to obtain your father's permission to return to Montreal immediately! Audley is like a perfect mad-man. He has heard somewhere that young Beauchesne is almost domesticated in your house, paying you all the while the most devoted attention; and he will have it that you are flirting outrageously with Louis, and entirely forgetting himself. He was here last night in a towering passion, and declared that if you remained in Valmont much longer, he would assuredly go there to see you, let the consequences be what they might. I have hitherto, in compliance with your urgent prayers, prevented him doing so; but I fear his patience and my influence have now reached their utmost limits. Who would have thought that such a dear, handsome, fascinating creature could so soon have turned tyrant! And yet there is something in his very violence, arising as it does out of the excess of his love for you, calculated, it seems to me, to render him ten times dearer to the one he has chosen from among all of her sex. How contemptible does the tame, philosophic love of most men appear when placed side by side with his stormy devotion!—Now, with regard to your visit here; how is it to be brought about? I think Mr. D'Aulnay and myself must drop in (of course unexpectedly) this week at the Manor-House; say we find you looking ill, which of course you do, or ought to do, separated from the being nearest and dearest to you in this world; and coax and worry Mr. De Mirecourt into lending you to us for some time. I will represent, that this being the season of Lent, I am doing penance for past gaiety in perfect seclusion—that you will meet no one at our house; and finally, if all else fail, I will invite Louis also. That last stroke of policy will I know decide the matter; for Uncle De Mirecourt will naturally suppose it will farther his own darling project of a union between you both.—But adieu, I hear Sternfield's voice in the hall, so I will not seal my letter yet. Of course, he also has a few lines, or rather a folio to send you. Your devoted, but greatly-worried, Lucille."

The lines alluded to were not calculated to diminish the mental trouble produced by the letter in which they were enclosed. They consisted chiefly of accusations that she had forgotten him, passionate protestations that he could not suffer to be much longer exiled from her presence; and a concluding assurance that he would endeavor to be patient for a few days longer, at the end of which time she must absolutely meet him at Mrs. D'Aulnay's.

Antoinette read and re-read the epistles with quivering lips, and covering her face with her hands, sobbed forth,

"Oh! Audley and Lucille, what misery ye have both brought on me!"

The words, melancholy-strange as they were, coming from the lips of a young bride, married to the husband of her choice, were not, as might have been supposed, the fretful complaining of a moment of trouble or anxiety, but the real outpourings of an overburdened heart. Yes, during the past few weeks, removed entirely from the fascinations of Sternfield's society—separated from Mrs. D'Aulnay's companionship and influence, she has leisure in the solitude of her own heart to look back on and to judge the irrevocable past. What the result of that stern scrutiny was, may be gathered from the exclamation that had just escaped her.

Had Audley Sternfield proved persistently gentle and considerate, there is no doubt that the passing fancy which she had mistaken for love, would ultimately have ripened into deep affection; for Antoinette's nature was loving and gentle, but the system of persecution and intimidation the bridegroom had so soon adopted after their ill-omened marriage, insensibly frightened away the dawning attachment she had felt for him; and with anguished fear for the future, despairing regret for the past, she now acknowledged to her aching heart that she only feared and trembled where she should have loved and confided. A dreary half-hour followed, during which she sat leaning her head on her hand, tearfully watching the bare branches of the trees as they swayed to and fro, or wildly tossed about, sport of the keen February wind; and thinking with a sort of broken-hearted apathy, how improbable it was that she would ever know peace or happiness again.

A slight tap at the door aroused her, and Mrs. Gérard gently asked admittance, mentioning that Mr. De Mirecourt and Louis were in the drawing-room, and had enquired for her.

"Please, go to them, dear Mrs. Gérard! I will be down in a few minutes."

After hurriedly bathing her eyes, and smoothing back her rich hair, yet damp with tears, she sought the drawing-room, tutoring her countenance as she went into a look of repose or indifference. Placing herself under the shade of the heavy crimson curtains, that the glow they cast might help to conceal her pallor (a precaution she had learned from the fair Mrs. D'Aulnay), she contrived to reply with apparent composure to the remarks addressed her. After a time, Mr. De Mirecourt was summoned to his private room by some neighbors who wanted his counsel and arbitration; and Mrs. Gérard, being occupied with some household details, the young people found themselves alone.

"What is the matter, Antoinette?" asked Louis, who had detected her mental trouble, spite of crimson curtains and assumed composure.

"Oh, Louis! I am very miserable—very unhappy!" was the agitated reply.

"I have seen that since the first hour of your return," he gravely rejoined. "You are not the light-hearted and happy being that you were, when you left us. But, dear Antoinette, is there anything I can do for you?"

"Oh, yes," she interrupted, clasping her hands together. "Obtain permission for me to return soon, aye immediately, to Montreal."

"Yes, to the fascinating society of the irresistible Major Sternfield," rejoined her companion with a jealous bitterness he could not at the moment overcome. "Surely, if he grieves over your mutual separation one half as much as you appear to do, your names will deserve to go down to posterity as illustrative of the noble devotion of the lovers of our day."

"Oh! Louis, spare me reproaches and taunts: I am already miserable enough. Help me, if you can; if not, pity me!"

Touched by her gentleness, young Beauchesne impetuously exclaimed, "Nay, Antoinette, 'tis you who must pity me, who must forgive my injustice. Say that you do so, and I will endeavor to prove myself worthy of the trust you have placed on me."

The assurance he asked was speedily accorded, and Antoinette then communicated to him Mrs. D'Aulnay's approaching visit and the object she had in view. Louis, of course, promised at once to do all in his power to further the project; and Mrs. Gérard entering soon after, he engaged her in lively conversation, in order to withdraw her attention from his still agitated companion.

Chapter XVIII.

On a pleasant bright morning, some days after, Mr. and Mrs. D'Aulnay dashed up in their handsome winter equipage to the door, greatly to the delight of Mr. De Mirecourt, who was equally partial to his graceful fashionable niece and her worthy philosophical husband. Antoinette brought her cousin to her own room, to take off her wrappings; and, once there, the latter carefully closed the door, saying: "Now, for home gossip; but, mercy on us! child, how dreadfully ill you look. What have you been doing to yourself? Why, you have not only grown thin, but your eyes and complexion have lost all their brilliancy. This will not do. You should never allow anxiety or grief to go farther than imparting a delicate pallor or pensive look to your features."

"Give me your receipt for thus restraining it within such moderate bounds," questioned Antoinette with a faint smile.

"Why, whenever you find yourself beginning to mope, stop thinking. Take a novel, or get up a flirtation, or overlook your wardrobe. If the latter be in a needy state, the remedy will prove infallible, for the one cause of low spirits will effectually neutralize the other. But, cheer up, darling child! We will obtain uncle's permission; and you will find yourself in Montreal to morrow evening, in my pretty sitting-room, with that dear tyrannical Audley at your feet. Hush, here comes Mrs. Gérard. Not a word about our project till after dinner."

The dinner was excellent, the wines choice, and Mr. De Mirecourt, conscious that everything was as it should be, was in a most propitious mood. Coffee served in the drawing-room, Mrs. D'Aulnay ably opened the campaign by a remark concerning Antoinette's pallor and delicate appearance.

"Yes, she does look ill," replied Mr. De Mirecourt, somewhat shortly, "but we may thank her town visit for that."

"Oh, dear uncle," smilingly rejoined Mrs. D'Aulnay, "she looked far better when she left Montreal than she does now. She is just moping herself to death here, for the matter of that, precisely as I am doing in town since Lent began."

"Very complimentary that, to Mr. D'Aulnay and myself," was the reply.

"But, uncle, you are very often absent, or occupied by important duties in your study, and Mrs. Gérard has her household duties to attend to, so poor Antoinette is frequently left alone."

"Let the little lady read, play, or sew, as she used to do very contentedly before her introduction to fashionable life," replied Mr. De Mirecourt in the same short tone; but the kindly look with which he regarded his daughter, contradicted the apparent abruptness of his words.

"Rather let her return to town with us, dear De Mirecourt," interrupted Mr. D'Aulnay, who had been previously tutored by his fairer half, "and I promise we will send her back after Easter, as merry and healthy as she ever was."

Mr. De Mirecourt laughingly shook his head, and Mrs. Gérard hinted that she did not think Antoinette would wish to leave home so soon again after her previous long absence.

What chance however had Mrs. Gérard of successfully coping with the able allies arrayed against her? Even

Louis, whom she had counted upon as a most efficient aid, incomprehensibly and treacherously went over to the enemy. What his motive in doing so was, she could not divine, unless it were, that, as Mrs. D'Aulnay had extended an invitation to himself, he wished to profit by the opportunity thus afforded him of becoming an inmate under the same roof with Antoinette. It escaped Mrs. Gérard's notice that Beauchesne replied to the invitation in question, in vague general terms, which left him perfectly free to accept or reject it hereafter, as best suited him. Antoinette herself, silent and spiritless, spoke very little, and, in spite of her cousin's warning looks, and significant hints, remained almost passive.

One appealing glance towards her father, accompanied by the simple sentence, "I would like to go," was all the help she gave. Had the young girl carefully studied however the most effectual means of winning her father's consent, she could not have adopted any more successful. The quietness amounting almost to apathy, the look of despondency clouding that girlish face, combined with the remembrance of his own severity in the matter of her marriage with Louis, touched him deeply, and inclined him to accede to her request. Mrs. D'Aulnay's assertion too, that they were living in due penitential retirement, as well as the knowledge that Louis was also invited, and could mount guard, as it were, over his promised bride, decided him.

"Well, child," he kindly said, drawing his daughter towards him, "we must make the sacrifice, I see, so we have only to endeavor to do it cheerfully. What, in tears!" he exclaimed, as Antoinette, overcome by his kindness and by the remembrance of her own ingratitude and treachery towards him, hid her face with a quick gasping sob on his shoulder. "In tears, little one! What does this mean?"

"Do not be so childish, Antoinette!" interrupted Mrs. D'Aulnay, more sharply than the occasion seemed to call for. "How ridiculously nervous you are today?"

"Well, it was yourself, fair niece, who taught her what delicate nerves were and how she might contrive to render herself miserable through them; but enough of this, Antoinette,—run up stairs and commence packing, or the half of the most indispensable things will be forgotten. 'Tis no use, Mrs. Gérard," he good-humoredly continued, as the latter commenced an earnest though respectful protestation against Antoinette's return to town. "'Tis no use. They have been too many for us this time. There, there now. Everything is settled. Give us some music, Lucille, if you can; but I am afraid the harpsichord is out of order. Our little girl has seldom touched it of late."

Shortly after Antoinette had sought her room, in obedience to her father's welcome directions, Mrs. Gérard entered. "I have come to see, dear Antoinette, if you want my assistance," she kindly said.

"Oh! I will not take much time to get everything ready. My wardrobe and drawers are in perfect order, thanks to your careful training, dear friend."

"Ah, my Antoinette," rejoined Mrs. Gérard, with a grieved anxiety of look and voice that she could scarcely disguise, "I fear my instructions on points far more important have been sadly deficient; and yet, God knows, I have ever diligently prayed for grace and enlightenment to accomplish worthily the important task assigned me."

"Dear Mrs. Gérard, why are you so anxious and unhappy?" soothingly rejoined the young girl, as she took the hands of her governess, and gently pressed them within her own. "You have been more like a mother to me than aught else. Ever kind, judicious, prudent"—

"And yet I have failed, signally failed," interrupted the elder lady in the same grieved, dejected tone. Nay, start not thus, Antoinette, but listen, for I am speaking truth. Where is the confidence I should have inspired and that should have brought you to me as to a mother, to relate your griefs, to consult me in your troubles? Alas, you place no more trust in me than if I were an utter stranger! You have cares and anxieties, but you weep over them in silence; you may have plans and projects, but you brood over them in secret. Oh, Antoinette, Antoinette, tell me, have I deserved that you should distrust me thus?"

The warm heart of the young girl, who was really fondly attached to the kind instructress of her youth, was deeply touched by this appeal. Flinging herself with a burst of tears into the arms of the latter, she sobbed forth, "Oh, my kind, dear friend, forgive me! Would that I had accomplished my duty one half as faithfully to you as you have done yours to me. Would that I had never left your side!"

"Then, why leave me again, dear one?" softly whispered Mrs. Gérard, smoothing back the rich hair from the fair young brow, leaning on her breast. "Let Mrs. D'Aulnay return alone to that gay town-life, in whose turmoil you have already lost your smiles and gaiety, your peace of mind."

"That cannot be!" ejaculated Antoinette, starting feverishly up. "Alas, I must go!"

"So be it, then, my child, and may God guide your steps aright. One word, my little Antoinette, one word more from the tried friend who first taught your tongue to lisp the name of our heavenly Father. Why is it that you, who were always so attentive to the duties and observances of our religion, have of late almost abandoned them?"

"Because I am unworthy of seeking their consolations now," was the girl's agitated reply.

"The very reason, my child, that you should the more perseveringly cling to them. Has not our Divine Master Himself told us that he came to seek, not the just, but sinners? But, surely, that term in its severest sense does not apply to my little, quiet Antoinette. Open your heart to me, my darling child; breathe in my ear the secret care that lies so heavily on it, and you will be lighter, happier, after."

Antoinette groaned in spirit. What would she not have given to have been able at that moment to whisper her hidden faults and griefs in the ear of that wise, prudent counsellor, to have shared the burden of that secret which was already beginning to prey upon her young life. But the remembrance of the vow of secrecy which Sternfield had extorted from her, sealed her lips, and, with another tender caress, she whispered, "Have patience with me, yet awhile, oh my kind, enduring friend; and, despite my seemingly ungrateful silence, love and pray for me still!"

"May I come in, Antoinette?" suddenly asked the silvery voice of Madame D'Aulnay; and without waiting for a reply, the new-comer entered.

"What is all this, my poor little cousin?" she questioned, glancing indignantly from Antoinette's flushed tearful face, to Mrs. Gérard. "You have been receiving a lecture, I suppose."

"Hush, Lucille! Do not speak so thoughtlessly," hurriedly interrupted Antoinette. "Are you going now?" she regretfully added as her governess rose.

"Yes, my child; but before I leave, I have one word of warning for you, Mrs. D'Aulnay. At your pressing instances, that innocent, inexperienced child was committed to your special care. To God you will have to answer for the manner in which you have fulfilled your trust. Whatever have been the snares into which her feet have wandered; whatever the errors into which she may yet fall, on your head, you, her guide and monitor, will fall the heaviest part of punishment."

"What a dreadful old creature!" exclaimed Mrs. D'Aulnay, shivering affectedly as the governess left the room. "She reminds one of a Sybil."[90]

"Spare your names and taunts, Lucille?" retorted Antoinette in a pained, indignant tone. "She has been

[90] Sibyls were female oracles or prophetesses in Ancient Greece. In English, the term was also used as a synonym for "hag."

friend, instructress, mothers, to me since infancy, and I would indeed be a shameless ingrate if I ever permitted her name to be slightingly spoken of in my presence, when I could help it."

"Oh, enough, my darling child! 'Tis a mere waste of indignation; for I am ready to speak of her, look on her in future as perfection, if you desire it. But let us not waste our time in quarrelling, when we have something more interesting to talk about. Have we not succeeded charmingly in all our plans? We are to start to-morrow morning early, to profit by the beautiful roads, which a sudden fall of snow may at any moment render heavy. Come, smile now, Antoinette. Look like your olden self, or your father will think of retracting his permission. And now that we have a moment to ourselves, why do you not overwhelm me, you icy-hearted bride, with questions about that dear, delightful, tyrannical husband of yours? Why, you start at the epithet as if it terrified you! You have really grown very nervous."

"Well, what of him?" questioned Antoinette, in a low tone.

"Well, what of him?" rejoined Mrs. D'Aulnay, playfully reiterating her words. "Is it thus an idolized bride of a few weeks should enquire about the handsomest, the most fascinating bridegroom that ever woman was blessed with?"

"I am not quite such an enthusiast as you are, Lucille; besides, you forget I received a letter from him two days ago, which informed me that he was quite well. But since you wish me to question you about him, tell me how he has been spending the time since my departure."

"Well, the truth is," rejoined Mrs. D'Aulnay, coughing, as if to conceal some sudden access of embarrassment, "it would not have done for him to have shut himself up like a hermit. People might have suspected something; so he has acted since just as he was in the habit of always doing."

"As he did the last evening of my stay in town?" rejoined Antoinette, whilst a flush of mingled pain and resentment overspread her features.

"Oh, yes: I know to what you allude. I observed myself his disgraceful flirtation with a couple of the girls present, and I roundly scolded him for it afterwards. Among other things, I told him that you had shown far too much gentleness and patience; and that your proper plan would have been to have flirted outrageously with some partner that suited your taste, thus combining pleasure and revenge. But, my dearest Antoinette, the dark, vindictive look he gave me, in return, almost froze me with terror. 'Listen to me, Mrs. D'Aulnay,' he said; 'as you value the happiness of your cousin, never give her advice to that effect. Should you do so, and she act upon it, the result would make you both rue the day she entered on so mad a career.' 'Why, Major Sternfield, you are a perfect tyrant,' I angrily retorted. 'Blue-beard[91] was not half as bad as you are.' 'Do not talk so childishly, Lucille,' he replied, impertinently calling me by my Christian name. 'I love devotedly, as a man ought, the woman I have chosen for my life's partner; and I could not forgive her trifling with my affections, much less my honor.' Is he not, spite of his faults, an irresistible creature, Antoinette darling?"

Antoinette made no reply, beyond what was conveyed in the faintest possible smile, and in a slight, very slight shake of her head.

"And who do you think was enquiring very particularly, very kindly about you, some short time since? Guess; I will give you twenty chances. What! you will not exercise your ingenuity at all? Well, I will tell you at once. The invincible, invulnerable Colonel Evelyn. What think you he had the coolness to say, one afternoon that he came up to speak

[91] Bluebeard (in French, "Barbe bleue") is a French folktale, best known in the version by Charles Perrault, first published in 1697. Bluebeard is the protagonist, a man who has been married six times and has killed all six of his wives.

to me whilst the carriage was drawn up near the Citadel,[92] to give me a chance of listening to the new band? After enquiring about you, and receiving the information that you were well, and that I expected to have you soon again with me, he launched forth into a diatribe something in the style of the one your governess has just favored me with, saying how inexperienced and guileless you were, and how jealously I should watch over—how prudently I should direct you. I think he must have been listening to some ill-natured remarks about yourself and Sternfield at the mess-table, though what can have given rise to them I cannot imagine. But, mercy on us! Antoinette, how flushed and feverish you are looking! Come, let us leave this packing to your maid, and go down to the drawing-room."

[92] Here, the author inserted the following footnote: "Now Dalhousie Square." The Citadel of Montreal was a small fortress built by the French in 1690 and torn down by the British in 1819 (with Irish immigrant laborers) to allow for the eastward extension of Notre-Dame Street. Part of the area thus freed was named Dalhousie Square in 1823 in honor of Lord Dalhousie, who was Governor General of Canada at the time (see Ferland-Angers).

Chapter XIX.

They found the gentlemen engaged in an animated political discussion, in which the grievances of Canada and the oppressive acts of the new government formed, of course, the chief topics. In deference to Mrs. D'Aulnay, who of late professed the greatest possible dislike to politics, nothing more was said on the subject, and the conversation turned to general topics.

The next morning was mild and pleasant, and the blue sky was beautifully dotted with soft fleecy clouds. In the farm-yards the patient cattle, released from the close confinement of stable and out-house, stood turning their wondering gaze on the white landscape around them, whilst flocks of tiny snow-birds hovered round, or settled down on the leafless branches of the trees. As arranged the day previous, the party started early; and Mrs. D'Aulnay, who was in the highest spirits, enlivened with many a gay remark their long though pleasant winter drive. In due time they arrived at their destination; and most comfortable did the well-furnished rooms, with their bright fires, look. The pleasant odor of an appetizing dinner, so welcome to the hungry travellers, pervaded the house; and the dining-table set for three, with snowy damask, cut crystal, and shining silver, told they were expected.

With that kindly good nature which formed so redeeming a feature in her frivolous character, Mrs. D'Aulnay hurriedly opened one of Antoinette's trunks, and taking from it a handsome, bright-colored dinner-dress, insisted on her wearing it.

"You know Audley will be here this evening, and I want you to appear to advantage," she whispered; "so now, as you have only ten minutes to dress, be expeditious. Mr. D'Aulnay, philosophic and patient on every other point, is the most irascible man in the world if kept waiting any time for his dinner."

Antoinette, ready within the prescribed time, sought the dining-room, where her host, watch in hand, was promenading the room.

"Oh what a treasure of a wife you will make, fair cousin," he smilingly said: "always ready to the moment."

The exhilarating effect of the long drive, with its natural result of an improved appetite, told with good effect on Antoinette's languid frame; and the lively sallies of the fair hostess, who was in one of her happiest moods, imparted to the young girl's spirits a cheerful tone which they had not known for many weeks past. She was freed, too, at least for a time, from the wearing fear, haunting her of late, that her lover would venture on some rash step, such as presenting himself unexpectedly under her father's roof; or, what she dreaded still more, arriving in Valmont under an assumed name, and insisting on, forcing her to grant him an interview.

After a half-hour's pleasant dinner-chat, Mr. D'Aulnay solicited permission to retire to his library, and Mrs. D'Aulnay and her cousin were left alone. The former, who was an ardent admirer of fancy-work in all shapes and varieties, brought out some new designs and patterns to exhibit to her companion. Whilst expatiating on the beauties of a certain vine which she intended reproducing on canvas, a loud summons of the hall-knocker sent the warm blood bounding through Antoinette's veins.

"Yes, that is Major Sternfield. 'Tis his impatient knock; but bless me, child, how rapidly your color is changing! Tell me truly," and she scrutinized the trembling girl more closely, "is it love or fear that moves you thus?"

"A little of both, I suppose," was the reply, uttered with a very poor assumption of gaiety.

His handsome face beaming with smiles, Audley Sternfield entered the room, and, as he gently drew his young wife to his heart, he softly whispered, "Arrived at last, my own darling. How happy—how blessed I am!"

Antoinette, remembering at that moment all the unkind thoughts, the bitter regrets that she had harbored since their last parting, forgot all her grievances, and, woman-like, accused herself of injustice and unkindness. Ah, had Sternfield been always tender to her thus, he might soon have rivetted her affections to himself as irrevocably as he had done her destinies.

The evening passed quickly and pleasantly, and unwillingly Sternfield at length rose to take leave. As he clasped his bride's delicate hand in his, his glance sought her wedding-ring, but it was no longer on the finger on which he had placed it.

"Where is *it*—your ring?" he asked, with a sudden contraction of his brows.

Antoinette raised her other hand, on one of whose fingers the golden circlet glittered, murmuring, "I used to color so deeply and feel so uncomfortable when any one even glanced towards my hand, I thought it more prudent to change it."

"Quite right, dearest; and now for another question equally allowable, and I hope equally easy to answer: Who is this Mr. Louis Beauchesne, with whom report says my little Antoinette has been so busily flirting of late?"

"Oh, poor Louis!" rejoined the girl, with a frankness which effectually disarmed his suspicions, at least for the moment.

"Why do you call him poor Louis?"

"Because I like him," she rejoined, smiling and slightly coloring.

"I hope you never call me poor Sternfield," returned her companion, divining, with a quickness peculiar to him, that Louis had been a suitor, though not a favored one.

"No, no," she gravely whispered; "you are one better calculated to inspire fear than pity."

"And love than either, I trust," was his equally soft-breathed reply.

"A truce to farther whispering, friends," playfully interrupted Mrs. D'Aulnay. "I want your attention for a matter more serious than any of your own private affairs."

"Speak your wish, fair lady. It shall be law for us both," and Sternfield gracefully bowed.

"Well, I wish to organize a sleighing-party to Longue Point or to Lachine. We can count on very little sleighing after a couple of weeks, the season is so far advanced."

"But we promised papa we should be so quiet and retired whilst I remained in town," hesitated Antoinette.

"And so we are, and so we will be, my very prudish little cousin. I do not intend proposing either ball, rout, or *soirée*,[93] but merely a drive, to profit by the present beautiful roads. St. Anthony himself[94] could not have objected to such a thing. Take this pencil and make a memorandum, Major Sternfield, of those I wish you to gather together."

Two or three names were mentioned and jotted down without comment, and then Mrs. D'Aulnay proposed Colonel Evelyn.

"Where is the use of asking him?" objected Sternfield. "He will not come. He did not the last time."

---

[93] Soirée is French for a formal evening party. The rout was more similar to a cocktail party, usually very crowded, in which members of high society came to pay their respects to the lady of the house.

[94] St Anthony the Great, also known as Anthony the Hermit (251-356), was the founder of Christian monasticism and famous, among other things, for the way in which he resisted temptations (a subject often represented in classical art). In 1856-1857, Gustave Flaubert (inspired by a 16th-century painting) published fragments from the second version of his dramatic poem in prose *La Tentation de Saint Antoine* (full version in 1874).

"Never mind that, Mr. Secretary, but attend to your duties," was the peremptory reply. "Invited, Evelyn shall be. He joined us once before."

"Yes, on which memorable occasion he lost the splendid bays he had brought with him from England, a reminiscence scarcely calculated to induce him to favor us with his society a second time. And besides, of what use will he be, now that he has neither horses nor turn-out?"[95]

"Nonsense, Major Sternfield," sharply retorted his hostess. "You know as well as I do that he has lately procured a pair of the most beautiful Canadian thorough-breds in the country. You are either jealous, or anxious to be the only irresistible beau of the party."

"Do you call him irresistible?" sneered Sternfield.

"No, but he is misanthropic—mysterious, which is a great deal better."

The gentleman shrugged his shoulders, and, after two or three minutes' farther discussion of their plans, took leave.

The morning appointed for their expedition dawned clear and bright; and whilst the two ladies were chatting over a somewhat late breakfast, in the pleasant little morning-room, Jeanne entered, and handed a card to her mistress.

"Why, I declare it is Colonel Evelyn!" exclaimed the latter, in tones of profound astonishment. "What on earth can he want so early?"

Antoinette's color slightly deepened, but she offered no solution of the problem.

"What are we to do?" continued Mrs. D'Aulnay. "The drawing-room fires are scarcely lighted yet. We had better have him up here. Yes, Jeanne, show the gentleman up. Do you know we both look charming in these graceful French

[95] "Turnout" is a term used today to refer to the way in which a horse-drawn carriage is equipped, but it also used to refer simply to the carriage itself.

morning-dresses?[96] and then this room, with my birds and flowers, is a perfect *niche* of comfort. Decidedly, 'tis the best place to receive him."

Stately and calm, the visitor entered. Probably aware of Antoinette's arrival, for he expressed no surprise on seeing her, he accosted her with quiet friendliness; and then, after apologizing for his matinal visit, said, with a tranquil smile,

"I wish to know from yourself, Mrs. D'Aulnay, whether your invitation was extended merely to my horses, or did it also include myself?"

"Why, what mean you, Colonel Evelyn?" was the indignant rejoinder. "I told Major Sternfield to ask you on my behalf, as I did not think it necessary to send you a more formal notice of such a very simple affair."

"Well, the invitation, to say the least, was a very equivocal one. I met Major Sternfield in the street yesterday evening; and after felicitating me on the acquisition of my new horses, and asking me if they were well broken in, he told me that Madam D'Aulnay was getting up a driving-party and could not do without them."

"How malicious of Major Sternfield!" ejaculated Mrs. D'Aulnay, with a heightened color. "I need not explain or deny anything, Colonel, for you know well I am incapable of such rudeness."

"I feel assured of that," he gravely rejoined. "The hospitality Mrs. D'Aulnay has so kindly shown to the strangers whom chance has brought to her native land, is alone sufficient refutation. But my chief purpose in coming was to know at what hour you wish my horses and servant (which are always entirely at your disposal) to be here. Major Sternfield, unfortunately, did not wait to inform me on that point."

"I will not accept either, well trained as I know they are, without their master," replied Mrs. D'Aulnay, with a pretty

[96] An elegant gown worn during the day (not in the evening). In the mid-eighteenth century, French fashion had women wear the "robe ronde" ("round dress") as formal day attire.

air of feminine *pique*. "I know you care, in general, but little for woman's society; still I am certain you are too kind to come in person to refuse a lady's invitation, especially when she tells you that doing so will both annoy and mortify her."

Colonel Evelyn looked perplexed. His chief object in calling that morning had really been, as he had said, to place his equipage at Mrs. D'Aulnay's disposal, and to ascertain at what hour he should send it. He may also have had a passing wish, unacknowledged perhaps to himself, to see Antoinette on her arrival; but joining the sleighing-party was a thing he had in no wise contemplated. Still, when the lady urged and pleaded, he at length rejoined:

"Of course, since Mrs. D'Aulnay so kindly insists, I cannot but comply with her wishes; but I much fear that, after the catastrophe which occurred during the last excursion of the sort that I joined, no lady will be found courageous enough to trust herself with me."

"Indeed you are mistaken. Without going farther, here are two ladies willing to share the glories and perils of your turn-out. What say you, Antoinette?"

The girl blushingly shook her head, but Colonel Evelyn, without noticing the slight movement, quickly rejoined:

"Oh! Miss De Mirecourt is a heroine in the true sense of the word; and if such an accident were ever to happen again, I could be almost selfish enough to wish her for my companion. It was her wonderful calmness that saved us both."

"Joined to Colonel Evelyn's own skill and presence of mind," replied Mrs. D'Aulnay with a winning smile. "But what say you, Antoinette," she continued, animated by a sudden desire to punish Sternfield for his late shortcomings,—"what say you to giving the world, and particularly Colonel Evelyn, a proof of your courage by driving out with him to-day?"

"Pray do, Miss De Mirecourt," he kindly, nay persuasively said. "I can safely promise that your nerves and resolution will not be subjected to such a severe trial as they were the last time. It will be a welcome proof that you have forgiven and forgotten the terrors of that dangerous drive."

"Of course, she will, Colonel Evelyn," interrupted Mrs. D'Aulnay. "Consider the matter as finally arranged."

Antoinette, timid and embarrassed, was ashamed to dissent farther; but when the visitor shortly after took leave, she burst forth, "Oh, Lucille, I am afraid Audley will be very angry with our arrangement."

"Just what he deserves, the impertinent creature, for misrepresenting me in such a shameful manner," retorted Mrs. D'Aulnay, on whose cheek a spot of indignant red yet lingered.

"But, Lucille, when he is angry, I feel so much afraid of him," remonstrated poor Antoinette.

"The very reason you must learn to brave him out; but if you should feel at all uncomfortable about it, I will tell him the arrangement was entirely my own—that you had nothing to do with it, which indeed you had not; so no more worrying about such a trifle!"

Chapter XX.

It happened, fortunately for the easy fulfilment of Mrs. D'Aulnay's plans, that Major Sternfield, owing to some unforeseen impediment, was somewhat late, and on dashing up in his fantastic but graceful cutter, he found the members of the party already in their respective places.

"Time is up, Sternfield! What kept you so late today?" exclaimed two or three voices, but the new-comer deigned no reply. When his eye fell on Antoinette, seated beside Colonel Evelyn, an angry flush mounted to his forehead; but, controlling his vexation, he approached Mrs. D'Aulnay, who sat back among her bear-skin robes, with a very provoking smile on her face.

"Am I to thank you for this arrangement?" he asked in a low angry tone. "Is it you who have condemned me to drive alone?"

"No need for that, Major Sternfield. Look at yon unfortunate Captain Assheton, with two ladies, crowded up in that nut-shell of his. Relieve him of one of his fair charges."

"Pshaw!" retorted the gentleman with a look of intense annoyance, "Mrs. D'Aulnay is not like herself today. However, you have punished me; now I shall retaliate, and inflict my ill-tempered companionship on you"; and, suiting the action to the word, he threw the reins of his horse to one of the men in attendance, and sprang into Mrs. D'Aulnay's sleigh.

"You are really becoming insufferably impertinent," she exclaimed, inwardly however, anything but dissatisfied with an arrangement which she had probably contemplated from the first.

A few smiles and satirical glances passed between some members of the party at this by-play; but Sternfield was an idol of the ladies, and do what he would, was generally sure of indulgence. Another five minutes' delay was occasioned by one of the gentlemen leaving his own already sufficiently freighted sleigh and stepping into Sternfield's empty cutter, into which he invited one of the over-crowded fair ones, vainly pointed out to the former's compassionate notice, a few moments previous. All were now ready, and, with jingling bells and nodding tassels, the cavalcade set out.

"Now, Mrs. D'Aulnay," abruptly questioned Sternfield, after a few moments' silence, "answer me frankly. Is this arrangement yours or Antoinette's?"

"Entirely mine."

"And why, may I ask? Why separate me from my wife when I have so much to say to her? when we have so little time to spend together?"

"To punish, Major Sternfield, for delivering so untruthfully and rudely my message to Colonel Evelyn."

"Ah, he has stooped then to explain and complain, our most potent, grave, and reverend Colonel," said Sternfield with a sneer.

"No such thing. It was by mere chance I found out your *supercherie*;[97] but, good heavens! do you want to break our necks that you worry and abuse my beautiful pets thus? Give me the reins at once! 'Tis dangerous to trust you with them whilst you are in such a dreadful temper."

Sternfield sullenly obeyed; and for a long time afterwards, nothing beyond an occasional monosyllable escaped his lips. Not so silent, however, were Colonel Evelyn and his fair companion; and it was well, at least for

[97] French for a deceitful act.

Antoinette, that she was removed from her bridegroom's immediate *surveillance*,[98] or she would assuredly have thoroughly expiated, at a later period, her own and Mrs. D'Aulnay's faults. Their conversation, on setting out, was confined to generalities; but as they entered on the Lachine road, the remembrance of their last eventful drive in that same direction, vividly rose up before the memory of both. A shade of emotion crossed Evelyn's brow, and he involuntarily exclaimed,

"What a narrow escape! Tell me, Miss De Mirecourt, what were your thoughts, that is, if you were capable of analysing them at such a moment, when we were dashing on at such fearful speed to what might have been our ultimate destruction?"

There was a moment's shy pause, for such frank communion with a comparative stranger embarrassed her, but then, half smilingly, half seriously, she rejoined: "I was thinking of death, and endeavoring to prepare myself for it."

"Well thought, well said," was the grave reply. "Though unfortunately I profess religion myself, neither in action nor in word, still, where I meet with it in others, I respect it."

"Are you not a 'true believe,' a Catholic like myself?" she questioned, smilingly though timidly.

"Why, Miss De Mirecourt, you are quite learned on all topics relating to my unworthy self," he rejoined, turning upon her with a suddenness that dyed her face with crimson. "I suppose the same charitable talker who informed you once before that I was a woman-hater, has also told you, that, though little better than an infidel in point of practice, I was born and brought up in the same faith as yourself. Well, I have no right to be angry, for much that

[98] "Surveillance" appears in italics because it was still a new word in English, having been borrowed from French at the turn of the 19th century.

has been told you is unfortunately too true. Do not mistake me, however. Though careless, indeed utterly, completely neglectful of all the precepts and duties of that Church of which I still and always will call myself a member, I have never gone so far in my impiety as to doubt even for a moment the wisdom and mercy, much less the existence, of the Sovereign Being who formed me. No, I am not an atheist, as many have charitably called me," he added with considerable bitterness, "but simply a bad Catholic. You are shocked—startled, Miss De Mirecourt," he said as he noticed Antoinette's color suddenly rise, and a pained expression flit over her face.

Not of his errors thought she then, but of her own. She the religiously-trained, the carefully-instructed girl, who had suffered a few months of fashionable, frivolous life to stifle in her heart all its best and holiest feelings, and to plunge her into a false step whose terrible consequences left nothing open to her save a long vista of future falsehood and misery. Again, Colonel Evelyn repeated his previous question, and his companion startled into reply, involuntarily rejoined:

"Has not our Divine Teacher said, Judge not lest ye be judged!"

Wondering at the gentle aptitude which alike charmed and surprised him in all Antoinette's replies, and won into farther confidence by her evident sympathy, he continued;

"And now, that I have proved to you I am not exactly an infidel or an atheist, may I venture on answering the other accusation laid to my charge, that of being, as you have already told me with an openness I prize in proportion to its rarity among your sex, a woman-hater?" Antoinette smiled, and the bright blush Evelyn almost unconsciously took such pleasure in watching, again rose to her cheek. He mused a moment in silence, and then, turning suddenly towards her, looked full in her face, and said:

"Shall I or shall I not give you a little insight into the story of my life? I cannot clear myself, or excuse my general avoidance and distrust of women, unless I do. Yes, I will tell it, but remember, not to be related again to Mrs. D'Aulnay, or any others of her stamp; a breach of confidence I feel convinced you could never be guilty of. I need no tell you—my misspent life would almost have done so of itself—that I never knew a mother's loving cares or counsels. Left an orphan in earliest childhood, I retain no tenderer recollections of my youth, than those with which college life, an indifferent guardian, and a handsome, haughty elder brother, furnish me. To be brief, I grew up to manhood uncared for, chose the profession of arms,—of course the family estate went to my brother John,—and entered on life with a heart, despite its harsh training, capable of yielding a rich return to whoever should win its love. The time and hour soon came. Chance threw me into contact with a young girl of good family and gentle bringing up. I will not vaunt her beauty, but will only say, that fair as you are, Miss De Mirecourt, she was still far lovelier. I wooed, and was soon accepted, both by herself and family; for though I was not wealthy, I had powerful family influence, which was certain to ensure my rapid advancement in the career I had chosen. The day was appointed, the bridal *trousseau* almost ready, and, having a few days' leisure, I determined on paying a visit to the old family-home to bid it and my brother farewell. He received me kindly enough, though he rallied me most unmercifully about my turning Benedict,[99] as he called it, so soon. Somewhat nettled by his satirical remarks, I drew forth in my boyish vanity, the portrait of my betrothed, which, like all model "true lovers," I wore about me, and triumphantly asked him, was not that face sufficient excuse for early turning Benedict? He looked long, earnestly at it, and at last returned it with the brief remark

[99] A newly married man, so named after a character in Shakespeare's *Much Ado about Nothing*.

that it was indeed a lovely countenance. When I came down the following morning, equipped for my journey, he was standing dressed in the hall, and carelessly informed me that he had business in—but names are unnecessary—in the same quiet country town in which my betrothed dwelt. Delighted at this, I expressed my satisfaction at the prospect of their so soon knowing each other, and of his being able to satisfy himself at the same time how far the reality eclipsed the pictured beauty of my bride-elect. There was nothing in the careless glance, the few indifferent words they interchanged on their mutual introduction, to warn me of coming evil. The time sped on. My brother, in his *nonchalant*, fashionable way, lounged in occasionally into the little drawing-room, but there was no reason to find fault with that: it rather gratified me. One evening he quietly said he wished to make me a suitable brotherly gift, to confer on myself and heirs for evermore the lands of Welden Home, a fine unentailed property[100] belonging to the family estate. My gratitude was of course as boundless as my credulity. I returned to the old house with the papers he placed in my hands, to seek an interview with the family lawyer. He was tedious, minute, detained me longer than I had expected; but what of that? I returned the eve of my appointed bridal day. Of course I went straight to her home. Secret consternation was depicted on the faces of the servants when I asked for her. Then came her mother, grayhaired and respectable; and told me to be patient, to be forgiving, but that my affianced bride was now the wife of John Evelyn, Lord Winterstow. I listened patiently, stupidly almost, so great was my woful surprise and grief, whilst she added that they had been privately married three days previous, and were now on their distant wedding-tour. Then I drew forth the miniature, with the papers which really and virtually conveyed to me the estate with which he

[100] Unentailed means not settled inalienably on a certain person or a certain line of descendants; thus, it could be gifted or sold.

sought to bribe me for my bribe, and cast them into the flames of the grate-fire before me. 'Tell them how I have disposed of both their gifts,' I said; 'tell them——'

"'Oh, do not curse them!' interrupted the pale trembling mother. 'Do not curse my child!' 'No,' I replied, as I turned away, 'I leave them both to the curse of their own remorse.' That very day I exchanged into a regiment ordered for foreign service. Since then I have served in India, Malta, Gibraltar; have sighed out five years of my manhood's prime in a French prison, the hard school in which I learned your language, Miss De Mirecourt, but for twelve long years I have never set foot on my native land."

"And what of them?" asked Antoinette, with a moistened eye and quickened breathing that plainly told how deeply this simple manly recital of a life's sorrow had touched her.

"Aye! what of them?" he rejoined bitterly. "In my early simplicity, I questioned like yourself, what of them, expecting that their perfidy would hourly meet with condign and striking punishment. Well, it has not been so. They are one of the happiest couples in England, with lovely intelligent children around them, she beautiful, admired—he happy, fond; whilst I am a lonely wanderer on the earth, a stray waif, a gloomy misanthrope. Do you wonder now, that I have lost faith in your sex; that I have avoided them almost as carefully as saint or anchorite has ever done?"

Antoinette made no reply, for she feared the tremor in her voice would reveal how deeply she felt, how earnestly she sympathized with the speaker; but the keen reader of face and character at her side, at once interpreted her silence correctly. After a pause he resumed:

"I have been strangely communicative with you, Miss De Mirecourt. What secret spell of yours has broken down so completely the barriers of my usual reserve?"

There was something peculiar in his tones, and Antoinette feared he was already regretting the frankness he had showed her.

Hurriedly he spoke: “I feel deeply grateful for the confidence you have deigned to repose in me, Colonel Evelyn, and it shall always be held sacred.”

“I know that, young girl. Think you if I had supposed for a moment that it could have been otherwise, I should have trusted you. From the first, I saw that you were a being as different to Mrs. D’Aulnay and others of her class, as I am different from that perfumed fop, that heartless Sternfield.”

Antoinette colored deeply; but that changing blush of hers came and went so often, that her companion attached no great importance to the circumstance.

Chapter XXI.

The party were now near the humble village-inn, at which they soon stopped for warmth and refreshments, the greater part of the latter being brought by themselves. Antoinette, somewhat chilled by the long drive, was sitting in a warm corner of the room, near an angle of the huge glowing stove, awaiting the return of Colonel Evelyn, who had gone to procure her a glass of warm wine. Here she was suddenly accosted by Major Sternfield, who stepped up to her, and whispered with that stern frown with which she was, alas! already so familiar:

"Much as you may have enjoyed the previous arrangement, Antoinette, I must insist on altering it. You will drive back with me and no other."

Without waiting for a reply he turned away, and, when Colonel Evelyn returned with the refreshments he had procured, he wondered much at the taciturnity and pre-occupation which had so suddenly taken possession of his young companion. Shortly after, Mrs. D'Aulnay floated gracefully up to them and exclaimed:

"I fear I come to change arrangements agreeable to all parties; but, my dear Antoinette, Major Sternfield tells me that you had promised to drive with him when this excursion was first spoken of. He feels very sore about his disappointment, so I think you had better console his wounded feelings by driving back with him."

Antoinette remembered no such agreement, but she was only too thankful to accept any subterfuge that afforded her an opportunity of deprecating the stern anger of which she stood so much in dread.

"Well, be it so," she quickly rejoined. "I know Colonel Evelyn will as kindly consent to this arrangement as he did to our former one."

"I have no alternative," he said with a somewhat formal smile. "And who is to be my homeward companion; or is it necessary I should have one?"

"Certainly. That young lady (and Mrs. D'Aulnay indicated, by a slight motion of her head, one of the over-crowded damsels on whose behalf she had vainly appealed to Sternfield in the morning) has been thrown again on the world by Major Sternfield's resumption of his sleigh, and she awaits the advent of some generous knight-errant to relieve her."

"I have long since given up knight-errantry," coldly rejoined Evelyn, "but the lady is welcome to a seat in my sleigh."

The latter, though a really very pretty girl, happened to be one of the most affected and insipid of her class; so the feelings of Colonel Evelyn during the return drive may be easily imagined. To her nervous little terrors, her pretty sentimentalisms, he opposed a silent grimness which made the young lady in question inwardly compare him to an ogre. "Faugh!" thought he, as the latter, on their arrival, determined to make an impression on his stony heart, thanked him with a die-away languishing glance from her really splendid, dark eyes, which had only the effect of inexpressibly disgusting him, "who could believe that this creature and that other rare young girl really belong to the same species!"

Poor Antoinette's homeward drive had proved even less pleasant than Colonel Evelyn's. Sternfield was in one of his dark, jealous moods; and he questioned, reproached, and taunted her, with a severity alike unjust and ill-judged. Mrs. D'Aulnay, also out of sorts, invited none of the party in on her arrival, and she and Antoinette entered the house alone.

"What a stupid affair!" she petulantly exclaimed, as she twitched off her rich furs, and threw herself down on a couch in her dressing-room.

"'Tis that ill-tempered Sternfield who spoiled all! I really think if I had not yielded to his wishes, and prevented you returning home with Colonel Evelyn, he would have made some dreadful scene or other, before the whole party. You cannot imagine how he annoyed and worried me. What did he say to you on your homeward *route*? Made love, I suppose?"

"Oh, that is unnecessary *now*," rejoined Antoinette, "it would be an idle waste of time!"

"Do not speak so singularly, Antoinette dear," hastily rejoined Mrs. D'Aulnay. "It alarms, grieves me. But you shiver, child, and how pale you are; I hope you have not taken cold. Lie down on the sofa, and I will send Jeanne to you immediately with a cup of hot coffee."

It was no cold or external physical ailment that blanched Antoinette's cheek, but mental suffering. That drive, both going and coming, had been a strangely eventful one for her. Thet powerful fascination Evelyn had exerted over her, whilst stooping to lay bare his proud heart to her gaze, and which she had earnestly, conscientiously, struggled against, still proved, alas! that she was capable of a far deeper, truer love, than that which she had bestowed on Audley Sternfield. Then the bridegroom himself, whose patient, thoughtful affection should have interposed an invulnerable shield between her inexperienced youth and the strange, dangerous snares that surrounded her peculiar position, yielding, instead, to jealousy, irritation, or any other unworthy feeling that happened at the moment to sway him, gave free vent to it, careless of the anguish he was inflicting on that sensitive young nature, to which the language of reproof was so new; or of the fearful rapidity with which he was weakening his own mental hold upon her.

The bitter hour of complete awakening from the feverish trance of her love-fit for Sternfield had at length arrived; and after a long hour's silent reverie, during which every little event and episode which had marked their acquaintance from its first beginning, down to the painful drive of that day, rose up before her, she suddenly clasped her hands, and murmured with a look of intense anguish, "God help me! I do not love him!"

What a terrible, but alas! what an unavailing confession for a bride to make!

But there were deeper abysses of misery yet remaining, and from which she should have prayed God on bended knee, night and morning, to preserve her. It was that of loving another. Yes, though her affection, or rather predilection, for Audley had vanished like a morning mist, still she owed him entire fidelity and allegiance, and every feeling of her heart belonged, of right, to him. Did any warning voice suggest that she should avoid Colonel Evelyn even as if he were her deadliest enemy—that that proud nature, which had so strangely unbent to her influence, was one, alas, too dangerously attractive, too wondrously fascinating? It must have been so; for suddenly, covering her face with her hands, as if ashamed of the weakness her words implied, she murmured, "I must see Evelyn no more—no more."

Chapter XXII.

A week passed over quietly enough. Sternfield, who had somewhat recovered his good temper, and who had received besides some very severe lectures from Mrs. D'Aulnay, behaved himself better. Colonel Evelyn had sent the ladies some interesting books, but he had not called to see them. One unpleasant, sleety afternoon, however, that they had settled themselves down to their work, certain that no visitors would disturb them, Jeanne brought up his card.

"What is coming over the man?" exclaimed Mrs. D'Aulnay. "He is surely in love with you, Antoinette. Is it not too bad that—" she suddenly stopped and bit her lip, but her cousin's rising color told her that she had easily completed the sentence, with its unexpressed regrets over her union with Sternfield. Alas! did not her own heart, not once, but daily, hourly now, waste itself in similar unavailing regrets.

Colonel Evelyn entered with a friendly kindness of manner, very different to his usual unbending reserve; and as Mrs. D'Aulnay watched the earnest gentle glance he bent on her young cousin, the genial smile with which he listened to her expression of thanks for the books he had sent, she was conscious of a secret wish, that the "irresistible Sternfield," as she had once delighted in calling him, was in the most distant penal settlement of his Sovereign's dominions.[101] With her unfixed principles, her lax ideas of right and wrong, it did not strike Mrs. D'Aulnay that there was any harm in permitting Colonel Evelyn to increase his evident admiration for Antoinette by intercourse with her. On the contrary, to a mind stored, like hers, with novels, love-tales of the most reprehensible folly, there was something inexpressibly touching in this dawning of "*un amour malheureux*."[102]

Fortunately, however, Antoinette's moral perceptions were of a keener character; and as Colonel Evelyn grew more attentive, addressing his conversation more exclusively to herself, her restlessness, and occasionally appealing glances towards her cousin, plainly told the latter that she wished her to come to her aid, by giving a more general tone to the conversation. Madame D'Aulnay, however, doing as she would have wished others to have done by her, and unwilling to stop so charming a little bit of romance in its very beginning, affected to be exceedingly engrossed by her tapestry-frame. Ere long, Jeanne came in with a message from Mr. D'Aulnay, whom his wife at once sought in the library. She shortly re-appeared at the drawing-room door, ready dressed for the street, and informed her astonished auditors that "she was going out with Mr. D'Aulnay for a half-hour, on business," an assertion which was really true. Antoinette's perturbation on this announcement became extreme, and Colonel Evelyn put his own interpretation, a flattering one to himself, truly, on her deepening color and nervous embarrassment. Involuntarily he drew his chair closer to hers, and his voice assumed a lower, kinder tone, which tended in no manner, however, to put his young companion at her ease. They were thus seated together, when, chancing to look up, they perceived Major Sternfield

[101] When Leprohon published her novel, Australia had become a British penal colony. However, in the 1760s (when the novel is set), Britain still transported criminals to the North American colonies.

[102] French for "an unhappy love."

standing in the half-open doorway, steadfastly regarding them. Antoinette gave an irresistible start of terror, which did not escape Evelyn's quick glance; but endeavoring to recover herself, she rose, and, in a somewhat faltering tone, welcomed Sternfield, and asked him to come in.

"No, I fear I might be *de trop*,"[103] he slowly rejoined, in accents of bitter irony. "It would be unpardonable on my part to disturb so engrossing a *tête-à-tête*." Colonel Evelyn's brow grew dark as the speaker's, and he fixed a stern, questioning glance upon him.

"Surely, Colonel Evelyn, you are not going to order me under arrest for my unwitting interruption," queried Sternfield, in the same mocking tones.

The Colonel hastily rose to his feet, but before he could speak, Antoinette gasped forth in tones of passionate entreaty, "Audley, for mercy's sake, hush!"

An actual storm of passion seemed to shake the young man's frame, but he evidently wrestled with himself to repress it. "Antoinette!" he at length said, in a voice hoarse from concentrated anger, "you shall account to me for this"; and then, as if afraid to trust himself longer, he turned abruptly away, and, a moment after, they heard the hall-door heavily clang to. Antoinette, white as death, and trembling in every limb, sank back in her chair, whilst her companion sternly exclaimed, "'Tis he, rather, who shall be called to a strict account."

"Just what I feared," she whispered, growing, if possible, whiter than before. "Oh, Colonel Evelyn, you will both meet in deadly conflict, I, the unhappy, unworthy cause, and one or both may fall."

"There is no fear of that, Miss De Mirecourt, if I choose to let the matter rest. Major Sternfield will scarcely challenge his commanding officer without some more tangible cause of provocation than I have given him."

"Ah, you cannot reassure me! I know that men of your profession generally hold the cruel code that the slightest

[103] French for "unwelcome, not wanted."

insult or offence should be washed out in blood. Oh, Colonel Evelyn," and she clasped his arm with her trembling hands, whilst her soft, speaking eyes sought his in earnest entreaty, "promise me that you will take no farther notice of this unfortunate affair—that you will not seek to exact from Major Sternfield an apology he may refuse to give?"

It was a new sensation to Evelyn to have that gentle, beautiful girl thus clinging to him in prayerful entreaty, and he inwardly rejoiced his heart was not yet so utterly insensible as to be able to resist its influence.

"For whose sake do you thus pray so earnestly," he smilingly questioned, laying his own powerful, sun-browned hand on the little fingers that lay like snow-flakes on his arm. "Is it for mine or Major Sternfield's?"

"For both," she rejoined, hurriedly, confusedly.

"Listen to me, Miss De Mirecourt, I will give the promise you exact of me—bind myself thus hand and foot, if, in return, you will frankly answer me one question, and pardon, at the same time, my indiscretion in asking it?"

"Speak," was the low-toned reply.

"Tell me, then, do you love Audley Sternfield?"

How that question flooded her heart with pain. She was asked did she love *him*, her husband, her future partner through joys and sorrows of earth, and she could not, anxiously as she sought to deceive herself, say "yes."

"Alas! I do not!" she rejoined, with a look and tone of indescribable anguish.

"Another question, Antoinette," whispered her companion, overlooking, in the delight which that earnest denial afforded him, the peculiarity of her manner, "another question," and he bent towards her till his thick brown locks almost mingled with her own shining tresses. "Do you think you could ever learn to love me?"

The tide of vivid burning scarlet that flashed over cheek, neck, and brow, the suddenly averted eyes, as if the girl feared he might read in their depths the secret feelings of her heart, rendered him careless of her startled, impetuous exclamation: "Do not ask me so idle, so wild a question, Colonel Evelyn?"

"Antoinette," he whispered, clasping her suddenly to his breast. "You do love me. It is useless to deny it. Oh to think that such a treasure of happiness is vouchsafed to bless my long-desolate heart, my barren, cheerless life!"

Ah! in that moment she felt that death would have been welcome, aye, pleasant. There was no chance of farther self-deception now. She loved with womanly love, not girlish fancy, the true-hearted man beside her, but she must leave for ever the support of those kindly arms that would have shielded her so carefully from life's trials and cares; she must reject that priceless devotion, and follow out alone her own dreary destiny, linked as it was for ever with that of the dreaded, heartless Sternfield. The regrets that crowded upon her overwhelming in their despairing intensity, and, with a countenance, furrowed at the moment with mental anguish, she slowly raised herself from Evelyn's embrace. "Words cannot thank you," she whispered, "for so great a proof of preference from one like you, to aught so unworthy as myself."

"But, I do not ask thanks, my Antoinette," he interrupted, troubled by her strange demeanor. "One little word of affection would be far more welcome."

"And that word can never be said. The love you deign to ask for, can never be yours."

"This is girlish trifling," he earnestly though gently rejoined. "I know you love me, Antoinette. I have read it unmistakably in your look, manner, and voice."

"So much the worse for us both, then," she solemnly rejoined. "I tell you, Colonel Evelyn, I can never be yours—must never listen to word of love from you again."

Terribly perplexed as well as grieved, he stood in silent trouble, regarding her; then it suddenly flashed upon him, that she might have entered into some thoughtless engagement with Major Sternfield, such as young girls often form as easily as they break, and that she regarded the engagement in question as an insurmountable obstacle to any other union, even though the fancy which first induced her to make it, had completely passed away.

"Sit down, Antoinette," he said. "We will talk quietly over the matter," and gently pressing her into a chair, he took her hand in his. She immediately withdrew it, but remained seated where he had placed her.

"You owe me a fair and patient hearing," he continued, and it will be better for us both that we should understand each other at once. I, who for long years past, aye ever since that first bitter trial of my life which I have already recounted to you, have avoided woman, shunned alike her love or sympathy, have suffered unconsciously to myself your image to creep into my heart and become very dear to me. Had you own sweet guilelessness of character not betrayed that my affection was in some slight degree reciprocated, notwithstanding the disparity of age, and the gloomy unattractiveness of my nature, I would have hidden it deep in my own breast, and none would ever have suspected its existence. Destiny has decreed otherwise; and it rests with you now to decide, whether this new-born love is to prove to me a blessing or a curse; it rests with you to decide whether the remaining half of my life is to prove as desolate as the first has done." She had covered her face with her hands and was sobbing bitterly, but he went on. "Antoinette, you are in the dawning of life, I at its meridian. Oh, you know how cruelly this heart of mine has been tried before—spare it now! Make of it no young girl's toy to be cast aside after it has been won, for some childish trifle, some exaggerated sentiment. Speak to me, tell me that my future life will be gladdened by your love!"

"Would to God that we had never met!" she passionately exclaimed, wringing her hands. "Was it not enough that I was wretched, without bringing misery on others? Oh, Colonel

Evelyn, I could kneel at your feet to crave forgiveness for the pain I have given, may give you, but alas! I must again say I never can be yours."

Keen and terrible was the suffering her words inflicted on her hearer, and he abruptly turned from her to hide the emotion every line of his countenance betrayed, but soon he returned to her side to make a last despairing appeal.

"Antoinette, you are sacrificing us both to some overstrained principle," he vehemently exclaimed. "You are trampling on my heart as well as your own, for some insufficient cause. You shake your head in dissent. Let me know then this obstacle that lies like a gulf between us. Give me the poor satisfaction, one accorded to the greatest criminal, that of knowing why I am condemned?"

"Alas! my lips are sealed by a solemn promise, by an oath, to never reveal it."

"Poor, innocent child! Some one has been practising on your youth and ignorance of life, to wind you into toils which may yet bring misery, if not worse, on your head. Break from them, Antoinette, turn from the false friends who would thus mislead you, and my arms will be your shelter, your home."

"Colonel Evelyn, you will drive me wild," she exclaimed, in a voice sharp with anguish. "Waste not your love or regrets on a wretched, guilty creature like myself."

"Guilty, wretched," he repeated with a violent start, whilst his face flushed. "These are wild words, Antoinette."

"Yes, but they are true ones. False to the holiest principles of my youth, false to ties which even the most hardened respect, what other epithets do I deserve?"

Earnestly, searchingly Evelyn gazed into her face, as if he would have looked into the depths of her soul, and then in an accent of indescribable tenderness, he said, "Poor wayward child, your looks belie your words; but it is time that this painful interview should come to an end. You have no gleam of hope to give me?"

"None, none," she reiterated. "I have only to say that my future lot will be far more miserable and cheerless than your own."

He looked at her a moment in silence, and what volumes of meaning, of emotion, were in that glance! No disappointed suitor's pride, no irritation, lurked there; but oh, such yearning love, such unbounded compassion for that fragile young creature on whom the hoarded affection of the best part of a life time had been lavished. "Antoinette, farewell," he at length said, and his tones trembled despite every effort. "Remember, in you hour of sorrow or trial, that you have a friend whom nothing can alienate."

Her hour of trial! Yes, it had come! Bitter, scathing trial, and he had in great part brought it about—infused into the chalice of her misery a bitterness which almost overtasked her failing strength to bear, and which left its traces so legibly stamped on her brow, that tender compassion for her almost predominated over his own wearing, hopeless disappointment. Silently he withdrew from the room, and she, stunned, almost bewildered, laid down her aching head on the arm of the couch, wishing that she might as easily lay down the burden of life.

Chapter XXIII.

Of the lapse of time she took no note; and when the well-known voice of Sternfield suddenly pronounced her name, she slowly raised her head and looked at him in silence. He drew a chair towards her and sat down, saying, in a low stern tone, "I have come to ask why I found my wife closeted, an hour ago, with Colonel Evelyn?"

The expression of heavy languor shadowing the girl's beautiful face remained unchanged, and in tones, strangely unlike her usual clear, sweet accents, she rejoined, "I was not closeted with Colonel Evelyn. I received him as I would have received any other gentleman in the public drawing-room with open doors."

"Where, pray, was your model *chaperone* meanwhile, the wise and prudent Mrs. D'Aulnay?"

"Gone out with her husband. I am not surely to be rendered responsible for that."

"No. I will only ask to hear the subject of the long conversation you held with this same gentleman visitor."

"That I cannot reveal to you, Audley. The secrets of others are not at my disposal."

"Is this your idea of wifely duty?"

No reply, save a moody silence.

"Answer me," he continued in tones of rising anger. "Is this ring," he caught up the small hand on which it glittered, "and the union of which it is the sacred symbol, a mere mockery?"

In his deep-restrained passion, he pressed, perhaps unconsciously, the small hand he had taken, till a line half livid, half scarlet, formed around the golden circlet.

"Press on," she murmured, giving no token, beyond a bitter smile, of the physical suffering that strong clasp caused her. "Why should not the outward symbol of our ill-starred union torture and crush the body as deeply as its reality does the soul?"

"You are complimentary," he rejoined, loosing his hold of the hand he had clasped, not in love but in anger, and tossing it from him.

"It seems to me that the union whose sorrows you are so eloquent over, does not weigh so heavily on you. It has neither taught you affection or duty to him you call husband, nor has it prevented you listening to the secrets or love-vows of other men."

"But whose is the fault, Audley?" she suddenly retorted with passionate earnestness. "Why have you placed, and why do you keep me in so cruel, so exceptional a position? I tell you I cannot bear this longer. I will acknowledge everything to my father."

"And break your solemn promise, your vow?" he interrupted. "No, Antoinette, you will not, you dare not do it. That promise made upon the cross received from your dying mother, is as binding as our marriage-vow itself."

"But why this continued secrecy and mystery? Oh, Audley, it is bad for us both. Do away with it. Acknowledge me before God and man for your wife, whilst a chance of happiness yet remains to us—whilst our hearts are not yet entirely estranged from each other!"

"Impossible child, utterly impossible."

"And why so?"

"Because," and his handsome lip curved with a movement of mingled sarcasm and irritation—"because I am not rich enough to afford the luxury of a dowerless bride."

"A dowerless bride!" she slowly, wonderingly repeated.

"Yes. Do you not know that if we were so infatuated as to confess our rash act to your father, the consequence would be your immediate disinheritance, and we would have nothing to live on but love, which would prove a most inadequate means of support. You may perhaps say that in three months, in six months, your father's resentment will be just as much to be dreaded as it is now. Perhaps not. Time brings many changes in its course, and before that period, other influences may be brought to bear on his prejudices, which will soften if not remove them. At the worst, Antoinette, you know that at the age of eighteen, nothing can prevent you coming into the enjoyment of your mother's small fortune, according to her dying wishes, which happily for us were legally expressed and recorded. Till then—'tis only a comparatively short time to wait—we may probably be obliged to keep our secret."

There was a long pause. New thoughts and fears were busy at work in Antoinette's aching brain, and for the first time the bitterly humiliating conjecture presented itself, that Sternfield had married her, not from any romantic feeling of attachment, but from cold calculation, from motives of interest.

Still with wonderful calmness she questioned, "Were you as well acquainted with my position when you married me, Audley, as you are now?"

"Of course, you simple child. Do you think that I, with an income which barely suffices to keep me in the necessaries of my rank—my gloves alone cost a dollar per day"—(Major Sternfield forgot to state what his gambling propensities cost)—"would have ventured on marriage, without previously ascertaining whether my wife possessed some golden charms as well as other more irresistible ones?"

"Thank you; I feel grateful for your candor. Now, I need not visit with such severe condemnation, nor expiate with such bitter remorse, my own waning love, my growing indifference, towards yourself."

"Whether your love wanes or grows, Antoinette," he carelessly said, "it does not matter so much, for you can never forget that you are my wife."

"There is no danger that the captive will forget the galling chain he is compelled to wear," was her bitter reply.

"A chain you assumed of your own free will, lady mine; but, a truce to heroics! I have a horror of them in private life. I have only to say before terminating this interview, which I fear we have already prolonger too far for our mutual comfort, that there are some things I will bear with—others I will not. With your indifference, or waning love as you call it, I can put up philosophically enough; but beware of rousing my jealousy by flirting with other men. Farewell. What, you will not let me take a parting kiss! Well, I will be patient: your mood may be more amiable at our next meeting."

Jeanne, who chanced to be in the hall at the moment, and let the gay handsome Major out, saw no tokens of disturbance on his smiling features; but she wondered much when she went up stairs shortly after to Antoinette's room, with a message from Mrs. D'Aulnay, who had just returned, at the ghastly paleness of the young girl's face.

"Tell Mrs. D'Aulnay, Jeanne, that I feel too ill to go down stairs this evening."

"Poor Mademoiselle Antoinette, you do indeed look very bad," said the kind-hearted woman in an anxious tone. "I will bring you up a cup of tea now, and some warn *tisanne* later,[104] which will make you sleep soundly all night."

"I fear that is more than your *tisanne* can accomplish, Jeanne."

"Indeed, Mademoiselle, you are mistaken: it is a most wonderful cure, especially in youth, for, thank God! dear young lady, at your age, you can have no thoughts able to drive sleep from your pillow."

[104] Today spelled "tisane" (French for "herbal tea").

Antoinette shivered as if a cold wind had suddenly struck her, but she forced herself to smile kindly on the woman as she dismissed her.

"My age!" she repeated. "Yes, young in years but old in sorrow," and she pressed her hands tightly on her burning, throbbing brow.

Jeanne soon brought up a daintily-prepared repast, with a message from Mrs. D'Aulnay, excusing herself for a couple of hours, as she was engaged with a friend of Mr. D'Aulnay, who had just arrived from the country.

The time passed heavily on, and Antoinette still sat motionless, her changing cheek alone giving token of the storm of agitated thoughts and feelings that worked within. Who could describe or analyse their intense bitterness? The full complete knowledge of Sternfield's unworthiness, and the certainty which brought so cruel a pang to her woman's heart, that she had been sought and won (her cheek burned as she recalled how lightly and how easily) from a paltry motive of worldly interest. Then came the thought of the deceit she had practised on a kind, indulgent father—of her own sad falling off from truth and goodness. But keener, bitterer pang, perhaps, than all else, was the agonizing remembrance of the priceless treasure she had lost in Colonel Evelyn's love. That brave, true heart, with its wealth of noble, generous affections; that clear, powerful intellect, and honorable nature, which might have belonged to her, and her alone, and which, alas! were for ever beyond her grasp. How contemptible appeared now the girlish feeling of admiration for Major Sternfield's handsome face and fascinating manners, which, combined with the flattered gratification of her own vanity, she had once dignified with the name of love.

It was a fearful consciousness to a wife, to a woman, weak, erring as she was, surrounded by temptation, and with nothing to save her from harm but the dim spark of religious faith that still burned in her breast. She thought of

Mrs. D'Aulnay, the unprincipled, ill-judging friend, whose counsels had ever led her astray; of Sternfield, her husband, who acted as if he wished to drive her to destruction; and then of her own miserable weakness, her luke-warm devotion, her undisciplined heart. From the very depths of her nature suddenly went up in the stillness of her room, an audible cry to Him whose ear is ever open to the accents of humble penitence: "Oh, my God, none but thou can save me!"

On her knees she repeated it, and in broken accents prayed, not in empty form as she had done for so long a time past, but in passionate appeal, that she and Cecil Evelyn might meet no more; that his love for her might pass away; and that God would give her strength and grace to preserve unsullied till death, even by one rebellious thought, the fidelity she had vowed to Audley Sternfield. In the luxury of that moment's free blessed communion with the Heavenly Father, she had, for a time, almost forgotten, she found strength to also ask for a wifely spirit of submission which would enable her to patiently bear all the bitter trials Sternfield's unkindness might yet inflict upon her. She was still engaged in prayer when the door softly opened, and Mrs. D'Aulnay entered.

"How are you, my poor darling? I had hoped you were asleep," she kindly exclaimed, as the girl rose from her knees. "Why are you not in bed?"

"I must take Jeanne's infallible *tisanne* first," was the reply, uttered with a smile that was inexpressibly sad.

Mrs. D'Aulnay, who was really very fond of her young cousin, watched her countenance narrowly a moment, and then whispered, as she threw her arm around her neck, and drew her gently towards her, "Alas! it cannot cure heart-ache. 'Tis that wretch of a Sternfield who renders you so miserable. I am really beginning to hate him. And the thought that you are tied to him for life sets me wild; now especially, that I have a secret conviction that that delightful misanthropic Evelyn loves you."

"Listen to me, Lucille," suddenly exclaimed the young girl, confronting her with a calm dignity, which awed for a moment the frivolous woman before her. "You have led me, by your counsels and solicitations, into a terrible step which will entail on me life-long wretchedness. I say not this to reproach you, for alas! I am far more guilty than yourself; but to tell you that having wrought me such misery, you should stop now and not seek to plunge me still lower into sin and sorrow. Mention Colonel Evelyn's name to me no more; and above all, never tell me, a wife, again, that he, or any other man, loves me. When you speak of Sternfield, too, if you cannot do so in terms of friendship, at least employ those of courtesy, for he is my husband. Oh, Lucille, if you cannot lighten my heavy cross, at least do not seek to make it more galling!"

"Antoinette, you are an angel!" enthusiastically exclaimed Mrs. D'Aulnay, touched by what she chose to regard as the lofty heroism of her companion. For every-day virtues she had no respect whatever,—in fact, as she often said herself, she had scarcely patience with them; but anything out of the ordinary routine of life, heroic or uncommon, filled her with admiration. "Yes, my child, your wishes, sublime in their self-sacrificing heroism, shall be law to me. And after all," she pensively added, "'tis perhaps better that Sternfield should try you as remorselessly as he does. You know a modern French writer has said that in wedded life, next to love, hatred is best; that anything is better than the terribly monotonous, hum-drum indifference with which so many married couples regard each other, and under the influence of which life becomes like a dull, stagnant pool, without wave or breeze ever breaking the surface.[105] Better the wild dash of the tempest, the sweep of the hurricane——"

"What, even though it scatter ruin and desolation around?" interrupted the poor young bride, won into

[105] A similar thought appears in the works of several authors of French classicism. The first to make it public was probably Thomas Corneille (1625-1709).

something like a smile, despite her misery, by this new and extraordinary view of connubial life. "No, no," she added more earnestly. "If I cannot have sunshine, let me at least have peace. I have not courage enough to cope with the storm or the tempest."

"Then, dear Antoinette, forgive my saying that you have not all the necessary qualifications for a genuine heroine. But here comes Jeanne with the *tisanne*, which has led to so singular a dialogue."

Chapter XXIV.

Antoinette found the two following days singularly quiet, after the terrible agitation she had recently undergone. Mr. Cazeau, the gentleman visitor already alluded to, was a quiet amiable man, with that gentle suavity of manner and cheerful, well-bred gaiety which characterized so generally the Canadian gentlemen of the time. He was a sincere patriot, too grieving deeply over his country's dark days, and Antoinette found a salutary distraction to her own sad thoughts in listening to him; the more so that his regrets and reveries were unmixed with the fierce, merciless denunciations of their conquerors, with which her own father ever alluded to their national troubles.

"Well, Miss Antoinette," exclaimed Mr. Cazeau, as the quiet little party separated the third evening of his stay, after a long, pleasant conversation, "when I see Mr. De Mirecourt, which I soon will, I must let him know how much report has misrepresented you, as well as Mrs. D'Aulnay. I was told you were always surrounded by a bevy of red-coats, plunged into the gayest fashionable dissipation, and totally inaccessible to common mortals, like ourselves. Now, I have been three whole days here, and I have seen you both constantly occupied with your needles or books, and asking no other amusement than the talk of a tiresome, old-fashioned man like myself."

"You forget that it is passion-week," interrupted Mr. D'Aulnay, with a very expressive shake of his head; "and these fair ladies, though passably fond of this world, have not given up all hopes of ultimately attaining to a better. Pay us a visit when Lent is over, and then tell me what you think. For my part, I could find it in my heart to wish that it were Lent all the year round. I would willingly endure the fasting and penance for the sake of the peace and quiet."

"Indeed, I do not believe him, Mrs. D'Aulnay," laughed the guest, in answer to a playful, though somewhat earnest protest on the part of his graceful hostess against Mr. D'Aulnay's last words. "I can only speak of what I have seen; and I can honestly tell my old friend that I have been charmed by the quiet domestic life you lead here, and that Miss Antoinette is all that he could wish her, only a trifle too pale."

"Do not say anything about that, dear Mr. Cazeau," pleaded Mrs. D'Aulnay; "for fear Uncle De Mirecourt should recall her to the country, out of anxiety for her health or complexion, a step which would certainly improve neither."

Mr. Cazeau's visit was so far productive of good, that Antoinette received a few days after a very kind letter from her father, saying that as she was leading such a quiet domestic life in town, she might extend her visit two or three weeks longer if she wished. He added, moreover, that he was going to Quebec on business matters, and would probably call himself on his return, to bring her home.

"Do you not find it very singular that Sternfield should be so long without coming to see us?" questioned Mrs. D'Aulnay, one afternoon, of her young cousin. "'Tis more than a week since his last visit; in fact, he has not been here since the day that *héros de roman*,[106] Colonel Evelyn, called."

Antoinette merely sighed, whilst Mrs. D'Aulnay resumed, with a yawn, which for the moment completely disfigured her pretty mouth, "He surely will come to-day. I hope so, for I feel in a most dreary discontented humor, and would like to see him, if only to have a quarrel. Pshaw! I am

[106] French for a gallant, leading man, like the hero of a novel.

tired of this stupid work," and, impatiently throwing down her embroidery, she walked to the window. Her remarks on the passers-by were anything but complimentary to the individuals in question, when suddenly she started, and, with a deepening color, abruptly exclaimed:

"As I live, there is Sternfield driving past with that pretty Eloise Aubertin, with whom he flirted so desperately at my last *soirée*. Is it not infamous?"

Antoinette's only reply was another sigh.

"How can you bear it?" questioned Mrs. D'Aulnay, indignantly. "A week without coming near you, and then to dare drive past our very windows with a young and pretty girl at his side. If you do not punish him well for it, you are utterly destitute of common spirit."

"What am I to do?" dejectedly asked her companion, thus energetically appealed to.

"What are you to do! Why retaliate in kind. Drive, walk out to-morrow, flirt with any handsome agreeable man. That will soon bring this refractory bridegroom of yours to his senses."

"Never, Lucille, never! I have erred and sinned enough. With Heaven's help I shall go no farther."

"Then the next time that he comes to see you, fly at him in a passion. Tell him that he is a tyrant—a heartless wretch."

"Scarcely the way to ensure his speedy returning," was the sad reply.

"Well, if you do not resent it in some manner or other, I frankly tell you that you have neither proper pride nor spirit."

"Lucille, nothing remains for me now but patience and gentleness."

"Antoinette De Mirecourt," exclaimed Mrs. D'Aulnay, with startling abruptness, "you do not love this man. If you did, your very blood would boil in your veins with indignation at his conduct."

There was no answer to this sally, and Mrs. D'Aulnay rapidly went on. "Good Heavens! this state of things is terrible—unnatural. Do you call this a love-match?"

"'Tis a match of your own making," bitterly retorted the poor bride.

"Yes, I acknowledge it," returned Mrs. D'Aulnay, slightly disconcerted by this unsparing home-thrust. "But who could have dreamed things would have turned out as they have done? Who could have dreamed that such a handsome, fascinating, chivalrous man as Audley Sternfield would have turned out such a wretch?"

"I have already told you, Lucille, that I do not wish to hear such epithets applied to him."

"Nonsense!" and Mrs. D'Aulnay tossed her graceful head indignantly: "I will give him his due once, at least, if you oblige me ever after to hold my peace. Husband indeed! He is certainly a singular illustration of the word. I tell you what, my poor little cousin, I see plainly you do not love him; and I do not think he loves you, or he acts as if he did not, which come to the same thing. No alternative remains for you but a divorce."

"A divorce!" re-echoed Antoinette; "since when has our church granted divorces? The most she has ever done is in cases of extreme urgent necessity to give permission to the parties to separate. But if they were living at the opposite ends of the earth, they would still be husband and wife. Ah! the chain I so madly forged for myself, however galling it may prove, I must wear to the end."

"But your case is an extraordinary one, poor child. We might appeal through our Bishop to the Pope."

"Of what use, when he holds not the power? Who or what am I, that I should expect an impossibility? What excuse for me is it that the senseless ill-judged passion which led me to infringe the sacred rules of feminine delicacy, the holy dictates of filial duty, has passed away as quickly as it rose. 'Tis but just that I should expiate my folly."

"But if Sternfield, on his side, wearying of the marriage, as you have done, should seek a divorce, obtain one, and then marry again,—a thing of sufficiently frequent occurrence, and permitted by his faith,—what then?"

"My chains would remain as firmly rivetted as ever, and in the eyes of God I would still be his wife, not only unable to contract any other union, but obliged to be as faithful in thought and deed to him, as if her were the tenderest of husbands."

"Good God! 'tis terrible!" exclaimed Mrs. D'Aulnay with a shudder. "Are you certain, Antoinette, that you are not in error?"

"Alas, I have studied the subject too well to be mistaken."

"But your marriage was secret,—the only witness myself,—no banns published, and you a minor."

"Alas, alas! all that helped to render it sinful, ill-judged, but it did not render it less binding."

"Oh, Antoinette, how little I anticipated so sorrowful a conclusion to a romance that opened so brightly. You are right in the stand you have taken, however, even though it may cause strife and unkindness to arise between you and Audley. A daughter of the De Mirecourts is not to be at the beck of any husband who is afraid or ashamed to publicly acknowledge her."

Chapter XXV.

"There is some one up stairs whom you will be very glad to see, Mademoiselle," exclaimed Jeanne, as Mrs. D'Aulnay and Antoinette entered the house on their return from an afternoon drive. "Mr. De Mirecourt has just arrived."

"Now remember, Antoinette," said Mrs. D'Aulnay in a warning voice, as her companion was hastening up stairs, "you must endeavor to obtain permission to extend your stay in town. Should you return to Valmont with your father, Sternfield will worry us both to death, and end by bringing about some grand *esclandre*[107] in your peaceful village."

Mr. De Mirecourt, who was in excellent spirits, received his daughter most affectionately, and dismissed the question of her delicate looks by a half dry, half-laughing remark that it was fortunate she had her husband Louis ready chosen and secured, otherwise her fading beauty might render it somewhat difficult to procure an eligible one.

Mr. D'Aulnay hastened to divert the conversation from Antoinette's personal appearance, a topic he well knew was disagreeable to her, by exclaiming: "But do tell us, De Mirecourt, how does Quebec look now?"

"How does it look!" exclaimed Mr. De Mirecourt, his expression instantly becoming grave; "just as a city that has been besieged and bombarded twice, might be expected to look—all ruins and ashes. The environs too, in which three sanguinary battles have been fought, the whole district

[107] A scene, a scandal (the French word is a doublet of "scandale").

itself, occupied for two years by contending hosts, all bear melancholy traces of our country's struggles and fall."

"Did you see any of our old friends?" questioned Mr. D'Aulnay.

"No, they all left the city after the capitulation of Montreal, and are now endeavoring, like many others, to occupy their time and repair their ruined fortunes by devoting themselves to their farms and lands. It will take a long time ere Quebec can rise Phoenix-like from her ashes."

"Did you meet any one you knew, going down?"

"No. I had but one fellow-traveller, an Englishman, as I at once detected by his accent, though he addressed the driver in excellent French."

"And what did you talk about, uncle?" questioned Mrs. D'Aulnay, becoming suddenly interested.

"The conversation would have been a very brief one, as far as I was concerned, fair lady, for I have no fancy for intercourse with our new masters, had it not been for an accidental circumstance, or, to be just, an act of courtesy on his part. Shortly after we started, a heavy snow-storm set in, accompanied by a sharp, fitful wind, which, notwithstanding my thick bear-skin coat, and woollen mufflers, so warmly knitted by my little Antoinette, soon searched me through and through. My chattering teeth plainly betrayed this to my companion, who instantly, with a kindness the more remarkable that I had previously repulsed most ungraciously his one attempt at conversation, unfolded the large cloak laid across his knee, (he had another one on him,) and insisted on my wearing it. After this, conversation flowed freely, and I soon found that my fellow-traveller was not only a person of high intellect, but also a just and liberal man, totally free from the prejudices that rule so many of his caste and race. We discussed the present state of the country with an openness certainly indiscreet on my part; but though I sometimes lost my temper, he never lost his, maintaining his point when he differed from me, with a manly courtesy which did him honor. On many subjects he thought with me, and, I could see plainly, had as great a horror of anything like oppression as myself. I had a practical proof of this at an inn where we stopped to change horses and procure refreshments. The man, Thibault, who formerly kept the place in question, embarked for France, last year, with many more illustrious than himself, and his successor is a person of the name of Barnwell,—one of the newly-arrived colonists who have come to lord it over ourselves and fallen fortunes. Just as we were resuming our seats, after partaking of some slight refreshments, our attention was aroused by the voice of our host, raised in loud angry tones. We looked round and saw him forcing back by the bridle of the horse of a poor *habitant*, whom necessity had compelled to stop for some little refreshment at his hospitable establishment. Poor Jean-Baptiste energetically protested, in his own tongue, that he had already paid twice the value of what he had received; whilst his adversary, with oaths and opprobrious epithets, insisted he should hand over the full price he asked, which was most extortionate. Emboldened by the countryman's evident terror, and the tacit encouragement or indifference of the lookers-on, Barnwell tightened his grasp on the bridle of the horse, and commenced at the same time lashing the poor animal about the head in the most merciless manner, threatening to do the same to the owner if he did not at once satisfy his claim. In a second, my fellow-traveller had leaped to the ground, wreathed his powerful hand in mine host's coat collar, and with the whip, he had just snatched from his grasp, administered him two or three sharp cuts. 'Your name!' gasped the fellow; 'your name, till I have you brought up before a magistrate at once!' 'Colonel Evelyn, of His Majesty's —th regiment,' he disdainfully replied, hurling from him the man, now thoroughly cowed and humbled."

"Colonel Evelyn!" breathlessly repeated Mrs. D'Aulnay; "dear uncle, we know him well."

"'Tis to be hoped you do; as you are acquainted with so many objectionable people of his cloth, it would be too bad not to know one who does it so much honor. Upon my word, my little Antoinette, I could have forgiven you if you had succeeded in winning this gallant Englishman's homage."

Poor Antoinette! She had but just received another illustration of the value of the heart which she had indeed won, but which was beyond her reach forever.

"And how did you find the roads?" questioned Mr. D'Aulnay.

"'Tis time for some of you to ask me that. My journey was as severe a one as I have ever yet made, though I have travelled many a mile on snow and ice."

"How is that? Tell us all about it!" exclaimed his listeners.

"Well, as I have just said, shortly after we started, it commenced snowing fast and heavily; and as it had snowed the whole night before, you may safely conclude the roads were anything but light or pleasant. Down it came in myriads of large soft flakes, darkening the air; and whilst my companion and myself were discussing Canada, its misfortunes and destiny, the snow was as effectually changing the appearance of everything as if sorcery had been at work. Fences, low stone walls disappeared entirely, and fruit-trees looked like mere shrubs. Fortunately for us, neither man nor animal was abroad, for no sight could have been more unwelcome just then than that of an approaching sleigh, which, by obliging us to yield half the track, would have probably sent us all floundering down into the depths of untrodden snow on either side of the narrow road. Had we been wise, we would have remained at Thibault's Inn, but I was anxious to press on, and so was my companion: after a minute's halt accordingly we resumed our journey. The cold soon became intensely severe. It ceased snowing, but the brilliant sunshine that had succeeded was perfectly powerless, imparting neither heat nor comfort. The wind used to catch the newly fallen particles of snow, now hard and glittering as diamonds, and whirl them back in our faces, blinding and suffocating us. Meanwhile we advanced at a true funereal pace. Large snow-drifts often lay right across our path, and we had to alight and take turns with the couple of wooden snow-shovels with which our driver's sleigh (probably with a view to such emergencies) was provided."

"And how did Colonel Evelyn act, uncle?"

"Just as a true man and soldier should. He neither grumbled nor wondered, but worked; and when the shovels came into requisition, handled his with as much skill and dexterity as one of your rose-water heroes, fair niece, would twist his ivory-handled cane."

"But, dear papa, you must have suffered dreadfully," exclaimed Antoinette.

"Yes, my little girl, I did. Every fibre and vein in my face ached and smarted, and my respiration became short and actually painful. And the roads—oh, how those poor exhausted horses of ours labored and floundered through the snow-wreaths, now plunging wildly forward, then bringing suddenly up. When we arrived at the little inn at which we were to pass the night, I was utterly, thoroughly done up."

"And your fellow-traveller?" Mrs. D'Aulnay asked.

"All I have to say is, that he has an iron strength of constitution, and, unused as he is to our climate, he seemed to bear its rigor better than even old Dussault, who has driven the stage for so many winters through all sorts of weather. He is most unselfish too, and showed as much wish to assist and relieve me as if I had some lawful claim upon him. But enough of this long story. Neither Colonel Evelyn nor myself will forget our winter journey for a long time to come."

Comments and suppositions followed on this narrative, and at a late hour the party separated for the night, in mutual good humor.

Mr. De Mirecourt, yielding to the united solicitations poured in upon him, consented to remain a few days, instead of starting the following morning with Antoinette, as he had intended. His stay proved very agreeable; and in witnessing the quiet regular lives the ladies of the household led, and partaking of their harmless amusements, he began to think matters must have been greatly misrepresented, and that there could be no great amount of harm in yielding to Mrs. D'Aulnay's petition, and leaving Antoinette with her till the return of spring.

Chapter XXVI.

Lent over, Mrs. D'Aulnay thought it but fair to repay herself for her late seclusion by giving an entertainment to her friends, though boisterous March with its rough winds and melting snows had already set in. The late temporary cessation of gaieties seemed but to add a fresh zest to present enjoyment; and perhaps the only heavy heart in Mrs. D'Aulnay's rooms that night, was that of the once light-hearted, happy Antoinette. Yes, there was one other also, the tone of whose spirits was somewhat in unison with her own; and Colonel Evelyn took himself secretly and severely to task more than once for his folly in thus seeking scenes distasteful to him, for the sake of a chance meeting with Antoinette, who, on her side, endeavored so assiduously to avoid him. There was always, however, a vague hope lurking in his heart that the obstacle which she spoke of as insurmountable, was not in reality so, and that some fortunate chance might yet set all right between them. For the first part of the evening he respected her evident wish to avoid any intercourse with him; but happening to see her seated alone in one of the pauses of the dance, he approached and accosted her on some general topic. Though he strove to interest and amuse, he had the tact to refrain from anything like an approach to subjects of deeper interest. This was fortunate; for Mrs. D'Aulnay, suddenly finding herself at a loss for something to say, called on him, with her usual thoughtlessness, to tell them "what he had just been whispering to Miss De Mirecourt."

"Most willingly. I was repeating the remark made by His Majesty George the Third to Madame De Lery, when she was lately presented with her husband at the English Court."

"Oh, the beautiful Louise De Brouage," replied Mrs. D'Aulnay, with lively interest. "Well, what did the King say? What did he think of her?"

"He must have found her very beautiful, for he at once said with considerable warmth, alluding of course to the recent acquisition of Canada, that 'If all the Canadian ladies resemble her, he had indeed good reason to feel proud of his fair conquest.'"[108]

"The more chance then for the mission of Mr. De Lery and his companions to prove successful," remarked her fair hostess.

"And what is that mission?" questioned one of the company.

"They have been sent to represent our interests, as well as to present the expression of our homage to our new monarch."[109]

"And behold it is His Majesty who pays homage instead, and with reason," exclaimed Sternfield, who had just joined the group.

"Oh, I suppose we shall be surfeited with compliments, now that King George has set the example!" coldly rejoined Mrs. D'Aulnay, as she turned away, for the irresistible Major was in anything but high favor with her just then.

Sternfield, who had heretofore been amusing as well as behaving himself tolerably well, no sooner saw Antoinette

[108] Leprohon inserted a brief footnote here: "Garneau." The story of the meeting between George III and Madame De Léry is indeed taken from Garneau's *Histoire du Canada*.

[109] This idea is also taken from Garneau's history. In reality, Gaspard-Joseph Chaussegros de Léry (1721-1797), who had fought in the Battle of the Plains of Abraham in 1759, had gone to France, where he was unable to find the opportunities he had been hoping for. He went back to Canada via England, where he arranged his return with the help of British authorities.

with Colonel Evelyn than his good humor vanished, and he commenced inwardly taxing his brains for some means of separating them. Being engaged for the next dance he could not ask Antoinette to be his partner, so he had the inexpressible vexation of seeing them conversing together during the long contra-danse which followed. Turning a deaf ear to his pretty companion's hint that she thought promenading infinitely preferable to dancing, he unceremoniously deposited her at the conclusion of the dance, on the first vacant seat, and hastened to Antoinette.

"May I request the honor of your hand, Miss De Mirecourt for the next?" he asked with an elaborate politeness which struck Evelyn as savoring more of mockery than respect.

What a vivid crimson dyed that young face, and what a mingled look of pained embarrassment and anxiety stole over it as she timidly replied that she was engaged. In the trouble of the moment she did not think of mentioning the name of the partner to whom her hand was promised, a very plain unattractive person as it happened; and Sternfield, at once inferring that it was Colonel Evelyn, notwithstanding that the latter rarely, indeed never danced, cast one stern vindictive look upon her, and turned away. His coming however had left its sting; and Evelyn soon saw that his companion's thoughts were now wholly occupied by things foreign to the subject of their conversation, which was the very harmless one of his late journey to Quebec with Mr. De Mirecourt. It was almost a relief when Mrs. D'Aulnay approached them, and, after some jesting remark to Colonel Evelyn, carelessly handed her cousin a small scrap of paper on which were traced a few words in pencil, saying, "A memorandum of yours, Antoinette."

The latter, the worst possible hand in the world at dissembling, took the paper, and hurriedly glanced over it. It was from Sternfield, and ran thus:

"You are trying my patience beyond all bounds! Meet me as soon as possible in the little sitting-room upstairs, for I have that to say to you which must be said without delay. At your peril refuse my request. If you do, you will regret driving a desperate man too far! Your husband,

AUDLEY STERNFIELD."

The tenor of this missive, as well as his recklessness in appending to it the signature he had done, convinced the unfortunate Antoinette that he was in no mood to be trifled with, and with trembling fingers she tore the paper into fragments. Her agitation was so evident that Evelyn could not help speculating on the cause, the more so as he had seen Sternfield give the note in question to Mrs. D'Aulnay to deliver, a mission which she had at first declined, but which his menaces had ultimately forced her into accepting.

"What can be the secret link between that handsome villain and this innocent girl?" he inwardly asked himself again and again. "It certainly is not love, for, apart from her explicit denial of the existence of such a sentiment at least on her side, her countenance expresses anything but that feeling when he draws near her. Well, I will watch, that I may render her service if possible, and protect her from his treacherous arts."

Seeing that his companion now evidently wished to be left to herself, he uttered some indifferent remark, and sauntered to the other end of the room. Another dance was beginning, and Antoinette greatly exasperated the gentleman to whom she was engaged by declaring she felt too much fatigued to join it. Taking advantage of the slight confusion consequent upon the dancers assuming their places, she contrived to steal from the room, as she hoped, unobserved. Up the narrow stair-case she sped, and entered the sitting-room in which Sternfield was already awaiting her, and which, unlike the rest of the house, was but dimly lighted.

"You have condescended to use haste in coming," he sarcastically exclaimed, as he handed her a chair.

"What do you want with me, Audley?" she asked, placing her hand upon her heart to still its rapid beatings.

"Have I not already warned you," he said, his brow growing darker and sterner as he spoke. "Have I not already warned you, that, though I may patiently put up with your coldness, your indifference, aye! if I read at times your feelings aright, your dislike, I will not stand quietly by, and see you, my wedded wife, coquetting and flirting with other men!"

"Ever the same unjust, unfounded accusation. With whom do you say I was flirting now?"

"With that deep, dangerous hypocrite, Colonel Evelyn. Do not attempt to deny it!" he impetuously continued, bringing his hand heavily down on the back of the chair beside him. "I watched you both narrowly. I saw your sweet down-cast looks, your varying color, and his undisguised bold glances of love and admiration. Curse him! Think you I will tamely suffer all this?"

"Why do you accuse and blame me thus?" She strove to look and speak calmly, though her hurried irregular breathing told how deeply she was agitated. "If a gentleman comes up to speak to me, to stand beside my chair, I cannot bid him begone; I must not tell him that I am a wife, and that my thoughts and smiles belong entirely to yourself. I will leave here to-morrow—bury myself in the country, there to remain till you judge fit to come forward and acknowledge yourself my husband. I may perhaps have peace there."

"Yes, flirting with your first love, Mr. Louis Beauchesne," was his moody retort.

Antoinette's small hands were clasped still more tightly over her wildly throbbing heart, as she whispered, "Audley, do you think you can continue to torture me thus, without life or reason yielding in the end?"

"No heroics, please," he coldly rejoined. "I am afraid Mrs. D'Aulnay finds you too apt a pupil in the science which she is so eminently qualified to impart."

The girl, too miserable, too heart-struck to reply to his taunt, covered her face with her hands in silent wretchedness.

"Listen to me, my Antoinette," he said with a rapid change of voice and manner. "You find me thus unkind and stern, because you have shown me on your side so little love or sympathy. Say that you forgive all the past; and let me, as a token of our perfect reconciliation—of my earnest intention to show you more gentleness in the future, press for once a husband's kiss on that proud brow, which has, heretofore, so scornfully refused it. Do not say me nay! I again repeat, 'tis wrong to push a desperate man too far!"

Feeling that she dared not, perhaps ought not to refuse him so trifling a concession, she made no reply, and Sternfield, interpreting her silence in his favor, threw his arm around her, and kissed again and again her brow, her silken shining hair. A sound between a startled exclamation and a half-suppressed groan, suddenly broke the silence; and Antoinette sprang from the treacherous arms that encircled her, in time to behold Colonel Evelyn standing, white as marble, at the door of the apartment. In another moment, he was gone; and as Antoinette's wild reproachful glance fell on her companion, she saw a triumphant sneer replacing already the tenderness his features had discarded as rapidly as they had assumed.

"Methinks the dainty Colonel Evelyn will be effectually cured of his love-fit by this wholesome lesson," he mockingly exclaimed. "You may flirt with him henceforth, Antoinette, as much as you like."

Slowly the girl confronted her tormentor, and in low thrilling notes exclaimed, "You have done your worst, Audley Sternfield. Profaning the sacred name of husband, you have been to me only a cruel, heartless tyrant. Prevented by sordid paltry motives of interest from acknowledging our marriage, you would yet wish to degrade me in my own eyes, in those of others. Now, listen to me. Till the day you shall come forward to claim me as your wife in the eyes of the world, I shall resolutely avoid all intercourse with you, and laugh your threats and prayers to scorn, for despair has made me reckless. I shall return to the country to-morrow; and if you follow me there to persecute me farther, the doors shall be closed upon you."

"Will you ever dare to say you love me after this?" he impetuously questioned.

"Love you!" she repeated with a short sharp laugh of bitterness. "Yes, as the criminal loves the instrument of his punishment, as the convict loves the other wretch to whom he is chained for life."

"Be silent, girl, or I cannot answer for myself," he said in tones hoarse with suppressed passion.

"Pshaw! Major Sternfield," she replied with calm disdain. "'Tis you who are acting now. A half-hour ago that speech would have made me tremble, would have kept me an humble suppliant before you; but I tell you that all sentiments of fear, hope, or any feeling save one, are dead now within my breast."

Sternfield glared fiercely at her. Calm, proud, she stood before him—so lovely in her graceful festal robes, so delicate and feminine in her girlish beauty; but there was an iron firmness of expression stamped upon her brow, which he had never yet seen there, telling of resolutions formed, resolutions to be rigidly kept; and with a wrathful pang he inwardly acknowledged that his own unhallowed violence had lost him, perhaps, for ever, the love of that matchless young creature.

"So be it, Antoinette; you have willed that strife should exist between us; but remember, that through weal or woe, in poverty or in suffering, in sickness or in health, till death doth part us, you are mine and mine alone."

Despite her calmness, her stoicism, she shuddered as the solemn words fell on her ear, but recovering instantly her late forced composure, she rejoined: "Do not fear, I can never forget that; but I will return to the ball-room now to enjoy myself as much as my present frame of mind will permit me."

Those who had chanced to notice the long absence of Antoinette and Sternfield, and saw them at last stealing back, one after another, inwardly judged it was a very decided case of flirtation; nor was there anything in the outward demeanor of either party to indicate the singular interview through which they had just passed. Antoinette was pale and quiet, but that she had often been of late; whilst Sternfield, as was usual with him, hovered about the fairest faces in the room, whispering words which ever won him the reward of smiles and blushes.

Chapter XXVII.

What Antoinette suffered during those tedious lagging hours, no words could express. Obliged to speak, to smile, whilst heart and brain were alike throbbing with agony; obliged above all, to hide her feelings from curious and cavilling eyes, there were times when it seemed to her she must drop the mask at once. To Sternfield, trained in deceit, triumphing in the success of his odious plot to degrade her in the eyes of Colonel Evelyn, a plot conceived and executed in the moment his keen eye had detected the latter approaching up the corridor, no great effort of self-command was necessary. Determined to pique and punish his refractory bride, he devoted himself with such assiduity to the young lady who had, on a previous occasion, shared his sleigh, that Mrs. D'Aulnay's indignation was excited to the highest pitch. Glancing around in search of Antoinette, she beheld her seated near a small table pretending to examine some engravings upon it. Resolved to punish Sternfield in kind, she beckoned Colonel Evelyn to her, and handing him a roll of paper, exclaimed,

"Pray go and show these new plates to Miss De Mirecourt, and examine them at the same time yourself. You will tell me afterwards what you think of them."

Evelyn looked for a moment as if he would have declined the commission; but meeting Mrs. D'Aulnay's dawning look of amazement, he took the engravings, and crossed the room to Antoinette's side. Abruptly, coldly, he said:

"Rather than excite Mrs. D'Aulnay's questions or suspicions, I have brought you these pictures as she instructed me to do."

"Oh, Colonel Evelyn, what must you think of me?" faltered the unhappy Antoinette.

"I will tell you," he rejoined in tones of suppressed bitterness. "My first love taught me to hate your sex; you, my second love, have taught me to despise them. She, though false to myself, was true at least to the one who had supplanted me; you, a few weeks ago, called on Heaven to witness you had no love for Audley Sternfield, and yet I saw you lie passive in his arms an hour ago, whilst he pressed his kisses on your lips and brow."

"Spare me! be merciful!" she implored with white and quivering lips.

"No, Antoinette De Mirecourt, for you have not spared me. Sternfield or his like might pardon you, for their love is as easily recalled as it is given, but I cannot. You have done me a woful wrong, young girl! destroyed the dawning confidence in human truth and goodness, beginning to spring up in my seared heart; dried up the springs of human sympathy there, and doomed back to hardened misanthropy the gloomy remainder of my barren life."

"Oh, forgive me, Colonel Evelyn!" and the speaker felt at the moment that she would willingly have laid down her life, if she could have saved him thereby one solitary suffering, one single pang.

Pitilessly he went on, "As much deeper in proportion as is my love compared to that of most other men, so is my resentment against her who has mocked that love to scorn. Oh what a wealth of affection have I not lavished on a worthless idol!"

"I have sinned," she rejoined in a low solemn tone, "and my sin has found me out; but, Colonel Evelyn, guilty in the sense you suppose me to be, I am not. Ten years would I willingly give of the life that spreads out such a dreary blank before me, to have my innocence made clear to you; but if in this life that may not be, there is another and a better world where it shall yet be made plain to you."

Evelyn gazed a moment on those clear truthful eyes, that fair youthful brow, and then hastily averting his gaze, exclaimed,

"Girl, ask of Heaven to withdraw from you that fatal gift of seeming innocence and candor, or you will win others to their destruction as you have won me to mine."

"And you will not spare me one kind or forgiving word?" she asked, clasping her hands together, reckless in the despair of the moment, who witnessed her agitation, or what construction might be put upon it."

"No. You have ruined, robbed me, and I cannot forgive you. If I were on my death-bed, on the point of appearing before my Maker, my answer would still be the same. I have loved you too well to show you mercy, but, hush!" he rapidly added, interposing his tall form between her and the other occupants of the room. "Your agitation may be noticed, misunderstood. Heavens! Miss De Mirecourt, what a finished, faultless actress you are. One would think now that my approbation or censure was a matter of life and death to you. I would believe it myself, only that I witnessed so memorable a scene in the sitting-room a short time ago. Oh, only for that terrible, damning proof of your worthlessness, nothing could ever have opened my eyes to it. Farewell now, and let us both mutually hope our paths in life may never cross each other again. You will hear that Cecil Evelyn is a greater misanthrope than ever, that he is more selfish and gloomily inaccessible to every social, kindly feeling; but knowing who has helped to make him so, you at least will hold your peace."

He bowed, turned away, and a few moments after left the house.

Sick at heart, Antoinette sat where he had left her, wondering if human breast had ever known such misery as her own; when Sternfield, who had been dancing and flirting in an adjoining room, came up to her. Narrowly he scanned her face, and then said,

"You look ill and sad, Antoinette."

"You cannot expect me to look well or gay."

"Perhaps you are angry with me for having flirted so much with that bright-eyed little Eloise?"

"I never noticed it," was the weary reply.

Sternfield bit his lip! This utter indifference was neither what he had sought or wished for, and he angrily rejoined:

"Doubtless more powerful interests and anxieties engrossed you."

"Ah, I have nothing left to hope or fear now."

"Are you really serious in your intention of returning to the country immediately, or was it merely an idle threat?"

"I go to-morrow."

"Shall I bid you farewell then to-night, or call again for a parting word in the morning?"

"As you wish. I think it would be better to say the parting word to-night."

"You are a loving bride, Antoinette."

"I am what you have made me," was the calm, passionless response.

"Then, since you wish it, Good-night," he abruptly, angrily rejoined. "I will not obtrude my unwelcome presence on you again."

He left her; and Antoinette, feeling she had suffered and feigned enough for one evening, quietly passed from the apartment.

How cheerful, how pleasant her own little room looked, with the bright fire, the wax-lights, the soft easy-chair drawn up into her favorite corner, but how heavy was the young heart of her who entered it! Closing the door, she threw herself into the fauteuil, hoping that tears might come to her relief; but that great solace was denied her, and she sat there in dry, tearless misery, recalling every trifling detail, every painful circumstance that could possibly add to the burden of her sorrow. Another hour passed, the last of the guests had taken their departure, and Mrs. D'Aulnay, as was her wont, stepped in to bid her cousin good-night. The latter looked strangely ill, but then she was very calm and quiet, so Mrs. D'Aulnay felt but little alarm.

"Are you sitting up, my dear?" she asked. "You should have gone to bed immediately."

"I wished first to tell you, Lucille, that I must return to Valmont to-morrow."

"Return to-morrow, and why? Have you had letters from home?"

"None; but I have decided on returning."

"This is incomprehensible, child! What cause, what reason have you?"

"I am heart-sick, weary, Lucille, and I must have rest, utter repose."

"You are ill, dear child. Aye, I feared so. You have looked wretched for some time past, and two or three remarked it to-night. Ah, I fear my poor cousin, you are very unhappy. And she anxiously scanned the pain-worn young face before her.

"Yes, I am indeed very miserable."

"And I need not ask the cause. I suppose 'tis in great part that miserable Sternfield?"

"I will tell you in a simple sentence. You were present when those solemn words were pronounced: 'Those whom God has joined, let no man put asunder.' Do you understand, cousin Lucille! The woful past is unchangeable, irrevocable!"

"Alas, do you really regret it so much, then? I suppose you must hate me at the same time; though, indeed, I did all for the best."

"Ah, no, I neither hate nor upbraid you; but it was an unfortunate hour for me when I entered beneath your pleasant, friendly roof."

"Tell me, what has Audley been saying or doing to bring you to such a hopeless state of mind?"

"'Twould be useless and painful for me to give any farther details than those with which you are already acquainted, but I have been sorely tried."

"Oh, as to that, dear child, so are all wives. There is André, who will sometimes get into a passion for the merest trifle, perhaps, a tardy dinner, at other times, say in his quiet way, the most sarcastic, cutting things you can imagine."

Antoinette smiled—a very bitter, strange smile—as she replied, "If Audley Sternfield never gave me greater cause of sorrow than Mr. D'Aulnay has given yourself, I would not grieve so deeply that our union is irrevocable."

"But to return to your lately formed determination, what will you gain, my poor darling, by returning to the monotony of your country life sooner than you can help? Here, at least, you have some distractions, some amusements."

"Do you include under that title the persecutions Sternfield daily inflicts upon me?"

"But he will persecute you in Valmont as well as here. You remember when you were there before?"

"Yes, but I have grown more callous than I was then, more reckless of consequences, and for his own sake he will not try me too much."

"Of course, dear, if you are decided on leaving, there is no more to be said on that point; but do you not think it would be better to brave your father's anger, violent as it may be at first, and acknowledge at once your marriage?'

"That would not suit Major Sternfield," rejoined Antoinette, with a sharp, forced laugh, that made Mrs. D'Aulnay start. "He told me he could not afford the luxury of a dowerless bride, having previously bound me by a solemn promise not to reveal my marriage till he allowed me, which will probably be on my eighteenth birthday, when I shall enter on the possession of my poor mother's fortune."

"He calculates closely as well as cleverly," was Mrs. D'Aulnay's sarcastic comment; "but, tell me, my poor heart-broken little cousin, would you like me to reveal all to your father, instead of waiting the pleasure of this tardy bridegroom? I care nothing for the promise he fraudulently extracted from myself."

"Oh, no," and Antoinette shuddered. "I begin to look forward to the period when he will claim me, with sickening terror. Let me enjoy my poor father's love, my own personal liberty, as long as he will allow me!"

"Oh, Antoinette, forgive me!" exclaimed Mrs. D'Aulnay, throwing her arms round her cousin, and bursting into a passionate flood of tears. "How greatly my unfortunate counsels have helped to bring utter misery on your bright young life. What would I not give to undo the mischief I have wrought! Handsome, fascinating demon, how I hate him!"

"Enough, dear Lucille. I am very weary—very ill. Leave me to rest."

With countless tearful protestations and caresses, Mrs. D'Aulnay parted from her, leaving her, not to repose, but to a night of sleepless wretchedness. The following day, notwithstanding her feelings of severe bodily illness, she persisted in her intention of leaving for the country. In passing before the parish church, not the massive, stately edifice which now bears the title, but an old-fashioned, though solid stone structure, situated almost in the centre of the French square, or Place D'Armes, she directed the driver to stop, and alighted for a moment.[110] On leaving,

---

[110] This is the footnote inserted here by Leprohon: "The church in question, which succeeded to the first simple wooden structure in which our early forefathers united in common worship, was built in 1672, and as we have already said, occupied a portion of the French square, standing awkwardly across the middle of Notre Dame street, which it divided into two nearly equal portions, requiring travellers to pass half round the church to proceed from one part of the street to another. The burying-ground was attached to the building, and occupied the space where the present parish church stands, as well as other parts of the Place D'Armes." One of Montreal's most famous landmarks, The Notre-Dame Basilica, in Place D'Armes, was built between 1824 and 1830, when the Notre-Dame Church, built between 1672 and 1682, was demolished. The Notre-Dame Church was located a little north of the present basilica.

shortly after, the sacred edifice, strengthened and consoled by a few minutes' closer communion with her Creator, she stood, leaning against the railings, gazing at the thickly strewn graves around her; and despite the cheerless aspect of the cemetery, covered, in some parts, by winter's icy mantle, presenting, in others, the muddy, sodden appearance with which the melting of the snow usually heralds Spring's approach, a wish, nay, rather a prayer, as earnest as heart ever framed, rose up from the depths of her soul, that death's dreamless sleep might be vouchsafed her before the arrival of the dreaded epoch when Sternfield should claim her as his wife.

In turning away, her eyes fell on the tall form of Colonel Evelyn approaching; but he passed her with a cold, though respectful salutation. A little later, she encountered a small party of the gay triflers she had often met in Mrs. D'Aulnay's drawing-rooms, and hats were touched, and bows made, with genuine respect, for Antoinette had ever been a general favorite. After she had passed, however, they wonderingly commented on her altered looks, and gravely marvelled if Canadian beauty was always as evanescent as hers had been.

Chapter XXVIII.

In the joy following Antoinette's arrival in Valmont, no one thought of wondering and questioning about her abrupt, unexpected return, and it was with something like a feeling akin to pleasure that she found herself in the calm atmosphere of her home.

Mrs. Gérard saw that her charge had returned to her, heart and world-weary; but she made no direct effort to obtain her confidence, contenting herself with surrounding the young girl with the tenderest marks of affection, which the latter, so far from shunning or avoiding, as she had done during her previous sojourn at home, now seemed to crave, to almost cling to. Passively she yielded to Mrs. Gérard's arrangements for the ordering of their time, and read, walked, studied, just as her kind friend wished. No more hours of lonely reverie now—no more long afternoons devoted to unknown correspondents. Letters she still received from town, but they were neither as frequent nor as heavy as formerly, nor did their reception bring in their train the swollen eyes and oppressive headaches which they had once done. There were times when the worthy governess became almost terrified by this passive submission, this apathetic obedience: it looked so like a species of despair. This thought struck her one evening with overwhelming force as she and Antoinette were seated near the open window, watching the dying glories of the setting sun, and listening to the liquid notes of that sweetest of all our forest songsters, the Canadian nightingale, or song-sparrow.

"Mrs. Gérard, mamma must have died very young?" was the girl's sudden but softly spoken question.

"Yes, my child. She married at eighteen and died on her twentieth birth-day, leaving you an infant of a year old."

"She died of decline, did she not?"

"I believe so," rejoined the governess, very unwillingly, for she did not like the turn the conversation was taking.

"Twenty," softly repeated Antoinette to herself. "Too long, too long! Oh, Mrs. Gérard, pray that I may never live till my eighteenth birth-day!"

Mrs. Gérard started, and looked earnestly, sorrowfully into her young pupil's face, but she tranquilly said, "That were asking perhaps too soon, my darling, for your heavenly crown. God may will that you should bear your earthly cross, whatever it may be, much longer than that."

"But mine is so heavy!" sighed the girl, more to herself than to her companion.

"He who sent it will give you grace and strength to bear it."

"Aye but He did not send it!" she rejoined, with a sudden irresistible burst of emotion. "It was I in my own blind folly that sought it out, that took it up."

"Bear it nevertheless, my child, with Christian courage, and exceeding great shall be the reward. Ah, my Antoinette! I seek not to penetrate your secrets, they shall be to me sacred; but all I ask is, that you should place your trust in no earthly arm or shield, but in God alone."

"You speak of secrets: young as I am, I have a heavy one, one which bears me almost to the earth by its merciless weight; and yet I was mad, rash enough to give my solemn promise on this doubly sacred symbol," and she touched the small gold cross she wore, "that I should never reveal it till permitted. Otherwise, my patient, unwearied friend, I should have confided all to you ere this."

"Thanks, thanks, dear child. How grateful I am to know that your silence has arisen from necessity, and not from any want of trust or confidence. Far from me any attempt to induce you to break your word thus solemnly given, but forgive me if I tell you to beware of the person who asked that promise. However dear they may have rendered themselves to you, however full of good or noble qualities, beware of them, for it was not for your sake but for their own it was exacted."

Some evenings after this conversation, Antoinette, unusually dull and preoccupied, sought the sitting-room where she and Mrs. Gérard usually sat together, but the latter was not there. On asking for her she learned that her governess was suffering from severe headache, and had gone to her room to lie down. Antoinette immediately proceeded thither; but seeing that the invalid required perfect rest and repose, she soon bade her good-night and returned to the sitting-room. It looked somewhat lonely; but the moonlight was streaming in, in floods of liquid silver, chequering the floor and furniture in lines of strange fantastic beauty.

"Do you want lights, Miss?" asked a servant, entering to close the windows and draw the curtains.

"No: I will sit in the moonlight for awhile. Does François expect Mr. De Mirecourt home to-night?"

"He is not sure, Miss. The roads are somewhat rough since the last rain, and 'tis fully a thirty miles journey."

The girl retired, and Antoinette sat down near the open casement, the fragrant breath of verbenas and mignionette[111] stealing up to where she sat, and adding yet another charm to the tranquil beauty of the still summer night. Soon her thoughts took the saddened character they ever assumed when she was alone; and painful recollections of Colonel Evelyn, Mrs. D'Aulnay, and bitterest of all, the worldly, heartless Audley Sternfield, rose upon her memory.

[111] *Reseda,* also known as "mignonette" (but Leprohon's is a common misspelling). The common mignonette, cultivated for its perfume, is called *reseda odorata.*

Suddenly her pulses gave a bound of terror, for surely she had just heard her own name softly pronounced in the well-known tones of Audley himself.

"It must be fancy," she thought, endeavoring to reassure herself, for she was trembling with agitation. "Perhaps the sighing of the night-wind."

Ah, again! This time it was not imagination. The word "Antoinette" clearly though gently pronounced, fell plainly upon her ear. Springing to the window, she bent her straining gaze from it, and between the acacia-trees growing close to the house, saw a tall, dark figure emerge. But surely this figure disguised in ungraceful cloak and slouching hat was not that mirror of elegant dandyism, Audley Sternfield! The remembrance of what he had once said to her about visiting Valmont in disguise, flashed across her mind; and without any farther doubt as to who the intruder was, she leaned forward, and rejoined in guarded but agitated tones:

"Oh, Audley, what brings you here?"

"What brings me here! Is that the only word of welcome you have for me?" was the rapid, irritated reply. "Do you intend coming out, or will you merely condescend to speak to me from the casement as if I were a lackey?"

"Heaven direct me," murmured the girl to herself, "what to do! Should I bring him in, and my father find him here in that disguise, what fatal consequences may not ensue; and yet to steal out to meet him and be perhaps discovered, misjudged, condemned!"

"Have you decided yet what farther reception you will give me?" The voice was louder now, less cautious, showing that the patience of the impetuous speaker was rapidly giving way.

"Hush!" she whispered. "I will be with you in a moment," and, unclosing the French window which opened on the low balcony, she soon stood beside him.

Coldly disengaging herself from his embrace, she again asked, "Tell me, Audley, what has brought you here?"

"Are you really flesh and blood, Antoinette, like others, or are you not rather made of marble?" he passionately retorted. "You ask me, your bridegroom and husband, after a wearisome separation of long weeks, what has brought me here."

"Have you come to claim me openly as your wife?" she shortly questioned.

"Not yet; not yet awhile," and his accents betrayed something like embarrassment. "You know the reason."

"Oh, I do, Major Sternfield, and doubtless you think it all-sufficient, all-powerful. It may be so, but in mercy do not talk of your love afterwards—'tis empty mockery. If from prudential, pecuniary motives you can defer for months, perhaps years, claiming me as your wife, your love is not so uncomfortably ardent that you cannot also refrain from paying me visits which can entail nothing else on me save annoyance and disgrace."

"You have a merciless, stinging tongue, Antoinette," rejoined the young man, baffled by the plain, straightforward manner in which his companion, once so childish and timid, spoke to him now.

"Listen to me, Audley. You have robbed me of nearly all I value in life,—my liberty, my happiness, the approbation of my own conscience. Nothing remains to me now save my reputation, and *that* no threats or menaces or yours shall induce me to risk in stolen interviews or secret meetings with you. If your love is so great," here the speaker's tones involuntarily grew sarcastic, "that you cannot exist without occasionally meeting me, come openly to the house in your own character of a gentleman, not disguised as you are to-night."

"Yes, and your father may seek perhaps to eject me, and bring matters to such a crisis that a full explanation and acknowledgment of our marriage would become inevitable. No, that would not suit me as well as it would suit you. But let me congratulate you on your tact: you are becoming a perfect diplomatist, my little Antoinette."

Without noting the taunt conveyed in this last speech, she rejoined, "Have you anything else to say to me, for I must return to the house? I expect my father this evening, perhaps this moment."

"There is no danger of that. They told me in the shabby apology of an inn where I put up last night, that he was absent, and would not probably return till to-morrow, on account of the bad roads."

"Believe me, you are mistaken; he may be here to-night: but in any case we have said all to each other that we have to say. I have no honeyed phrases to whisper; and if you have them for my ear, they will prove at best but unwelcome."

"Do you not fear that you are laying up a terrible reckoning for a future day, lady mine?" he asked in a low menacing tone. "Think you that Antoinette De Mirecourt's bitter revilings, her scornful disdain, may not yet be remembered to Mrs. Audley Sternfield?"

"Very probably. I have seen enough, Audley, to know that you will not spare your wife more than you have done your bride; but I do not think that in any case you could make me more wretched, more hopeless than I am now."

He smiled—a cruel, meaning smile—and it was well for the grail young girl at his side, that the shadow of the acacia-boughs hid his face, or that smile would have haunted her long afterwards.

"Well, 'tis to be hoped I never will; but you have only a very slight idea of the troubles of life, young lady. Your bark has always glided over a sunshiny sea; but it may meet with storms yet, such as you have never dreamed of. Do you intend returning to Montreal soon?"

"No. Not whilst I can help it. I suffered too much during my last visit there; but I am living as secluded and quiet a life here as you could wish. I rarely go out alone, have few visitors, and am nearly always with my governess. Believe me, for both our sakes, 'tis better to leave me in peace. Let this visit, Audley, be your last."

"It certainly ought, for my reception has not been such as to encourage a renewal of it; but I will make no rash promises, lest I should be tempted to break them hereafter."

"Hush!" suddenly exclaimed Antoinette, grasping his arm tightly. "My father has arrived. Do you not hear the voices—the noise?"

A moment after, lights were glancing from the sitting-room window, and Mr. De Mirecourt's clear, pleasant voice was heard, loudly summoning his daughter.

"Oh, we shall be discovered! He is coming this way," said the girl in an agony of terror.

"Go forward, and meet him as usual, foolish child," whispered Sternfield. "He will suspect nothing."

Slowly, hesitatingly, Antoinette went forward into the bright moonlight; and had Mr. De Mirecourt's trust in his daughter been one degree less unbounded—had his suspicions in any way been previously aroused—he could not but have noticed the singularity of her manner. Fortunately, however, he was in high spirits, jested her about her sentimental love of moonlight musings, and then enquired for Mrs. Gérard, which afforded Antoinette an opening on a subject about which she could trust her voice.

Sternfield waited till father and daughter had re-entered the house, and then advancing a little closer to the open window, but keeping still in shadow of the trees, he listened.

"I thought her a much better actress," he said to himself, after a moment. "How is it her father does not see there is something the matter? Pshaw! she is a mere child yet, and still how thoroughly, how completely she keeps me in check," and a stern, dark look crossed his features. "Do I love her, or do I not? At times when her rare beauty, her wondrous grace, rises mentally before me, I feel she is a creature to be madly worshipped; then again, when she stands forth opposed to me, with that relentless firmness, that iron will, so strangely at variance with her usual character, her feminine loveliness, I feel as if I almost hated her. Still, there is a wayward charm, too, in that very coldness, which makes me rejoice in the thought that she shall one day be mine; but I cannot afford to hasten that time, even if my love were ten times as fervent as it is. My gambling losses fetter me as completely as her secret marriage fetters her. I certainly love her more now than when I wooed and won her. I wonder will she venture out here again to-night! I shall wait and see. Ah! I have wofully bungled matters to have allowed her love for me to die out so completely. I must try another course, and coax it back again."

The lights soon passed into a front room. Mr. De Mirecourt was about to partake of what, according to the customs of the time, was a singularly late tea; and the opening and closing of a door, followed by the light rustling of a woman's dress, fell on Sternfield's quick ear. Yes, it was as he had expected—Antoinette had returned,—and, stooping from the window, she hurriedly whispered,

"Audley, are you still here?"

"Do you think I could have gone without a farewell word?" he gently, though reproachfully rejoined.

"I have come to say good night. Of course you leave to-morrow," and her tones plainly betrayed the intense anxiety she felt.

"Yes, since you appear so strongly to desire it."

"Oh, thank you, thank you. I cannot tell you how much I dread anything like a scene between you and my father."

"Is your health not better since your return to the country?" he enquired, with real anxiety.

"No; still I have no decided ailment—merely weakness."

A sudden fear flashed across Sternfield's mind as he remembered how sadly changed Antoinette was from the bright blooming creature he had first met in Mrs. D'Aulnay's drawing-rooms. What if Death snatched his bride from him before the time her intended claiming her had arrived! He had heard it said that Antoinette's mother had died in early youth of decline, and that her daughter strongly resembled her in her delicate beauty, but he had paid little attention to the rumor at the time. Now it occurred to him with painful force, and he inwardly determined to spare his bride the agitating scenes, the wearying persecutions, which he felt had strangely helped to undermine her physical health as well as happiness. Pursuant to this resolve, he gently said:

"As I know my presence in Valmont alarms and annoys you, I shall leave it to-morrow at daybreak. I will not seek to see you again for fear of discovery, so I will say farewell now."

She leaned still lower from the low casement, and extended her hand. It was of a dry burning heat, and his conscience smote him as he pressed it to his lips.

"If you should wish to see me, Antoinette, write me word. Till then I will not trouble you."

"God bless you, Audley!" she falteringly whispered, for his unusual gentleness touched her. "I will write to you often, and live as quietly as you yourself could wish."

In a moment he had vaulted on to the low balcony, through the open window, and was beside her. Not for long, however. One ardent, passionate embrace, and he was gone as rapidly, as silently, as he had entered.

Shortly after, Antoinette returned to superintend the tea-table; and Mr. De Mirecourt, noticing the scarlet flush on her cheeks, laughingly enquired "where she had stolen her *rouge*."

Chapter XXIX.

Summer had mellowed into autumn. Not the autumn of other lands, with its leaden gloomy skies, and dark, withered foliage, but our glorious, glowing Canadian autumn, with golden, hazy atmosphere, and gorgeous woods and forests.

Has it not often struck you, reader, how wondrous is the change wrought by the first severe autumn frost? You have retired to rest, giving a pleasant parting look to green hills and emerald woods,—you awake and find earth and wilderness flooded with new lights and colours. Here the rich scarlet of the glowing maple contrasts with the pale gold of the delicate birch; there the quivering, silvery leaves of the poplar with the dotted saffron of the broad sycamore. Farther on, the crimson berries of the ash and the gorgeously dyed vines, looking yet more bright against a gloomy back-ground of firs and evergreens. If ever beauty smiled brightly forth in the midst of decay, it is certainly in the foliage of our autumnal woods.

Looking languidly out from the window of her room on the scene before her, sat Antoinette; and the pillows heaped upon her chair, the tiny vial and glass beside her, as well as the painful delicacy of her whole appearance, betrayed she was an invalid. By her side sat Mrs. Gérard, who, with a cheerful smile, exclaimed:

"Do you not wish to hear what Doctor Le Bourdais says, dear child?"

A faint smile and an inclination of the head was her only reply.

"Well, he declares that your lungs are perfectly sound, and that all you require is cheerfulness and variety. He finds the life you lead here too dull and quiet for the present state of your health, and recommends an immediate visit to town."

"To town!" repeated Antoinette, in consternation. "The worst thing he could advise. No, I will not leave home. Here, at least, I have peace and quiet—all I can wish or hope for on earth."

"My darling Antoinette, you will go since it has been judged necessary for you to do so. You need only remain a few weeks, just sufficiently long to satisfy Dr. Le Bourdais' wishes, and the engrossing anxiety of your poor father."

The young girl, either too docile or too spiritless to offer farther resistance, soon yielded, and that day week[112] she was seated in the easiest, softest *fauteuil* in Mrs. D'Aulnay's drawing-room, submitting, like a passive child, to the congratulations and caresses of that highly delighted lady.

"What a treat to have you again with us, dearest Antoinette! I am determined you shall enjoy yourself well."

"Our ideas of enjoyment are now very different, Lucille, and you must not forget, that being an invalid, I must have quiet, and early hours."

"No such thing, child; you have been moped to death in that dreary old Manor-House, and you require a little gaiety to bring you round again. Did not the doctor tell you as much himself?"

"Not exactly: he said my illness almost baffled his skill, that he could not arrive at its origin, so, *en désespoir de cause*,[113] he ordered a change, to see what effect that would have. Remember the conditions, dear Lucille, on which I came here."

"Oh yes, I remember rashly promising that you should remain as isolated and unsocial as you liked, so I suppose

[112] Old-fashioned way of saying "one week from that day," "exactly one week later" (see also note 81).

[113] French expression meaning "as a last resort," "having no other choice."

I must respect my promise for awhile. Of course, you will make an exception in Sternfield's favor?"

A delicate flush rose to the girl's cheek, as she said, "Yes, I must not refuse to see him."

"Indeed, you had better not," was the somewhat significant reply. "It may serve as a sort of check upon him."

A look of painful enquiry rose into Antoinette's eyes. "Perhaps I should not tell you, my dear, but you would hear it more abruptly from other quarters: report says he has been leading a very wild life lately."

The anxious look in Antoinette's eyes deepened.

"Yes, not to speak of other failings, perhaps still more unpardonable, and which I will not even hint at, it appears he is becoming a confirmed gambler. They say his losses are enormous. 'Tis probably his complete separation, amounting almost to estrangement from yourself, that has driven him desperate."

Antoinette sighed—a long, weary sigh. Oh, how every shade deepened the gloom of the future! This reckless gambler, this libertine spendthrift, whose faults were in every one's mouth, was her life's partner, he husband; and she awaited but his will, his word, to leave the loving, tender friends of youth, her happy home, perhaps, her native land, to follow his ruined fortunes. One gleam of hope presented itself, her own failing health; and it was with a strange quickening of her pulses she remembered that death might yet free her from a union, to whose consummation she now looked forward with inexpressible aversion.

"I have no doubt," continued Mrs. D'Aulnay, "that Audley will entirely reform when your marriage is publicly acknowledged, and will probably make an excellent husband."

"Peace! peace!" implored Antoinette, tortured almost beyond her strength by the ill-chosen remarks of her companion.

"Certainly, darling child. I will not touch on the topic again since it annoys you. To speak of another, and very different character, Colonel Evelyn: you must know that he has become the most gloomy misanthrope, the most confirmed savage, you can imagine. To the several invitations I sent him after you left town, he returned the shortest, most peremptory refusals possible, never paying me the civility of a call afterwards. Like St. Paul's relapsing sinners, the last state of the man is worse than the first.[114] Ah, I hear carriage-wheels at the door. 'Tis Sternfield. I thought he would not prove tardy in paying his devoirs.[115] But I must go up stairs for a moment: I shall be back immediately."

Whatever had been Sternfield's late mode of life, his sins, or his anxieties, no traces of either rested on his gay, careless features when he entered; and as he stood there, so marked a contrast, in the pride of his strong, handsome manhood, to the fragile delicate, girl beside him, the latter could not help bitterly thinking, that she, and she alone bore the heavy burden of their mutual fault. With the bright smile of old, he threw himself on the low ottoman at her feet, exclaiming:

"So they have sent you to Montreal to recruit, my little Antoinette? The best thing they could do, for the dreariness of Valmont is enough to destroy the strongest constitution in less than six months."

"I have never found it dreary, Audley. I was born and brought up there, and the place is inexpressibly dear to me."

"For the matter of that, so is, to the Esquimaux, the barren waste he inhabits; but you will acknowledge I have not troubled or worried you much lately. I formed the good resolve during my first and last moon-light visit, that no act

[114] The sentence mixes Paul's discourse on the struggle with sin in his letter to the Romans with the parable of the unclean spirit in Matthew 12:45.

[115] Duties. The word (borrowed from French) only became obsolete around the turn of the 20th century.

of mine should disturb your mental peace, and thus retard your recovery."

"Thank you. You have indeed been considerate, and I feel grateful to you for it."

The young man coughed as if slightly embarrassed, and rejoined, "I must tell you, though, whilst Mrs. D'Aulnay is out of the room, that, naturally feeling very lonely whilst thus separated from yourself, I sought distractions and amusements which a rigid moralist might censure; but I will take courage and hope from one of your own charming French proverbs,—*à tout péché miséricorde.*"[116]

Antoinette was silent, and he went on, "Mrs. D'Aulnay, who is as indiscreet and ill-judging as she is graceful and fascinating, took it into her fair head to bring me to a strict reckoning about my conduct, threatening at the same time to make a formal complaint to yourself about me. I told her it was quite enough for me to render an account of my actions to my wife, without having also to do so to my wife's friend. Was I not justified in telling her so?"

"I have never assumed the right to find fault with your actions, Audley."

"Adhere always to that determination, and you will make one of the most perfect little wives in the world. But to change the subject to one more agreeable: I suppose you have returned to town for a little gaiety, not to immure yourself here as you have done in the country. In furtherance of so laudable a purpose, I shall call for you to-morrow afternoon, and we will take a long drive in whatever direction you may prefer; but Mrs. D'Aulnay must not be of the party."

"In that case, I dare not go."

"Pray give me your reasons then?" he irritably questioned.

"In the first place I do not wish to offend Lucille, who is always so kind and considerate to myself; then it would not

[116] French for "every sin shall find mercy."

do for me to be seen out driving alone with any gentleman, the very day after my arrival. It might come to papa's ears, and——"

"In short, Antoinette, you are the most prudent and circumspect of young ladies. No danger of your heart or feelings ever running away with your judgment; but, since you will not accept my offer, do not be offended if you should see me out with some less particular and cautious young lady than yourself."

The entrance of Mrs. D'Aulnay put a stop to the conversation as it was taking this most unpropitious turn; and after a half-hour's general conversation, Sternfield took leave.

The following day was one of those glorious October days which almost reconcile one to the flight of birds and flowers, and which possess a peculiar charm in their mellow beauty, beyond that of the blooming luxuriant Summer herself. Mrs. D'Aulnay's carriage was at the door early in the afternoon, and vainly Antoinette begged to be excused from accompanying her, repeating Sternfield's request of the preceding day, and her own refusal.

"The very reason you should go with me, child. You must show him that you intend going abroad, keeping a strict watch over his actions. Come, I will take no refusal."

Mrs. D'Aulnay carried her point; and with a sad heart, which neither golden sunshine nor bracing pleasant air could enliven, Antoinette took her place beside her cousin in the latter's small though handsome carriage. Arrived in Notre Dame street, Mrs. D'Aulnay, as usual, had some shopping to do, and, promising not to delay more than five minutes, she alighted before one of the dingy, narrow-paned shops, so different to our present large-windowed, handsome establishments. She had scarcely entered the store in question, when Sternfield's light, graceful equipage passed. By his side was seated a smiling blushing beauty, one of the many who shared his attentions and his flatteries, and in passing Antoinette, she bestowed an unmistakable glance of triumph on the latter. Scarcely recovered from the unpleasant sensations which this last meeting had excited, Antoinette beheld advancing towards her a tall figure, the first glimpse of whom caused her heart to beat with unwonted rapidity. It was Colonel Evelyn, and, supposing he would probably pass her without any sign of recognition, she turned away her eyes from him. Yielding however, to an influence which he rarely allowed to sway him, that of impulse, he suddenly stopped, and with scant words of introductory courtesy, asked her when she had arrived.

Recovering from her agitated astonishment, she briefly told him.

"I have heard that you have been very ill since I last saw you."

"Such things are always exaggerated," she rejoined, with a wretched attempt at carelessness.

"You do not, however, look like one in health. Is it mind or body that is ailing, Miss De Mirecourt?" and his eyes earnestly scrutinized her face. Then bending towards her, he said in a low tone, "You told me once before, that you were very unhappy, and I scarcely believed you; now I read in your face that you spoke truth. In expiation of my incredulity, and on account of the deep powerful love I so lately bore you, I wish to whisper a word of counsel in your ear. Will it be of any use to warn you to put no trust in Audley Sternfield? He is unworthy of any woman's love."

"Too late, too late," she faltered: "the past is irrevocable!"

"Aye, after what I had seen, I ought to have known it must be so. Well, you have chosen a frail support; but regrets are unavailing. Farewell." Touching his cap, he strode off just as Mrs. D'Aulnay, having completed her purchases, left the shop where she had been tantalizing master and clerks about a certain indefinable shade of lilac, in search of which nearly all the goods in the store had been overturned.

Antoinette, agitated by her late interview with Colonel Evelyn, was in no mood for conversation, and, after taking a turn up to Dalhousie Square, in which the hill or citadel then stood, surmounted by its flag, and the few rusty cannon which had been almost the only defence that Montreal had to offer against the three besieging armies that had invested it, they returned homeward. Again, Sternfield and his blushing triumphant partner passed them. To the bows of both, Mrs. D'Aulnay only returned a cold, disdainful nod, which mortified Sternfield almost as much as Antoinette's quiet, self-possessed bow. Mrs. D'Aulnay was in a fever of indignation, and she abused Sternfield and his companion with a fervor and energy which could not have been exceeded if she, instead of Antoinette, had been the aggrieved party.

"May I tell Jeanne that you are not at home, when he calls the next time? Do not shake your head—I will. This insolent bridegroom must be brought to his senses in one way or another."

The next day, Dr. Manby, one of the army surgeons, and a frequent visitor at the house, called, and he enquired so earnestly about Antoinette's health, and expressed so great a desire to see her, that Mrs. D'Aulnay, despite her cousin's avowed intention of receiving no visitors for two or three days, went to her room, and half coaxed, half forced her down. Dr. Manby was a quiet, middle-aged man, neither handsome nor accomplished, simply respectable, so Antoinette felt no anger at his questions, nor scrutinizing looks. As he rose to go, he kindly said, retaining in his grasp a moment, the small thin hand he had taken:

"If I were your physician, Miss De Mirecourt, I would prescribe neither quinine nor tonics, but a daily dose of heart's ease."

"But is that remedy found in every apothecary's store?" she rejoined, endeavoring to laugh off his remark. "Or have you any doses ready done up for use?"

"I am afraid not; but at your age, my dear young lady, it is easily procured. The best means is to take plenty of exercise—see agreeable, cheerful people, and religiously avoid all dull or melancholy thoughts. I will call again next week to see if my prescription has been followed, and to ascertain the results."

"What a good-natured, officious creature," said Mrs. D'Aulnay, as she watched the Doctor's short, thick-set figure traversing the street.

"Kind-hearted, and amiable, though," returned Antoinette.

Neither dreamed for one moment, that Colonel Evelyn, unable to subdue the anxiety which the sight of Antoinette's altered appearance had awoke in his breast the day previous, despite his outraged love, despite that never-to-be-forgotten scene which he had witnessed between her and Sternfield, had asked Doctor Manby, one of the chosen few with whom he was on anything like terms of intimacy, to pay a visit of apparent civility to Mrs. D'Aulnay, and ascertain as much as he possibly could about her young guest. It must not be inferred from this, that Colonel Evelyn had at all relented in his feelings of estrangement towards Antoinette, or in his severe condemnation of her conduct. No, her offence was one which that sensitive, honorable nature never could forgive; but, at the same time, there remained a feeling of powerful interest in her, one which, perhaps, he could never wholly overcome; and a deep intense sentiment of regret that the man for whom she had sacrificed so much was so utterly unworthy of her. No one was better acquainted than Colonel Evelyn with the lawless recklessness of Sternfield's career; and as he thought over the future misery of the young girl, when united for life to a man who set all moral laws at defiance, it was more with the anxious grief of a father than with the irritation of a rejected suitor.

Chapter XXX.

Mrs. D'Aulnay did not obtain as speedy a chance of saying "not at home" to Major Sternfield as she had expected, for several days elapsed without his renewing his visit; and whilst she wondered and scolded, Antoinette grew thinner and paler every day. Doctor Manby, who, without having been formally adopted as the latter's physician, took the liberty of questioning and prescribing during most of his frequent visits, began to get anxious and irritable. One day that he found himself alone with the lady of the house, he took her roundly to task, for the rapidity with which her young friend's health was declining.

"But what can I do, Doctor?" was the indignant rejoinder. "'Tis you, a physician, who should be able to suggest and prescribe something that would be of service to her."

"So I could and would, madam, if this were an ordinary case, but it is not. 'Tis the mind that is ill with her, and you should endeavor to soothe, cheer and solace her."

"But I repeat, what can I do?" questioned the lady despairingly. "If I propose a *soirée*, dancing, or other amusement of the sort, she says she is too ill, and menaces to shut herself up in her room till the entertainment is over; if I seek to engage her in visiting, shopping, or novel-reading, or indeed in any other feminine pastime," the Doctor smiled grimly at this choice of amusements, "she begs off with such a coaxing way, that I cannot find the heart to insist. The only point on which I invariably remain firm is to bring her out driving every day, and a difficult task it sometimes is."

Doctor Manby, convinced that the case was a serious as well as difficult one, departed without another word; and Mrs. D'Aulnay set herself earnestly to work to think what more effectual means she could adopt to amuse and divert her young guest. She was highly delighted, therefore, when, that very afternoon, a clear pleasant voice resounded in the hall, and Louis Beauchesne entered, all smiles and gaiety. Antoinette, too, was pleased to see him, for she had always looked on him as a brother, and there was something almost contagious in his exuberant spirits and kindly genial humor.

He informed them "he had come to spend some weeks in Montreal, having business of importance to transact, and that he had promised Mr. De Mirecourt at the same time to keep a strict watch over their movements."

Mrs. D'Aulnay laughingly declared that "as she wished to afford him every opportunity of prosecuting his researches, she gave him *carte blanche* for visiting at the house. Morning, noon, or night—to dinner, breakfast, or tea, he would be always welcome without farther invitation."

This pleasant species of challenge was smilingly accepted, and that evening, as well as many succeeding ones, saw Louis a welcome guest at Mrs. D'Aulnay's. Something of Antoinette's olden look and color used to steal over her face whilst listening to Louis and his mirthful sallies. His conversation awoke no disagreeable thoughts or reminiscences; it brought back only the happy golden past: and his careful, delicate avoidance of any illusion to his own ill-starred passion for herself, which he seemed apparently to have completely mastered, removed the only unpleasant feature that by any chance could have attached itself to their intercourse.

One evening the three were seated together in Mrs. D'Aulnay's drawing-room, and never had Louis been more entertaining or his companions more highly amused.

Antoinette had asked him to hold a skein of floss whilst she wound it off; and to assume a convenient position, he had thrown himself carelessly at her feet on one of the low stools with which Mrs. D'Aulnay's rooms were filled, and which, that lady's enemies maintained, were intended for such purposes. The heat of the fire had flushed the young girl's face; and as Louis, perhaps wearied of his task, fidgetted about, rendering the winding of the silk a very difficult thing, she laughingly chided him for his impatient awkwardness. At that moment the door opened, and, without warning or announcement, Sternfield walked in. He stood a moment on the threshold, glancing darkly on the group before him. He had come there that evening, magnanimously thinking that he had sufficiently punished Antoinette for her obstinacy in the matter of the drive, and expecting to find her ill, pale, and spiritless. He saw her instead, with a glow on her face, and smiles on her lip, such as neither had worn for many weeks past; whilst by way of climax, Louis was seated at her feet, his gay, handsome face upturned to hers.

Mrs. D'Aulnay, who easily divined the jealous angry feelings of the new-comer, fairly revelled in the triumph of the moment, and, with a look of smiling *badinage*[117] which he found inexpressively provoking, inquired where he had been lately, and what he had been doing with himself?

Scarcely replying, he walked over to a chair beside Antoinette, and, throwing himself into it, sarcastically expressed his delight at the improved state of her health. Of Louis he took no notice whatever; but the latter revenged himself by adjusting his low seat more comfortably, and inquiring how many more skeins Antoinette had to wind, announcing his willingness at the same time to hold any amount of them. With all his arrogance, his self-esteem, Sternfield felt somewhat disconcerted. Mrs. D'Aulnay's mocking smile, Louis's easy not to say impertinent

[117] French for playful banter.

indifference, and Antoinette's constrained embarrassed welcome, formed a reception such as he had not calculated upon. But Major Sternfield was not a man to be easily vanquished; and whilst Mrs. D'Aulnay was yet triumphing in his mortification, he had determined how to bring the latter to an end.

Giving ample time to Antoinette to finish the winding of her floss, he waited till Louis rose from his seat in obedience to a look from the young girl, and drawing his chair nearer to hers, hemmed her in in such a manner as to isolate her entirely from her companions. Then addressing her in a low familiar tone on matters which he knew could not but chain her attention, contrived to engross her completely. Louis watched this palpable and singular flirtation with mingled surprise and indignation. That Antoinette should permit such a thing astonished him beyond measure; and yet, the more he watched them, which he did very narrowly, the more leniently he judged her, and the more intense became his feelings of dislike for her companion. There was a constrained unhappy look about her, a restless glancing around, as if she were weary of her position, and longed for release, which seemed to speak of fear more than of love; and though Sternfield bent so closely over her that his dark curls almost mingled with the braids of her hair, and his eyes beamed glances that might have awoke emotion in the heart of any woman who entertained the slightest feeling of affection for himself, the coldness of her manner never wavered, nor the glow which had faded from her cheek shortly after his entrance, never mounted to it again.

Sternfield however had accomplished all his intentions: he had changed the pleasant cordiality which reigned on his entrance into embarrassed dullness, and, whilst inflicting ample mortification on his supposed rival, had punished at the same time Antoinette for having dared to be gay or amused during his absence. Mrs. D'Aulnay, however, was eagerly watching an opportunity of retaliation, and when Major Sternfield said,

"I will call to-morrow for you, Miss De Mirecourt, if you will do me the honor of driving with me," she hastily interrupted, "Impossible! Antoinette and I are engaged to drive out with Mr. Beauchesne in the country, to see a mutual friend."

Sternfield glanced at his bride, but her eyes, determinedly bent on the carpet, warned him he would get no assistance from her; and too wise to enter on a contest in which he ran the risk of defeat, he bowed and withdrew. In doing so, however, he managed to tell Mrs. D'Aulnay, in a low whisper, to beware of making Antoinette as independent and careless a wife as she was herself, for that he assuredly would not prove as tame and blind a husband as Mr. D'Aulnay."

"Audacious!" muttered the lady with crimsoning brow; but before she had time to collect her thoughts, the offender was beyond reach of her voice.

The fierce unreasoning jealousy of Sternfield's character had been strangely roused by finding Louis on such intimate terms in Mrs. D'Aulnay's house; and the fact of subsequently meeting him a few days later, driving the two ladies out, still farther increased his anger. Shortly after the visit during which he had contrived to render himself so disagreeable, Mrs. D'Aulnay half coaxed, half worried Antoinette into promising that she would enter into the details and preparations for a small *soirée* with which she wished to enliven the present monotony of their lives. The appointed night came, and the young girl in her gauzy white robes looked so delicately lovely, but so fragile, that Jeanne, remembering how full of health and bloom that young face and form had been one short year previous, sadly and forebodingly shook her head.

Aware that many unpleasant remarks regarding her altered looks had been whispered about, Antoinette spared no effort to appear gay and cheerful; and Doctor Manby, who was among the guests, quietly rubbed his hands, and murmured to himself, "That what his young friend really wanted after all, was distraction and amusement."

One of the liveliest of the gay assemblage was Louis Beauchesne; and there were few whose reserve of manner did not yield more or less to the influence of his frank, joyous gaiety. Sternfield, on the contrary, was in one of his worst moods. Heavy gambling losses experienced the night previous had greatly ruffled his temper, and rarely man sought a festive entertainment with feelings more ill-suited to the occasion. Pre-determined to find fault with his unfortunate young bride, he felt angry with her for looking so unusually cheerful, angry with her for the calm even friendliness of her manner towards him. Availing himself of the opportunity afforded by the dance for which he had secured her hand, he contrived to effectually damp her assumed cheerfulness by favoring her with a chapter of reproaches and upbraidings such as she was now, alas! too familiar with. The dance concluded, he abruptly left her and sought out one of the budding young beauties with whom he was so fond of flirting. Whilst bending over the latter, looking and whispering tender things, he inwardly congratulated himself on the means and power he thus possessed of punishing that rebellious girlish will that ever dared to place itself in opposition to his own.

Antoinette, however, was not left to a wall-flower's fate, and eager partners thronged constantly around her. Among these, Louis was naturally one of the most attentive. Her greater degree of intimacy with him, the freedom from restraint, from the necessity of keeping up that appearance of cheerfulness or interest which she was obliged to assume, whilst dancing with others, induced her more than once to grant his demand for her hand. Still there was nothing which an unprejudiced eye would have regarded as even approaching to flirtation between them; and when Antoinette two or three times chanced to meet Sternfield's glance angrily fixed upon her, she though the looks were merely the supplement of the lecture he had previously given her. Strangely dispirited, however, by those threatening glances, she refused Louis's request to join a cotillion then forming, declaring that she felt too much fatigued to do so.

"Then I shall sit beside you and wait for the next, for you have promised me a dance," he rejoined, carefully adjusting the cushions of the silken ottoman on which she was seated.

Kindly solicitous to make her forget the sadness which he saw stealing over her, the young man strained every faculty, though unavailingly, to interest and amuse her. Antoinette's glance was either wandering wearily round the room or stealing towards Sternfield, who stood some distance from them, apparently engrossed by his pretty partner, for he never danced with any but very young and handsome women. His companion's look strangely puzzled Louis. There was sadness, anxiety, pain in it, but no jealous anger, none of the *pique* which a girl might naturally be expected to feel or show, in witnessing her lover devoted to another. Suddenly, after studying her countenance a moment in silence, he impulsively exclaimed:

"Pardon the remark, but I think Major Sternfield is a recreant wooer. Oh! Antoinette, can it be possible that you really love that man?"

She blushed deeply, painfully at the question, but made no reply beyond a reproachful glance.

"Forgive me, dear Antoinette," he earnestly continued, "but it seems to me there is something in his manner and character that should prevent him winning, much less retaining, the love of such a heart as yours."

"And yet is he not handsome and fascinating, envied by men and admired by women?" she replied with a touch of bitterness which but confirmed Beauchesne's supposition that whatever tie still linked her to Sternfield, it was not that of love.

"I acknowledge he is all that, but methinks there is much in which he is still wanting. However patiently women may put up with slights and frowns after marriage, they rarely tolerate them before."

"Because, probably, they have then a remedy in their own hands, and can turn the despotic lover adrift; but here is the object of your doubts approaching."

"Yes, and with a stormy looking brow too," thought Louis.

Sternly, Audley drew near them, and, unceremoniously leaning across young Beauchesne, whispered in Antoinette's ear, "How much longer do you intend rendering yourself ridiculous by flirting with the brainless puppy beside you?"

"What do you mean, Audley?" she inquired in turn, her face flushing.

"I will tell you if you will favor me with your hand for the next dance," he rejoined, in a somewhat louder key.

"Miss De Mirecourt is engaged to me," said Louis, stiffly.

Sternfield cast a supercilious, negligent look at the speaker, and repeated, "Do you hear, Antoinette, you will dance the next dance with me?"

"Pray, Miss De Mirecourt, do not forget that we are engaged," interrupted Louis, still more firmly than before.

Antoinette, infinitely distressed and perplexed, glanced entreatingly from one to the other. Louis's countenance was proud and determined, but Sternfield's brow was like marble, as cold and unrelenting.

Again stooping towards the young girl, the latter menacingly whispered, "I swear if you set me aside to dance with that fool, I shall teach him with a horsewhip to come between me and my wishes."

The unmanly threat was worthy of him who uttered it, but it had its effect; for Antoinette, dreading not only the menaced insult, but the deadly satisfaction which was sure to follow, turned with a blanched cheek to young Beauchesne.

"Are you ready, Miss De Mirecourt?" inquired the latter, "I do not like to hurry you, but the dancers are taking their places."

Sternfield deigned no farther remark, but, with an intolerable sneer on his lip, waited for Antoinette's decision. The latter suddenly placed her hand on Louis's arm, and, as he bent towards her, whispered:

"Oh, Louis, dear Louis, I implore you let me dance with him. I am very wretched. Do not help to make me still more so."

The pale cheek, the tearful eye, the voice of the speaker, touched the generous heart of Beauchesne, and he mutely bowed in assent. As Sternfield abruptly, almost roughly, drew his partner's arm within his own, he cast a disdainful arrogant glance upon his momentary rival, which the latter's kindling eye returned with interest, speaking of something more than mere anger,—of menace, of future revenge.

"What sweet words have you been whispering in that idiot's ear to make him yield his insolent claims so easily?" harshly questioned Sternfield.

Antoinette dared not reply, for her lashes were heavy with unshed tears, and there was a suffocating feeling in her throat that was almost growing beyond her control: a scene she did not wish to make, and she felt that she was on the verge of one.

"Take a word of friendly warning, sweetheart mine," resumed her companion, "and bring your present flirtation with that young gentleman to a speedy close, or I shall do it for you in a more summary and unpleasant manner than either of you could desire."

Antoinette shuddered, for well she understood the threat conveyed in his words; but the music commenced, and with what composure she could gather, she had to go through the lively dance and endeavor to look careless and indifferent, in default of looking gay or amused.

"Hang that fellow Sternfield!" inwardly soliloquized Doctor Manby, who had noticed how entirely Antoinette's tranquillity had given way since the former had accosted her: "his shadow, like that of the upas-tree,[118] seems fairly to blight that poor young creature."

The dance at length came to a close, and Antoinette was meditating flight to her own room, but Sternfield had no intention of allowing her to escape so easily. Bringing her to a small alcove, he drew forward a chair for her, and then placed himself in front of her. "I want a word of explanation with you, for I do not think we understand each other yet. You have braved me pretty well in this last flirtation of yours with Mr. Louis Beauchesne."

"Audley, cruel and unjust as you always are, will you not believe my solemn, sacred asseveration, that Louis is nothing more to me than an old and esteemed friend?"

"Tush! the man loves you heart and soul; and as you do not care one iota for your wedded husband, it is hard to say on whom your wandering affections may be placed."

What could she say to this heartless, merciless tormentor, who scoffed at her denials, sneered at her protestations? Words were unavailing, and with hands tightly clasped, and colorless lips, she sat, determined to listen and suffer in patience. Had she not in her own blind folly filled up this cup of misery, and was she to murmur now at the bitterness of the draught?

Either encouraged or exasperated by her silence he went on: "You have hitherto been firm and unyielding as

[118] *Antiaris toxicaria,* a tree from whose bark the natives of Java used to extract a poison in which they dipped their arrows. The tree's poisonous powers were grossly exaggerated in 18th- and 19th-century literature.

bronze on your favorite whim. Tender word, caress, or kindness, such as the most scrupulous young ladies often accord their lovers, you have perseveringly refused me. Well, so be it. You have been true to your hobby, so I will be to mine. You shall walk, drive, flirt, with no living man of whom I could possibly be jealous. If, neglecting this, my explicit command, you disobey me, I shall walk up to your cavalier of the moment, Master Louis, or whoever else it may be, and publicly insult, strike him. On your own head be the result! If you will not love, I shall at least teach you to fear me." He uttered this last sentence with the menacing sternness peculiar at times to his voice, and which was in such striking contrast to his usual rich musical tones.

"Well, God will perhaps show me that mercy that you refuse me," she said, whilst an expression of anguish momentarily convulsed her features.

At that moment her eyes encountered the fixed, sorrowful gaze of Louis, who stood at some distance, apparently watching the dancers, but in reality concentrating his attention entirely upon herself. Instantly however he turned away; but another scrutinizing pair of eyes was also fixed upon them—the light blue orbs of the worthy Doctor Manby, who with a face purple with suppressed indignation, suddenly stalked up to Major Sternfield.

"What disagreeable nonsense are you whispering in Miss De Mirecourt's ear, I should like to know?" he said, in a low tone. "You have chased smiles and color from her face."

The young man drew himself stiffly up, and "wondered what Doctor Manby meant."

"Doctor Manby means what he says," was the testy rejoinder. "And he does not like to see a young lady, whom he looks on as one of his patients, frightened and worried out of her health and wits, without interfering. Come, Sternfield," he added, more good-humoredly, "you have scolded Miss De Mirecourt sufficiently for one evening, whatever her offence may be; so let me replace you, whilst you go and relieve that pretty little girl in white over there, looking out so disconsolately for a partner."

Knowing that all farther chance of private conversation with Antoinette was now at an end, (for Doctor Manby was equally tenacious and outspoken,) Sternfield rose, and, after telling her, with marked significance, that he gave her free permission to flirt with Doctor Manby, but with no one else, he turned away.

"How is this, my fair patient?" kindly enquired the good-natured physician, secretly noting and grieving over the suffering, pain-worn look of his companion. "Have you been dancing too much? you look sadly exhausted."

"Because I am unhappy, wretched!" she rejoined, with that reckless candor which great misery often induces. "Talk to me no more of drugs or palliatives, Doctor, unless you can give me one that will set this weary heart at rest for ever."

Inexpressibly shocked at this sudden confidence, as well as at the depth of mental misery which it revealed, he hurriedly, but soothingly, said: "Courage, courage, dear child. We cannot throw down life's burden because in a moment of depression we may find it heavy. To-morrow all may be light and pleasant again."

"Never, never!" she rejoined, with a slow, hopeless shake of the head.

"Listen, dear Miss De Mirecourt, to the advice of a man old enough to be your father, and do not let a lover's quarrel prey on your spirits thus. Major Sternfield is hot-tempered, but he soon forgets and forgives."

As he uttered the name which had proved such a woful sound to her, a shudder ran through her frame, and, more perplexed and troubled than ever, he inwardly thought, "She does not love the handsome villain. What does it all mean?"

In a quiet, indifferent tone he soon resumed: "You seem so weak and nervous to-night, my dear young lady, the best thing you can do is to retire to rest at once. Take my arm, and I will pilot you to the hall, after which I will tell our friend, Sternfield, that I insisted on sending you off."

Arrived at the foot of the stair-case, Antoinette gratefully, falteringly bade him good-night, and hurried to her room. Shall we follow her there, reader? Shall we watch her during the course of that long, weary night, during which no slumber closed her burning eye-lids; no temporary unconsciousness brought its blessed balm, even for one half-hour, to that tortured heart and spirit? The lesson would be a painful, though, perhaps, a useful one. She had erred, but how speedy had been her retribution; she had violated the dictates of conscience and religion—trampled on a daughter's most sacred duties, and what had it brought her? That which guilt and wrongdoing will ever bring to those who are not utterly hardened in evil,—remorse and wretchedness.

Chapter XXXI.

Mrs. D'Aulnay, who had just risen from her couch, was seated in her easy-chair, the morning after her *soirée*, her feet thrust into her quilted satin slippers, whilst Jeanne was preparing to disentangle and smooth the thick masses of her hair, when a loud, prolonged knock, whose echoes reverberated through the whole house, startled mistress and maid.

"Heavens! what can that be? Run, Jeanne, and see," ejaculated Mrs. D'Aulnay.

The messenger soon returned with a small note, which she said "Mr. Beauchesne's man had just left. He must be in a great hurry, Madame, for he never waited to ask how you and Miss Antoinette were, as he generally does, but thrust the letter in my hand, and hurried away."

The note was crumpled and ill-folded, the address carelessly and illegibly written; and with a presentiment of evil, which caused her heart to throb more rapidly, she opened the missive. It ran thus:—

"He who writes this, dear Mrs. D'Aulnay, is now flying from justice, and, if not overtaken, will soon have left his native land for ever. Major Sternfield insulted me last night, goaded me to ungovernable passion by his insolent cruelty to our poor unhappy Antoinette, who seems—Heaven help her—to be strangely in his power. I controlled my anger at the moment, and waited my time. It soon came; for shortly after he left the house, which I took good care to do at the same time with himself, I went up to him and asked for an apology, which of course he was as little disposed to give as I was anxious to obtain. This morning we met, and fell, mortally wounded. They tell me he is dying. Say to Antoinette, that if, contrary to my secret suppositions and thoughts, he is really dear to her, I implore her, by the memory of the deep, true love I have ever borne her, to forgive me. Deeply I regret the mad act of which I have been guilty, not so much for the consequences it has entailed on myself, as for the terrible responsibility thus incurred of hurrying a fellow-creature, in the strength of manhood, into eternity. Ah! before the deed was done, I could never have dreamed that the remorse would have been so bitter—so weighty: but time presses. With earnest thanks for all your past kindness to myself—I dare send no farther message to Antoinette,

Yours,
Louis."

Deeply agitated, Mrs. D'Aulnay perused and re-perused this painful letter, and then, suddenly starting up, hastened to her cousin's room. The latter, who had thrown herself on the bed about an hour previous, was lying motionless, her eyes listlessly fixed on the pale rays of light streaming in between the parting of the curtains, her face looking as wan as that chill, pale light itself.

"Antoinette darling, I have something terrible to tell you. Are you strong enough to bear it?" tremblingly questioned Mrs. D'Aulnay.

Neither the warning of coming evil, contained in this mysterious announcement, nor the evident agitation of the speaker, aroused anything like anxiety or emotion in Antoinette. She was too ill in body and mind at the moment for that.

"Well, child," sharply continued Mrs. D'Aulnay, with an irritability springing from her own intense agitation, "have you no question to ask, no wish to enquire farther? It concerns chiefly yourself, or rather one nearly related to you. 'Tis of Audley Sternfield I would speak."

"What of him?" languidly questioned the girl.

"There, read for yourself," and she placed Louis's letter in her cousin's hands. "But Antoinette, darling, for Heaven's sake be calm: do not faint or go into hysterics."

The latter did neither, but her cheek turned to an ashy hue, and her very lips became white as she read. The letter perused, she sprang from her couch, and, without a moment's thought or hesitation, proceeded to dress.

"Why this hurry? Where are you going?" asked Mrs. D'Aulnay.

"To poor Audley," was the whispered reply.

"Have you taken leave of your senses, child? How do you know where he is, or even whether he is still living?"

"I must ask, find out. They have probably brought him to his quarters."

"And do you mean to say that you, a young girl, will seek him in his own rooms?"

"But you will come with me, Lucille?" was the imploring rejoinder.

"You are certainly out of your mind, poor child," and Mrs. D'Aulnay's accents betrayed both irritation and compassion. "Why all Montreal would ring with it to-morrow if we were to do such a thing. Our names would be in every one's mouth."

"So be it, Lucille: I shall go alone."

"You shall do no such thing. After quarrelling and disagreeing with that unfortunate Sternfield ever since he wedded you, about the preservation of your fair name, are you going to uselessly, recklessly forfeit it now?"

"'Tis my duty; and whatever be the consequences, I must go."

"But you do not love, you do not even like him, thoughtless child,"

"Oh, the more reason that I should seek his dying bed without delay. Alas! remorse is busy enough at my heart already, without my adding farther to its weight."

"But what good can you do him?" persisted Mrs. D'Aulnay.

"My presence may smooth, may solace him. Would you have him die," and a convulsive shudder ran through her frame, "with anger towards me in his heart, perhaps curses on his lips, as might happen if I kept away from him, forgetful of his claims and my duties?"

"Well, at least wait awhile. Mr. D'Aulnay is out, but I expect him in every moment, and I will then boldly ask him to accompany us."

But Antoinette had no intention of wasting priceless moments, any one of which might be Sternfield's last on earth, in waiting for a chance that might in the end fail her, and, hastily completing her toilette after her cousin's departure, she stole softly down the back staircase, and thence through the narrow passage which led to the out-houses and court-yard. As she had partly hoped, she saw one of the servants lounging about the stable-door, and in a low tone she told him to harness one of the horses to the plain light vehicle usually employed by Mr. D'Aulnay. In a short while it was ready; she got in, and they quietly passed through the gate without attracting the notice of any of the household, save one of the maids, who saw nothing very unusual in the fact of Miss De Mirecourt's going out at so early an hour in the morning; her destination, as the girl at once decided, being of course to church.

"Now," thought Antoinette, pressing her hand to her aching head, "my first step must be to call at Doctor Manby's, and, though he will probably be with poor Audley, I may learn from some of his people where the latter is."

Arrived at the quiet boarding-house which Doctor Manby made his home, she was told he had gone to Major

Sternfield's quarters, to attend the latter, who had been dangerously wounded that morning in a duel.

Major Sternfield, and three or four of his brother officers, occupied a plain, though comfortable, stone house, situated towards the east end of the city, now included in that portion which we call the Quebec Suburbs.[119] A small garden, environed by a wall, whose rough masonry was concealed in great part by the spreading maples that kindly drooped over it, sloped from the back of the building towards the bank of the broad, blue St. Lawrence, from which it was divided by a very narrow road. Directly in front lay the graceful, picturesque island of St. Helen's, then belonging to the Barons De Longueuil,[120] affording a pleasant resting-place to the eye, when weary of dwelling on the sparkling, dancing surface of the river.

Before the door of this residence, Mrs. D'Aulnay's coachman drew up the reeking, panting horse, which he had driven at a merciless pace, moved by Antoinette's unceasing and urgent appeals. A terrible fear had taken possession of the young girl's heart, that she would arrive too late—arrive, but to learn that the man to whom she had sworn life-long love and fidelity had passed from earth, hating and cursing her. Without waiting for assistance, she sprang to the ground, and, heedless of the amazed looks of a couple of soldiers, officers' servants, who were loitering about the door-steps, plied the knocker with what strength her trembling fingers permitted.

A soldier opened it, and she hastily exclaimed, "I wish to see Major Sternfield. Show me to his room immediately."

Lounging in the hall, with a cigar in his mouth, stood the Honorable Percy Delaval, and had Medusa herself

[119] The Quebec Suburbs were an area just east of downtown Montreal (initially between Bonsecours Street and Place Viger and then extending farther east).

[120] St. Helen's Island is an island in the St. Lawrence River, today the home of several tourist attractions. It was sold to the government by the Longueuil family in 1818.

suddenly appeared on the threshold, enquiring for the sick man, he could not have looked more utterly astounded. In an adjoining room, the door of which was open, two other officers were seated, and the expression of intense astonishment that suddenly overspread their features rivalled the wonder depicted on Lieutenant Delaval's countenance.

"Do you hear me? I wish to see Major Sternfield," repeated the new comer, with feverish agitation.

The man hesitated, fearing to introduce so unusual a visitant, without, at least, previously announcing her to the patient.

Antoinette, chafing at this additional delay, instantly turned to Mr. Delaval, and entreatingly exclaimed:

"You know me. Tell him to bring me at once to Major Sternfield."

"Certainly, Miss De Mirecourt," rejoined the young man, with an embarrassment which contrasted strangely with the young girl's fearless earnestness. "Certainly. Here, sirrah,[121] show this lady immediately to Major Sternfield's room. I take all responsibility upon myself."

Of course the man obeyed, and Antoinette followed him with trembling limbs up the steep, narrow staircase.

"Well, I call this a case!" whispered the young honorable to his two brother officers, who had joined him in the hall as soon as Antoinette had disappeared. "A young lady who would do that in England would certainly be tabooed."

"And that poor girl will just as certainly be tabooed here," rejoined one of his companions. "They are not more indulgent to woman's weaknesses in Canada than they are at home."

"I can scarcely believe the evidence of my own senses," said a third, a clever, gentlemanly man, whom Antoinette had often met at Mrs. D'Aulnay's. "I repeat, I can scarcely

[121] An obsolete form of address for someone younger (a boy) or of inferior rank.

believe it, for Miss De Mirecourt was such a gentle, modest little girl, the very last one I would have thought capable of venturing on such a step."

"Oh, love works miracles, Thornley,—changes people's very natures sometimes."

"Sternfield is a lucky dog," groaned young Delaval. "Living or dying, he always contrives to make a sensation. No danger of any of us, if we were at the last gasp to-morrow, having such an angel visitant."

"Well, poor fellow, it will not do him much good," resumed Captain Thornley. "He is almost beyond earthly consolation now. And I must say, that I for one do not think the less of the true-hearted girl who has had courage enough to brave smiles and sneers, in order that she might bid a last farewell to the man she loved."

"But I really do not think she loved him. She showed him no very decided marks of preference; and I have seen her sit near him for a half-hour at a time, with a look so cold, a glance as distant, as if she were made of marble."

"Oh, that was perhaps put on. At any rate, she has just given proof of a love surpassing that of most modern young ladies."

But we will leave the group to their discussion, and follow the object of it on her way."

Chapter XXXII.

Arrived at the landing-place, the soldier who acted as guide silently indicated a door, and then, as if fearing to venture farther, disappeared. Antoinette, faint, sick with agitation, knocked hurriedly, though lightly. It was opened by Doctor Ormsby, the clergyman who had performed the marriage-service for herself and Sternfield.

"Does he still live?" she gasped, looking wildly up into the kind, though sad face that met hers.

"Yes, but his hours are numbered," he whispered, glancing sorrowfully towards the bed, on which, ghastly and deathlike, Sternfield lay.

"Oh, Audley, my husband!" sobbed Antoinette, suddenly springing to his side, and sinking on her knees beside the couch, careless in that supreme moment who might be there to learn the long jealously-guarded secret of her breast; unconscious that another, and that other, Cecil Evelyn, stood at a distant window, listening awe-struck, spell-bound, to that strange confession. Every thought or fear of hers then was absorbed in the overwhelming consciousness that the man who had been the bane, the curse of her life, but to whom nevertheless she belonged by the holiest of earthly ties, lay there before her, dying.

With an effort of strength, wonderful in his exhausted state, the wounded man raised himself on his elbow, and gazed at her a moment with a look of intense astonishment, which speedily changed to an expression of passionate anger; then he hoarsely said:

"Away, hypocrite, away, mocking dissembler! How dare you utter the word husband? Have you ever been wife to me in aught but name? Have you ever shown me wifely duty, love, or submission?"

"Audley, Audley," she wailed, "be merciful, be just. Embitter not this solemn moment by cruel upbraidings."

"Why have you come?" he interrupted, in a still harsher voice. "Is it to gloat over my dying agonies, and to assure yourself by witnessing them, that you are really free at last? It is not love that has brought you; for if one spark of that feeling for me had glowed in your heart, you would not have mocked at my prayers and tenderness, trampled on my rights and claims, as you have so insolently done, since the hour I placed the wedding-ring on your finger."

"But whose was the fault?" she asked, with clasped hands and streaming eyes. "Did I not tell you that the instant you would acknowledge me for your wife before the world, and have our marriage solemnized again, without which my creed and belief told me it was not lawfully completed, I was ready to follow you to the ends of the earth."

"Mere hair-splitting," he sneered. "No girl, it was not that, but it was because the short-lived fancy that had led you to consent to our secret union, had died out as suddenly as it had arisen."

"Forgive me if I interfere," said Doctor Ormsby, advancing, moved alike by compassion for the agonized suffering depicted in the girl's colorless face, and with anxiety for the unchristian state of feeling into which the dying man had lapsed. "Forgive me if I interfere; but as the clergyman who solemnized that marriage, which has been, alas! so fruitful in misery to both, perhaps I may have some slight claim on your mutual attention and confidence."

Here Colonel Evelyn, suddenly recovering from the stupor of astonishment into which this singular dialogue had plunged him, and becoming at the same time awake to the grave impropriety of his remaining there, a witness to an interview of so strange and delicate a nature, stole from the room, closing the door noiselessly behind him; and as he passed through the hall, the loungers there wondered much what had occurred in the sick chamber to move Evelyn's iron nature so greatly, and to leave such traces of deep agitation on a countenance usually impassible as marble.

"May I speak, Sternfield?" gently questioned Doctor Ormsby, seeking to soothe the fiercely roused passions of the wounded man.

"Say on," was the sullen rejoinder. "What I could listen to from no other earthly being, I can bear from you."

"Well, my dear friend, it seems to me that you are severe, nay, unjust towards this young girl," and he kindly laid his hand on the shoulder of the still kneeling Antoinette. "I remember well her telling you what she has just said, and calling on me to witness it."

"The old story, ever the old story," peevishly ejaculated Sternfield, turning aside his head. "Go home, girl; go home: and you, Doctor, leave me in peace. I am growing weary of you both."

As he spoke, a deadly pallor stole over his face, and Antoinette, terribly started, sprang to her feet.

"Do not be alarmed," Doctor Ormsby reassuringly exclaimed. "'Tis a temporary faintness. He had a similar attack shortly before you entered, when Dr. Manby was here. Here are restoratives."

Their united efforts soon brought back something like life to Sternfield's pallid features; and the clergyman, fearing the sight of Antoinette might renew his agitation, motioned her to place herself behind a high screen which stood in one end of the room.

After a moment, the dying man glanced restlessly around him, and then muttered, "Where is she gone, my wife, Mrs. Sternfield? Ha! ha! Doctor," and he laughed in a ghastly manner. "Let me at least give her the title once before he who conferred it will be turned to lifeless clay."

"You told her to go home, just now."

"But why did she listen to me?" he retorted. "Why did she go? Of course she was tired of so dull an affair as a death-bed, and having made *son apparition*,[122] as Mrs. D'Aulnay would say, prudently retired."

"Shall I send for her again?"

"No, by——: I am not fallen so low as that. Had she remained, it would, though I hate almost to acknowledge it, have been a solace, a comfort to me."

"I have not left you, Audley. I am still here," said Antoinette, timidly, as she emerged from her retreat, and approached the bed.

Something like an expression of satisfaction stole over his features, imposing still in their death-struck beauty; but when she faltered out "Dear Audley, may I remain beside you?" he answered, with the olden sneer, which habit had rendered almost natural to his handsome lip, "Since it pleases you to act the part of a sister of charity, I will not say you nay. It amuses me, though, to see you shower on my dying hours, attentions and tender cares which you never vouchsafed my living ones."

She bowed her head submissively,—no taunts of his could move her now,—and, after a few moments' silence, gently said:

"Had you not better try to sleep? I will watch beside you. Are there any medicines to be given?"

"Pshaw! I will take none. I told Manby so. My case is beyond human skill, and why should I torture my palate with any vile drugs or mixtures?"

Knowing that insisting farther would only irritate him uselessly, she drew a chair close to his couch, and silently seated herself. After quietly watching her for some time, he suddenly exclaimed:

[122] French for having made an appearance.

"So you have fairly installed yourself here as my nurse—determinedly taken up your post! Are you aware of what the world will say, of what men will think?"

"Oh, dear Audley, what is the world to us?" she sadly said. "Do not think of it. Do not torment yourself about its opinions."

"Aye! it is nothing to me now; but to you, girl, it is everything. Why, before two hours, this mad step of yours will be repeated, with exaggerations and commentaries in every corner of the city; and the fair name, of which you have been so jealously careful, will be at every one's mercy."

"If so," and the mournful eyes and voice became yet more sad, "'twill be but the just punishment of my past folly: I have sinned, and I must expiate my fault."

"You have done so severely enough already," he rejoined, the first approach to anything like feeling which he had yet shown, softening his voice. "I have not spared you; and few young brides have ever passed through as bitter and ordeal as yourself. Well, the close of my rule and the dawn of your liberty are both at hand, sooner by thirty or forty years than you might have dared to hope for."

"Audley, talk not thus. Do not agitate yourself unnecessarily—"

"Stop lecturing, child: here comes a higher authority than yourself."

As he spoke, Doctor Manby entered the room. The new-comer's amazement on seeing Antoinette seated at his patient's bed-side, was almost ludicrous.

"God bless my soul, Miss De Mirecourt!" he ejaculated, involuntarily starting back.

"Not so, Doctor, but Mrs. Audley Sternfield," said the patient, with a forced laugh, that grated most painfully on all ears. "Nay, do not stare, man, as if you were moon-struck. Our good friend, Ormsby, here, who performed the interesting ceremony, can corroborate my words. Speak out, fair bride. Do you deny my ownership?"

Antoinette's cheek had turned from white to deep scarlet, and then to white again, at this address; but though her eyes were welling over with tears, she contrived to rejoin, with tolerable calmness, "I do not seek to deny it, Audley. Why should I? It is you, not I, who have always insisted on keeping it secret."

"Well, I acknowledge it now; so you see, Doctor, I shall, at least, have something about a young and interesting widow to round off gracefully the paragraph announcing my decease. Do not look so reproachfully at me, Manby," he continued, as Antoinette, cruelly wounded by the mocking strain in which he persisted in addressing her, hurriedly rose, and turned away in tears. "You know the proverb, 'ruling habit, strong in death';[123] and I have been so much accustomed to torment and worry my bride from the first, that I can not resist the temptation even now. But sit now, if you have sufficiently recovered from your amazement to do so, and tell me how many more hours this thread-like pulse of mine promises me."

Scarcely recovered yet from his first overwhelming astonishment, the physician took the chair which Antoinette had just vacated; but in the midst of all his bewilderment, he was conscious of a deep feeling of indignation excited by the mocking manner of Sternfield towards the unhappy young creature whom he called by the sacred title of wife.

"Well, speak out, man! What does my pulse say? Ah, you need not mince the matter. I am no school-boy to be frightened by a few hours' advance or delay. You will not answer? Never mind: that shake of your head tells enough. I supposed that I am booked to start on my last journey before to-night."

The physician made no reply. He could not conscientiously contradict him; for, despite the strength of

[123] "Ruling passion strong in death" (from Alexander Pope's "Epistle I on the Knowledge and Characters of Men," III, 263).

the wounded man's voice, and his fluency of utterance, the faint, irregular pulse told that sudden reaction, followed by the *end*, was at hand.

"I can do no more for you, Sternfield," he said, hurriedly rising to his feet, his late feeling of irritation completely merged in compassion. "A few drops from this vial when you feel faint is all I can prescribe; at least, all that would be useful to you. Good bye. God bless you!" and after a long, friendly grasp of the hand, the kind-hearted Doctor hurried away, more agitated and grieved than he cared to show.

For some time after his departure, the patient maintained a moody silence which he at length broke by sullenly asking, "Do you know, girl, whose vile hand laid me here? Of course you do. It was that smooth-faced country lover of yours. If I have not spoken of him before, 'tis because at the very thought of him curses rush to my lips, throng through my brain. But I have a word to say to you about him. It is this: He may hereafter return, hereafter renew his suit, and I would have your solemn promise ere I enter eternity that you will never lend him a favoring ear."

"Dear Audley, could you think that the hand stained by a husband's blood—"

"Pshaw! no girlish sentiment. I want not protestations nor speeches, but a promise, aye! an oath," he added more fiercely, "that you will never be aught nearer to him in any circumstances, than what you have hitherto been?"

"Willingly," she eagerly rejoined. "With heart and soul."

"Then, kiss that," and he indicated by a look the chain to which was attached her small gold cross. "The promise you made me once before on that, has been so religiously kept, that I can put faith in any other, framed in a similar manner."

She drew forth the cross, and with an earnest solemn look kissed it.

"'Tis well, Antoinette: I can die now without cursing him and hating you."

"Oh, Audley, my husband," she entreatingly exclaimed, presenting the cross to his lips, "kiss it also; not as I have done, merely to add solemnity to an earthly promise, but as the blessed token of salvation, of future pardon and peace."

"No, no, Antoinette," and he faintly smiled. "'Tis too late to try proselytizing now. I have settled my spiritual affairs already with Doctor Ormsby, who has read prayers to me, and prevailed on me, though with great difficulty, I must acknowledge, to refrain from heaping curses on the wretch who has cut short my life."

"But it will do you no harm to allow me to say a prayer at your bed-side."

"I am here, my dear young lady, to accomplish that grave duty which is peculiarly my own," exclaimed Doctor Ormsby, in a firm though gentle voice, as he advanced towards them. "I have hitherto refrained from intruding on you, knowing that you must have much to say to each other; but if you wish for prayer or reading now, Major Sternfield, I am ready."

"Of course you are, Doctor," rejoined Sternfield, with a somewhat equivocal smile. "It would be a terribly mortifying affair if I should slip from your pastoral care at the last moment, into the pale of Rome."

"Oh, dearest Audley, do not talk so lightly, so mockingly of all that is most solemn and sacred on earth. If your heart leans to the faith of my fathers, do not allow—"

"Tush! child, enough of such folly! I will die in the creed in which I was born and brough up."

"Then Doctor Ormsby will read you some prayers at once: your time, my dear, dear husband, is very short."

"Do not commence croaking, Antoinette: it will do me no good. Doctor, I am ready, but excuse my saying I hope you will not be too diffuse."

"Your present state of weakness will prevent that. Believe me, I will not overtask your strength."

At that moment a knock was heard at the door of the apartment, which Doctor Ormsby instantly opened. "A messenger for you, Miss De Mirecourt," he said.

Antoinette glanced through the half-open door-way, and instantly recognized Jeanne; so whispering to Sternfield that she would return in a few moments, she went out to the new-comer.

The latter told her in a low tone that Mrs. D'Aulnay had sent her with strict injunctions not to go back till Antoinette should return with her. "But, *mon Dieu*,[124] Miss De Mirecourt, what does all this mean?" enquired the old servant, drawing her farther into the passage so that the sound of their whispering might not disturb the clergyman who had commenced reading aloud. "Mr. D'Aulnay, always so quiet, is like a madman. He says you have disgraced us all, and that your father will die of grief and shame; and has been scolding my mistress all morning, saying that she is to blame as much as yourself,—he, that to my knowledge never said a downright cross word to her since they became man and wife. *Madame* at last told him that if you had gone alone to see Major Sternfield, you had a right to do so, for that you were his wife. It was that stupid Paul, who, on being asked by Mr. D'Aulnay as he met him driving into the yard, where he had been, told at once. But is it true, dear young lady, what Madame said?"

"Yes, Jeanne," said the girl, sadly. "Major Sternfield, who is now dying in yon room, is my wedded husband. I was married to him secretly."

"Oh, Miss Antoinette! Miss Antoinette!" ejaculated the old woman, clasping her hands in overwhelming distress. "I could not have believed that a pious young lady, so carefully brought up as yourself, could ever have consented to such

[124] French for "my God."

a thing. What will poor Mr. De Mirecourt and Madame Gérard feel? What will the wicked slanderous world say?"

Antoinette shuddered. "Alas, I have mourned over my folly bitterly enough, but that has not repaired it. I have still a long expiation before me."

"And how long will you stay here, poor dear child?"

"'Tis all is over if he will let me," was the faltering reply.

"Ah me, Miss Antoinette, of what service can your presence be to him now? Come home, come home. How unseemly it is for a young lady of your age to be alone in this house with none but soldiers and gay young officers around you."

"Jeanne, if my dear and much-wronged father were to come himself to bring me away, I could not, would not go."

"Well, I suppose 'tis no use arguing with those whose minds are made up not to see the right; but it was an evil day for us all that we caught the first sight of a scarlet coat in our quiet home. Go in now, Miss Antoinette, dear; I will just sit down here: for that handsome Major, who always looked so scornfully at me, would'nt like perhaps to see me in his dying room."

"But, Jeanne, you will feel ill at ease here,—so many strange faces passing and repassing."

"And what harm can they do beyond staring at me, and what does an old withered woman like me care for their curious looks? It is'nt like if it was your own pretty face they were peering at. Go in, go in, and call me whenever I can be of any use. I will sit here till then."

Doctor Ormsby was still reading when Antoinette re-entered, and the young girl knelt down in a corner of the apartment and poured forth in silence her own earnest prayers to Heaven in behalf of that soul trembling on the verge of eternity. Meantime, a sort of drowsy torpor was stealing over Sternfield; and when Doctor Ormsby, having finished his ministrations, addressed a few words to him, his answer was confused and almost unintelligible.

"I must leave you for a time," said the clergyman, closing his book; "and I think, my dear young lady, you had better bring that respectable woman in, provided she is willing to assist you. If poor Sternfield should recover his consciousness, which is improbable, she can leave the room if her presence annoys him. I will return in a few hours."

Acting on this advice, Antoinette brought in Jeanne; but unwilling to run any risk of annoying the patient in case he should suddenly recover consciousness, she pointed to the latter to seat herself behind the screen which had already afforded temporary concealment to herself. Slowly the time wore on, no sound breaking that deep, hushed silence save the laborious breathing of the dying man. Prompted by a delicacy and kindliness of feeling that did them honor, the other occupants of the house permitted no loud voice, or hurried, careless footstep, to intrude on that heavy stillness.

Shortly after noon, a single knock was heard, and Jeanne hastened to answer it. It was a soldier bearing a tray containing some simple refreshments which he said, "Doctor Manby ordered him in the morning to bring to the sick room."

"I begin to think in a kindlier way of these redcoats than I have ever yet done," inwardly soliloquized Jeanne, as she arranged the things on a small table, and carried the latter close to Antoinette. "Ah, I fear me, yon handsome-faced one was the worst of the lot," and she glanced towards the calm statue-like countenance of the sleeper.

Earnestly, anxiously she pressed the young girl to taste some of the refreshments she placed before her; but the heart of the latter was too heavy for that; and she was obliged at length to remove the untouched tray, consoling herself by the reflection that if her young lady did not eat, it was not at least owing to that most deplorable of all earthly reasons, the having nothing on which to exercise her powers of appetite.

The sun had set behind thick banks of clouds, leaving here and there a sullen crimson streak, and the twilight was stealing rapidly on, its gray shadows rendering still more wan and ghastly that white upturned face lying so still and motionless on its pillow. Suddenly it stirred, the heavy eyelids parted, and Sternfield's voice, so hoarse and changed as to be scarcely recognizable, exclaimed, "Are you there, Antoinette?"

A gentle pressure of his hand, a softly whispered word of kindness, answered him.

"Determined to see me through the last stage of my journey? It must be near its close, for my sight is growing strangely dim."

"The twilight is coming on, dear Audley. It may be that."

"No, 'tis that twilight which will never know another sunrise. Well, 'tis not the death a soldier would have chosen, but it might have been worse. I am at least free from pain."

"And you have had time, dear husband, to reconcile yourself with God?"

"Yes, yes, and to dictate a short letter of farewell to the two fair-haired sisters living in that quiet town in Warwickshire in which I was born. Ah! I had not dreamed a year ago, of finding a grave amid the snows of Canada; above all, a grave at so early a period of my pleasant life. Perhaps it would have been better for me had I never exacted that promise of secrecy from you; but you had told me so often our marriage was not lawfully completed, that I dreaded such was really the case, and feared if our secret became known, that your friends would prevail on you to seek a divorce. Meantime, whilst waiting thus securely for the day which would put you in undisturbed possession of your mother's fortune, many things favorable to me might have happened: your father's death—in this solemn hour, I speak openly, Antoinette—or other circumstances which would have placed yourself and reputation completely in my power. But my dreams, like my life, are at an end."

A long silence, broken only by Antoinette's sobs, followed.

"Listen to me, child; bend nearer, for I have that to say to you which I once thought my proud lips would never say to mortal. Your patient gentleness has touched me at last, and before I go hence, I would ask you to pardon me for all that I have made you suffer, for all my past cruelty and injustice?"

"From my heart," she whispered, stooping over, and pressing her lips to that death-damp brow. "May God forgive me all my own errors as freely as I forgive you."

He faintly smiled, and his fingers tightened on the small hand that rested in his own. The twilight gloom deepened. Colder and colder became his clasp, darker and darker grew the shadows round his eyes and mouth; and when his pale young watcher, at length startled by his fixed gaze, loudly uttered his name, no look or word gave response.

"Jeanne, here, come here," she shrieked.

The woman hurriedly drew near, and, after a glance at that marble face, she gently disengaged the girl's fingers from the icy clasp in which they were still twined, and whispered, "How peacefully he passed away!"

A wild, hysterical fit of sobbing gave some relief to Antoinette's overtasked feelings; and a moment after Doctor Ormsby entered the room.

"Take her home, poor child," he compassionately said, raising her from the bed on which she had thrown herself. "Take her home: she has been sorely tried. I will see to everything."

Passively, almost unconsciously, Antoinette yielded to Jeanne's guidance, and suffered herself to be dressed, and placed in the vehicle which one of the officer's servants had procured. Arrived at home, the kind-hearted woman undressed her now almost helpless charge, and put her to bed; previously warning Mrs. D'Aulnay that she must on no account even enter her cousin's room that night. Neither all these tender cares nor the calming potion which she passively took, sufficed to chase away that grim shadow of impending sickness which was brooding over her pillow. From a heavy lethargic sleep, she awoke up delirious. A physician was sent for, and the startled household learned that she was dangerously ill of brain-fever.

Chapter XXXIII.

Whilst the young girl lay on that sick bed, unconscious of every thing passing around her, battling with the strength of youth against death and disease, the mortal remains of the handsome and fascinating Major Sternfield were committed to their last home. Very busy were gossiping tongues with his name and that of the hapless Antoinette; and had the latter but known half of the false rumors which malice or thoughtlessness invented and repeated, it would in all likelihood have prevented convalescence from ever revisiting her sick couch. Everything of such a nature however was carefully kept from her, whilst watchful care, medical skill, and judicious nursing were all enlisted in her cause; and after eight or ten days of anxious suspense, she was pronounced out of immediate danger. Wofully weak and altered was she though, and friends and attendants ominously shook their heads and whispered each other that she would never get wholly well.

Mr. De Mirecourt had hastened to Montreal immediately on hearing of his daughter's illness; and whatever may have been his first feelings of anger and humiliation on learning the sad tale of her secret marriage, her severe and dangerous attack of sickness, calling forth his deep parental tenderness, shielded her not only then, but even after recovery had set in, from rebuke or reproach. About two months after Major Sternfield's death, one afternoon that the invalid had yielded to Mrs. D'Aulnay's entreaties, and ventured into the latter's cheerful morning apartment, her hostess was summoned to the drawing-room to see a visitor. She soon returned, and coaxingly exclaimed:

"My little Antoinette, an old friend prays for permission to see you. 'Tis Colonel Evelyn. Will you not admit him?"

How rapidly Antoinette's color came and went, how wildly her heart throbbed at that name; and Mrs. D'Aulnay, taking advantage of her involuntary silence as implying consent, hastened away. A moment after, a firm, manly tread resounded through the ball,—a mist arising from weakness or agitation swam before Antoinette's eyes, and, when self-possession returned, she was alone with Colonel Evelyn, both her hands in his, and his kind, friendly glance bent earnestly on her countenance.

"You have been very, very ill," he exclaimed, in accents as gentle as his looks.

"Yes, but I am rapidly recovering," she rejoined, with a desperate effort at composure, and withdrawing her hands as she spoke.

A silence followed, silence almost insufferable to the nervous, agitated girl, for her companion's earnest searching gaze was still fixed upon her, and beneath it she felt her color come and go, and her eyes droop in painful confusion. At length he resumed in tones whose involuntary tremor betrayed that he too was moved in no small degree:

"Will you pardon me, if, at the risk of agitating you, I allude to the painful past and to that strange secret which brough so much misery to more than one? Was it—was your marriage with Audley Sternfield your only cause for rejecting my own suit?"

Antoinette became deadly pale, and, clasping her hands to her breast as if to keep down her deep agitation, she faltered:

"Colonel Evelyn! Do not speak of my past madness till at least I have acquired sufficient calmness to bear allusion to it. How you must wonder at my folly, condemn and despise me!"

His only reply was to clasp her quickly, closely to his breast, whilst he whispered, "My much-tried, long-suffering Antoinette! Mine own, at last!"

Ah, no farther need of disguise then, and, in broken accents and with panting breath, she faltered forth her gratitude, her joy, her happiness. Much had they to say to each other; and with a childish truthfulness, for which that stern proud man could have knelt and worshipped her, she recounted the history of that long period of dark and bitter trial. True, she hesitated when she came to the part in which he himself had become an actor, when she had to acknowledge how very dear he became to her heart; but still bravely she went on, telling her ceaseless struggles against that new-born love, her temptations and her sufferings; but sparing all the while, as much as was possible, the name of him who had wrought her all that misery.

Her tale concluded, she bowed her head on the arm of the sofa, but he tenderly drew it towards his bosom, whispering, "Here is your resting-place henceforth. O, my beloved, as gold out of the furnace, so have you come purified and perfected out of your fiery trial—all that I had first thought, first hoped you were."

"But, Colonel Evelyn," and she raised her head with a sudden anxious start, whilst the bright rich glow on her cheek faded to a marble pallor, "report must have said so many and such bitter things of me. How can you so fearlessly brave the world's judgment, and make the object of its censure, perhaps scorn, your wife?"

"I have long since ceased to care for the world's opinions or its judgments, and certainly I will never suffer it to influence me where the happiness of my life is at stake. Do not worry your mind with trifles or phantoms, my Antoinette. Thanks to that merciful God whom I so sinfully ignored in the dark days of life's adversity, and to whose love and service your counsels and examples will guide me back, the future lies happy and bright before use. Your father's consent is already obtained." Antoinette joyfully started. "Yes, before renewing my suit to yourself, I thought it but right to speak to him. Without much demur he consented; frankly assuring me at the same time, that, had not circumstances banished Mr. Beauchesne from his native land for ever, he could never have listened affirmatively to my prayer."

"Oh, Colone Evelyn, I feel almost too blessed," she whispered, tears swelling from her eyes despite every effort. "Leave me now awhile, for I am almost giddy with excess of happiness."

"Not happier, my own, than I am," and he tenderly raised to his lips the hand on the second finger of which Sternfield's wedding-ring still glistened. As his glance involuntarily rested on it, the girl's face deeply, painfully flushed, but he softly whispered:

"Another will replace it, beloved. One which will bring you, let us humbly hope, more happiness that it has ever done. But I must leave you for awhile now, for this interview has been an agitating one, and I must be careful of my new-found treasure."

Rapidly to her room sped Antoinette to give vent in tears, in earnest eager prayers of thanksgiving, to the joy which was filling her young heart to overflowing. Ere she had yet half recovered her calmness, a slight tap came to her door, and Mrs. D'Aulnay, half sobbing, half laughing, folded her in her arms.

"Is it not like a romance, a fairy tale, my poor little Antoinette?" she exclaimed. I have this minute come from Uncle De Mirecourt, who is in the library with that darling Colonel Evelyn, and everything is going on as smoothly as heart could desire.

"And my dear father has really given a cheerful consent?"

"Well he might, child," was the significant reply. "He knew that after the *éclat*[125] accompanying Sternfield's death

[125] Unlike the English loanword, the French *éclat* can mean "scandal."

and the promulgation of the secret which had previously been so carefully kept, he might find it very difficult to get a suitable husband for you. Colonel Evelyn's conduct too was so manly, so honorable throughout. Whilst you were still struggling in the early stage of your terrible attack of fever, he called here almost wild on account of your danger. Your poor father, bowed to the very dust with humiliation and grief, chanced to be in the room into which he was shewn by the half-distracted Justine, who, in common with the rest of the household, seemed to be at her wit's end at the time. The two gentlemen exchanged a few words together, having become acquainted during Uncle De Mirecourt's memorable winter drive to Quebec; and I know not exactly what brought it about, but Colonel Evelyn laid open his heart to your father, exposed his fears, his hopes, his feelings, and received the latter's sanction to his suit if you ever recovered, which at that time was indeed very doubtful. We all agreed we would not agitate you by speaking on the subject till you were sufficiently recovered to let your lover plead his own cause. And now what do you say to my matchmaking talents? Two husbands in the short space of one year! All the young girls in the country will be wild to partake of my hospitality. But here comes that dear old tyrant of a Doctor. He will be puzzled by the rapid rate at which your pulse must be beating now."

Despite the opinions of friends and acquaintances, who had obligingly decided that Antoinette should at once enter a convent, or retire immediately to Valmont, there to live and die in the strictest seclusion, she was publicly united a year after to Colonel Evelyn. It is hard to say whether surprise or indignation predominated; and more than one fair lady expressed unmeasured wonder and contempt at Colonel Evelyn's mad infatuation for a girl who had rendered herself so notorious as the bride had done.

Over Antoinette's future destiny we will not linger. Happiness soon restored to that youthful frame the health which had commenced to give way so rapidly under her early cares and trials. To her devoted, idolizing husband she brought that unclouded domestic felicity he had for so many years of his life despaired of ever knowing, and in assuring his happiness, she assured her own.

Louis Beauchesne, who, through the connivance of friends, was fortunate enough to escape from Canada, notwithstanding the strict search instituted for him, never returned to it. He was kindly received in France, which welcomed at that time with open arms the Canadians who chose to leave their native land for her own sunny soil. After a time he formed new ties and friendships which brought him happiness, though they never obliterated from his memory those of his youth and childhood.

The philosophical Mr. D'Aulnay returned with renewed ardor to his books and folios, after the strange period of trouble and bewilderment which had hovered for a time over his household. His fair wife smiled, dressed, and flirted as of old, ever willing to help any of her young lady friends in their love-affairs, but entertaining to the last moment of her career, a prudent horror of secret marriages.

THE END.

A School-Girl Friendship

A School-Girl Friendship

CHAPTER I.

The school bell had just summoned the pupils of Miss Judson's select and aristocratic female seminary, situated in one of Montreal's widest and shadiest streets, to their respective class rooms. Slowly and lingeringly—for the day was oppressively warm—they filed past into the large, bare-looking apartments, where so many weary hours of the long summer day were passed. Without unnecessary delay, for the Lady Principal of the establishment was a strict disciplinarian, they seated themselves at their desks, some with gay mischievous faces, others with weary, discontented looks; whilst the teachers, rigid and formal, sat upright at their different posts, showing but little indulgence to the indolent or ignorant.

When the afternoon hours, with their tiresome hum of study and repetition, were over, and the pupils had joyously closed their desks and left them, two girls still remained standing in an angle near a window, engaged in low, earnest converse. One was a tall bright blonde of eighteen, dressed with a careful elegance that had often drawn down on her cold reproof from Miss Judson, that lady regarding a marked love of dress as almost incompatible with love of study; her companion was a slight delicate girl, attired with great simplicity, and apparently two or three years younger, though in reality of the same age.

"How is it, Charlotte," enquired the latter, with a tired, discouraged look, "that though I studied this weary task," and she glanced towards a book she held in her hand, "for nearly an hour yesterday evening, how is it that you, who read a novel during that time, repeated the lesson so well to-day, and received praise, whilst I reaped only disgrace and rebuke? I cannot understand it at all."

"Oh, you darling simpleton, did you not see that I had placed loose leaves containing the task between my atlas and handkerchief, where I could fortify my memory with a peep when necessary; said leaves, to deepen the measure of my iniquity, as that odious Miss Judson would phrase it, being torn from my book for the special purpose?"

"Surely a dishonourable action," rejoined her companion, her pale cheek slightly flushing. "I wonder that some of the girls did not tell on you."

"Because, friend Gertrude, I took good care that the hateful things should not see me do it. As for you, I do not mind, knowing that your sense of honour, or what might be called your want of sense, will not allow you to expose your friend."

"'Tis all very tiresome," sighed Gertrude, "and now, with a blinding headache, I must commence studying again."

"Go boldly to Miss Judson, saying that you are suffering, and she will let you off. You look wretchedly ill and pale to-day."

"I have not courage enough. She might tax me with pretence or indolence. Oh, how I wish the vacations were commencing this very day!"

"For the matter of fact, so do I; but, in the meantime, I shall endeavour to make life endurable by all the means in my power, honourable or not; and if you were not a silly little puss you would do the same. But to turn to pleasanter subjects than our school worries, I want you to tell me when you are to see or be seen by this newly-arrived lord of the creation to whom you have been promised in marriage, without your tastes or wishes having been in any degree consulted?"

"My last home letter told me I might expect him and papa this very week, but I do hope they will not come to-day. I feel neither well nor in spirits—"

"And consequently not in condition to make a proper impression on Mr. Arthur Rodney, the sultan to whom you find yourself promised and given. Frankly, in your place, I would never have tamely submitted to such a high-handed measure."

"There is nothing high-handed about it, Charlotte. My poor mother, with whom Mr. Rodney was a great favourite, being also a distant connection, thought she could best insure my happiness by betrothing me to him, under condition, however, that the step should be kept quiet, and that at the end of the first year that should elapse after my leaving school the engagement would be regarded as void if either party felt the slightest disinclination to fulfil it."

"Which will not be likely on your part, at least," and Miss Brookes smiled satirically. "Your suitor is rich, of good family, and possesses what must be a rare treasure, since people talk so much about it, a remarkably upright, honourable character. I only wish my future lay before me as clearly and pleasantly marked out as yours seems to be. But by the way, have you any idea what the man is like? How long is it since you last saw him?"

"Three years; about the time of poor mamma's death. He has been absent in Europe since then, and when he landed in Canada a short time since, papa wrote, telling me to soon expect them both."

"Pray let us hear what you thought of him when you did see him. I have always found you strangely reticent on this topic, considering the extent of our friendship. Do speak out frankly!"

"I saw him but very seldom, owing to the critical state of my poor mother's health at that time, which rendered me almost indifferent to everything else. I remember well though that he was handsome, cleaver,—indeed, much too good for an insignificant, plain girl like myself."

"Nonsense, Lady Gerty! You have youth, are of good family, and have had careful training. Then you have money, and though he has also a large share of the same useful commodity, your having it will not prove detrimental to your marital prospects. But what a bearish suitor he must be to not have written you a line immediately on his arrival. A Turk could not have acted worse."[1]

A vivid blush suddenly dyed Gertrude's cheek, imparting a wonderful charm to her pale, girlish face, and she unclosed her lips as if about to speak, yet still hesitated.

"Ah! little traitress, you are concealing something from me, and have been doing so all the time! Be truthful, now, if you wish me to condone your deceitful past."

"I have but little to tell. When papa wrote last I also received a few lines from Mr. Rodney, accompanied by his likeness."

"And you have never shown me either. Is this what you call friendship and confidence? Quick, tell me all, show me all, or our Damon and Pythias friendship[2] is for ever at an end."

Reluctantly Gertrude opened a morocco pocket-book and drew from it a letter and richly chased locket.[3] This latter Miss

---

[1] In 1877, when the story was published, Turkey (a former British ally) was widely condemned for atrocities committed in Bulgaria. William Ewart Gladstone (several times British prime minister) had published in 1876 the influential pamphlet *Bulgarian Horrors and the Question of the East*.

[2] Damon and Pythias were legendary best friends in ancient Greece.

[3] Morocco is a type of soft leather, usually made from goatskin; chased means embossed or engraved.

Brookes, in her eager curiosity, almost snatched from the hands of her companion, and, after gazing long and earnestly on it, closed the costly case, and returned it with the simple exclamation, "Too handsome by half!"

"Well, as I have no beauty to pride myself on, it is fortunate he has enough for both," and Gertrude smiled faintly as she spoke.

"O my poor little friend, it does not matter much, for a man with a face like his will be always too much taken up with it to think of any one else's physiognomy. Now for the letter."

"My dearest Gertrude,—Returned at length from my long wanderings, I hope to have the pleasure of soon seeing you and assuring myself that you are both well and happy. I send you my likeness, and will put in a claim in person for yours as speedily as possible. Till then, yours most devotedly,

A.R."

"What a priggish, stilted effusion!" commented Miss Brookes. "Just what I would have expected from the owner of such a face."

"It is neither one nor the other, Charlotte! Give it back to me, and let me tell you it was certainty that you would pass some unkind remark on it that prevented me showing it to you when I first received it. Do you suppose he should have written me a long diffuse love letter, knowing as he does that our epistles run a chance of being subjected first to Miss Judson's scrutiny?"

"Hoity toity, friend Gertrude, Mrs. Arthur Rodney that is to be, you are unusually warm. Already the foreshadowing of the dignity so soon to be yours has fallen upon you. But I shall endeavour to be more prudent in future, so meanwhile forgive——"

"Enough, enough, dear Charlotte! I am irritable to-day and my head is aching intolerably. Oh! I must ask leave to lie down!"

A sudden hush fell on the two girls for a tall stately figure, dressed in dark olive silk—the formidable Miss Judson herself—loomed up suddenly in the door way.

"Miss Brookes and Miss Mildmay infringing the school rules which forbid pupils remaining after hours in the class rooms! Young ladies, I shall take note of this; in the meantime you are both wanted in the drawing-room."

Gertrude naturally timid and quite overpowered by the magnificent stateliness of the speaker, ventured on no interrogation; but Charlotte, always undaunted, hoped in her sweetest and most insinuating tone that Miss Judson would permit her to enquire if it were their late fellow pupil, Miss Lewson.

"'Tis Mr. Mildmay and Mr. Rodney," was the cold, brief reply. "No unnecessary delay, young ladies! 'Tis ill breeding to keep visitors waiting," and the Lady Principal swept from the room.

"What shall I do? I cannot go down in this condition," helplessly exclaimed Gertrude, her soft gray eyes betraying more nervous anxiety than pleasure. "I must smoothe my hair, put on another frill or ribbon."

"To please His Serene Mightiness, Mr. Arthur Rodney, I suppose?" questioned Miss Brookes. "Why Gertrude, you sly little creature, I had no idea that the conquest of his priggish lover of yours was an aim so near your heart. There, there, you look well enough, indeed too good for him. If we delay another moment that old martinet, Miss Judson, will be down on us again!"

Playfully seizing her companion's hand she drew her away with her. Poor little Gertrude! how suffocatingly her heart beat, her courage sinking lower and lower till it reached its last ebb. Often had she pictured the coming interview to herself, looked forward to, longed for it; and now that the moment had arrived, she was conscious of no feeling save dismay. Very dear to her heart was Arthur Rodney and in her innocent girlish dreams he seemed a being so far above her that she scarcely dared hope, notwithstanding their betrothal, he would ever seek to win her love. Often as she had thought of him, frequently as she had pressed her lips to his likeness, she had carefully concealed within her own breast the affection with which he had inspired her, and contrary to the wont of most young ladies, rarely entertained her "bosom friend" with the subject.

Still holding Gertrude's hand Miss Brookes playfully drew her on, and arriving at the drawing-room door, threw it open. Gertrude was at once enfolded in her father's arms where she seemed to gain some degree of courage and self-possession. Then after that warm embrace, her hand was kindly grasped by a dark, stately-looking man whose keen dark eyes gazed with intense though respectful interest into hers, even while his lips uttered some simple words of friendly courtesy. The shy embarrassed girl returned but cold response, and after a time, Mr. Rodney's gaze wandered to Miss Brookes on whom it rested with admiring surprise.

What a contrast the two girls presented! On the one hand Charlotte with her graceful ease of manner and patrician bearing, regular features and bright complexion, her attractions still further enhanced by a toilet which if too elaborately elegant for a school girl, imparted nevertheless, to its fair wearer, a remarkable prestige: on the other, Gertrude, timid and shrinking in appearance, pale from emotion and recent illness, dressed with a simplicity too stiff and rigid to prove becoming; a foil in all things to her brilliant friend. Chancing to look up and see in a mirror opposite a full reflection of herself and her companion, she then and there broke down completely. Vainly Mr. Rodney addressed her kindly remark or conventional question, he obtained no reply beyond a low monosyllable, till wearied or discouraged, he turned to her friend.

Mr. Mildmay though a well-meaning, kind-hearted man, was not very penetrating in character, so he scarcely noticed his daughter's embarrassment; her whispered intimation that she was suffering from headache satisfactorily accounted for the absence of certain demonstrations of tenderness which she usually showered upon him, but of which she proved unusually chary on the present occasion. After a protracted stay the guests rose to go, promising to return early on the day appointed for the breaking up of the school whence they would all proceed together to Mildmay Lodge, Mr. Mildmay's abode, one of the handsome residences gracing the picturesque town of ——, Canada East.[4] Both girls were unusually reticent on the subject of the visit, almost tacitly avoiding it, but that evening, Charlotte whilst bending apparently over her books was weaving a rose-colored dream of which she was the heroine, her friend's affianced lover the hero; Gertrude, on her side, cried herself to sleep.

CHAPTER II.

Charlotte Brookes, left an orphan at an early age, found herself entrusted to the sole guardianship of Mr. Mildmay, a relative of her mother. She met in him a generous protector who injudiciously, perhaps, allowed her to spend a considerable portion of the small income she possessed, in purchasing the rich toilettes she so dearly loved, making up from his own purse what was necessary to pay for the costly education she was receiving at Mrs. Judson's boarding

[4] A term used between 1841 and 1867 for the Province of Quebec.

school. It was tacitly understood that she should reside with her guardian till she had attained her majority or changed her maiden state, an event that young lady was quietly determined to bring about as speedily and in as advantageous a manner to herself as possible.

Gay, handsome, winning, she had made herself very dear to Gertrude Mildmay, all the more so that she indulged at times in a certain unceremonious abrupt mode of expression or action that seemed the offspring of unwavering frankness, and which rendered the pleasant speeches and affectionate praises she generally employed, doubly welcome on account of their apparent sincerity.

The education of the girls was now nearly completed, or at least the time of probation allotted for their studies was near its close, and they were already joyously looking forward to their return to Mildmay Lodge, to enter probably on the career of frivolous pleasure to which so many young girls give themselves up on leaving school, unfortunately for that society amid which they will soon be called to fill the high and important offices of wives and mothers.

A dramatic and musical entertainment was given by Miss Judson's pupils preparatory to their final dismissal, and a leading *rôle* was assigned to Miss Brookes, she having acquired by dint of application, considerable proficiency in singing and elocution, the only two branches to which she had ever really applied herself. A secondary but still sufficiently effective part had devolved to Gertrude, with every appearance that she would acquit herself creditably; when unfortunately, just as she appeared on the temporary stage and intoned the first notes of an *aria*, well adapted to her clear sweet voice, her glance fell on her father and lover who had just entered, and were listening and watching with breathless interest. This was more than enough to put poor Gertrude's composure to flight, and in school phraseology she "broke down." An effort to resume her song only ended in her taking it up in a wrong key, and the first verse finished, she retreated to her seat, overwhelmed with shame and mortification, Miss Judson glaring at her meanwhile with a stony look of concentrated anger which ought to have made Gertrude thankful, if she had not been too perturbed to remark it, that the term of the Lady Principal's authority was at hand.

It was now Miss Brookes' turn, and her keen eye also discovered, near the door, the two gentlemen whose entrance had proved so fatal to her friend's self-possession. On herself their appearance had quite a contrary effect, and seemed but to inspire her with additional power and ease. Magnificently did she acquit herself, and murmurs of subdued but universal admiration sounded through the room, Miss Judson's brow recovered, in some measure, its serenity, and she felt that life was no tall a blank.

The representation over, and farewell words to teachers and school-mates spoken, Gertrude clad in her plain dark travelling suit, and looking pale and dispirited, entered the small sitting room where Mr. Rodney and her father awaited her.

"You look ill and nervous to-day, little one!" kindly exclaimed Mr. Mildmay, as he took her in his arms. "Don't be put out, because you missed in that *opérette*,[5] as they called it. A fig for it all!"

This sudden allusion to what the young girl regarded as a most overwhelming disgrace was too much for her self-command, and still smarting from the keen mental suffering it had inflicted on her, she hid her face on her father's shoulder and burst into tears.

Rodney, all sympathy, hastily whispered: "Courage, dear Gertrude! Let me help you into the carriage now waiting at the door. You will soon be at home."

Roused by the tones of the voice already so dear to her, the girl silently, shrinkingly obeyed, seating herself in the farthest corner of the comfortable roomy vehicle. Of course Mr. Rodney had to return for Miss Brookes, who stood awaiting on the hall-steps, attired in a handsome écru-suit[6] of stylish make and material, and looking radiantly happy and handsome.

To spare Gertrude's perturbed feelings no allusion was made to the events of the morning, but the conversation embraced various topics on most of which the charming Charlotte discoursed with a sparkling ease and fluency that found ample encouragement alike in the hearty laughter of Mr. Mildmay and the amused attention of Arthur Rodney. Though really deficient in point of intellectual acquirements, Miss Brookes possessed considerable natural quickness, and a superb self-possession that enabled her to appear with more advantage than many far superior in point of actual knowledge. If the conversation verged on topics, in discussion of which her ignorance was likely to be exposed, she had a way of adroitly turning it into another channel, or starting some new subject with which she happened to be more conversant.

---

[5] French for operetta. This type of light opera (and precursor of the musical theatre) had recently been recognized as a new genre in Paris, mostly due to the efforts of Jacques Offenbach.

[6] Écru (from a French word meaning the color of unbleached or raw linen or silk) is very similar to the color of sand.

Meanwhile Mr. Rodney, seated opposite his young betrothed, was anything but forgetful of her, and frequently bending over, addressed her pleasant words or friendly remarks, to all of which the shy-constrained girl responded with oracular brevity, or maintained a cold silence. Annoyed by conduct which he totally misunderstood, the young man after a time turned his attention to Miss Brookes.

Very glad was Gertrude Mildmay when, the journey over, she found herself seated in the school-room at Mildmay Lodge, surrounded by her three little brothers, and responding to their lavish caresses and childish prattle. After a time, however, Mrs. Wells, who held the posts of governess and directress of the household even for a considerable time anterior to the death of the late Mrs. Mildmay, now entered, and after some kindly pleasant words with Gertrude begged the latter to dress for dinner. This she willingly rose to do, having forgotten, in the happiness of finding herself again in her own pleasant home, the humiliations the morning had brought her.

That day and many succeeding ones passed over the inmates of Mildmay Lodge, filled apparently with gaiety and happiness, but poor little Gertrude's sunshine was in reality sorely clouded, and in the devotion Mr. Rodney paid her brilliant school friend and the persistence with which the latter challenged that attention were to be found the origin of many secret and bitter tears. No allusion to their conditional betrothal ever passed between the two parties; and though the young man's manner and voice were always kind and deferential, he did not hang over Gertrude's chair when she was reading or sewing, or seated at the piano, as he generally did when Miss Brookes was in question, nor ramble with her for hours in field and shrubbery[7] as he did with the fascinating Charlotte.

Of all this Mr. Mildmay took but little note. If Arthur Rodney liked Charlotte better than Gertrude and wished to marry her, why, let him. His little girl, with her handsome dowry, could easily find a suitable bridegroom; and for his part he was in no hurry to give up his dear little girl whose presence so pleasantly brightened his home, to the guardianship and authority of another. Besides she seemed to care very little for the recreant wooer, and viewed with perfect indifference the flirtation carried on between him and Miss Brookes. Ah! Mr. Mildmay knew not that his daughter

[7] The shrubbery was a feature of 19th-century gardens designed in the English manner. It was a part of the garden consisting mainly of shrubs (rather than flowers) arranged so as to provide walking paths.

buried deep in her own heart feelings of wounded affection, bitter beyond measure. Once that she had remonstrated gently with her false friend, regarding the latter's persistent efforts to win Rodney to herself, Miss Brookes loudly protested that she was in no way to blame, and that if Gertrude were about to grow jealous she had better assert her claim to her betrothed at once, and take and keep him to herself.

From an approach to such a step our heroine's whole being recoiled, and the mere fear that Charlotte might allude in some way or other to the subject, in Mr. Rodney's presence, prevented her from offering further remonstrance to the false friend who continued to spread her Circe-like snares,[8] serenely careless what unhappiness they brought to others. Day by day her hopes rose higher, and to induce Arthur Rodney to commit himself by some plainly spoken word of love or devotion was now her constant aim. Lightly pressing him into her service for the purpose of gathering ferns for a fancy basket she was making, she set forth with him one bright morning, leading the way to the belt of stately woods that bounded the view at the back of Mildmay Lodge. The walk must have proved a dangerous one to Rodney, for his companion attired in the daintiest of morning dresses, looking lovely and bewitching beyond measure, seemed determined to try his stoicism to the utmost. Soft and appealing were the looks she from time to time directed towards him from beneath her long heavy lashes, and more than once his *empressé*[9] manner quickened her heart beats, whispering that the propitious moment was at hand. Still talking vague sentiment, still exerting every effort to bring about the wished-for result, Charlotte strolled on with her companion till they arrived at a charming little shady dell.

"Here I must rest," she said, advancing a few steps accompanied by Mr. Rodney, when a scene somewhat unexpected was presented to the gaze of both.

Seated on the greensward[10] was Gertrude, her hat beside her, whilst two of her brothers[11] were sportively showering leaves on

[8] In Homer's *Odyssey*, Circe is a goddess who lures Ulysses' men to a lavish meal and uses a magic potion to turn them all into swine.

[9] French for "zealous."

[10] Though better known as turf or sod (the upper layer of earth covered with grass), it can also mean a meadow.

[11] We have corrected here the original, which read "her two brothers."

herself, and the youngest of the band, laughingly clasped in her arms. The picture—comprising the bright smile that rested on the girl's innocent youthful face, the animated looks of the children, and the beauty of their greenwood surroundings—was a pleasant one, and Rodney stood a moment, silently surveying him.

"Why, Gertrude, playing good sister, I see," said Miss Brookes, by no means pleased with the expression of Mr. Rodney's face.

Gertrude who had colored deeply on first perceiving the intruders, hastily brushed off the leaves whilst Norman, the eldest of the three brothers, quickly rejoined before she had time to speak:

"Gertrude does not play at good sister—she is always good."

"Aptly said! my young friend," was Rodney's gay rejoinder, "but will sister Gertrude, who I feel assured is always good, as you say, join us this morning, and bring her little court with her?"

"No, indeed, Mr. Rodney," was Master Norman's prompt reply. "She comes here with us nearly every morning, and after we play some time, reads to us, so you see she cannot go with you."

Rodney smiled. "You seem very sure of your point, young gentleman! But what does Miss Gertrude say? I must have my answer from her own lips."

The young girl, secretly sore at heart, quietly rejoined:

"What Norman says is just. I have promised them a portion of my morning, and they have consequently a claim to it."

"And have I no claims, dear Gertrude, of any sort?" asked Rodney, in a low significant tone.

A blush, a rapid averting of her head was the only reply he received to the first indirect word of love he had ever whispered her. Miss Brookes perceiving that the situation was growing critical, with one of her sweet smiles interposed.

"It is not fair, Mr. Rodney, that we should interfere with Norman's claims or pleasures. Please bring me back to the house, for I really feel ashamed of my idleness, and am determined to sew or study for the remainder of the morning."

The young man lingered a moment, as if expecting Miss Mildmay would join them, or at least express a hope that they should stay, but Norman threw himself on the grass beside his sister, saying:

"Yes, you had better go, for Gerty will read to us now."

Gertrude's silence proving conclusively that she acquiesced in this decision, Rodney and his companion turned away and for some time he was unusually silent and preoccupied. But Miss Brookes taxed every power of witchery, and soon had the satisfaction of bringing back his smiles and devotion.

Weeks passed, and though our heroine seemed outwardly happy, she was nevertheless growing thinner, and losing a little of the lightness of step that had first distinguished her on her return to her home. One evening that she was lying on the sofa in her own room, the latter lighted only by the faint twilight that came in through the gauzy curtains, Miss Brookes entered, and seating herself beside her, took her hand tenderly in hers.

"Gertrude, dear, you look dull to-night. What is the matter?"

"Nothing whatever," and the girl gently disengaged her hand from her friend's clasp. "I have a slight headache."

"Ah, a heartache, darling, I begin to fear. Surely you are not fretting for Rodney who seems to trouble himself so little about you?"

There was a time when Gertrude Mildmay would have thrown herself into the arms of the young girl beside her and sobbed out an avowal that such was indeed the case; that his indifference, if not faithlessness, was breaking her heart, but now, after a moment during which she silently struggled for self-command, she quietly replied:

"Why, Charlotte, I thought you did not believe in aching or breaking hearts. You have always laughed at such thing heretofore."

"Perhaps I have had cause to change my opinions of late. I certainly believe in them now."

Gertrude made no reply to this. The subject was painful, and one on which she scarcely ventured to trust her voice.

"Forgive me, dearest," resumed Miss Brookes as if determined to probe her companion's feelings to the quick, "forgive me if I say I do not think that Arthur Rodney loves or ever will love you."

Constrained, yet calm, the answer came:

"Well, and what then?"

"This, Gertrude! Well I know that you have too much maiden-pride to waste the treasure of your love on one who cannot, who will not respond to it."

"Why, Charlotte, you are both eloquent and sentimental to-night. 'Tis almost the first time I have heard you speak in such a vein."

Ah, and it was perhaps the first time that sarcasm had ever fallen from Gertrude's gentle lips!

Miss Brookes steadily resumed: "Has it never struck you, dear friend, that Arthur Rodney loves another; and that, bound in honor to yourself, he is wearing out his life in ceaseless regrets over his bonds?"

A pause, and then Gertrude rejoined: "Mr. Rodney seems both happy and cheerful—not all like one who was wearing out his life in the very poetical manner you have just described."

"Gertrude, you speak like a child. Do you think a proud, reticent nature like his would go about baring his griefs and troubles to every eye? No, he will give no sign, no matter how much his chains may gall him."

"How am I to know he really entertains the sentiments you so pathetically attribute to him?"

"Gertrude! mine are no idle words spoken at random. More I must not say than that I have good ground for what I advance."

Our poor little heroine winced. Did not this speech seem to intimate that the wily Miss Brookes had already won from Rodney an avowal that such were really his sentiments?

After a painful silence, she questioned, half raising herself from the sofa: "What would you have me do?"

"Restore him his liberty freely and unconditionally. Tell him that in your eyes a betrothal contracted in such unusual circumstances is not binding, and that you release him from it."

"Well, when the fitting time comes, I may do what you so earnestly counsel, so warmly urge upon me; but, till then, Charlotte, remember that the subject must never again be mentioned between us."

With some effort Miss Brookes restrained the secret irritation awakened by this firm reply, and imprinting a kiss on her friend's cheek, which caress, despite her efforts, was somewhat cold, swept from the room.

"Perhaps 'tis better to follow her counsels—better to give up all my cherished hopes and dreams, and the young girl fell wearily back on the arm of the couch. "I am clinging to a hope illusive as a shadow. But I must have a few hours more to school my heart to this last most bitter ordeal. Ah! Charlotte, false friend, you have won from me my one pearl of price—the heart I had every right to call my own!"

That evening Miss Brookes, as if bent on proving to Gertrude the hopelessness of her affection for Arthur Rodney, exerted every feminine art with such winning grace and tact as to centre his attention completely on herself.

Other admirers there were who fluttered around the fair young hostess, but, destitute of anything like coquetry, she neither cared to attract or receive their attention. She sought her own room that night with a heavy heart, determined to restore her betrothed his liberty on the morrow, a step her womanly pride loudly insisted on; and have a final parting interview with him.

CHAPTER III.

An opportunity of putting her project in execution was soon likely to offer itself to our heroine, for an expedition had been planned for the following day to visit some neighbouring woods remarkable for a waterfall of great beauty.

As usual, Miss Brookes, even whilst still standing on the piazza[12] in the morning sunshine waiting for horses and carriages to be brought round, called Mr. Rodney to her side, careless of the fact that he was conversing with his young betrothed and enquiring with real interest if she were ill, a solicitude the latter's palor amply justified. The truth was the very thought of the cruel task before her, and the mighty sacrifice it would entail, made Gertrude's heart throb suffocatingly and blanched her cheek. She felt it would be like signing her own death warrant. Just as Mr. Rodney was on the point of offering himself as her escort, the irrepressible Charlotte gayly spoke out, reminding him in her clear sweet tones of his having promised to act as her guide to the Silver Creek Falls. After a moment's hesitation, a quick glance towards his betrothed, whose eyes were studiously averted, he accepted Miss Brookes' challenge, the latter little dreaming that she had thus defeated, at least for a time, her own most cherished desire—a parting and final explanation between Arthur Rodney and her friend.

The vacant place at our heroine's side was immediately taken by a Mr. Rowan, a wealthy, good-looking, though tiresome young gentleman; and if Gertrude had possessed a wish to make reprisals, a favourable opportunity was now offered her. Such was not, however, the case, and though she listened politely to Mr. Rowan's heavy remarks on the weather and the scenery, she never entered on anything approaching to flirtation.

[12] In New England and southern Canada, this term (now dated) referred to a veranda or a porch.

Arrived at the Falls, a general halt was called, and exclamations of real or simulated admiration were heard on all sides. The scene was indeed charming: a canopy of fresh green foliage overhead, through which the sunbeams flickered down in golden lines, moss smooth and soft as velvet beneath the feet, wild flowers showing their frail lovely heads at the foot of every old tree or mossy stone, and the chief object of attraction, the pretty cascade itself, crowned with silvery foam, leaping down the brown rocks and filling the air around with delicious coolness. Through the intervening trees glimpses of the rude masonry of an old mill were discernible, and the deep, solemn stillness of the woods was relieved by many a musical note from the boughs overhead.

Suddenly a commotion on the outskirts of the grove became perceptible, and a voice exclaimed, "By Jove, there goes Maitland's turn-out!" just as a powerful black horse, dragging a small but elegant phæton,[13] dashed suddenly into a car track leading into the wood.

After hurriedly excusing himself to Miss Brookes, Rodney was off to the rescue, followed by two or three of the gentlemen. When the little excitement caused by the incident had subsided, the remainder of the party either seated themselves beside the spray-covered rocks or dispersed to explore the woods. Some twenty minutes afterwards Mr. Rodney rejoined the sojourners by the waterfall, and to their enquiries regarding the result of the affair, returned an assurance that all was right and the horse properly secured.

"But where are Miss Mildmay and Miss Brookes?" he asked, his quick eye at once detecting their absence.

"Gone on a voyage of discovery with Mr. Rowan. They said something about visiting an old mill in the neighbourhood."

An uneasy feeling shot through Rodney's breast. He remembered having heard that the mill in question was in so ruinous a state as to have necessitated the boarding up of the entrance. Fearing that Rowan, whom he knew to be very careless, might have removed the slight barricade and penetrated already into the interior of the ruin with his companions, he bent his steps in its direction, and soon came in full view of it. Yes, the rough boards that had barred the entrance were lying on the grass, and a flood of

[13] A phaeton (more popular at the turn of the 19th century) was a light carriage drawn by one or two horses and made conspicuous by its big wheels. For "turn-out," see note 95 of the main text.

amber sunshine streamed in through the aperture, lighting up the gloomy, cavernous recesses and rough angles of the building. One rapid, anxious glance at its ruinous aspect and he sprang forward to the doorway. At the farther end of the large square space stood Charlotte, while directly above her head, lit up by a ray of golden light, was a long narrow crevice, from which tiny rivulets of dust and mortar were trickling down, unperceived by the temporary inmates of the mill. Not far from the spot in question young Rowan, encouraged by the enchanting smiles of Miss Brookes, was engaged on the arduous task of dragging a heavy block of wood towards a small window pierced somewhat high in the wall, so as to enable the lady to enjoy the view it commanded. The situation was most critical, and Rodney took in its danger at a glance. The fissure was rapidly spreading, dust and mortar were lightly falling in every direction, unaccountable detonating sounds made themselves faintly audible, whilst Mr. Rowan, in his hasty struggles to effect his object, was precipitating the crisis. Entering with a quick yet light step, Rodney strode towards Gertrude, who stood watching her companions, and amazed expression on her face, and quickly raising her in his arms, turned towards Rowan, exclaiming, "For God's sake take Miss Brookes out of this; the mill is about to fall!"

Rowan, thus suddenly appealed to, and in no circumstances ever remarkably bright, stood staring mutely at the speaker, but Charlotte, every quick where her own safety or interests were at stake, heard the warning, and in two bounds was at the door, reaching it at the same time as Rodney and his burden, followed by Rowan, who, on seeing the rapid flight of his companions, sped after them, impelled more by instinct than reason.

Just as they had cleared the portal, the wall in which Rodney had perceived the fissure fell inwards with a thundering crash, and the whole four were enveloped in a cloud of dust, crumbling mortar, and falling stones. Not a word was spoken till they had put a tolerable distance between the dangerous building and themselves, when Rodney asked, in a low agitated tone,

"Gertrude, for God's sake tell me are you much hurt?"

He had seen a stone strike her just as they had passed through the doorway.

"A little," was the faintly-whispered reply. "My head feels sore."

"O my arm! I fear it is broken!" moaned Miss Brookes, as she raised her elaborate trimmed sleeve and revealed some scratches on the white skin. "What shall I do?"

"Mr. Rowan, what are you about? Why don't look after Miss Brookes?" sharply interrogated Rodney, as he nervously tore off our heroine's hat to examine what injury she had sustained.

"How can I look after Miss Brookes pray, when my own shoulder is nearly dislocated?" was the gruff retort.

An angry gleam shot from the fair Charlotte's eyes at this double desertion, and experience somewhat novel in her case, but she wisely held her peace. By this time Rodney had removed our heroine's hat, parted the thick silky hair, and discovered a long red gash, from which the blood slowly oozed. Water, however, was at hand, and dipping his handkerchief in the little stream that had once moved the mill, he staunched the wound with a skilful, tender hand, Gertrude thinking all the while in a dizzy confused sort of way, that she had never felt so happy as now, thus tended and cared for by her betrothed.

The crash of the falling mill having been heard by the other members of the party, stragglers soon began to arrive on the scene of action, and assistance was proffered on all sides. Miss Brookes immediately became the centre of a sympathizing circle, and the trifling scratches she had received were loudly lamented over. Rodney allowed of no interference with his charge beyond accepting for her a glass of water, and as he held it to her white lips he saw at last the colour return in some degree to them.

"How shall I thank you, Mr. Rodney? You have saved my life," she whispered.

"Why should you thank me for doing my duty?" was the half gay, half serious reply.

There was something in his answer that jarred unpleasantly on the girl's ear. Ah! it was duty then that had dictated the preference he had given her over Charlotte Brookes, a preference that had secretly filled her heart with joy. Shortly after, Miss Brookes came up to them, accompanied by one of the kind, fussy matrons of the party, who then and there insisted, despite Gertrude's faint remonstrances and Rodney's more outspoken objections, on taking possession of her dear young friend, who must be kept perfectly quiet, remain with and return in the same carriage as herself.

Fearing a refusal might be construed into a desire to continue in the charge of Mr. Rodney, who might perhaps be already wearying of an office undertaken through duty, Gertrude complied, evidently to the annoyance of her betrothed.

"Well, Mr. Rodney, what do you think of our recent adventure?" asked Miss Brookes, looking up into Rodney's face with her most winning smile. "Was it not in the highest degree sensational?"

"Yes," he answered, smiling despite himself. "But who was the Fatima whose persevering curiosity[14] brought such an adventure upon us?"

Miss Brookes turned the tip of her dainty lace-covered parasol towards herself, thereby mutely replying to his interrogation.

"Ah! indeed. Well, 'tis fortunate the results have not been more serious."

"Yes, thanks to Mr. Rodney's gallantry," and the fair speaker gracefully bowed. "With what bravery and promptitude you rescued our poor timid Gerty, who would never have had courage to save herself."

"Miss Brookes flatters me. I merely did my duty."

"That is more than Mr. Rowan can say. He remorselessly left me to my fate, as indeed did every one else."

"Oh, that tacit reproach is for me, Miss Charlotte, but please bear in mind that Miss Mildmay was standing alone, and it was natural to suppose that, as Mr. Rowan was so much engrossed attending to your behests, he would also see to your safety in the moment of danger."

"Ah! Rodney; jealous at last!" thought the lady, with secret exultation, replying, however, with outward calm:

"Very true; but to make amends for having left me completely to my fate, you must really take charge of me on the way home, without expecting, however, another exciting adventure like that of this morning to enliven the route."

It was impossible to resist the winsome gaiety of this appeal, so Arthur Rodney offered his arm, which was triumphantly accepted.

CHAPTER IV.

The adventure of the mill created a great stir at Mildmay Lodge, and its master poured forth a series of exclamations, ejaculations

[14] Fatima is Bluebeard's wife (see note 91 of the main text) in the popular 1798 play *Blue-beard; or, Female Curiosity! A Dramatick Romance* by George Colman the Younger.

and interrogations that fairly bewildered the listeners, whilst Mrs. Wells, the housekeeper, took possession of our heroine at once, tenderly put her to bed, and hovered around the gentle patient till the latter fell asleep. A physician's verdict that no danger was to be apprehended had previously reassured all parties.

After two hours of deep slumber, Gertrude awoke, and the first object her glance rested on was Miss Brookes, who, wrapped in a large shawl, occupied an easy chair which she had drawn close to the bed.

"How are you, dearest?" was the visitor's tender query. "So you feel better?"

"Much, thank you," and as the events of the previous hours rose upon her recollection, bringing with them pleasant reminiscences of her betrothed's devoted care and gallantry, a pleasurable feeling mingled with the deep gratitude she felt for her safety.

"We had a narrow escape, Gerty!"

"Very," and the speaker shuddered.

"I suppose you feel very grateful to Arthur Rodney for his opportune assistance?"

"Surely with good cause, Charlotte!"

"Hem! yes, but he gave me to understand, remember, darling, this is strictly confidential, that he sprang forward to rescue you, impelled by a sense of duty."

Our heroine winced. Had he not already intimated the same to herself, but looking calmly in her companion's face, she asked:

"What is your motive in telling me this?"

"Friendship, dearest; can you doubt it? You are not as sharp a reader of character and conduct as I am, and I wish to give you the benefit of my clear-sightedness. Rodney, of course, till formally released by you from the tie that binds him, will consider it his duty to guard, honour and protect you. I must say, dear love, that in your place I would long since have flung him back the freedom he seems so ardently to covet."

"So that he might be free, Charlotte, to accept and wear your own chains. I do not possess, as a rule, your clear-sightedness in judging people and their motives, but I can plainly see that, regardless of the friendship you have always professed for me, you have done your best to win the affections of my betrothed, and to urge me into finally discarding him, probably for your own purposes."

Miss Brookes grew perceptibly pale, for she dreaded a rupture with the young girl whose friendship afforded her so many advantages. Accustomed to rule and influence her friend so long, she forgot that a time might come when the latter would see, judge and choose for herself. In a soft, almost supplicating voice, she murmured:

"Surely, dearest Gertrude, we will not allow the true and tried friendship of our girlhood to be shaken or alienated by any new interest or influence! If I have offended, it has been most unwillingly. Pray forgive me!"

"Willingly, but henceforth leave me to judge for myself in all matters wherein Arthur Rodney is concerned."

"Certainly, darling!" and here Miss Brookes fell on her friend's neck, wetting it with penitential tears and murmuring: "O Gerty, if our friendship were severed it would break my heart, I love you so very dearly!"

Poor little Gertrude, regretting already her unwonted severity, and touched by this eloquent appeal, kindly met these pluvious demonstrations of affection, and softly returned her friend's good-night kiss.

Gertrude's rescue by Rodney did not tend in any manner to draw the two together. The young girl, fearing her betrothed might misconstrue any increase in friendship on her part into a wish to assert her claim on his affection, became, with the instinctive pride of a true woman, more retiring and undemonstrative than ever, a fact patent not only to Rodney, but to others as well. The succeeding weeks of summer brought but little change to Mildmay Lodge. Miss Brookes, though more prudent in her friend's presence, continued to secure a great portion of the fickle Rodney's time and attention, and succeeded through her judicious manœuvering in conveying the impression that he was the one who planned their walks, talks, and flirtations. With simple, quiet dignity Gertrude withdrew each day more and more from the unequal contest, and avoided now, completely, all private interviews with her betrothed. Bravely but deeply she suffered, for, thrown constantly into intercourse with him, she found it impossible to overcome the affection so strongly rooted in her heart, and she felt that her eighteenth birthday, now at hand, was destined to find her sadder and less happy than that pleasant anniversary had ever yet done.

"Good morning, my darling," tenderly exclaimed Mr. Mildmay, as he entered the breakfast room somewhat earlier than usual. "I trust you are as well to-day, in mind and body, as your fond old father could wish?"

Gertrude replied by an affectionate caress. Mr. Mildmay went on: "Though you would not allow me to celebrate this, your birthday, as I had wished, by giving an entertainment surpassing anything Mildmay Lodge has yet seen within its walls, I can at least bestow on you the wherewithal to purchase a gift worthy of the occasion," and the speaker placed in her had a check for a considerable sum. "You will know best what to buy. I would only have made a bungle of it. But you look very thoughtful, Gerty; what is the matter?"[15]

"Why, when I proposed travelling two months ago, you declined."

"Yes, but I have changed my mind since then—a girl's privilege, you know—and would like now to make an extended tour."

"Very well; but in what direction, Gerty, would you like to go?"

"Very, very far, papa, dear; so far that I have scarcely courage to state it. 'Tis to Europe."

"Europe! well, that is indeed a distance," and Mr. Mildmay stroked his chin reflectively. "And how long would we remain there?"

"As long as would suit you, dear father, but I hope not shorter than six or eight months."

"Phew!" ejaculated Mr. Mildmay, drumming energetically with his fingers on the table. "That is a somewhat serious proposition, but it can and will be done, little girl. I have always intended to take you to visit the other side, and would perhaps have spoken of it before, but you seemed averse to travelling somehow."

"Well, there is nothing I desire more now, and I will be ready whenever you are prepared to start. The sooner the better, dear, dear papa," and a little soft hand caressingly smoothed down Mr. Mildmay's sandy and somewhat bristling locks.

"All right; but what about Arthur Rodney? I suppose he will come with us, also Charlotte?"

"We will settle all that later; the great point is that we should leave here as soon as possible."

"That is easily accomplished, child. The house and boys can be left—as they always are—in charge of Mrs. Wells, with whom they will be perfectly safe. My banker can furnish the necessary funds, and I see no cause for delay, unless you have not a sufficient stock of feminine frills and frippery laid in."

---

[15] Gertrude's line in which she was supposed to state her desire to travel has not made it into the original text.

"I have quite sufficient for the present. I can make additions to it on the other side, if necessary. But do not tell this good news to any one, please, dear father, for a day or two."

"Certainly not, if you wish me to be silent; and now for breakfast; I feel sharp set[16] this morning."

The meal over, from which Miss Brookes was absent, a not unusual occurrence with that young lady who never sought to emulate the feats of the lark in early rising, Gertrude passed out into the garden whither she was immediately followed by Arthur Rodney.

"Rest here awhile, Miss Gertrude," he said, stopping at the entrance of a small arbour, thickly overgrown with honey suckles and vines.

The young girl, who had reasons of her own for seeking an interview with the speaker, assented.

"Do not think I have forgotten what anniversary this is," he softly said, laying on the rustic table before her a tiny but richly chased agate casket, on which her name was inscribed.

With a flush more eloquent of pain than pleasure Gertrude opened the case and surveyed the costly brilliant diamond cross it contained, composed of gems of the purest water. At length she spoke.

"'Tis too beautiful, Mr. Rodney, too costly, and I cannot decide on accepting it."

Noting the cold questioning glance he bent upon her, she hurriedly added:

"However, I have a present to give you in return, more valuable, perhaps, even than this!"

"And that is——" he questioned, his late look of annoyance giving place to a bright smile, whilst he strove, tough unsuccessfully, to take her hand, "that is——"

"Your liberty. To-day, Mr. Rodney, we will mutually efface certain passages in the past from our lives. Within a few days I leave for Europe with my father, and you will be henceforth utterly free, untrammelled even by my presence."

A pause followed, during which Gertrude, though her cheek was deadly pale, affected to examine with great interest the jewel case.

"Is this announcement, Gertrude, merely a result of feminine pique or of mature deliberation?"

[16] An obsolete way of saying "very hungry."

"'Tis both serious and irrevocable; and now, Mr. Rodney, do not feel hurt if I return your beautiful cross, which will be a fitting gift later for her whom your vows and heart belong."

He looked very earnestly down in her face, and then seizing her hand held it tightly imprisoned in his own, whilst he whispered:

"Gertrude, my darling, they are, gems, vows and heart, your own. Ah, you know not how closely I have studied for months past your matchless worth, nor how warmly I have felicitated myself each day, that such a treasure was destined to be mine."

"O, Arthur, how can I believe you? Remember the attentions you paid Miss Brookes."

"I merely accepted the challenge to flirtation extended to me by that lady. Another thing, I strove to enkindle in your cold little heart, by exciting its jealousy, a small portion of the love that filled my own. However, I have a lifetime before me to win the coveted prize; and now say that you forgive me for my past apparent inconsistency, knowing the motive that dictated it? You will never have cause to complain of me again."

"But, Rodney, Charlotte is so handsome and accomplished, and you seemed to admire her so much."

"My darling think you I could prefer her beauty, with the vain frivolous arts through which I read so plainly, to your own sweet womanly gentleness and truth; qualities which have displayed themselves more clearly and brightly every day, since our sojourn here? Gertrude, love, we will carry out your project of going to Europe, and that as speedily as possible; but," and he gently raised the fair blushing young face that had bowed itself on his shoulder, "the trip will be our wedding journey."

THE END.

WORKS CITED IN THE FOOTNOTES

Colman the Younger, George. *Blue-beard; or, Female Curiosity; a Dramatick Romance.* London: Cadell and Davies, 1798.

Ferland-Angers, Albertine. "La Citadelle de Montréal (1658-1820)." *Revue d'histoire de l'Amérique française.* 3: 4 (March 1950), 493-517.

Gadoury, Lorraine. *La Noblesse de Nouvelle-France, Familles et alliances.* Montreal: Hurtubise HMM, 1992.

Garneau, François Xavier. *History of Canada, from the Time of Its Discovery till the Union Year 1840-41.* Translated by Andrew Bell. Second Edition-Revised. In Two Volumes. Montreal: John Lovell, 1862.

Gladstone, William Ewart. *Bulgarian Horrors and the Question of the East.* London: John Murray, 1876.

Hendricks, Bonnie. *International Encyclopedia of Horse Breeds.* Norman: University of Oklahoma Press, 2007.

Larin, Robert. "Les Canadiens passés en France à la Conquête." *Revue d'histoire de l'Amérique française* 68: 1-2 (été-automne 2014), 101-124.

MacGregor, John. *British America.* In Two Volumes. Edinburgh: William Blackwood; and London: T. Cadell, 1832.

Stevenson, John James. *House Architecture.* In Two Volumes. London: Macmillan, 1880.

Vergnes, Sophie. *Les Frondeuses: Une Révolte au Féminin.* Seyssel: Champ Vallon, 2013.

www.ingramcontent.com/pod-product-compliance
Lightning Source LLC
Chambersburg PA
CBHW070637310726
48982CB00001B/308
* 9 7 8 1 9 8 8 9 6 3 7 0 9 *